Sexual Secrets and the Forbidden Scroll

N.R.R.P.

ISBN:: 978-1-9995070-8-4

Title: Sexual Secrets and the Forbidden Scroll

Author: N.R.R.P.

Publisher: Between the Sheets Publishing

DEDICATION

To my partner and all those couples who need to spice up their life, and not just in the bedroom. To couples who desire a deeper level of connection with their partner.

ACKNOWLEDGMENTS

Thank you to my partner who is a motivation.
Thank you to all the readers.

1

The bodies of both men were lying on the king size bed with their arms and legs sprawled out and hanging over the edge. The red silk blankets barely covered their naked bodies. They were dead. Dead to the world.

She finished putting on her black sexy see-through lingerie that was thrown to the floor next to the bed just four hours earlier and glanced at both men in the bed with a quizzical look and forced a smile while putting on her silk rope. She shook her head, then sauntered to the kitchen to retrieve the already brewed espresso from her prized Jura Giga espresso machine.

She sipped it slowly to savour the flavour while meditatively walking to the spare bedroom that was converted to a personal art studio overlooking the city. Placing the cup of espresso down on the table next to the sculpture – a work in progress, she unpacked the clay and dipped her fingers in the water before handling it. It felt sensual in her hands as the wet clay oozed out between her fingers. Playing with it until it was soft enough to shape it, she embodied the saying, "like putty in the hands." Anything in her hands softened, or hardened, depending on what she wanted. She placed the newly molded piece onto her sculpture to finish off the artwork.

She wiped her hands on a towel that was on the table then walked to the corner of the room and rinsed her hands in the sink. She removed a plush towel hanging on a ring next to the sink and dried her hands off as she walked over toward the window to look out and scan the city with her eyes – it helped with introspection.

It was not unusual to see very little traffic this early in the morning, and it lent to a feeling of solitude. After replacing the towel on the ring, she took another sip of the espresso and admired the peace and quiet over the city as the sun barely kissed the horizon. A struggle had been brewing for a long time. There was an internal conflict between feeling a shallow contentment and being deeply unsettled.

Turning her attention to the next unfinished sculpture that needed to be painted, she picked up a brush to moisten it and dipped it into a bowl of water and tapped it clean before coating the brush with paint. She exhaled slowly every other stroke of the brush. Each long brush stroke took her deeper into thought. Every stroke that was made, and every breath that was taken was slow – methodical - calculated. She was lost in her own mind, aroused by her imagination and creativity and the control she had over the creation of the art.

Thirty minutes went in the blink of an eye, so she put the brush down and took the espresso to the kitchen and opened the fridge to grab a bottle of water. She walked to her bedroom and placed the cup and water on a table next to a window and went to the closet for a change of clothes.

She looked over her shoulder teasing the men in bed and undressed slowly as if doing a strip tease, making sure to bend over slowly, mocking the fact that they missed a free show of her tight body, her round plump ass and perfect size tits. A handful or mouthful size, that any man would die for. She scoffed while putting on the jogging outfit.

She took the water from the table but left the espresso and went down the hall to another spare bedroom that was converted into an exercise studio. Turning her stereo on to play music that hyped her up, she warmed up on the treadmill.

The treadmill started slowly and picked up speed. In a matter of seconds, she was running full tilt and then adjusted the program to run a steady pace for the next 20 minutes while the sweat dripped down her face and down her neck and into her top. She finished the workout and wiped the sweat away from her face and gulped the last of the water while walking back to her bedroom.

The men hadn't moved that whole time and it didn't matter how much noise she made for the past hour - they didn't hear a sound. She walked over to the table and took another sip of the espresso and gazed out the window briefly.

The sun had risen above the horizon. There was a deep admiration of its beauty, akin to admiring her expressive art and it made her inhale deeply, as if smelling a bed of roses.

"Time to shower." She said out loud. She's a soft-spoken woman and heard it from both men and woman that she had a sexy voice. Her friends asked if she ever considered being the voice on the other end of a telephone sex line. Most of the men she knows admitted to calling her just to hear her soothing voice.

She turned and walked toward the foot of the bed while stripping her clothes off. Standing briefly at the edge of the bed to look at their naked body before going to the shower she said, "Time to get up."

Kicking the base of the bed to shake it she raised her voice, "Hey! Get your asses up. Are you ready for round three?" She was kidding, but if they had woken, she would have fucked the shitbags back to sleep again.

She wanted them up and out before she had to go to work. They weren't dead after all because they finally stirred – one of them groaned.

Her body language displayed dissatisfaction and muttered under her voice as she turned and walked toward the bathroom, "Pussies. That's why I invited two of you. Maybe I should have gotten a third as backup."

She went to her oversized bathroom and turned on the rain-flow shower. Her body is tight - fit and toned. Men acknowledged in the middle of orgasm that she had the perfect tits. She had curves that would make a Ferrari sweat with apprehension on approach. The reflection in the mirror showcased her body as it glistened with sweat. She was proud of her physique, not because it looked good, but because she felt good. In her line of work, she needed to be in top shape.

After blasting music, she stepped into the shower to wash her hair and lather her neck and shoulders. The soap ran down between her tits and down her back until it settled momentarily at the base of her back - covering her tattoo before it made its way to the crack of her ass. The soap ran down past her belly button and she massaged the soap into her skin, pushing it down until it dripped across her pussy.

The music took her mind somewhere else and she found herself massaging her tits and squeezing her nipples. She took her time massaging her body and took another handful of soap to create more bubbles.

She lathered her pussy and squeezed her lips then brushed her clit until she could feel herself throbbing. She was slow and methodical about scrubbing herself, moving to the beat of the music like she did in the art studio. The lather made her skin silky smooth – slippery. The feel of her own skin was erotic, and it made the craving intensify.

She washed her pussy gently, slowly sliding her wet fingers across the lips, pinching it between her fingers, just like she did when she shaped the clay. The throbbing intensified as she slipped her fingers inside. It was instinctive for her to lean her head back and close her eyes to enjoy the feeling. She kept the pace that she wanted – she was in control. You couldn't hear the moaning above the music. The breathing got heavier every slip of her fingers inside until she was satisfied and cum on her fingers.

After she was finished, she rinsed herself off completely and stepped out of the shower and covered herself with a thick plush robe and walked into the bedroom where the men had wakened and gotten out of bed. She glanced at their hard-naked bodies for a moment and walked over to her large custom window and took the last sip of her espresso to enjoy the view outside.

The sun had risen over the city skyline. It held her attention and she found herself staring out the window longer than she expected and never felt the urge to turn her head to watch either man getting dressed. She wasn't enamored by the clean-cut taller man, who had chiseled good looks and could easily impress most women with his Armani suit as he adjusted his tie. Nor was she impressed with the other man who had long blonde hair and a tanned beach body. He took his time putting on his designer jeans, T-shirt and leather jacket.

The smile on their face suggested they both wanted to see her again. She was more than what they expected in the bedroom, and they nodded to each other as if they were affirming to each that they gave her good time – pleased that they satisfied her curiosity.

The man in the suit cleared his throat to get her attention, but she didn't bat an eyelash and kept staring out the window at the rising sun. Instead, she waved her hand like an empress giving them permission to leave.

The man with the suit smirked, while the designer jeans man scoffed. They found their way out of her penthouse with a false sense of being able to sexually gratify her. They were fooled by the satisfaction of their own sexual fantasy. They wanted more of her but knew it wasn't going to happen. The man with the jeans muttered under his voice to the other on their way out the door, "Fuck her. I got what I wanted."

Just then, from the other side of the house they heard her yell, "Don't kid yourself dickweeds. You're fucking homeless clowns looking for a circus to join and I'm your ringmaster. Now you know what toilet paper feels like, so take your limp shit somewhere else."

They adjusted their coats in disbelief – victims of "shock and awe" as they left the penthouse in silence with their tail between their legs. That was the last time they showed their face.

She turned to gaze at the scroll above her bed and sighed. She couldn't help but wonder – what am I missing? She got closer to take a look at the scroll which behind an eloquent frame. It was artwork for her, recently added several months ago, and it was also the most important find in her whole collection. She was an avid collector of all forms of art, but this one was special. For millenniums, it was believed that the scroll was a myth. A legend that began before civilization.

She admired it, but a puzzled look appeared while staring at the scroll. It was supposed to reveal the mysteries of sexual ecstasy. The myth suggested that it was a secret reserved only for the gods.

She believed it was possible to experience a deep, mental and emotional connection – and that sex was an avenue that made it possible. Great sage spoke of the legend and the ability to experience ecstasy, but that level of intimacy felt allusive to her. Having a satisfying fuck wasn't enough. Her craving for ecstasy and a deeper connection felt like a myth to her. It made her feel unsettled and unsatisfied. Because of that, she was willing to search the globe for answers. Her work made it possible to tap into the resources needed to find the scroll that had the answers.

The yearning to fulfill her fantasies made her willing to take the journey that led her around the world, no matter what the cost or the level of danger. The closer she got to finding the scroll, the more real the legend became. It was more than a myth.

For the one who learned its ways, it would violently thrust heaven to the earthen plane with the power of an earthquake or an erupting volcano. These methods became forbidden, concealed from humanity because it was believed nobody could survive this method of sexual intimacy, specifically the moment heaven was ushered in, and nobody understood why it couldn't be endured.

Scanning the scroll unsympathetically to figure it out, she affirmed that it wasn't going to defeat her. She fought that feeling of having lost a battle since finding the scroll. She even went so far to convince herself that possessing it alone or hanging it in the bedroom would make a difference. Like it was some kind of ancient relic imbued with powers.

Shit! I don't fucking understand this shit. I mounted it right here above my bed so I can study it every day hoping that something would click. Hell, I figured maybe if I just have it in the same room with me, it would at least bring some kind of power or intervention. I've studied it forwards and backwards and I'm doing everything I think it suggests. Maybe it was interpreted wrong. Maybe I'm not doing it right.

For fuck sakes, how the hell can anyone get sex wrong? Shit, I had two guys here for 4 hours doing it right. But I still have that hollow feeling of being unfulfilled. It drives me crazy sometimes to feel this way and I hate it. The craving for something deeper is insatiable.

I should probably google it to see if there is something wrong with me. I'm sure I'll find a few clinical terms out there that describe me or can pinpoint what they think it is.

Is it so wrong to want a real man to hunger after my body, to be ravenousness after my soul so that I could surrender and submit myself to him for his pleasure? Is it so wrong to want to be taken beyond the sexual limitations that this god forsaken world imposes on me? Maybe once I learn the scroll's secret, I'll be satisfied the moment I cum, and only then will it leave me fulfilled for more than a day.

I've always had an unquenchable thirst of wanting to see a hunger in a man's eyes and to feel his desires, his lust for me - to know that we could satisfied each other. I want him to be able to see my soul and read me like a book. I want to see in my lover's eyes that I am everything to him even if he has everything, so that when I subjugate myself to him, he will take me to places I've never been, beyond just an amazing fuck. I want to experience a completeness, but I feel like it's eluded me for years.

Shit! What the hell am I doing? If I overthink this or dwell on it, it can be so fucking maddening.

She scoffed at her own thoughts and turned her attention to the time on the docking station on the nightstand.

"I gotta get ready for work." She said to herself.

She turned the radio on while it charged her phone. " ♪ I need your body, it's my canvas to express myself. Where are you baby?"

She heard the lyrics and agreed, "I hear ya. Where are you baby?" She let the music play while she put lotion on and got dressed.

Her phone buzzed without her noticing it at first. It

buzzed a second time and it got her attention, notifying her of a text.

"You got the approval to take on the Morocco mission. You leave tomorrow morning. You'll be briefed on the operation. See you in a bit."

She read it, fist pumped and yelped with an unorthodox show of orgasmic delight. She made the request for this covert operation to Morocco months ago. The intel gathered specifically for this mission's success required only top tier agents who were specialized in tactical combat.

It was a highly sensitive operation that planned a 'catch and release' method without alerting the public, politicians or any other top-secret agency for that matter. This went beyond the standard, "Can neither confirm nor deny" operation and there was room to eliminate the target if necessary, according to their unwritten motto.

She was a critical component to the success of this campaign and was one of only a few agents who could be briefed 24 hours before a mission and still pull it off.

The elated response wasn't because of this mission alone. She was on a personal mission to gather more intel on the scroll, and all of her sources pointed to Morocco for answers.

From what she learned from scholars, sages and mystics, there was a chance that there was another part to the scroll. Maybe it contained the answer to her questions. Maybe that was the missing part of the puzzle to achieve sexual ecstasy and fulfillment. She reasoned that the other half was somewhere in Morocco. This was the perfect opportunity to take some time for herself after the covert operation to look for it.

Clearly pleased with the text message, it put a bounce in her step as she finished getting ready and left her penthouse to the parking garage. The news added to the pleasure of driving her black Lamborghini Urus to work. It heightened the intoxicating feeling of stepping on the accelerator knowing that power like that had unprecedented control as it turned every corner. She loved the way it handled and enjoyed the luxury feel of her SUV and planned to push it on the highway to get to work today. After all, when you have that much power, why not use it?

She could feel her heart pounding in her chest and heard a thumping in her ears the moment she turned the corner and accelerated onto the highway. Her smile grew, the faster she drove. It was the perfect morning to ride with the driver side window open and let the music play loud enough to excite her while her long silky hair waved in the wind.

She created an environment for herself to be aroused. Just then, she glanced in the rearview mirror and saw a black 1969 Chevy Chevelle SS coming up to her rear. The rumble of the exhaust could be heard as it caught up to her - it gave her goosebumps as it pulled up next to her on the passenger side. She couldn't see who was driving. The windows were tinted just dark enough to show a silhouette. They couldn't see in her car either. They tested each other's power on the highway, teasing each other as they took turns pulling ahead and then slowing down. She glanced at them, sneered and stepped on the throttle and forced the engine to rumble and engage the turbo.

She had the edge in this race and gave a smug chuckle as she pulled away. In a moment of her gloating, it stunned her when the Chevelle pulled up next to her unexpectantly. It paced her long enough to give her the impression that they were toying with her. The thunder of the Chevelle boomed and it jetted forward past her.

"What the fuck? Oh, hell no!" She was surprised and pleased at the same time by the brief encounter with this stranger with muscle. She stomped on the petal but just as she did her cell phone buzzed - distracting her.

It wasn't her burner phone from work, it was her personal burner phone. She groaned with frustration because someone interrupted her arousal – killing the mood of the moment. She eased up on the gas to pull over to the rest area to read the text message, thinking it was an important message she was anxiously awaiting.

She unlocked her phone to see a picture of a man's dick with the message, "You know you want this baby. Call me so we can hook up later."

"What the fuck!? I don't have time for this shit." She said while turning the radio down because it annoyed her.

She was infuriated that an asshole like this would interrupt her perfect morning while she watched the Chevelle drive off into the distance. She groaned looking for the name of the sender.

The only thing on her mind now was ripping this guy a new asshole.

Who the fuck is this anyway?

She read the name and was puzzled.

I don't even remember who this is.

She scrubbed through previous messages from this guy to see how long they've been texting each other. Her thoughts were screaming.

Don't you clueless clowns get it? I'm gonna ghost your ass when you send me dick pics, or when you send me inflated ego pictures as you pose shirtless with your six-pack abs. I don't care how tight you are or how big your dick is.

As it turned out, the messages sent back and forth between the two of them were only one week old.

She shook her head and said out loud with surprise, "One week?! What the fuck?!"

She texts him back before deleting his message.

"Hey clown! How 'bout you go fuck yourself. Your dick is long enough to reach your ass. You must be proud of that. And you're wrong! I don't want that nasty shit. I'm sure there's a hoe slut out there that appreciates a clown like you. I'm good."

Right after it was sent, she could see that it was read and that he was in the middle of texting her back when she texted him back first, "You fuckin' moron. Why you still texting me. I said goodbye."

I'm tired of these motherfuckers.

She put him on the ignore list. Then threw her phone into her purse and tried to get back into the zone again so that she could enjoy the rest of her ride into work.

She's a sophisticated, no nonsense, experienced woman who thinks of herself as a complex person that needs to feel adrenaline course through her veins on occasion to feel alive, but she also wants to be treated like a woman. Her friends joked with her one time and called her an adrenaline junkie. She didn't deny it. Letting go of all her inhibitions with everything she did was what she expected of herself and wanted someone she could share that with, who craved the same thing. But he didn't exist.

She grudgingly settled for living in a fantasy world, chasing after anything that took her to the edge. Feeling like she was the only one in the world that lived like this, and it made her feel lonely at times, despite having any man she wanted. Her father, who she looked up to, was an adrenaline junkie too who lived on the edge most of his life as well. That's where she gets it from.

The sound of the turbo kicking in got her out of her head. Driving fast put her back into a meditative space, helping clear her mind. She reflected on everything she went through to find that scroll. The search began years ago for this ancient secret of ecstasy, and it took her to exotic lands during the height of her career as she was able travel frequently. She spoke to less than a handful of scholars, elders and shamans from different cultures who heard about this secret. After centuries of looking, most of the adventurers, historians and scholars gave up believing in its existence and stopped looking for this mythical scroll, passing it off as being a mere fable.

At the time, she felt like she was getting closer to finding the answer to ecstasy and gathered enough evidence to ignite the belief that these ancient scrolls - passed down since biblical times, might be real, she wanted to see for herself if it was true.

After acknowledging and confirming the story around the world and in different cultures, it seemed like it was no longer a myth. This was real and it felt like she was the only one getting closer to finding it. She was exceptional at tracking things down and finding the answer to the truth that allude people for eons. That skill set came in handy for her work. That ability came from her father as well.

Six months ago, she was compelled to search a forgotten cave in a desert somewhere in Israel. A few scholars suggested that a scroll was locked away in a clay earthen jar and buried there for safe keeping. That's where she found it. She happened upon it after searching for months in the bowels of the earth. She wouldn't have found it if it weren't for the earthquake that hit the day before she was scheduled to leave. It exposed the jars hidden in the walls of the cave.

Finding the jar was one of the most exhilarating moments she ever had. Finding and holding the scroll was like having an orgasm – it was the first time she had experienced a mental and emotional orgasm. To wrap her fingers around the scroll and feel it in her hands was an incredible moment. To touch a myth was surreal. The satisfaction she felt to prove all the naysayers wrong brought her an inner satisfaction that was difficult to explain to anyone. She couldn't help but cry, laugh and feel relieved. It was almost an outer body experience holding the scroll that wasn't supposed to exist. Nobody would understand how she felt. This moment - this exhilaration and release, was something that could only be understood by experiencing it.

She opened the scroll gently and held it like a lover. On the scroll were ancient text and images that spoke of the untold powers to unlock and connect the gates of heaven to earth through sexual expression. She couldn't make out the language on the scroll despite speaking six languages fluently herself. She needed a brilliant mind or a group of minds to decipher what was written on that ancient paper.

All the brilliant linguistics professors around the world could only give her parts and pieces of the text. In the end, they suggested that there was more to the secret – a second scroll that completed the text. The writings mentioned a seacoast – a high traffic area somewhere in Africa. It appeared intentional to separate the two scrolls. But there were clues left on the scroll to one day bring them together.

That's why she wanted to go to Morocco. All the signs pointed to an ancient land in that area, long before Morocco was named. The Phoenicians claimed that territory 1000 BCE and they may have hidden the scroll somewhere in that area. It was suggested that it could be found in the ruins of a temple that was buried by the sands of time.

Snapping out of her meditative thought - she realized that it didn't take her long to get to headquarters. She parked in her usual spot and entered the building still excited about the assignment. Before she could enter "A-wing" she placed her eye in front of the retinal scanner. The door beeped and then opened up for her. Immediately she was greeted by two female colleagues – the one's she considered friends.

She was briefed on her mission and it lasted more than half the day because it was a high-profile operation approved by the Commander in Chief himself – President Trump. She was given whatever resources she needed to carry out the mission - to guarantee her success. She was ready to fly to Morocco in the morning.

The mission alone had the potential to give her the adrenaline she thrived on. "Operation Collaborative Silver Stone – Blind Ambition," is what it was called. It required her to locate and track high profile and heavily guarded targets, to disengage their security so that she could peg "tangos" for extraction.

She was to take out communication and blind her target's security for the success of a collaborative effort on the part of

China's "Snow Leopard Commando Unit," Israel's secret service, "Unit 269 – Sayeret Matkal" and United States "A-team - Navy Seals."

Each country had a vested interest in this mission and her success would allow the teams to enter hostile territory with weapons hot to subdue and retrieve their perspective targets at any cost without raising local or international attention.

Everything was riding on her shoulders. Just the way she liked it. She savoured the rush – the craving intensified. Not just for the mission, but for the scroll and its secrets, because her sexual appetite would finally be satisfied, and it was going to be found in the second part of the scroll – which was sure to be found somewhere in Morocco, miles from her mission.

Later that night, sprawled across her couch, she sipped on her herbal tea in front of the fireplace and reflected on the mission and the rush she was going to get from it. She couldn't help but feel a moment of appreciation for her life. It brought a contentment that covered her like a warm blanket and helped her to wind down quickly. It made her sleep like a baby that night. She needed all the rest she could get, to get her through one of the most intense seven days of her   career   yet.

2

She caught her plane early in the morning and arrived in Morocco at the safe house and prepped for the mission before going out into the field.

The entire mission took approximately three days to prepare for but only took 12 hours to complete and each country accomplished their mission alongside of each other and she was the glue that held it all together. Not a single shot was fired and she still wreaked havoc on the targets and their security.

Over two dozen men were going to be waking up with a migraine headache feeling nauseous, not realizing what hit them, thinking they got sick from food poisoning and experiencing a loss of memory. And not a single agent knew how she did it without breaking a sweet or getting caught. A few argued it was her sexual prowess, referring to her as a "Siren."

Then an argument ensued among the agents on what to nickname her, it was either "Eris" the Greek goddess of chaos or "Kali" the Hindu goddess of destruction. The United States unleashed their secret weapon on the enemy, and she created hell for them.

The Chinese agents made a strong case for their nickname for her, "Xiwangmu" the Chinese goddess who was once a ravenous, ferocious and animalistic spirit that lived in the mountains and created cataclysmic disasters. Later, she transformed through enlightenment and became a goddess and married the Jade Emperor, the benevolent ruler of heaven. Together, their love for each other created humanity.

She heard everyone's argument and the Chinese nickname intrigued her the most and it seemed somewhat fitting for her life at the moment. Instead, she accepted the easiest to say, and how she felt at that moment, "Eris".

She butted into their conversation, "You guys are crazy...but call me 'Eris.'" Everyone laughed.

The mission went off without a hitch. It gave her the rush she was looking for. She was commended for her efforts and personally recognized for her talents and commitment to her country. The commander in chief himself, along with officials from China and Israel acknowledged her as well. This was a big deal for her, and everyone involved.

It's a weird feeling to be one of only a select few people who knew about this covert operation while the rest of the world went about their business, oblivious that this mission had international implications.

Operations like this, occasionally led to a feeling of loneliness and being disconnected from the rest of the world. She was an unknown and unappreciated hero that lived among the common with a life that seemed like a fantasy and a genuine rush, and she couldn't tell anyone about it. It didn't help that feeling much, when the people you knew back home didn't even know your real name.

It took a long time get used to that feeling. Everyone at headquarters understood this. That's why they honored her and most importantly gave her some personal time, and this gave her the opportunity to vacation in Morocco.

She was in a popular local restaurant talking with her guide, her only connection to assist with finding the ancient temple when she noticed a gentleman in the corner of the restaurant. She could tell he was out of place. He was too clean cut and had an air of mystery about him. He was deeply engaged in a conversation with his Moroccan friend. It appeared they were long-time friends.

She made her way to a table at the back of the restaurant with her acquaintance, engrossed in conversation oblivious that he made his way to the table too. Each of them stood at the table focused on their discussion. She glanced briefly at the table to gage where the pineapple was and then refocused back on the guide.

With their head turned in the direction of their conversation, they reached for the food on the table. She was surprised to touch a hand also reaching for the same pineapple, who also had his head turned in the direction of his friend as they spoke. It surprised him that someone touched his hand.

What the hell?! I was startled to grab a hand – because it was completely unexpected. I turned and noticed it was him, the guy from the corner of the room. I don't normally lose track of my surroundings, but I must have let my guard down, that's why it surprised me. Probably because I'm excited about going out to find that scroll. Besides, I'm in a safe place and I'm relaxing – coming down from a high and an adrenaline rush after that mission.

He looked down at our hands as they hovered over the pineapple briefly. I felt an electricity coming from him - from a simple touch. I couldn't help but leave my hand there briefly, hesitating from pulling my hand away, and I noticed he did too. When we pulled our hand away, I noticed we slid our hands across each other to keep constant contact, to maintain the electricity for as long as we could without it being awkward. It wasn't just my imagination that he felt it too because I could see a glean in his eyes and look on his face like he just had an orgasm.

I was a little surprised when he spoke to me, "'Afwan. Min faDlik. Aafek. TafaDDal," as he gestured to the pineapples.

I understood the customary greeting in that area. He greeted me and had offered to let me go first to take food.

I couldn't hide the fact that I was pleased by his mannerisms. So, I nodded and reached for a slice of pineapple.

She scanned him up and down - checking him out, then looked him in the eyes as she placed the fruit in her mouth, and with purpose she slowly wrapped her lips around the fruit. He watched her with intrigue.

He greeted her as per local customs, "As-salaam 'alykum."

She took her time eating the fruit before responding, then

lowered her head, "Wa alaykumu as-salam."

"Do you speak English?" He asked.

"Yes. I do," and then took another bite of pineapple, but not before smiling seductively.

"Is it good?" He gestured to the pineapple on the table.

She nodded her head, "mmm hmm. Do you know one of the delicious benefits of eating pineapples regularly?"

There was a silence while the sexual tension ignited between them as she gestured for him to eat some.

I could sense that he had an answer in mind but withheld it from me, almost like he was teasing me. I'm pretty good at getting an answer from people but this man was different. I could tell by the look in his eyes and the smirk on his face that he knew from experience what I was talking about. He simply nodded his head and sampled the fruit, while I glanced down at his crotch making sure he noticed that I was looking.

She nodded her head slightly, pursed her lips and squinted her eyes as he ate the pineapple, "You should fill your plate then." Then brushed her hair back and exposed her neck.

He didn't hesitate. Grinning as he helped himself.

"My name is Naffilia," she said with an inviting smile before she took another bite.

I noticed he was looking at my lips. I had a deep shade of red lipstick on today. Men have told me that I had full sexy lips and that the red made them stand out even more. I haven't seen a man drawn lustfully to my mouth like that before. Still, he didn't a say a word about them. It made me wonder why he didn't say anything.

She took advantage of the moment and used the tip of her tongue to touch the pineapple first, to taste it, then closed her eyes as she wrapped her lips around the succulent fruit while it dripped down her hands.

She opened her eyes to catch him lost in the moment. He took a breath and said, "Nice to meet you Naffilia. My name is Tye."

He reached out to shake her hand, "Are you from around here?"

He had no regard for the fact that my hand was still dripping with juice. I wasn't sure if he didn't notice that it was dripping, or if he didn't care – as if he liked it wet and dirty and it turned him on. I didn't feel compelled to wipe it first before shaking his hand, because I wanted to see how he would respond. I was curious now. "No. I'm not from around here. I'm from Boston."

His eyes widened, "Really? I'm from New England myself. Actually, I was born and raised in that area, so I know it very well." He licked his fingers while offering her a napkin before wiping his own.

Oh my gosh, what the fuck?! Did I just see him lick his fingers? That's obviously suggestive and erotic or he's fucking bizarre with no sense of hygiene. I read it as erotic, and I could feel a pulse in my pelvic.

I shifted my thoughts quickly to avoid showing my astonishment, besides, I couldn't help but wonder what brought him here. What are the odds that I would meet someone from my neck of the woods halfway around the world, "What brings you to Morocco?"

"I'm here on business and pleasure. I'm looking for something - and someone," Tye said.

I was curious what he meant by that, and I had the urge to flirt with him, "Did you find what you were looking for?"

He annunciated every word, "I think I may have found the person…" and gave me a smile that made me blush, "…but I need the rest of what I'm looking for to make sure I have everything I want."

I knew what he was doing, I've seen it before - the charm and masculine seduction was breath taking. But he did it very well. So, I played the same game, "Now that you found the person, what exactly is the thing you want?"

Tye leaned in closer to me and put his mouth close to my

ear to answer my question as if telling me a secret. With a tone that was soft but edgy he spoke with a sexy bass and said, "I want something that everyone said I can't have."

Naffilia's pupils dilated when his breath penetrated and tickled her ear and felt the vibration of his voice on her neck. She dragged her words out slowly, "Really?" was all she could say as she turned to look into his eyes. She lost herself in his hazel coloured eyes – they more green than brown.

"You seem stirred by my response." He said with curiosity.

I probed him to find out what he meant by that. I couldn't tell if he was talking about finding a woman he could fuck or if there was something else. I got the feeling he wasn't in Morocco for pleasure. He seemed like he was here for business. He has an air about him, like he is used to getting what he wants. What piqued my curiosity was the way he said it. Like he was after something, and he was confident that he was going to find it.

Tye gestured with his right hand toward the table of food as if offering a feast, "Do you care to join us at our table?"

I didn't want to mix business with pleasure. I was here looking for the second part of the scroll and my guide and I were about to discuss our plans. As enticing as it was to take him up on the offer, I declined. But I was very curious about who he is. "Perhaps we can do this another time? I have business to tend to."

"Of course. I understand. It would be my pleasure," he said with a smile as he placed his hand over his heart.

They filled their plate with food and sat at a distance from each other and continued their conversation with their guests. For the remainder of the time, they noticed they were glancing at each other occasionally.

I tried to stay focused on the conversation with the guide, but it was a bit difficult. Honestly, is was a bitch to focus. I don't usually lose my concentration but for some reason

Tye's voice and what he said to me kept me pre-occupied. My imagination started to take me to places I've never been before. The more I looked over at him talking to his friend, the more I imagined what he was like in bed. It made my pussy throb.

This is unusual for me. I have to admit that. It was the way he had control over our conversation and had control over his emotions when I flirted with him – it was like he was immune to me. The confidence he had come through in the way he spoke to me and it captivated me. I felt wet and gushy when I imagined what he would be like with me.

He passionately sucked and licked my inner thigh until the tip of his nose pressed my clit, where he stopped to inhale the aroma of my dripping pussy that matched my oriental musk perfume.

I can tell the smell of my pussy ignited his imagination which was a turn on for me. He closed his eyes and inhaled deeply my fragrance and tasted my moist lips. It gave me a sense of power knowing that he was losing control over his body – that his dick was hard, and his heart was pounding.

At the same time, I felt desired, that he would lust after me and I wanted him to have power over me – I wanted to let go and let a man like him take charge. He grabbed my ankles as though I was his capture and he was a bit rough as he ran his big strong callused hands up my legs to grab me by the waist and flip me over to fuck me from behind.

I heard a moan when he slowly slid his cock inside and noticed the tattoo on my lower back which was covered by goose bumps. He was letting go of the control he had over his mind and emotions while he watched my tattoo violently shaking as he pounds my pussy with perfect rhythm. His auditory senses were heightened as I screamed with every rhythmic thrust. It almost pushed him over the edge as I spoke with a quiver in my voice, "Oh god babe, your cock feels so good. Fuck me harder. That's it babe, fuck my craving pussy."

He appeared hornier when I talk dirty to him, "Oh shit, I'm gonna cum. Stay inside. Fill my pussy with your cream and give your baby what she wants."

He was turned on by the electricity generated when he touched my tattooed silky skin and slapped my heart shaped ass and then wrapped his hands around my waist to pull me forcefully into his pelvic. I gave him command over my body, and he took it. He never felt a chemical electricity like that before as he touched my soft skin, now forming beads of sweat and pooling at the base of my back. Fuck! I never felt an electricity like that before.

To make sure we cum together, I reached between my legs to lovingly caress his balls and gently scratch the base of his cock. All of his senses were engaged while he fucked me hard and we both felt a deep unbreakable inner connection between us - it felt like heaven on earth.

All of this heighten his arousal and it engorged his cock so that it filled my swollen wet pussy and brought both of us to ecstasy. I arched my back to make sure he could fuck me deeper. He pulled my hair with one hand and slapped my ass until his body stiffened, his eyes rolled up, and he threw his head back while he thrust his hips forward and it made me scream with pleasure while he filled my fucking hot dripping pussy with his cream.

I could feel the pulse of his cock deep inside me while I squeezed it and he shot his cum inside me. I kept squeezing my pussy around his cock so that I could get every last drop of it inside me.

The ultimate form of ecstasy was felt – we were lost in the moment and knew we more than enough for each other as we collapsed into each other's arms - dripping in sweat. This was only the beginning of the rise of sexual hunger for each other. It began a graving on par to the animalistic appetite of an alpha wolf for raw red meat.

The sudden sound of the paper map being cracked open as the guide pulled it out snapped me back into reality and out of my fantasy – it got me out of my head. The guide pulled out the map to discuss where we were going to go in the morning. The guide knew I was lost in another world and he nervously chuckled as he put it down in front of me.

"Miss. Are you ok?" He said, knowing that I was daydreaming, because I was looking right at Tye. After that fantasy, I was fucking ready and more passionate than ever about finding that scroll – Tye definitely had something to do with that. My panties were wet, and I could feel the residual pulse happening deep inside my pussy, working its way to the edge of my lips.

Shifting her legs, she turned her attention to the guide. She was so focused on the map that she didn't notice Tye walking up to her. He placed a napkin on the table in front of her on top of the map, "It was a pleasure speaking to you. Perhaps we can meet again?"

She turned the napkin over. His name, number and email address were handwritten on it. She shook her head and said, "It was a pleasure. Perhaps we can."

That was the last I saw him for the remainder of my time in   Morocco.

3

I stayed in Morocco for a few more days searching for the scroll. By the third day, we found a temple that I believed held the second scroll. Finding the temple itself was surreal. It had been hidden from sight for generations, buried deep in the sand far from civilization. We searched the temple for two days but couldn't find it. The temple was searched in places that most people wouldn't think of hiding things.

Since I couldn't find it, I brought the temple to the attention of the antiquity's division of National History for African art, museum and culture. They were astonished at my find and sponsored the rest of the dig. I was handsomely rewarded for the discovery. Close to a million dollars handsomely!

However, the disappointed was very heavy – it shook me deeply that the scroll wasn't there. I was certain that it was. Maybe there was something in the first scroll that was translated wrong. I needed to gather my thoughts and find someone who could point me in the right direction.

I stayed long enough in Morocco and it was time for me to get back home. My flight was leaving in the morning, so I tried to enjoy the remainder of my time and relax.

It was a long 8-hour flight back home. Long enough for Naffilia to contemplate the past week – the mission, finding the temple and the heartache of not finding the scroll. She scheduled a meeting with another expert in linguistics and art history who had connections in the archeology field - Dr. Martin Shraver. He came highly recommended because he had written a few books about myths and legends and the connections they had to language and culture. It wasn't a best seller like his other books. In fact, it became an obscure resource that never panned out for him financially. It was that book that caught the attention of people she had worked with to discover the first scroll.

Dr. Shraver is perceived as an odd person. After the release of that book, it almost cost him his credibility. He mentioned the scroll in a chapter – because of it, he was shunned in academic circles. Some suggested that he had lost his mind. I didn't think so. In fact, I had the scroll that would prove him correct. He didn't know I found it. Very few people knew I had it in my possession. This would be the perfect opportunity to get his help and maybe restore his name, but the world wasn't ready for this secret, that's why I didn't tell anyone I had it.

She landed in New York for a layover before heading back to Boston. She took this time to contact Dr. Shraver and scheduled a meeting for the next day. He was curious as to why she wanted to talk about a book that almost cost him his career. Specifically, about an obscure mention in a chapter. Nevertheless, he obliged.

After getting off the burner phone, it buzzed immediately. It was work. They had another mission for her. She had a couple more days off before having to return to work to be briefed and prepared for the next two weeks. This mission was going to take her to the exotic land of Dubai.

The reality of her daily routine was coming back to her, and the everyday part of life that grounded her, brought her back to life as normal. It made her aware of her craving for a connection and a sexual expression that she long for.

Fuck! I haven't gotten laid in almost a week. I almost forgot why I went to find the scroll in the first place. It feels good to be home and I can't wait to get back to my place and lay in my own bed.

Just then, her phone buzzed a few more times, it was a few guys she met over the past month. They wanted to meet for a date. She smiled, "Perfect timing boys. I'm gonna have some fun tomorrow." She arranged a date with each man – three of them. She spread out the date so that she met each one at different times of the day.

In the morning she would date a millionaire who owned his own diamond distribution company. He would fly in from New York and they would spend the morning talking over breakfast just to get to know more about each other. His tenacity and business knowledge impressed her, but he had a tough time keeping his head in their conversation the last time they met.

In the afternoon, she would date a professional athlete who played football. He was a high-profile player who could have any woman he wanted, but he wanted to date her. She was curious as to why he was interested. They had met at a party months ago and he remembered her. His inflated ego was one thing she didn't care about, but he was good looking, built and had potential, that gave her reason enough to go out on a date with him.

In the evening, she would date a corporate lawyer from California – he owned his own firm and represented some of the most well-known corporations in the US. They had met through a friend of a friend. He was drawn to her. She didn't know much about him and was curious. Of the three of them, he had the most potential to meet all her needs. He was a gentleman, good looking, very smart and a promising future. In her mind she saved the best for last.

It was time to board the plane and head back to Boston. It felt like she was getting back into the grove of her life. Sometimes these missions take a toll on her, as though she was living two separate lives. On occasion it feels like her fantasy world crossed over and became her reality, and vice versa. Getting into a routine helped bring balance. She took a quick nap on the way home.

She arrived in Boston and went to the overnight parking garage to pick up her SUV. Her automobile made it feel good to be home. As she was driving along the length of the airport she drove past the far end – the side where private planes had their own hangers. That end of the airport was always filled with exotic cars – luxury cars, limousines and corporate transportation.

Today she slowed down to take a closer look at this part of the airport and noticed in the distance there was a black muscle car driving out from that area. She couldn't make it out until it drove off the property and made its way toward her.

Oh shit! It's the muscle! What the hell are they doing in there? She could feel her body tingle as she recalled seeing them on the highway just a week earlier.

She slowed down on purpose in order to meet with them at the merge. It worked. They met at the merge and it was obvious they recognized her because they started to pace her. They at least recognized her car, because they started to pace her again. She pulled out in front and then let up on the throttle until they caught up. They pulled out in front of her and she caught up. They paced each other perfectly.

"Who the fuck are you?" She couldn't make out who he was through his tinted window. They were a mere silhouette and probably couldn't see her either because their windows were tinted as well. It didn't matter. She was going to kick their ass this time and cranked the music to set the tone and a big shit eating grin appear on her face.

He was going in the same direction as her. They exited the area and got onto the highway. The moment they had a straight away, their engines throttled. It was like the thunder of a storm as both cars jolted forward.

She howled with excitement, "wooo hooo…let's go muscle. Show me whatcha got."

The race was on and they took the lead, but only by a foot. Both cars weaved in and out of traffic. She laughed with excitement, "Ha haa…whoever you are, your ass is mine this time. Let's see how much muscle you got." She stepped on the throttle and sling shot forward. With a smile plastered on her face, she turned her head to find out where he was.

She spotted him at least a car length back. The power of his classic muscle car was no match for the modern power of her turbo car.

She belted out with a tone of satisfaction, "Ha." She was pleased with her win. The competitive side of her hates to lose. "You're not such a badass after all." This time, it was her driving off into the distance while she watched them in the rear-view mirror take the off ramp 2 exits before her.

Still reveling in her victory, she couldn't help but feel intrigued that they came from the airport from the private sector. "Who the fuck is this guy? What the hell are they doing there?"

Naffilia pulled into the underground parking. "Ahh. It feels good to be home." She made her way toward her private parking space where her red Porsha 911 and her black Suzuki M109R motorcycle were parked. "I love my life. I'm grateful for everything in it, and gratitude keeps me young and young at heart."

She parked her car and made her way to the elevator. Why does it feel cold between my legs? Oh my gosh. My panties are wet, and I feel gushy. What the fuck?! I didn't even notice that while I was driving. Ha. Oh well - the price you pay for an exciting life like mine. At least I beat that muscle and they welcomed me back to Boston in style with a mental orgasm and a race to remember.

She entered her house and called out, "Alexia...lights on and play music." The lights came on and soft music played in the background.

Kicking off her shoes she dropped onto the couch, ordered takeout and settled in. Before the food arrived, she took a hot shower to wind down for the rest of the day, sipped on wine and make a few phone calls. Dr. Shraver was on the list of people to get in touch with, along with her three dates tomorrow. She text Dr. Shraver and confirmed where and when to meet.

"We'll meet at the Boston Museum tomorrow at 2:30 pm with the curator and 2 collogues."

She texts her three dates and arranged to meet them tomorrow, the first one at 7 am, the second at 12 pm and the third was scheduled for 6 pm. In her mind, she saved the best for last and wanted to get to know him more because he had potential.

She took her shower and got into her plush bathrobe to relaxed for the remainder of the evening and watch the latest series on Netflix until she fell asleep.

Tomorrow morning was going to be a busy day, she was excited for the possibility of getting the answers she was looking for. She was growing more restless and frustrated by the fact that she couldn't find the second scroll, especially since she was convinced that it was in Morocco. Everything pointed to that fact that it was at that location and it made no sense that it wasn't.

Contacting Dr. Shraver was the right thing to do. He may have an answer that may have been overlooked by everybody else. In the morning as she was getting ready, she text Dr Shraver to confirm her 2:30 pm appointment.

Naffilia's first date was set for 7 am. Having a breakfast date would seem out of the ordinary for everyone else, but not for her. She grew tired of the typical date, and meeting for breakfast made things more interesting. Because they were meeting for the second time and going to a well-known restaurant in the heart of the city, she dressed to impress but kept it a few steps below formal.

Roger Clayton flew in from New York on his private jet to meet Naffilia at an exclusive restaurant overlooking the city. He was punctual, just like her. They met in the waiting area. Roger was a clean-cut man and was dressed as if he were going to a business presentation. Naffilia was impressed, "You look handsome. Nice shoes!"

Roger warmly replied, "Thank you. You look beautiful."

He motioned for her to lead the way, "Shall we?"

Roger was a well-known distributor for diamonds across

the globe. The conversation was captivating for both of them. However, the more comfortable they got with each other, the more eager he was to share his profession than he was about sharing his personal life.

He was obviously a driven, successful businessman who took pride in how much he achieved over the years. It showed in the way he kept talking about his next business move and how many times he turned from their conversation to answer his text messages.

Naffilia was impressed with his achievements and the vast wealth that he acquired with little help from his family, but there was something about his state of mind that told her that she would have been nothing less than a collection to him, that barely stood out from his diamonds and business dealings.

For being an exclusive restaurant, Naffilia wasn't impressed with the food. Breakfast is breakfast. You can only prep eggs so many ways. The atmosphere and the view made up for it. Although, she found herself looking at her watch to check the time because the second date was at noon.

The moment they were done eating breakfast she said, "Roger. I appreciate your invitation to breakfast and getting to know you better. I would like to express my thanks for this time this morning." She reached into her purse and pulled out a gift for him. "Please accept this rose and bottle of cologne as a token of my gratitude."

Roger's face was surprised. He had never been given a gift on a date before. Naffilia was truly unique and it showed where her heart was. "Thank you for this. I appreciate it."

Roger took care of the bill and they made their way toward the exit. Naffilia motioned with her head toward the exit, "I have an appointment for noon, so I should probably get going now. Again, thank you Roger and it was a pleasure to meet you."

Roger nodded his head because he understood that they didn't connected as he had hoped, but he didn't stop trying. He reached into his pocket and gave her his business card, "If you would like to meet up some time in the future, here is my number. Have a good day."

Naffilia nodded as she took his card.

Her next date was with a pro athlete with the local football team. In her eyes, he was a prize. He was popular and well known. He was an athlete which meant he had a "hot bod" and he probably had enough stamina to please her, and he was independently wealthy. On the surface, he seemed to have everything going in his favour.

They agreed to meet at the popular seafood restaurant at the pier in the heart of downtown Boston. She loved seafood and he picked her favorite place to eat. Because of that, he was already one foot in the door to her heart.

He offered to pick her up, but she didn't want to miss her 2:30 pm appointment with Dr. Shraver and his colleagues and told him that it was best to meet him there.

She was prompt and paid for valet because it was convenient for her. There was no sign of him for 15 minutes as she waited outside for her date. She rechecked her phone messages to make sure the time was correct and to see if he might have text her. Just as she looked up from her phone, she could hear loud music blaring from a yellow Porsche with black details as it sped down the road to the parking lot. As he pulled up, she could hear the lyrics from hard core rap – 'You're on my dick when you need my money. You're on my dick when you need my shit. You're on my dick when you need my ride…'."

She watched in horror as the car pulled in, and mumbled to herself, "What the fuck? 'You're on my dick?' Oh no, please don't let that be him. Shit. Shit. Shit."

Yup, it was my date. I hope I didn't just walk into this clown's ring to be a part of his tricks. Please don't let this set the tone of our date.

She looked around to see how many people were staring at him as he made a fool of himself pulling into an exclusive restaurant with his music blaring.

He poked his head out of the window as he turned the music off, "Hey! Sorry to keep you waiting. I was later than I expected at my photo shoot for Nike. Plus, a few fans stopped me on my way here."

What the fuck?! He's attracting attention like flies on shit. This dude is way too much into himself. I gotta play this off somehow.

Naffilia shrugged her shoulders, "It happens. I'm glad you made it."

Bucky Stoner was his name. As soon as he stepped out the car, I noticed that he was dressed like a fuckboy, and he seemed pleased that he carried himself like one. I couldn't help but laugh and remark under my breath without him hearing, "What the fuck?"

As he was walking toward me, he barked into his key fob, "Lock the doors."

You could hear the car respond – click - beep-beep.

He looked at me with a smirk on his face, clearly showing off. He motioned with his thumb over his shoulder, "It's the latest model with all the bells and whistles."

I tried not to make it obvious from my facial expression and did my best not to roll my eyes, knowing that this date was off to a bad start.

What the fuck! This guy is an asshole and I could smell his shit through his cheap ass cologne. He probably can't even fuck a woman the right way. This dickhead is likely to get lost in his own world looking for my clit.

He pranced up to her gesturing to the peer, "This is a hot spot. It's a kickin' restaurant. The boys and I love hanging out here after practise. They have a great bar here overlooking the peer."

Just then a few fans came between him and Naffilia and he

soaked it up like a sponge. It was the giddy women who pleased him the most.

He stopped to give his autograph and nodded toward Naffilia, "Hey. You go in and get our seat. I'll be right in."

Naffilia scoffed and shook her head as she looked at her watch.

Damn, I still have 2 hours with this fucking prick.

She went inside to get their seat on the deck while he took his time signing autographs in the parking lot.

I'll find something to appreciate right now. I have to admit that the view overlooking the peer is breathtaking. There's one thing that I've always loved, and that's taking walks along the peer or along the beach. It reminds me of my family, especially my father and the precious times we shared when I was younger. I've always loved this spot to eat for this very reason. I like to watch the boats come in with the catch of the day while I lose myself in solitude.

She lost herself temporarily in the peace that the ocean waves created as they crashed into the port. The waiter approached her, "Hi. My name is Kody. Welcome to Seaport Eatery. Are you waiting for someone or are you ready to order?"

She paused briefly to think about what he said, "I'm not waiting for anyone. I'll get the seafood platter and the house beer."

He nodded, "Very good ma'am."

Just as the waiter walked away Bucky came in and sat down. He seemed pleased with himself, that he contributed to society. "So. Naffilia. Thanks for meeting with me today. I'm excited that you reached out to me. For a little while I thought you forgot about me after the party. Do you wanna order before we get too deep into conversation?"

Naffilia motioned to the main part of the restaurant, "I

already ordered."

Bucky raised his eyebrows, "Oh. Ok." He scanned the menu quickly before the waiter came over to him.

Against my better judgement, to get a conversation going, I figured I'd ask him what position he played for his team.

He put the menu down and leaned back in his chair and rested both arms on his seat as though he were sitting on a throne. "I play line backer."

He made a sad attempt to joke by speaking cryptically to her, "My job is the stuff the runner." He chuckled.

Naffilia tilted her head, "That's funny. So basically, if you run a 4-3 defense your job is pretty limited, and with the way the coach is running the defence these days you're probably seeing less action than you did when you were younger. Plus, I read that the coach drafted younger players for this season, and he is considering more experienced talent to bolster the defense next season and run a 3-4 defense. Seems like the coach doesn't trust your skills. Aren't you a bit concerned for your job?"

Bucky's face looked as if he saw a ghost. Just then the waiter introduced himself and asked if he was ready to order. Still a bit stunned from her response, "Oh. Yeah. I'll take the grilled swordfish with fries and a Bud."

Bucky motioned to Naffilia for her to order.

She smirked, "I told you, I already ordered while you were with your fans."

Naffilia's order came out before his and she started to eat while he did most of the talking, mainly about himself and didn't ask about her. This gave her plenty of time to eat and listen to, "The wonderful world of Bucky."

She finished her meal by the time he was halfway through his and she made an attempt to talk about herself, where she was from, and what she was all about. He seemed more interested in how good the swordfish was than what she had to say. Just then, his phone started pinging.

He held up his finger, gesturing for her to wait one second

while he answered the text. When he was done texting, he invited her to talk again. He made an attempt to pay attention to her, but his phone rang louder than she was speaking, the ringtone was from a popular song called, "Bitches."

He stopped and turned away from the table to answer the phone. "Hi mom."

He nodded his head and pointed to the phone and mouthed, "It's my mom. I gotta take this." He laughed as he turned his body away from the table and took his time on the phone.

Naffilia winced, "I wonder what my ringtone is."

She looked at her watch. It was 1:30 pm and she had enough. It was time to leave. She didn't hesitate to call the waiter over, gesturing him not to speak too loudly, and handed him $100, "This is for my part of the meal if 'Homey the clown' doesn't cover it. You can keep the change."

The waiter snickered as he received the money.

Then she gave him a $50 bill, "This is for you. Thank you for your service. Can you tell valet to have my car ready?"

"I will. And thank you for the tip." He glanced at her date and then back to her, "I hope you have a good day."

"Thank you." She chugged the remainder of her beer and got up from her seat without bringing attention to herself. Bucky didn't notice she had already paid for her meal and stood up at the table until he finished his call just in time to see her starting to walk out.

He was in shock as he took a long hard look, at her toned, tight, heart shaped ass in her skin-tight skirt while she walked away from the table and left him in the restaurant.

She didn't bother to look back while she purposefully shook her ass on the way out and mocked him, "That line backer won't be getting this tight end."

Bucky shoveled down the rest of his meal and threw money on the table and left the restaurant to catch her. As he ran after her, three women stopped him. They were giddy for an autograph and a selfie and bounced up and down until their tits caught Bucky's eyes. He didn't hesitate to privilege the woman with his signature and a picture with them. After he posed for a selfie with them, he looked over to see a Lamborghini Urus pull around the corner. He was stunned that an expensive car like that was even in this part of the city. He was even more stunned to see Naffilia getting into to it.

She was smiling as she got into her car, then glanced back at him briefly and scoffed. She rolled down her window and turned on her radio with her own hard-core rap song blaring, "You're not worth a dime if you can't respect my mind. Respect my heart and respect my soul, then I'm gonna treat you like you're worth more than gold. Show me that you need me, as much as I need you..."

He stood in astonishment as the song caught his attention, it was the same artist that he seemed to admire.

Naffilia revved her engine. The rumble of the car could be heard through the whole restaurant. She deliberately stretched her arm out the window with her hand clenched in a fist and slowly raised her middle finger to Bucky.

She shouted over her music, "Stick this up your ass."

He stood there with his jaw open as he watched her drive away in a car that he himself couldn't afford. He never felt like an ass like that before, until he crossed her path.

She arrived at the museum a little earlier than she expected so she took her time to look at some of the artwork along the long hall as she made her way toward the curator's office. There was one piece that looked unfamiliar to her. Since she was an art enthusiast, well versed in most mediums and from different eras, she recognized that this new image was new to the art world, something that nobody has seen before. She stopped to examine it and noticed that it came from the same era as the scroll, it was oddly familiar.

It had an insignia on the bottom right-hand corner. This was done by an unknown artist, yet all of the elements of the art looked similar to the scroll. It was more like illustrations of erotic art, erotic sexual positions of lovers.

On the background she noticed something that looked very similar to a few things she's found in the temple in Morocco, as well as etching she found in the cave in Israel. It looked like an insignia of some sort. She recalled seeing it worn on high profile people - elitists around the globe, and she wondered if there was a connection. They wore them as pins or buttons. These were people of influence, shakers of the world.

The image reminded her of Dubai, and it struck her as odd that something so ancient would have a Dubai and an Israeli connection, yet there remains and odd disconnect. She studied every detail and took out her cell phone to take pictures of the image and zoomed in on the icon and took a picture of it.

After a few minutes of studying the new art, whispers could be heard echoing in the great hall, coming from outside the curator's office. It was Dr. Shraver, the curator and two other people. They took note of Naffina looking at the image and kept glancing in her direction. They were curious to know if she was the one they were supposed to meet.

Their whispers caught her attention and she walked over to them with an air of confidence as their whispers waned. She announced herself, "Hello. I'm Naffilia. I'm looking for Dr. Shraver."

Dr. Shraver extended his hand, "I'm Milton Shraver. These are my colleagues Dr. Ian Van, doctor of linguistics and History." Dr. Van nodded.

"This is Brian Wicker, a friend of ours. He's a myths and legends enthusiast, author of several books and an expert in urban legends and culture."

Shaking Naffilia's hand, "Hi. Nice to meet you."

Dr. Shraver gestured, "This is Dr. Anne Price, doctor of antiquities and art history. She is very well known in her field and has written a number of books as well." She nodded her head.

"And this is the curator of the museum, Dr. Mark Spencer. He's very well connected in the art world. This guy really knows his stuff.""

Mark reached out and shook Naffina's hand, "I noticed that you were looking at that art over there. Is there something about it that intrigues you?"

She gestured to the painting, "It looks like a new piece of art that the world hasn't seen before."

Mark raised his eyebrows in reply, "I'm impressed." He shook his head, "You know your art. That's actually true. It was just discovered four months ago in the area of Dubai and nobody knows for sure about its origins yet."

Mark captivated everyone's attention by subtly waving his hands like a conductor, "You see?! Most people don't know that Dubai has an inhabited history that goes way back almost 2500 BCE. In 35 CE the Persian Gulf was an important fishing and pearl harvesting location. There's speculation that this artwork has influence from that area. The interesting thing about it is, that it's not your typical art depicting history, culture or lifestyle. It seems to serve a purpose."

"A purpose?" Naffilia asked.

"Yeah. Think of it this way. I noticed that you took a picture of the art. Why did you take the picture?" Mark asked.

"I was curious about something and I wanted to keep in my phone to check it out later and study it." She said matter-of-factly.

Mark nodded, "You have a purpose for the image being on your phone. You didn't take it for the sake of art. I'm assuming you're not making it your background on the phone. That's what this artwork is. It served a purpose other than art." He said with conviction.

Brian raised a question. "So how could something like this be hidden from the world for so long? Where 'bouts in Dubai was it found?"

Mark replied, "It was found in a desert area outside of Dubai as they were digging for oil. For religious reasons there was one tract of land that couldn't be touched for centuries. When they finally had access to it, a rigger found a shrine buried almost 150 feet below the sand. Excavation found a shrine probably as big is this hallway. The only thing they found in the shrine was that piece." He pointed to the art.

Dr. Shraver interrupted the conversation. "I'm sorry to interrupt this fascinating story, but Miss Naffilia called me about something equally intriguing."

He motioned to her, "Please. How can we help you?"

Before I address these brilliant minds, I have to gather myself because I'm really curious about this art piece now. I feel like I'm about to blow my fucking mind with what I just heard. What are the chances of me finding something like this in my own back yard? Mark made a great point that it looks to serve a purpose. I can see that there's a connection to the scroll.

She cleared her throat, "Thank you all for hearing me out. I just want to begin by acknowledging and agreeing that this art…"

She pointed to it, "…doesn't look like traditional art."

I couldn't tell them that it looked eerily similar to the map I found several months ago, around the same time they found this art. I'm pretty certain there is something about this piece that may answer some questions I have. I hope someone here can help me. I have to use my interrogation skills to get the answers I am looking for without telling them I found a scroll.

One the one hand, I didn't want to tell anyone about the scroll - it was too monumental of a find that I wanted for myself before anyone else could get it, but I was running out of options to get the help I needed to translate it. I got this far with limited help, but If I wanted to find out its secrets, I would have to trust at least a few people to help me.

"Dr. Shraver. You wrote a chapter in your book that piqued my interest. You wrote about a myth about sexual ecstasy. I understand that you took some heat for it. For closed minded people, it seems like foolishness, but I consider myself an adventurer and an optimist. Could you, and your collogues expound on that myth?"

A look of curiosity came over Dr. Shraver's face and his posture became more erect, "Certainly."

He looked around at his friends and they gave him their attention as well.

Dr. Shraver addressed them, "I've done years of research for various myths, legends and culture and I happened to come across this one particular legend of sexual ecstasy. Of all the legends I've come across, this one was the most elusive. Hell, the Loch Ness monster, sasquatch, area 51 and Stonehenge looked more like accepted facts and accepted truths compared to the legend of a scroll that connected heaven to earth through sexual expression."

The whole group laughed in agreement. Most of them shook their head in agreement while Naffilia mimic them to appear that she agreed.

He continued, "I happen to come across this legend but I decided not to pursue it because there wasn't enough evidence to warrant writing a whole book about it, but I came across a handful of sage and shaman around the world and in different cultures who alluded to this legend."

He raised one finger to emphasis his next point, "That alone was enough to warrant a mention in one chapter. How could people around the world who have no connection with each have the same story? I just mentioned it in passing. It was my duty to bring it to light."

Naffilia asked, "So, you really don't have any more information other than you think there is a possibility that it exists?"

"I'm sorry to disappoint you, but that is the case. Perhaps my collogues can paint a bigger picture for you." He made a gesture to open the floor for discussion.

Mark spoke first, "As I already mentioned, the only reason

we found that art on the wall there…"

He pointed in its direction, "…is because there was a tract of land near Dubai that was under religious protection. It was a sacred place for unknown reasons. I don't know the details."

Mark was a captivating storyteller. He continued, "The shrine they found had inscriptions on the walls. Come, let me show you the pictures."

He directed everyone to the conference room where he showed them pictures of the inscriptions.

I took a closer look at the inscription and gasped. I hope that nobody noticed. Shit, I could feel my heart skip a beat. The inscriptions were similar to the ones on the scroll I had at home that nobody could interpret for me. The fact that they had something like this in their possession told me that these guys are the real deal. I couldn't resist and I had to ask.

"Has anyone been able to translate the inscriptions?" She asked inquisitively.

Mark shook his head, "Not yet. We're still looking for someone who could actually read it, rather than give their opinion."

Dr. Anne Price gasped, "Oh my gosh!" She covered her mouth.

Dr. Milton Shraver was surprised by her reaction, "What?"

Anne squinted her eyes as she stepped closer to read the inscriptions, "I know this language. It's a rare Hebrew language that hasn't been seen since biblical times. This goes back almost 3000 BCE. It's based off an original Hebrew dialect, an untouched version of Hebrew, unlike that which is spoken today."

She motioned with her hand around the text, "The best way to explain this inscription is this – it's like having the original language without any slang or derogatory suggestions mixed with another culture's language. It's a true reflection of the culture and the heart of the people that spoke it. But this looks like there are Egyptian symbols mixed in as well. As though it's an attempt to mix cultures and create a new language. That's why you haven't found anyone who can interpret it. It doesn't exist in the known world."

All eyes in the room were locked in on her and what she was saying. Everyone was on edge as to what she was about to say next.

With a smile of admiration and awe she said, "It's an attempt to write and speak the language of gods. When the gods speak, it is out of purity, love, power and spiritual enlightenment – what ensues is power in the purest form. This seems like some kind of mystical prayer."

Brian the enthusiast who hadn't spoken much to this point, grabbed his head in excitement, "Holy Fuck! This is real Indiana Jones shit! Like finding the Ark of the covenant."

Everyone looked at Brian with different reactions – contempt, humour and excitement. Their air of formality seemed to melt because of his reaction.

He continued, "Seriously! It's like that scene when they opened the ark and all these spirits came out and turned the Germans to dust. That kind of power...that kind of mind-blowing find. It makes me wonder if the scroll is real - with this kind of high-level power."

Dr. Shraver reached out with his hand to calm him down, "Easy my friend. We don't even know what it says yet." He turned to Anne, "Can you translate it Dr. Price?"

She squinted her eyes to concentrate, "I think I can read a portion of it..." This part here says, "The two will become one."

They were puzzled by the translation. There was a pause in the room before Brian spoke up. "Isn't that a phrase from Jewish sayings?"

Naffilia spoke up, "It comes from the book of genesis. Specifically, genesis 2:24 - alluding to when a man and woman come together to become one flesh."

The room when silent with her insight along with this newfound information and find. It captivated everyone's mind and they were stunned to the point that nobody could speak.

Mark broke the silence, "There's deeper meaning to this. This isn't just about sexual ecstasy. I think there is something else to this. Hear me out for a moment."

He paused to gather his thoughts, "Dr. Shraver. You made a valid point that around the globe snippet of the same story is told. If you think about this, they each hold a piece of a puzzle – a truth if you will. If we were talking about a truth or god, then no single person is capable of grasping the whole. So, the truth or god is easier to understand from parts and pieces, the truth or god is more bearable to grasp in small pieces, but the drawback is that you aren't getting the bigger picture."

He paused to let it sink in and then gestured by opening his arms wide and brought them closer together to make a point when he said, "Bring those pieces together – like pieces of a pie then you get a big picture. You get the complete understanding of truth or the full revelation of god. What if, this hidden scroll serves the same purpose. What if these inscriptions and that new art we acquired are a part of the mystery of this legend you speak about? What if there were more than one scroll?"

He stunned everyone with the question and then continued, "They would have to remain separate to preserve its integrity but also help in some way to understand fractally the bigger picture. Yet, to get the bigger picture, you have to bring them together. The moment you bring them together, the full power of truth or god is understood – the full power of ecstasy if experienced. What if there are two scrolls?"

There was a hush in the room, then Mark continued, "Let's think about this for a second. Gather all the knowledge together in a single place and we can accomplish anything. Yet, it would take the collective mind of every human to come close to having even a speck of truth of who god is. If you bring people together and sort through to find the truth, you get a single picture, you get one big truth."

Mark motioned like he was gathering people together, "Suppose you gather all the minds together, and somehow tap into all of them simultaneously and re-direct them into a single source, you can funnel heavenly experiences into temporal minds – you usher into our time and space a speck of god or truth."

His excitement started to spread, "People! We are looking for two scrolls. There's another part of the scroll."

He paused to reflect on what he said, "There's two parts of the scrolls. Both parts together become one map and it tells the secret! That art that you have hanging out there might be a snippet of something more."

Brian raised his clenched fists and paced the floor, "Fucking A! The legend is real! There's two parts of the scroll somewhere in the world. Secrets of the gods. Are you shittin' me?!"

Dr. Shraver abandoned his proper ways and chimed in with uncontrolled elation, "Son of bitch. I almost lost my career over this and it actually exists!"

Dr. Price became the voice of reason, "Now let's not get ahead of ourselves here. We can't go running around telling people we have information on something we really have no confirmation about. The scrolls have never been found. We have very little information where to find them and we only have these pictures as proof of a legend, and nobody can truly translate this."

Dr. Price deflated the room with a single stroke of reasoning. But I knew something they didn't. I could barely contain myself. My excitement level was on the same plane of having an orgasm. The feeling was like having a full body orgasm in public and you are trying not to show anyone that you're having one. It was like holding back the power of rushing water, and you are the damn.

The translation told me two things. Two scrolls existed, and that the possessor could tap into sexual ecstasy, to touch heaven, and all of it was real! Fuck! I couldn't hold back my excitement. If my panties were going to get wet, now was the time. I had to get my focus back and draw everyone back into the important matter at hand.

Naffilia asked, "This photo of the inscriptions you have and the art on the wall out there, has anyone or any of the best analysts had a chance to see all of this before us?"

Mark replied, "A select few. All they discovered is that this ancient art comes from Biblical times and some think it has Babylonian influence. Some suggest that it is rare Jewish art."

Naffina questioned his findings, "Yeah but I don't recall the Jewish culture having art like this to depict their culture."

Dr. Price agreed, "Yeah you're right. The Jewish culture didn't have this kind of art, that's why it's rather odd and intriguing. From what we discovered just now, it's more an illustration or instructions of some sort."

The room went silent to ponder the words spoken.

My curiosity heightened again because there was a symbol on the illustration. It looked familiar. I've seen this in Morocco in the temple, I've been to Dubai in the past and saw it there before. Now that I think of it, I've seen that symbol in other places. I just don't remember where. It was like my subconscious was recalling it. I glanced at my watch and realized that the time for my third date was close.

"Excuse me lady and gentlemen. I have an appointment to tend to. But I would like to thank all of you for coming together today for this. I'll get in touch if I have any more questions or information. I'll keep this close to my chest until we all have conclusive evidence of the scroll."

They bid her farewell and stayed a few more minutes to talk among themselves about the scroll and if it had connections to what they discussed.

On her drive home she thought about the conversation. She started to connect the dots.

That art was about sexual expression, but it seemed like it

was laid out in such a way that it was more of a map than art and it pointed to Dubai. There was an icon on that image. I have no idea what it means or if it has any significance whatsoever. Anyway, it looks like I'm going to Dubai the next time I get an opportunity.

In mid thought her phone rang. The display on the dash showed up as Stanley Bradby. Stanley was her third date for tonight. He was old school and talking on the phone to confirm a date was his way. She liked that about him. He was a gentleman who crossed all the "T's" and dotted every "I." He had his shit together, and from what little she knew about him, he didn't have any emotional baggage and was financially and emotionally independent.

She was excited to get home and take her time getting ready for this date. Because Stanley was a corporate lawyer and owned his own firm it made him come across as being very intelligent. The thought of his intelligence, especially coming from a meeting surrounded by academic minds turned her on. This was something new for her – arousal by intelligence.

She had heard about sapiosexual arousal but thought it was a fabrication by self-proclaimed sex experts who were simply internet junkies, and that it was unsubstantiated. At the very least, she thought it was a rare occurrence. The more she thought about these intellectuals and the thought about going on a date with one, a low pulsing throb could be felt in her panties.

What the hell? I'm actually turned on by the thought of this date and the conversations we might have. I'm getting fucking horny because of their brilliant minds.

The more she thought about this rare type of sexual arousal, the more she felt it rise. There was something about a man who saw the world differently and who could use their imagination and creativity. It reminded her of herself. Maybe these guys understood her better than most of the men she's dated, and that in itself was a turn on. That they challenged her mind.

Her foot instinctively pushed the peddle a little harder to race home and get ready. She wanted enough time to be ready for Stanley. She took her shower and got dressed. This was a semi-formal date, so she looked her best and was particular about the jewelry she was going to wear.

In the meantime, her mind kept bouncing back and forth between her date and the conversation about the art, the scroll and Dubai.

She was making plans in her mind to travel and what she was looking for when she got there. She was mentally putting all the pieces together about the art when Stanley called her phone again to let her know that he was going to arrive at the restaurant in 30 minutes.

Oh, fuck I'm going to be late. I'm never late. How the hell did I lose track of time?

She finished getting ready and left in a hurry. She wasn't far from the restaurant. The restaurant they agreed on was a popular steak restaurant. Only the finest chefs of Boston worked there. Out of courtesy she called Stanley to let him know that she would be outside shortly. She barely made it on time and gave her car to valet and called Stanley to tell him she was outside getting ready to walk in.

He came out to greet her and kissed her on the cheek. It sent tingles down her spine to be greeted that way, to know that he was focused on her and greeted her in a classy way.

He seemed genuinely pleased to see her, "I'm glad you made it. I've already been seated. Shall we?"

Stanley grabbed her hand and led her into the restaurant. He was a gentleman by every sense of the definition. The bonus was that he paid attention to how he took care of himself and what he wore. The women who watched him walk by in his Ermenegildo Zegna custom tailored suit knew exactly what I mean by that. His presence caught the attention of both the men and the women as he walked by to be seated.

He pulled her chair out for her so she could sit down. She was pleasantly surprised that chivalry wasn't dead, and it turned her on.

Stanley was classy. He spent time grooming himself, and I could tell it wasn't just for our date. This appeared to be something he did regularly. It helped him to carry himself very well.

Everything on the outside tickled my senses and I couldn't help but wonder if he was a bad boy deep down inside and covered it up well. There was something about a nice clean-cut guy who held back the freak inside waiting to unleash himself in a moment's notice in the bedroom. I guess that's what I'm going to find out and I have every intention to find out tonight.

Before they even ordered their meals, they talked about their day and a little about themselves, with a noticeable smile on each other's face. Their conversation was engaging from the get-go. He had lots of questions for her and wanted to get to know her.

Before they went any further, he paused, "Tell me what you're in the mood for."

He motioned to the menu.

Stanley mentioned that he was starving. Unintentionally he gave her a look that she had seen before as he said, "I have a craving for meat today. But first, I'd like an appetizer before the main course."

It seemed like he was teasing her. It sounded naturally sexual to her and Naffilia's mind started to buzz.

The way Stanley gestured with his hands as he spoke made him seem expressive and it was oddly similar to the man I met in Morocco. If I remember correctly, his name was Tye. He was captivating and Stanley's mannerisms made me start to think about that encounter.

Stanley asked her a question so she could do the talking first and then slowly put a piece of bread in his mouth. In an instant, Tye from Morocco flooded her mind.

She remembered the moment when he put the pineapple in his mouth slowly. Stanley's voice had bass just like Tye. The atmosphere with all the sounds and the smell took Naffilia back to Morocco in an instant. In her mind flashed an image of Tye with his rock-hard naked body fucking her in a bed in the middle of a desert as red silky sheets engulfed them as they fluttered in the desert wind. Her thought and imagination felt real, she would swear she heard both of them moaning with ecstasy over the sound of their flesh pounding as he fucked her from behind.

I could feel my breath quiver and my heart beating at the thought of Tye pounding my pussy - which I could feel pulsing as I was sitting across my date. The thought of Tye's dick filling me as I straddled him, subjugating myself to him, made me lose control. Every forceful bounce on his cock sent a wave in my body so that my tits bounced in his face, swiping his extending tonged and teasing my nipples until they were hard. The thought of fucking a man I couldn't have, in the middle of nowhere in a desert, in the open like that for everyone to see, made a bead of sweat form on my nose.

I couldn't tell if I was daydreaming or having a vision of being with Tye. I couldn't separate this vision from reality because his touch and his voice imprisoned my body and soul in timeless space.

Stanley's voice sounded muffled. "Are…m…ay" He had to repeat it twice, "Are you OK? You seem a bit lost in thought there."

Stanley is a good-looking man and within minutes was able to trigger something in me. He seemed like a brilliant man and I was getting turned on by his intellect. I couldn't pull myself out of the thought that Tye had this effect on me as well. It suddenly made sense to me why I was turned on by

Tye when we first met, there was a part of me that was sapiosexual. Holy Fuck! And I can feel it in my body.

I looked down at the menu, and the design elements reminded me of the art I saw today. In an instant, my mind transitioned to the new lead I got from my meeting today with the intellectuals at the museum. The excitement of the thought that another scroll existed, the meeting of the minds, the man who sat across from me and the vision of Tye all pooled in one place at the wrong time, right now over dinner, and all of it overwhelmed me.

My date's voice was muffled, "Hello?" Stanley repeat. "My dear are you here with me?"

She shook her slightly to get out of her mind and looked him in the eyes and smiled. "Yes. I'm sorry. You reminded me of something. I found out some good news today and I was just thinking about it."

She noticed the sweat on her nose. "Pardon me Stanley, but do you mind if I go to the lady's room for a moment."

He took a breath and let out a noticeable sigh, "No, I don't mind."

I could tell by his voice that he was mildly frustrated with me for not paying attention to the conversation. He was genuinely interested in me, an unusual trait in the men I've dated lately, but I can tell that I came across like I was blowing him off while he was talking to me. I needed to get my bearings.

She walked into the lady's room quickly and stopped abruptly in front of the mirror to powder her nose, as she did so, she paused to look at her reflection.

Get your shit together. Get your mind into this date. He's a good guy. He's a really nice guy Naffilia.

She took a deep breath and returned to the table where Stanley was ready for dinner. She still wasn't herself. She struggled most of the night to get her head into the date.

Stanley was a gentleman the whole time. I could tell that he made every effort to enjoy himself despite my lack of presence. He made every effort to get to know me. The questions he asked were deep and I enjoyed getting to know him. We ate our meal, which was amazing, but I could read his face and it told me that he thought it was rude of me not to live in the moment with him and share this time together.

As the evening with him drew to a close he came out and asked me, "Is there something or someone else your thinking about tonight because you seemed a bit distracted?"

"No. I'm really sorry about that. I didn't know how distracted I was until you mentioned it." I kissed him on the cheek like he did to me when he greeted me. I reached into my purse and gave him a red rose and a bottle of cologne as a gift.

He was surprised at my gesture, but he also tried to hide how disappointed he was, "Thank you. It happens. Perhaps another time would be better."

Naffilia nodded, "Yes. I would like that. We have each other's number. I'm going to be away for a little while for work but when I get back perhaps, we can meet again."

He nodded.

I knew I fucked this one up. Stanley did everything right, and I never did find out if the nice guy he is had an inner sexual secret. Of all the men I've dated, he has qualities that I should have acknowledged. He was head and shoulders above the asshole Bucky was from earlier today, and I certainly don't remember much from my first date…well…the meal was fantastic.

It was uncommon for Naffilia to lose herself on a date like that, and she recognized that the conversation at the museum and being surrounded by academic professionals made her excited and horny. The urge to let go was overwhelming. The multitude of emotions - including frustration, filled her whole day, and it put her in a state of mind that all she could think about was dick and getting fucked to ease and cover that itchy feeling on the inside.

The regret of fucking up this date and the intensity of

thinking about Tye pushed her to the edge. She thought about going to an exclusive club for excitement and release for herself.

In the financial district of Boston there was a hidden exclusive club known as Orgy. Getting in was by invitation only. Naffilia knew about the club because her agency kept tabs on all the underground businesses in the area. Knowing about the underground world of business, technology and connections paid off many times for her during her career. But tonight, it was about pleasure.

She kept some clothes in the back of her car in case she ever needed a change of clothes. Naffilia parked in a garage less than a block away from the club. She stripped down in her SUV and put on her sexy and almost revealing outfit. After she got dressed, she walked down an alley way to an obscure door with no handles, obviously it was meant to open from within. The only way you could tell that it was the right door was by the small insignia at eye level. It had an eerie similar look to the icon she saw on the map today. She brushed it off as happenstance.

She knocked three times and then paused, then knocked twice. The door cracked open and a deep raspy voice of a man could be heard. "What's your business?"

"Pleasure. Pleasure hides the pain." Then she held out 3 crisp $100 bills near the crack of the door.

The man's fingers reached out and took the bills and the voice said, "Who's your invite?"

She whispered, "Tiny Thong" and then chuckled and held out another 3 more $100 bills.

You could hear a chuckle on the other side of the door, "It's an older member but the invite is still good." The fingers took the bills and the door shut.

Naffilia stood back to look around and down the alleyway to make sure nobody saw her, then the door squeaked as it opened slowly to a dimly lit red room. The door opened all the way but the man behind the door was gone. It was like a scene from a movie – a psychological thriller or horror movie.

The only light in the room came from the stairs that were lined by LED's. As she walked up the stairs, she could hear the bass of music getting louder the closer she got to a second door. It was muffled but she could hear it. She couldn't tell if the vibration from the bass made her chest pound or if was the excitement of not knowing what she would find on the other side of the door.

She only heard about this club from work, rumors mostly, and thought it was the perfect time to go. She knocked 3 times on the door, paused and then knocked once. The door opened slowly, as if going in slow motion. Suddenly a gust of wind whooshed by her head and she could smell sex in the air – the smell of sweat, wet dick and pussy was thick, and it got thicker when she took a few steps into the purple lit haze of the night club.

The music was erotic and sent a chill down her spine when she heard it. It was mesmerizing. The smell of the air intensified the feeling of being transcendent as the bass thumped in perfect harmony with her heart. The music was slow moving – it was enough to put you into a hypnotic state. Slow enough to create the perfect atmosphere to fuck, which was happening everywhere around the room, with the occasional dancer scattered here and there lost in the music, dancing as though they were having sex with nobody.

Naffilia vigilantly walked up to the bar to order a glass of Cabernet. She took a few sips while scanning the entire floor in a state of disbelief but in awe. The atmosphere was surreal. There where custom-built chairs and sofas all over the place so that couples could fuck in the perfect positions. Through the dimly lit room you could see exquisite room deco to add to the atmosphere. This place spent money on the deco to add to the pleasure of the club. They spared no expenses to create the atmosphere. After a few more sips she was ready to explore the club.

She was getting turned on by all the sex around her, getting horny by watching all the people letting go of their inhibitions. She could feel their ecstasy as they let go, to escape the monotony of their world. Some people were in costumes, others wore masks, while the rest were naked to showcase their shit.

Her pussy was throbbing deeply because her senses were overwhelmed by everything – the music, the sound of pounding flesh, the moaning and the nakedness everywhere she looked. She closed her eyes to intensify the taste of the drink and the smell the sex in the air to put herself into her own sexual fantasy.

She walked around the club like a lioness on the hunt with hunger in her eyes and a craving from deep within - like a shark who could smell blood from a mile away, looking for a man good enough to fuck.

I'm gonna get me some dick now, not just one though. I can have all the dick I want.

She found two guys that were suitable to get her fuck on, one of them was looking at her from the other end of the bar. She stuck her chest out to display her cleavage and bit her lip to let him know that it was him she wanted. She walked up to him and didn't say a word as she pretended to spill her drink on his crotch to get an outline of his dick.

Yeah. He'll do. That dick will be just fine.

He looked down at his pants with surprise and started to wipe them off.

Naffilia grabbed his hands and said, "Don't bother wiping it because I'm gonna make those pants more wet with your pre-cum."

The shock on his face was priceless. Then Naffilia rolled her eyes toward another guy standing a few feet from him.

She led the first man by the hand and walked up to the second one and said, "Think you can handle this pussy with another man?"

He didn't flinch when he asked her, "Is this a gang bang?"

She leaned in to seductively touch his earlobe with her red plump lips to whisper, "It is. You wanna join our fuck team?"

His eyes widened and looked at the first man who nodded.

He gulped and nodded, "Yes. Definitely"

She reached down to grab his dick as her facial features transitioned from curiosity to an animalistic expression – like a carnivore after its prey and snarled, "I want you to fuck me hard, like you've never fucked a woman before. Don't hold back. Nothing is off limits. Can your dick handle this?"

She looked him in the eyes and stood there until she got an answer.

"Yes. I understand." He said sheepishly.

She placed her empty glass down and led both men by the hands to the bathroom. Her boldness caught the attention of the other guys around her. She was deliberate with every step she took to make sure that it shook her ass and tits to showcase her body to everyone in the room.

The guys heart where pounding faster than pace of the music as they made their way to the back of the club, and they started to unbutton their tops as they made their way to the bathroom.

She pushed the door open and turned to the first man. Naffilia undid his pants and unleashed his cock, he was already hard. She pushed him onto the counter, "Sit down."

She turned around to the second man and pulled his pants down to free his dick as well. She turned around in front of him and bent over to display her round ass as she slipped her panties off.

"Take a close look at my ass. When I tell you, fuck my hole as hard as you can."

Naffilia was right about making him pre-cum. His dick was dripping. If she hadn't taken his clothes off, he would have wet his pants already by the way she talked and how she displayed her ass and pussy to him.

She climbed up on the first man and slid her already steaming pussy down around his dick until her pussy settled at the base of his cock and road him hard. She rode him up and down until the breathing got heavy. While grinding the shit out of the first man who was moaning uncontrollably, she turned to the second man, "You. Fuck my ass now."

The second man didn't hesitate as he spit in her ass to lubricate her. The rhythm of the music and the motion of every thrust was in sync. It was all perfect timing as she raised her body up and lowered it down, feeling the fullness of both men.

Oh shit. As long as they stay hard, I'm gonna enjoy this time. Mmm…nice, hard and long. The double penetration is deep enough to make me forget my day, but not enough to rid the thought of Tye fucking me like a slutty hoe.

A flash of her and Tye came to her mind. She shook her head to get back into the moment of getting fucked by two cocks.

Her pussy and her ass were tingling like never before. The double stimulation was intense. The heavy breathing from all three echoed in the bathroom as though they were in a sex chamber. She lost control of herself as she imagined being a porn star, putting on a show for everyone to see, but knew she couldn't be seen, or she would jeopardize her career. She couldn't take that chance to let anyone know who she was, and this was the perfect place to let go…and let go she did.

The double fuck was too intense for the man from behind and he pulled out to cum on her back. She could feel the hot cum dripping down her back to the crack of her ass and it made her cum on the first man's dick. The sound of her scream made him blow his load and he pulled out to spray her belly and it dripped down her thigh.

The three of them didn't say a word to each other as they wiped themselves with the plush towels that were supplied. They looked at each other in disbelief as they got dressed.

The men reached into their pocket and pulled out their phone and pointed to it. Naffilia knew what they wanted but started to walk out the door. They grabbed her soft silky hand and motioned to her phone. She nodded and they gave her their phone number. They wanted to see her again. They motioned to their phone, but she refused and shook her head.

She walked out of the bathroom and passed everyone in the room to walk out of the club with her head held high, ignoring the sex all around her.

The moment she got outside the club door, she looked down into her phone and deleted their numbers while smiling.

"It was an experience, boys…but not enough to do it again. At least not with you."

4

The next day, Naffilia was scheduled for a special combat training exercise where secret agents participated in cross training with other agencies. Only the elite recruits who have top secret clearance are invited to the training to protect everyone's identity within that circle of training.

When she got to the academy, she prepared herself for the training. Her and a handful of other women and men from their unit were hosting the training. They didn't wear your traditional workout gear; they wore form fitted material that was breathable. It made their division, including Naffilia, look like models on a photoshoot. Naffilia stood to the side while her division took the lead to warm up the group before the teacher came out.

Despite her attempt to not bring attention to herself, her athletic body was a distraction to some of the recruits as they stole glances in her direction while she bent over to stretch and warm up. A few of the men licked their lips while she bent over and her plump round ass was on display. The men gulped when she stood up to stretch her arms and her tits became prominent under the light.

After the class had warmed up and were told about the various combat techniques by the men and woman standing at the front, Naffilia walked from where she was standing and took center stage in front of the class and interjected her own words, "Ok. Let's get down to the crazy shit we all came to learn. How to kill a person in under 10 seconds."

There was confusion in the room as she started to talk. None of them knew who she was, nor expected her to be the teacher. Because of her small frame, other than her large tits, they made an assumption that the largest muscular man in the group at the front was the teacher. Nobody knew that she is one of the country's most esteemed teachers specializing in combat and assassination techniques and is often commissioned by her division to hold teaching seminars for FBI, CIA, NSA and Select Military units.

Everyone was in awe in the way she took command of the class and the authority in which she spoke about real combat situations. She emphasized some of the stealth techniques and demonstrated kill points on a body, how to strike and how to use weapons in certain situations.

She invited volunteers to the front to practice what they have learned, but she wanted to demonstrate what it looked like in a real situation.

Nobody volunteered so she picked out a man from the back of the room, "You in the back! What's your name?"

He shouted out with an air of arrogance, "Titus."

She gestured him to the front, "Titus. Come up and attack me full force."

He made his way to the front and stood briefly at a distance and hesitated because she was smaller than him.

Smugly he said, "Sorry, but I can't come at you with a full attack. I don't want to hurt you."

Naffilia's division chuckled and the largest guy in her group belted out, "You'll probably be the first to die in a combat situation because you're a pussy and you have shit for brains. That kind of thinking will kill you in a real situation."

The crowd began to laugh. It embarrassed him and he lunged at her in anger, not pulling his punch as he aimed for her chin to knock her out with a single blow.

In one quick move she deflected his punch and jumped up to wrap her legs around his neck and take him down to the floor. He didn't even see it coming and she proceeded choke him with her legs and held his arms so that he couldn't move or tap out. He gasped for air while his face was press against her pussy.

She kept him on the floor in that position while he breathed heavily, gasping for air. Naffilia could feel her panties heating up from his breath.

He had no way to tap out as he was gasping, trying to tap out using his tongue, flicking her pussy. "Hmmph. Hmmph."

She looked down at her prisoner and then up to the recruits, "Never attack your opponent in anger. Always keep your composure. Your emotions will get the best of you."

She held her dominate position over this big guy and it started to turn her on while he was trying to tap out with his tongue, it got her more excited to see his face turning red while his nose and mouth was pressed into her pussy and he made an attempt to talk. It felt like he was eating her out. The fact that she was able to dominate a man twice her size fed her ego and made her feel in control of her surrounding and her life.

She let go of the man and asked for the next volunteer to demonstrate more techniques. Every man in the room raised their hand so that they can experience the raw power of Naffilia up close and personal. Hoping to get a sniff or two, or maybe have to tap out using their tongue.

The class lasted for approximately two hours and she demonstrated dozens of kill techniques and it captivated all of the classmates.

After the training session, the men where in the locker room raising a ruckus. One man shouted from across the room, "Hey Titus! I've never seen a man get pussy whipped like that before."

Everyone laughed, including Titus, "At least I got some pussy today. When was the last time YOU got some?"

The locker room roared with laughter, and in the middle of it all another man yelled out, "Did you eat that pussy or get a whiff before you passed out?"

Titus had to have the last laugh, "Oh I got a whiff alright. Smelled like she just got poked by a tuna." The laughter could be heard through the gym.

Meanwhile in the lady's locker room the women were having fun of their own as they shouted out to Naffilia, "You just had to wrap your legs around that guy's head, didn't you?"

Laughter broke out, "She's like a black widow, let him sniff your snatch, then crush his head like a melon and kill him."

Naffilia chimed in, "There's nothing like making a man eat

you out and then popping his head like a zit. I tried to squeeze his tongue out so that he can at least do it the right way."

The women's laughter filled the locker room as they talked about the worst tongue they've had.

After her training session and shower, she went to a 2-hour briefing for the newly assigned mission to Dubai. This one was going to require a team that spoke the native tongue fluently and looked like a local resident. They were to execute an assassination on a prince's second in command who used his royalty influence to cover the fact that he was head of a terrorist organization that was on the verge of starting a global economic crisis via biological warfare.

The briefing was thorough and intense. It included training for a specialized technique to eliminate the target in close proximity. It was going to require two other women from her team to make this work. They would need to disguise and infiltrate the palace. It was a technique that has never been done before because they needed to seduce him to make it happen. This mission was her biggest adrenaline rush to date.

They were finishing up with their briefing when the director interrupted the meeting, "Pardon the interruption, but we have a break in locating a high-profile target in connection with the Dubai mission. We've tracked him for the past 8 months and he's in Miami. We got word that he's been hired to assassinate a number of political dignitaries."

The room was silent as he briefed them on the sudden mission to Miami. This had to be done swiftly and silently. The director continued, "This has to be done tomorrow. We've already assembled the team." He looked at the women and nodded in their direction.

The girls smiled when the director told them, "Our motto is in affect for your girls. Let this play out as it may."

By the end of the day Naffilia had worked up an appetite that required a release. She had a favorite massage therapist that knew how to help her relax and recover from strenuous workouts. He was an Egyptian man with years of experience in his field, but he had a few other tricks up his sleeve. He had a large client following. Naffilia made an appointment with him.

Their services were open to the public and it was called, "King's Temple Spa." It was held privately by a select group of people for their own purpose. Membership was sold to those who could afford it.

The spa was surrounded by exquisite art from around the world. The environment was pristinely decorated, and the music induced relaxation the moment you walked in the door. The whole environment was hypnotic. A light meal was provided after the massage as part of the experience.

Naffilia announced herself, "Naffilia. For 6 pm."

The reception replied, "Please confirm services."

She looked over her shoulder, "Maximum release."

Reception looked down at her computer and wrote something on a piece of paper and handed it to her. It had the words, "Max Release," on it.

"Give this to Fadil and he'll take care of you. Please go to the end of the hall and take a seat." She motioned for her to walk down the hall.

She walked to the end of the hall and took a seat. The wall opened next to her; it was the entry into a soundproof room. It resembled something from the garden of Eden. Everything about the room perfectly resembled peace.

Fadil greeted her with an accent, "Welcome back Miss Naffilia."

Naffilia handed him the paper. He read it and threw it into the fireplace that was roaring at the end of the room.

He gestured to the hot tub waiting for her, "Please. Take your 15-minute soak before we get started. Your water and herbal tea are within your reach. When you are done, do not dry off. Lay on your stomach on the bench and cover your hair and body with these towels." He pointed to the massage bed.

"I'll be back in 16 minutes." He exited another door.

The relaxation was exactly what she needed after a physically and mentally demanding day that she had. She almost fell asleep listening to the crackling fire and the soft music.

The sound of chimes rang when her 15 minutes were up, and she laid on the table. Fadil knocked on the door and came in, "Are you ready for your massage?"

She could barely get the word out, "I'm ready."

As he prepped the oils, "How was your soak in the hot tub?"

"Always fantastic. Thank you Fadil," she replied.

"So, we'll give you the regular massage from head to toe and if you should fall asleep, that's okay. I'll wake you when time is up."

He started by massaging her feet and then her hands. He massaged her neck and her shoulders. He massaged her shoulders and the tension melted away. Fadil was intentional about the way he massaged her.

I could feel myself drifting off, but I didn't want to fall asleep. I wanted to stay awake to enjoy the feeling. Fadil leaned in closer to my head and I could see his erection. Every time he massaged me; it didn't take long before it became obvious that he enjoyed touching my body. He really loved his job. He purposefully put his dick in my face while he massaged out any knots in my neck and shoulder. His strong hands gave me goosebumps.

I could feel a sense of strength and pleasure rising within me knowing that I had this kind of power over a man, and it turned me on. My pussy was throbbing, and I was getting horny with every stroke he made. I had to fight the urge to reach out and undo his pants and put his dick in my mouth. It wasn't protocol here and he could lose his job. That made it all the more exciting, that I couldn't touch, but he could do whatever he wanted to me. I guess that added to the service he provided here.

The various oils he used smelled so good. He gripped the towel in his hands so that it didn't move, "Please roll over."

The towel barley covered my tits and pussy. Being partially exposed while he still had access kept the arousal in motion. He continued to massage my shoulders and then without warning slid his hands under the towel and he pinched my nipples.

I was glad that the room was soundproof because it surprised me, and I vocalized my pleasure with a moan. The heavy breathing would have been heard down the hall if this was a normal room. This helped me to let go even more.

He went to the other side of the bench to massage my thighs. Oh shit, there was no way I was going to fall asleep now. He worked his hands toward my pussy. I knew for a fact that I was dripping cream already. I felt it drip to my ass and onto the towel underneath me.

He reached underneath the towel and massage my lips. The natural cream from my pussy helped him massage me perfectly. I gave him access by removing my towel and letting him touch my tits and pussy all he wanted.

He slipped one finger in first and it sent a shiver up my body. I could barely moan out the words, "Put two fingers in."

He did as I requested and stroked me perfectly. He made sure to put the right amount of pressure on heaven's curve and moved with timing that made by body quiver, making sure that my clit was stimulated at the same time. He had years of fingering women, and he did it very well.

I couldn't hold it anymore and he pulled his fingers out just in time to avoid getting shot by my fluid. My body spasmed out of control for what felt like hours. I could feel my toes curl up and my back arched to enjoy the feeling. I looked down to see my nipples erect. I instinctively wanted more. I wanted his cock in my mouth and then to have him fuck my pussy hard, but my time was almost up. He finished the massage with light touching everywhere and helped me to come down slowly and relax.

I couldn't help but notice that Fadil had a stain in his pants. This was his best massage yet and he obviously enjoyed it to. It melted all of the tension away.

I took a quick shower and sat in the seating areas to curb my now growing hunger. They had a healthy snack waiting for me. I listening to soothing music and not a thought entered my mind. To have this kind of rest was exactly what I needed.

Fadil came out to see me off, "Thank you for visiting us today. It was my pleasure to help you relax."

As I normally did, out of good business practise and to express my gratitude, I reached into my purse and presented Fadil with a red rose and bottle of cologne along with a $100 tip for his services. That's always been my way to express my heart. I learned that from my grandfather and my father. It's an uncommon practise and people will remember this gesture for a long time.

Fadil lowered his head, reached for my hand and kissed it, "Thank you. You are a treasure. May you be blessed and prosper this day and the remainder of this year."

She finished her snack and ended her day relaxing at home watching Netflix and working on a new sculpture.

5

Tye was walking on a fine white sandy beach. Each step he took squeaked as the sand covered his feet - it looked like crystals between his toes. He held a picture in his hand, a map of some sort. It was beautiful. Something amazing to behold and it made him smile. He let out a deep sigh of pleasure looking at it.

He was breathing heavily. He began to moan with pleasure as he looked down at it. In an instant he found himself in the sea, surrounded by beautiful under water creatures. He watched them swim around him. They synchronized their swimming, up and then down. The motion was slow and methodical. He was mesmerized by their hypnotic movement up and down as they swam around him. He heard someone moaning with pleasure, so he scanned his surroundings.

He listened, looking for the direction in which it was coming when he realized he was the one moaning. The pleasure he felt was intense. He closed his eyes and leaned his head back and let his own sea spill out.

When he opened his eyes, he looked down toward his thighs and a brunette was moaning while licking the cum that just spilled from his cock. She licked his dick up and down until it was clean. Then sucked his balls until all of the cum was gone.

She was moaning while cupping his sack in her hand massaging it, then wrapped her lips around his balls until he moaned again. She didn't get enough of him and raised her head above his cock and stuck her tongue out and then lower her head until the tip of her tongue covered his dick hole.

She swallowed his cock slowly to deep throat his dick and it made him moan louder. She shook the bed with every bob of her head. He could barely whisper, "The sea is coming."

She didn't want to stop, she wanted to do more for him. She guided his hands to the back of her head to control the motion and speed and went ham on his cock, up and down until she started to gag on his engorged cock.

She turned him around and puts her tongue in his tunnel to give him pleasure and tongue fucked him. His breathing was uncontrolled. His groan became louder from every touch she made and couldn't hold it back anymore. She climbed up on him and hover over his erect dick. She reached down to position him, putting the head of his cock in her pussy just deep enough to give her pleasure and to tease him until her juices dripped down and covered his head. Then in an instant dropped down onto his lap so that his hard cock filled her steaming hot pussy. She leaned into him and rode him hard so that her tits bounced in his face.

Her pussy was hot, and her juice ran down his dick like honey being poured from a jar. The sound of her wet thick pussy and the pounding of their flesh made both of them lose control.

He grabbed her ass to help her move, "Fuck me harder. Go harder. Faster, faster. Fuck me harder." They both drove each other crazy with the moaning and deep thrusts. He positioned both her legs over his shoulders while he supported her back and ass. She widened her thighs to bounce on his lap and grind him hard.

She was craving dick in her mouth so she stopped and deep throat his dick so that she could taste her own juice on his cock.

It turned him on so much that he made a demand on her, "Open your mouth and swallow the sea." He unloaded in her mouth with every pulse of his cock. He filled her mouth and she swallowed to please him. He thrust his hips upward and kept going until he watched it spilled out of her mouth.

His body went limp and closed his eyes to enjoy the relief. They both sighed with satisfaction. He slowly opened his eyes and smiled, "Mmm. Now this is a way to start the day. Thank you."

He stretched and moaned before rolling out of bed. He walked to the bathroom to take a shower and get ready for his annual fundraiser. This was an important day for him, and it started off in style.

The moment he stepped into the shower memories of Naffilia flood his mind. It was triggered by the brunette who gave him head. Naffilia's black curly hair pinned up to expose her neck and her soft silky skin was easy to remember. Her gorgeous smile and sparkling eyes captivated his mind.

He snapped back into reality the moment he stepped out of the shower with a towel wrapped around his waist and walked into his room on a luxurious yacht docked at Boston's exclusive beachfront just outside the financial district, minutes from the heart of everything the city has to offer.

The brunette was still in his bed waiting for him smiling seductively and said with her soft-spoken voice, "Are you ready for round two?"

He refused and told her that he has to get ready for work, "I left you something on the table" he said as he pulled out his designer jeans and a dress shirt.

He sat down to put on his casual brown shoes and reached for his brown trench coat. "I'll text you later tonight."

She watched him dress, obviously pleased that she was living in her own fantasy romance novel. She watched with great pleasure while he put his belt on, slipped on his Cartier watch and put his Cartier wallet in his back pocket. He walked over to her to kiss her on the cheek goodbye.

She whispered, "Oooo, you smell so good." She took a deep breath, "Oh shit, what the fuck are you wearing?" She reached out to pull him closer to kiss him.

She kissed his cheek and he smiled as he pulled back gently, "Ok. I gotta go. I have an important meeting to attend. Help yourself to something to eat. I already took care of your bank account."

She glanced down at her phone briefly, then looked up at him and smiled. "You didn't have to do that. We're friends, yet I feel like I'm getting all the benefits."

He turned to her and gave her a smile before leaving, "I'm benefiting too."

He made his way to the deck just as his driver pulled up to

the dock. Tye took a deep breath of the ocean air, pausing briefly to acknowledge that he was grateful for the life he was living. As he walked toward the car his driver got out to greet him and opened the door for him, "Good morning Mr. Wolf."

Tye adjusted his jacket before getting in the car, "Good morning Michael, how's the family?"

"They're doing fantastic sir. I just wanted to say thank you so much for the scholarship you gave Megan. We're grateful that you gave her the opportunity to go back to school." The driver closed the door.

Tye leaned forward to ask Michael a question, "What did your wife decide to major in?"

Michael started the car and then turned around to address Tye, "We thought about what you said, and she's going to go into business finance. She could go anywhere and have a job."

He leaned back in the seat, "That's fantastic. I'm happy to hear that."

"Thank you, sir. I'm gonna roll up your window now for your privacy." The window between them closed and he drove him through the busyness of the downtown area while Tye voice activated a phone call to his secretary.

Her voice came over the speaker, "Good Morning Mr. Wolf. How can I help you?"

He cleared his throat before speaking, "Were you able to get the guest list from Morocco?"

His secretary responded, "Sorry Mr. Wolf, but I wasn't able to get the information you requested."

"Ok, no problem. Maggie, I have a meeting and a conference call scheduled today before my charity event tonight. Can you move both of them to tomorrow? I need to make an important stop before I come in this morning."

"Yes sir. Will that be all?"

"Yes. That's all for now, thank you. I'll see you in a bit."

"We'll see you later Mr. Wolf."

The sound of her phone being placed on the receiver

could be heard over the speaker.

He pushed a button to speak to Michael, "Mike? Let's go to the Boston museum by the pier."

"Yes sir."

Tye was meeting with a dealer for some art pieces to add to his collection. He had arranged a meeting with the curator and a few of his colleagues a week earlier to discuss some art he had found. While he was there, he ordered a piece. He was going in to pick up the delivery of his art.

Prior to arriving, he got a text message about going to Dubai to take care of additional paperwork about an oil deal that he had negotiated months ago for his corporation.

Just as he responded and put his phone down, he got another text. "Hi dear, I miss you so much. The thought of you cumming on my face is how I'm starting my day. Lol."

He grunted and replied, "Dear, I'm very busy today and heading to a meeting. I'll text you later."

She replied, "Okay honey."

Initially, he didn't know who was texting until he realized that it was Sabrina from Seattle.

He put his phone down to listen to some music when his phone pinged again.

Katy was the sender, "Hey baby how u doing? U ready to party?"

His reply was short and sweet, "Dear I'm busy in a meeting. Let's chat later."

Katy replied, "kk baby text me later."

While he was texting his reply, another text came in and he shook his head and let out a deep sigh.

He leaned his head back and looked at the roof of the car and let out a moan before looking down at his phone. When he checked the message, he seemed relieved, "Oh."

It was his secretary confirming that the meeting and conference call had been changed.

He said out loud, "Ok...I got a second phone for a reason. One for business and one for pleasure. I better keep them separate."

He put his phone on silent and tossed it aside so that he could spend some time in peace. He thought about the woman he met in Morocco. He decided that he would make a phone call later to his friend, Aasim in Morocco, to help him find her and ask if he had seen her since he left.

They pulled up to the front of the museum. Tye told him to drive to the back entry instead. Tye let himself out of the car and tapped on the driver side window. Mike rolled the window down.

Tye said playfully, "I'm gonna be about an hour. Play some video games or something."

They both laughed.

Tye started to walk away but stopped abruptly and turned back to Mike and handed him a $50 and pointed to a group of eateries nearby, "Grab yourself something to eat. I'll text you when I'm almost done."

"Thank you, sir."

Tye walked to the back entry and pressed a buzzer. A guard opened the door. "Good morning Mr. Wolf. Dr. Spenser is expecting you."

Dr. Mark Spenser greeted Tye, "Good morning Tye. How's things with you?"

Tye nodded his head, "Going very well. How's the new wing coming along?"

Dr. Spenser gestured toward the new wing under construction, courtesy of Wolf Enterprises.

"Everything is on track. Thank you so much for your donation."

Tye gave a look of approval in the direction of the new wing where the work was being done, "It's my pleasure. I wanted to do something special in honor of my parents."

Dr. Spenser looked at him empathetically, "They seemed like remarkable people from the limited stories you told me about them. Again, I'm sorry for your loss."

Tye nodded, "Thank you. They were remarkable. I wouldn't be where I'm at today, if it wasn't for their love and support. I have amazing memories of them."

Dr. Spenser replied, "Were they lovers of art?"

Tye chuckled, "Nope. The only art they knew was all of my comic book drawings I did when I was a kid. I hung them up all over my walls in my room. That was the extend of all the art any of us knew in our house."

They both laughed.

Tye paused to look out the window to reflect, "I have very fond memories of them. The art that was important to them came in the form of family pictures everywhere."

There was a brief solemn silence in the room.

Tye cleared his throat and turned toward Mark, "I came here to pick up my art. I was told the piece came in and it was waiting for me."

Mark and Tye walked to the curator's office, "Yes. It arrived a couple of days ago."

They looked at the art with admiration and Tye spoke up, "Wow. It's more exquisite than I remember."

Mark agreed, "Remarkable…the detail. You don't find that in modern art these days."

They stood in silence looking at the painting before Tye took out his phone and transferred money into the museum's account via donation.

After the transaction Tye asked, "Did you manage to mull over the question I asked a few weeks ago about that art I was telling you about?"

Dr. Spenser remarked, "I did. And I got in touch with a few people I know. As a matter of fact, they came in a week ago. We had a meeting with a woman who had some questions about some art. When we were done, I proposed the question to them to see what they thought. These guys are brilliant. They came up with a few possible scenarios."

Tye noticed a new piece on the wall, "I heard you got a new piece of art recently," Tye commented.

"Is that it?"

Dr. Spenser brought him to the new addition. They both

stared at it intently in silence.

Then Tye's brow frowned as if he were confused, "Hmm." He took his phone out and took a picture of the art and took a close up of what appeared to be an icon in the image.

Dr. Mark Spenser looked at him, "What?"

"This doesn't seem like your typical art does it?" He gestured to it. "It's missing elements of cultural connection."

Mark remarked, "That's what most of us were discussing. Although, it seems to have connection to Saudi Arabia. Maybe even Egypt. It was also suggested that there seems to be a connection to the Jewish culture as well."

Tye looked at him intently, "I've never known the Jewish culture to have their own art. They strictly adhered to the second commandment to not worship any graven images and that kind of influenced their decision not to participate in traditional art as we know it."

Mark agreed, "That's what baffles us. It's a bit of a mystery to all of us."

Tye tilted his head as he asked, "Us?"

"Yeah. There were a few of us," he nodded.

Tye was inquisitive, "So, did you present my question to your sources? Who did you ask?"

He put his hand to his chin to remember the names, "Dr. Milton Shraver, Dr. Ian Van, Dr. Anne Price and a mythology enthusiast - Brian Wicker."

"What was their conclusion?" He asked with curiosity and excitement.

Mark took a deep breath, "They said, 'Yes. It is possible that a scroll exists about the secrets to sexual ecstasy. That it was relegated to a myth. Nobody could confirm it, but various cultures around the world have their own folklore that suggests that it might exist.'"

Tye's demeanor changed. He seemed to have given in to his excitement. "What else did they say?"

Mark said in a curious way as he pointed to the new art, "The woman they met with suggested that this art was more instructional. It made those guys think that it was more of a map than anything else. The question you proposed about the existence of secrets to sexual ecstasy stunned them. They had heard of this legend of the scrolls that speak of it and concluded that they do, in fact, exist..."

Mark paused and raised his finger in the air to put emphasis on the next point, "...but, they felt that it was in parts or pieces and scattered to who knows where. They think there is connection to biblical times. After much debate, they felt there was some sort of connection or a bond of some sort, between two completely different cultures."

Tye looked confused and asked for clarification, "They concluded that a scroll does exist, but it's been divided?"

Mark shook his head, "Yes."

Tye continued, though deep in thought, "And that two unrelated cultures know about this scroll or at least are connected in some way because of the scroll?"

Mark nodded vehemently, "That's what they are guessing."

"That's remarkable." Tye turned to ponder this information as he walked toward his new art acquisition, "Interesting."

Mark responded, "That's pretty much what they concluded. And they are very curious about why you were asking."

Tye quickly responded, "I'm just curious because I heard about it for years." He reached out to shake Marks hand. "Thank you for your help."

Mark shook his hand, "No problem."

Dr. Spenser watched Tye with curiosity as he left his office.

Tye paused as he walked by the new wing and turned back to Mark, "If you need anything else, let me know."

Mark nodded his head appreciatively.

Tye text his driver to let him know that he was done and took his painting to the back door. He waited briefly before Mike pulled around to the back and popped the trunk for Tye to put his painting in.

Dr. Spenser could be seen from his office window watching Tye with benevolence and appreciation as he put his art in the trunk of the car before driving away.

Tye called his secretary, "Maggie. I'm sending you a file right now for my speech. Can you print it out and have it ready for me? I'll be there shortly."

The phone call was brief, "Yes sir."

Tye sent the document to his secretary and then sat back to relax for the rest of the drive in to work. He took in the scenery that buzzed by him in a blur, it triggered memories of his hometown of Worcester and he drifted into his thoughts.

In a flash he recalled the many summers he spent on a reservation in Canada where his father grew up. His father was First Nations. Here in the states, the politically correct wording was Native Americans or Aboriginals.

Growing up on a reservation was an experience unlike no other. There was a sense of community and family. Being on a reserve, everyone took care of each other. One thing it did for him was that it nurtured a sense of family and entrepreneurship and creativity. Most families found a way to make a little extra cash on the side while they collected social assistance.

In an instant Tye was brought back to memories of him and his father fishing from his father's canoe. They used that same canoe in a number of local races and won a few trophies.

His father was a WWII vet who served in the Navy. After getting out of the Navy his father met his mother and they settle in New England in a city outside Boston. That's where he grew up most of his life.

Being a blue-collar work with an entrepreneurial spirit, his father invested in an apartment. In New England, they were known as 3-Deckers. It was the perfect arrangement to raise a family for years. Leaving the nest and going out on your own meant you simply moved into the second or third floor. Family was just one or two floors down.

Tye's father was a seasonal laborer all his life working in the construction business. He worked hard to take care of his family but there were times that sacrifices had to be made. A roof over their head was more important than buying the latest gadgets. Bills were a regular topic around the house. Looking back on his life, he came to realize why baked beans and hotdogs was served almost every Saturday in the house. It wasn't just a tradition; it was all they could afford. His father would get caught on occasion eating a midnight snack – a tomatoes and mayonnaise sandwich.

There were simple pleasures in life that his father enjoyed that brought cozy memories for Tye. His father loved music. Often times, late into the night the record player could be heard playing music from every genre, from big band to country. Tye even remembers names such as Glenn Miller and Conway Twitty.

The holidays were very special for his family. That's when they took the time to spend money on each other. It was the one time of the year to appreciate the escape of living on the edge of poverty. His father and mother did their best to provide for him and he didn't go without, but it could be felt the rest of year, that they were more than a dozen paychecks away from taking a vacation or buying luxury items for themselves, and they were one paycheck away from not being able to buy essentials in their life. That's why Tye doesn't remember going on vacation when he was younger.

A warm smile came to Tye's face as he remembered the festive times with his family. A pleasant feeling engulfed him as he remembered walking several streets over in the cold to pick out a Christmas tree with his father and siblings. The car lot was converted to a tree lot and it was lined with stringed white lights, and in the background Christmas music played softly over a vintage cone speaker. What added to the power of those memories was the smell of pine needles. The aroma got stronger the closer they got to the tree lot. Tye, his father and sister carried the tree all the way home, excited about the family time that was planned for that weekend. The whole family participated in decorating the tree.

For most of his adult life, Tye wanted to show his appreciation for his mother and father for their commitment to him while growing up. On top of the scholarships he got, his parents scraped every dollar they could to send him to University. His mother and father were believers in hard work, but his dad was a believer in taking chances as an entrepreneur and it started with strengthening your mind with wisdom and knowledge.

Set back and struggle brought the whole family closer and made them stronger. Love was the glue that bind them together. By the time Tye graduated from University, he didn't get a chance to take care of his family and his world came crashing down.

Suddenly, the sound of an accident in the distance startled him and snapped him out of his memories and back to the moment. He shook his head to get his bearings just in time, because they arrived at the office moments later.

That evening, around 5pm Tye hosted a fundraiser near and dear to his heart. The fundraiser was unique in that it wasn't just for one charity but two. One of the foundations directly supported a scholarship program for underprivileged families that wanted to send their kids to college, and the other program was for blue-color workers who needed that little extra help to cover essential needs such as electricity, water, gas and money at Christmas time.

These programs gave hard working parents with kids the chance to ease the stress they feel during the winter months and especially around the holidays.

The fundraiser included catered meals from his restaurant business and music by local bands. During dinner, in honor of his father, he hired well known big band players for background music and an occasional dance. He held both silent auction and regular auction that offered various products and services from businesses from all around New England.

Later on, in the evening the party got going with live music from special celebrity guests that were hot and in demand for today. What made it unique and successful was that after each singer gave a private concert for the special guests at the charity fundraiser, they went across the street to sing for paying fans who had purchased tickets for a concert that had multiple artists playing.

There were high profile guests, from politicians and professional athletes to actors and business owners. In all, it was a success as they raised over 17 million dollars for the charity event. This was Tye's most treasured way to remember his mother and father.

Later that evening, after his fundraising event he retreated to his office. It was 2 am. He made a call to his good friend Aasim in Morocco.

He greeted his friend as per his culture, "Al-salaamu 'alaykum Aasim."

Aasim replied "Sabaah al-khayr. How are you friend? I am very good thank you. How can I be of some services to you?"

Tye was apologetic, "I hope I didn't wake you up. I know that it's early there and I know that you like to wake up before the sun. I need a favor from you Aasim. Do you remember when we met in a restaurant the last time I was there? I had a conversation with a lady there."

He replied, "Yes, I do remember her. I remember you talking to her."

Tye replied, "Do you know how I can get in touch with her? I'm guessing she stayed in the area after I left and maybe you bumped into afterwards."

Aasim answered, "No. Sorry. I never seen her before. I only met her that one time when you and I got together. I haven't seen her since. I can tell that you got along very well immediately. She's very beautiful."

"I thought that maybe she was at the convention I held while I was there. I had my secretary check the guest list and nothing came up."

"Yeah. Sorry my friend. I can ask around for you. I'll see what I can do." Aasim said.

Tye's call was brief, "Thank you. But if it's too much trouble, no worries."

Aasim replied, "No worries and no troubles. Let me see what I can do for you. It's my gift to you."

"Thank you Aasim you're a good friend." Tye ended the call.

He turned around in his chair that was overlooking the city. It was a beautiful clear evening and he admired the beauty and let out a sigh.

Tye took his time going home and sauntered toward the elevator. He got on and pressed the button to the garage. The elevator music put him into a serene mood. He wanted to spend the night at his penthouse instead of the yacht, and took his time driving his Lexus home listening to music his father used to listen to – big band.

It was a long day, but a noteworthy day. When he got to his penthouse, he felt accomplished but ready for bed. It took him less than that 30 minutes to fall asleep after his warm shower. Tomorrow, it was business as usual.

6

Naffilia woke up earlier than usual. This usually happened when she had something on her mind. She moaned after looking at the time on her phone.

She stretched, "Ahhh."

She chuckled as she remembered an old TV commercial from her younger days and said out loud, "Time to make the donuts."

Might as well work out to get the blood flowing. Nothing like a quick shot of adrenaline in the morning.

She went to her workout room for a 30-minute run on the treadmill then hit the shower afterwards.

The steam in the shower had a nice relaxing effect on me. After a good workout, it always put me in a zone. I needed that sleep last night. Today is the day for the Miami mission. I wasn't nervous, but I could feel the adrenaline start to ramp up last night before bed. That's probably one reason for the early rise today. It's going to be a long Saturday with the girls.

Naffilia put on comfortable pants and suit and ate something light while she logged in to the Uber app to schedule a pickup. Before heading out the door she grabbed her burner phones and her work phone.

Naffilia looked at the app and it showed that the driver was 5 minutes away. She went down to the front lobby to wait with her suitcase by her side. When the driver arrived, he confirmed the pick-up and destination. He loaded her luggage in the trunk of his car and headed towards Logan airport.

She text her friends - the other agents, who confirmed that they would meet her at passenger drop off. They arrived at the Uber drop off point where the other agents were just arriving. The driver retrieved her luggage for her and wished her well when she reached in her purse and tipped him $50.

He looked at the tip with surprise, "Oh…wow, thank you ma'am. You have a pleasant flight today."

She smiled, "Have an awesome day."

Her friends greeted her with delight, "Good morning Naffilia."

She hugged them, "Good morning ladies. Are we ready for some fun today?"

Chloe, a mild-mannered woman with a sense of humor and a consistent off and on relationship with her boyfriend greeted Naffilia, "Girl this mission is going to spice up my sex life."

They all laughed.

Mya was the single extrovert type and loved to party, she was always the loud one in the group, "Girlfriend…I hope we get to fuck 'em and then fuck 'em up."

The girls stirred up the morning silence a bit with their laughter.

Chloe and Mya were always partnered with Naffilia whenever they did missions that involved a possible assassination. The three of them together brought a sexiness that can't be matched, and they used this to their advantage on all the mission they were paired up in.

This mission to Miami had significant implications to United States and China and the three women were commissioned to make this swift. This was going to be a big money maker for all three of them - over 3 million each. There were multiple contracts on the target and multiple countries and their government was willing to pay big for this mission. The agency paid their agents well for dangerous missions like this.

They processed through the VIP express area with minimal holdup. Before boarding, the three of them sat in the waiting area lost in their own world of texting. They stood out from the rest of the women with their boujee attire, Gucci and Louis Vuitton carry-on luggage and were made up like they were going to a mile-high party. There were several eyes gawking while the women were checking their make-up or caressing their soft legs.

Over the speaker they called out for VIP and Senior

81

citizens, along with women and children to board first. They waited for the women with kids to get in front of the line along with the senior citizens.

They boarded and took their seats in business first class. The captain welcomed everyone aboard and asked the flight attendant to prepare the cabin for the flight to Miami.

When they arrived, they picked up their luggage and went to a limousine that was already waiting to take them to the Baltimore Coral hotel.

Naffilia nodded her head, "Alright girls. Notify HQ that we'll be arriving at the Baltimore in a few minutes and you're turning off your phones. We are going to radio silence from this point forward."

Normally a mission like this would have been planned for weeks but this one was sudden due to the level of urgency. However, there were other agents who were already on top of it. They've been ready for a week and prepared secure packages for the agents and it was already waiting in their room. They were designed as a beauty box for makeup. To open them, it required their thumb print.

When the girls got to their room the secured packages were already on the bed waiting for them. They placed their thumb on a scanner and it opened the box. Each of them took a deep breath when they saw what was inside. Chloe announced, "Oh my! Just look at these toys…Girls, it's like having an orgasm without the man."

They laughed as they reached in and took out an assortment of guns, silencers, knives, single shot darts and an assortment of chemicals for killing or knocking the target unconscious.

Mya grabbed a gun, "Mmm hmm. Nice and hard. Ready to shoot with raw power." She stroked the barrel of the gun and started to moan.

Laughter broke out in the room while each of them prepped their weapons. There were three special weapons disguised as lipstick which gave them a single shot. It had to count.

Naffilia belted out, "Lock and load ladies." Three simultaneous cocking sounds filled the room.

They retrieved a laptop from the bottom of one of the boxes and cased out the surrounding area and went over the mission again, making sure to identify emergency escape routes.

They put on the outfits they would wear tonight and admired how each of them looked. They pinned up their hair and put on styled wigs and dressed up to party. Each of them put on a racy leather outfit with fishnet stockings.

Chloe and Mya were pleased with what they saw and said, "Mmm hmm. We look good."

Mya said with emphasis, "If our sexy looks don't kill 'em…by Glock will."

Naffilia announced, "That too much to go to the mall in, but good enough for tonight. It's time to go shopping girls. We got some time to blend in with the locals and maybe shop for a party to tonight."

Naffilia started to take her outfit off, "We gotta save this for later. We can't shop in these."

Mya found some sexy music to stream and turned up the volume while they got undressed. She started to do a sexy erotic danced and grabbed her tits through the leather outfit, "Momma feels sexy Daddy."

Naffilia laughed, "What the hell are you talking about bi'atch? You're not a mother, let alone married!"

The agent shrugged her shoulder, "I've always wanted to say that. It just sounds sexy."

Naffilia smirked, "Is that the best dirty talk you can do? Shit! No wonder you're not married yet."

The room belted out with laughter as each of them did a sexy dance and moaned like they were fucking the air.

It was time to execute the first part of their mission after they had their sexy mission rally - shopping at the galleria. They discussed the objective of the mission one more time as they changed into something less attention grabbing.

Naffilia announced, "Ok girls, if you want, we can find another sexy outfit at the store and even do some casual shopping to pass the time. I personally want to get in and get out, and then come back here to chill. We have time to memorize what our target looks like and then go over our escape plan. Easy peezy baby."

They left the hotel to pick up their rental car outside the hotel lobby. Naffilia led them toward a four seat Ferrari.

Chloe gasped and tried to contain her excitement and said, "Oh shit…this is our rental?"

Naffilia, "Are your shittin' me? This stands out like sore thumb."

She pointed past the Ferrari, "Over there. That's our rental." She pointed to a VW bug.

The girls started laughing, "What the fuck?! We'll look like clowns in a circus coming out that piece of shit."

Naffilia started laughing, "I'm just joking girls. That's our car." She pointed to a BMW 4 Series Cabriolet convertible.

Mya nodded her head, "Ok. I can live with that. Mmm mmm good."

Naffilia tossed the keys to Mya and sat on the passenger side. She put the coordinates into the GPS for the popular galleria. They needed something the locals wear so that they could blend into the crowd for the rest of the day and not bring attention to themselves. Maybe they could find something racier than what they already had for tonight's party.

Naffilia sat on the passenger side to play some music and relax. She turned the radio on, and it blared music suddenly. It startled the woman as the radio played, "You're on my dick when you need my money. You're on my dick when you need my shit. You're on my dick when you need my ride …"

"Are you fucking kidding me!" Naffilia belted out.

The girls look at her a bit confused.

Naffilia chuckled, "That's the song the football player was playing, when he pulled up to me on our first date in front of the restaurant…"

She cringed as she finished her sentence, "…that everyone could hear."

Mya winced, "Are you serious? Ahhhh"

They all groaned and then filled the car with laughter.

Chloe added, "Sounds like that date was memorable."

Naffilia sniggered, "In more ways than one. I gotta turn that shit off."

She turned off the radio and used her Bluetooth connection to play her favorite songs. Hard rock and metal blasted the speakers as they drove off.

The women sang with approval and enjoyed the warm sun on their skin and the wind in their hair as they drove to the mall.

They maximized their girl time at the mall shopping for shoes and an outfit. It was both rewarding and relaxing, but they worked up an appetite, so they stop to eat at the popular restaurant on their way back to the hotel.

They had the time of their life and they had enough time to rest at the hotel. They spent the remainder of the evening napping, meditating and recharging for the energy they would need for tonight.

It was 11:30 pm. Time to get dressed. Each of them puts on a different wig and dressed in their new outfit that they purchased at the mall and concealed their weapons.

They left the hotel at midnight. They were 10 minutes from the mission location when they pulled into a burger joint to park near the rear of the parking lot, away from any lights or camera. They changed again but this time into their sexy outfits that they had on earlier. It was clothes that hugged their curves and revealed enough flesh to intoxicate any man. They topped it off with perfume befitting of the environment they were going to.

They drove 5 minutes from the kill zone and parked the car in an inconspicuous place and called for an Uber to take them the rest of the way. With a mission like this, especially with a criminal with this level of influence, every movement needed to be covered. Every car they got into and each change of clothe was to cover their tracks.

The driver arrived and they got in. The driver confirmed their drop off point because he thought it was a mistake, "So, ladies. Just to make sure I got this right, we're going to 'Gitchie Gitchie' gentleman club, right?"

Chloe and Mya turned on the charm and belted out, "That's right baby. We're gonna have some fun tonight."

When they arrived, the line was out the door and down the street. Naffilia and her friends walked past everyone and unbuttoned more of their top to show more cleavage and pressed her tits against the bouncer and whispered in his ears, "Me and my friends wanna get in. Here's $500 from each of us."

She slipped the $1500 into his pants and left her hand in his pocket long enough to get a response from him.

The bouncer smiled and looked into their purse for security purpose and didn't think much of the lipstick case. He gave them clearance and then radioed them in for VIP services.

He didn't bother frisking them because their dress was so tight, they couldn't possibly hide anything on them, especially with their tits almost hanging out.

Mya said with a sexy voice as she stuck her chest out, "Do you wanna frisk me baby?"

The bouncer chuckled, "Go inside. There's a VIP spot for you."

The girls smiled and walked past him, "Thank you baby. You have a good evening now."

Chloe was walking close to Naffilia and Mya and just before going inside whispered, "Girls, I'm getting turned on by the gun between my legs."

Naffina whispered firmly and with authority, "Easy girl. Keep your shit together and play it cool. We've got some trash to take out and I need you here and now."

The door man opened a second set of doors to the club. The music was thumping - every beat can be felt in their chest. The lights were flashing around the club with spotlights on the nine girls at the center stage dancing, bouncing their tits and shaking their ass for the men up close. To the side of the room, in all four corners, women were dancing on small platforms with poles. The men packed the room so tight that there was hardly any room.

There was an excitement in the air as the music vibrated off the floor and the girls were walking around topless with a tray of shots for everyone. The guys in the club were letting loose and there was a general feeling of mass hysteria as Miami's most gorgeous woman convened in this room to dance on as many dicks as they could, putting a smile on everyone who got a lap dance.

There was the occasional drunk guy folding a $20 or $50 bill on his nose so that the women can sit on his face and pick the bill up with her ass or pussy just so that he can get a hard-on from a sniff. By the looks of it, each woman was covered with a few dozen 20's and 50's.

They scanned the strip club, taking in every detail of the place, looking for their target. They made their way through the crowd to the private room for VIP members only. The smell of their private room smelled like pussy and dick. It didn't come as a surprise that they used this as a fuck room.

They sat down to scope the area while the waitress brought over drinks for them. They waited until the club was overcrowded. By 2 am you could barely walk around the club.

The girls drank slowly. By their second beer, Naffilia spotted their target. He was making his way toward the men's room. The other agents confirmed that it was him.

Spike Clearwater was his birth name, but he is known in the underground world as 'Stone Heart' – to the agents at HQ his code name was Bojangles. He's a sought-after arms dealer in the underworld. He recently supplied 88 billion dollars in arms to Iraq through a connection he has in Dubai. The agency was trying to find out who his connection was in Dubai. They had originally suspected that it was a prince who used his royalty to cover up arms dealing but recently found out it was his second-hand man.

Bojangles is not just an arms dealer, he's also a hitman for hire and he does it for the thrill. Bojangles is hardcore and there is no telling how quickly he'll pull a trigger on anyone who gets in his way. He once agreed to kill a man for a dollar, just because he didn't like the way he looked.

Spike Clearwater was a hard man to kill even among the underground world because he was always one step ahead of everyone. Most people in the underground world and any agent who kept track of him heard of his largest paid hit – a whopping $5 billion. It's known in the agency that he killed a number of politicians, but they couldn't prove it to convict him.

The most recent intel led them to believe that he was hired to take out the Chief Financial Officer for the White House in 15 days when he was to negotiate trade with china. He took the job because he had a vested interest in his death because the CFO stood between him and his next lucrative arms deal. The hit was supposed to take place on Chinese soil. If he succeeded, it would likely to be deemed as an act of war and it would incite global chaos, sending the United States into an economic tailspin and a provoked war.

He was hired by four criminal organizations and two terrorist sects - all of whom paid a portion in advance for a sum of three billion dollars. The agency was keeping tabs on him, and right now was a critical time to act on the agency's motto.

Bojangles made his way to the men's room. Naffilia signaled to both girls with her head to go in after him while she stood guard outside the door. Both girls followed him into the bathroom, "Hey good looking. Are you looking to go home with somebody tonight?"

They startled him. He turned around to bark at them, "Who the fuck are you? Get the fuck outta of here!"

Chloe and Mya knew that Bojangles was a hard guy and he displayed that immediately. They had to soften him up quickly.

Mya raised her hands and said, "Whoa baby! I was telling my girlfriend here that I was looking to have some fun with her and thought you would be a suitable addition to our party tonight."

Chloe undid her button lower and ran her fingers over her tits as she spoke to Mya, "That's ok darling. He's probably not the kind of man who can handle us."

Mya smiled and glanced at him, "Too bad baby…you could've gone home with us tonight and had some fun."

He looked miffed and pointed to his crotch, "You can't handle this…girls. Maybe we can some fun tonight."

Chloe swayed her hips as she walked over to him and grabbed his dick and licked her plump red lips. She pushed him into a stall, "Let's get a taste first."

Meanwhile Naffilia stood outside the door. A man was about to enter when she stopped him, grabbed him by the arm and pulled him aside, "Tom. I haven't seen you in a while."

The man looked confused, "But I'm not…"

"Hey!" She interrupted him by guiding his hands to her tits and she grabbed his dick, "I missed you so much. Why didn't you call me?"

Back in the bathroom, Spike looked down at his crotch to unzip his pants so get some head, as he did his head leaned closer to Chloe's face. Then Mya handed Chloe the lipstick needle lace with a muscle relaxer and stood outside the stall. Chloe poked his neck with the needle.

Spike yelled, "Ow…you fuckin' bitch. I'm gonna beat the fucking shit out of you."

Mya and Chloe punched him in the throat, and he leaned over to gag. They took his belt off and tied his hands.

Chloe left the bathroom to give Naffilia an update.

She walked past Naffilia and shook her head, signaling that

it wasn't done yet. She gestured with her eyes and her head up toward one of the cameras in the hallway.

Naffilia understood and gave the stranger enough pleasure to keep him out of the bathroom until the hit was made.

The Chloe walked nonchalantly toward the security guard who was oblivious to her as he left the security room to walk his rounds. She made it seem like she was going into the women's bathroom but waited for him to pass her.

He walked past her, then she quickly made her way to the security room and pried open the door with a knife and entered.

She scanned the room and noticed on the monitors all of the camera placements in the club. Without hesitation she hacked the computer system and deleted the recordings from the whole facility for the past 60 minutes, hiding evidence that they were even near the men's room. She downloaded a virus into the system so that if anyone tried to retrieve the last few hours they were in the club, it was be activated and corrupt all of their files.

Chloe came back out and took Naffilia's place, "Do you know this guy?"

Naffilia looked at him and let go of his arm, "No! I mistook him for someone else."

Chloe motioned to let him go. The man turned to use the bathroom.

Chloe said to Naffilia as she motioned toward the bathroom, "It's your turn."

Meanwhile, in one of the stalls, Spike's head was leaning against Mya's shoulder and he started to lose consciousness while she gagged him with a handful of toilet paper.

The man went in and used the toilet and heard moaning in the stall and thought it was someone struggling to take a shit. He snorted and left the bathroom after he finished.

Chloe prevented anyone else from entering the rest room.

Naffilia walked in and called out to Mya, "Bring him out."

Spike was barely conscious and was irate as he belted out a muffled threat while he had a mouthful of toilet paper.

You could barely understand him, "Foonkin' brauds. I'll kill'f broff of yooo."

Naffilia motioned for him to be quiet as she put her finger over her lips and shoved more toilet paper in his mouth.

"Mr. Stone…I'm gonna recite our motto to you and you have a decision to make. We give all of our victims the option to choose a new path in life…"

Naffilia smiled at Mya and looked at Bojangles, "You are either with us or against us. Do as we demand, believe as we believe, or choose your fate. There is no room in this conversation for free thought. We will do your thinking for you - this is your last chance to choose your fate now…"

He looked at her with confusion and muffled incoherent words, "Hmm dee ooky ooo?"

Naffilia wrapped her hand with toilet like a glove and pulled out most of the toilet paper from his mouth, and he immediately yelled, "Who the fuck are you?"

Naffilia stuffed his mouth and ignored him, "You have a choice to make right now Mr. Stone. You can die by our hands or you can choose to live, but just so that you know, you will lose everything."

She leaned in to look him in the eyes, "…and I mean everything. Your home, your identity, your way of life and…"

She paused briefly to take a breath and savor the moment, "…and the billions of dollars you just made from the hired hit…"

Naffilia waved her hands as if conducting an orchestra, "…and we will distribute your money and all your assets to worthy causes as part of your payback to society."

Mya chimed in, "Choose life. Choose life. We have some great charities you can sponsor. We got homeless shelters, food banks, scholarships and the list goes on."

Stone Heart laughed and muffled the words, "Fuck you. You can't do jack shit to me. Kill me…if you think you can."

Naffilia nodded to Mya, "Ok. We gave you a chance to

change your ways."

Naffilia opened her lipstick case and she placed it on his forehead and pushed on the bottom. A quick popping sound echoed in the bathroom.

He slumped over into her arms and she place him on the toilet seat, "Here. Let me get that zipper for you baby. You obviously can't unzip your own pants," she pulled his pants and underwear down.

She reached between her legs and pulled out the silencer and placed it on his heart and pulled the trigger, confirming that the 'Tango' was down.

She walked out of bathroom and gestured to Chloe with a nod. Just then, Mya exited the door and gave a nod of approval as well.

The women avoided the remainder of the cameras and proceeded to kitchen area. They walked past the chef who was engulfed in his work that he didn't see them walk through. As they were walking through the kitchen, Naffilia arranged an Uber pick up.

The ride was close by waiting outside of another strip club, so it took less than a minute to arrive.

They took Uber back to their rental car and drove to a safe house for the rest of the night. Before going inside the safe house, they slipped out of their skin-tight dress and into casual clothes while a male agent stood by and held out his hands to take their clothe and wig to incinerate them.

He pretended to look away as they were stripping down but couldn't resist seeing them naked. They removed their wig and put it in his hands, and he put everything in a paper bag and dropped it into a garbage bin designated for the clean-up agents.

Early the next morning they drove back to the hotel, wiped the car clean and ordered the clean-up crew to finish the job. They gathered all their items and packed their guns in the make-up box and sealed it up and left it at the front desk. Naffilia left instructions, "Someone will be picking these up within the hour. Can you make sure they get this? They'll ask for the make-up box specifically."

They had an early morning flight to leave Miami and an Uber driver was waiting for them after they checked out. He drove them to Miami international airport.

On their drive to the airport Naffilia contacted HQ by text and confirmed Tango down – "Bojangles is dancing with the devil – eating worms together. He chose not to share his wealth and went with option B. He refused to live by our motto. Objective complete."

The text came back, "Affirmative. Clean-up crew is complete. The media is being brainwashed right now. We have secured most of his funds and it is being distributed as we speak. Great job. See you soon for debriefing."

They arrived at the airport and the driver assisted with their luggage. Naffilia gave him a $100 tip, "Thank you for the ride."

The driver was stunned and could barely speak as he stuttered and squeaked out the words, "Th…Th…Thank you. My thanks to God and blessings on you. Thank you so much."

They took their carryon and made their way to the seating area. The plane to Boston was on time and boarding would begin momentarily. Just then there was an announcement for VIP business class to board.

Once they were seated each of them were given a pillow to rest their head and it only took the other agents a few minutes to fall asleep once they were in the air.

Naffilia checked her messages. She turned on her burner phone to see all the missed calls and text messages. As she scrubbed through the messages, one of them caught her eye, that said, "I miss you hun and miss that pussy."

The message was surrounded by dick pics. She shook her head in disbelief and zoomed in on the pictures to get a better look at his dick and noticed it had blisters with white bumps.

Oh hell no. I had to looked over my shoulder to see if anybody was looking at my phone. In disbelief I had to get a better look, so I zoomed in again. Oh shit. I gotta throw up. This guy has got to go.

I had to text this asshole back, "You, Mr. Nasty Dick, have no class to send me dick pics. I told you before, that I'm not into that and I won't be sending you pics of me either. This pussy that you miss, won't be riding that pony anymore. I'm looking for a stallion. And I'm not talking about dick size. I'm talking about class size. I'm looking for a man who understands me, feels me and has a good head on his shoulders, not just a good head on his shaft. Find yourself a nasty pussy to match your nasty dick. Thanks. I'm good."

I'm getting tired of these clowns who get their degrees from Ringling University, majoring in self-absorption. I'm tired of finding men with no balls. It's becoming clearer that a man-child like this can't put their heart and soul into making a difference in the world, and can't love and respect themselves properly, let alone me. At some point, a real man is going to come along.

She blocked him, and the other half dozen messages that sent dick pics. She copied and pasted that same message to them as well. She sighed deeply and felt her eyes closing slowly. She turned her phone off and took a nap.

It felt like she closed her eyes for just a minute or two when she felt her friends gently touch her, "Hey. We've landed. Wake up."

She stretched and retrieved her carryon bag and made her way through Logan airport and scheduled an Uber to pick her up. When she went to the pick-up area, Uber was already there.

Mya's ride was already there as well, but Chloe's boyfriend wasn't there to pick her up. Naffilia offered to share her ride. The driver confirmed her drop off point but Naffilia told him to reroute to take her home too.

He acknowledged, "It's going to be added to your

account. Is that ok?"

Naffilia agreed, "Yes. That's fine. I'll make it worth your while."

They dropped Chloe off at her condo first and then they went to Naffilia's penthouse. She tipped the driver $50 and bid him farewell.

Taking a deep breath as she walked toward the lobby - a sense of peace and calm engulfed her.

Ahhh. Home sweet home. There's nothing like a mission like that, or a day like that to make you appreciate your life even more. I couldn't put it into words about how I felt, but everything around me looked crisper and clearer. It feels like everything is in its proper place. Even walking to this elevator and as I make my way to my house, I feel like there is nothing more that I want right now, right here and now.

It feels like all of my senses are heightened and I'm sensitive to everything around me. The touch of the button on the elevator. The music playing. The peaceful walk toward my penthouse and the sound of the keys as I pull them out. This is living in the moment. When nothing goes unnoticed. I can feel the gratitude well up from deep within me as I open my door and look at how beautiful everything is in my home.

Ahh. Time to strip naked and take a steaming hot shower. I wonder if this is what finding the right person feels like. Someone who can satisfy every part of me, that makes me feel like a woman. I wonder if this is what it will feel like to live in the moment with a man who can share this same mental, emotional and sexual space as me.

She put her carryon bag and personal effects on the floor near her bed and looked at the scroll over her bed out of curiosity.

Shit, I can't help but to think about that scroll. Does it really hold the secret to the perfect life of fulfillment of sexual satisfaction with a partner? After reading the text from those clowns, I don't just want sex. I want a sexual experience that heightens all my senses. The way I feel right now. That makes me feel so alive. I want an experience that takes me out of this world.

Naffilia got out of the shower and put on a tee shirt and panties. She went to the fridge and looked inside, and then looked in the direction of her phone, "Time to order in."

Just as she ordered, the weather turned without warning, and the sky turned various shades of grey. She could hear the sound of the rain hitting the windows around the penthouse and it was hypnotic. It put her deeper into a state of relaxation.

She took in a breath slowly, "This is the perfect time to binge watch Netflix while I eat some Greek food."

She poured herself a glass of red wine and sprawled across the couch looking through the latest movies on Netflix.

The buzzer rang. Over the speaker you could hear the concierge, "Miss Rosebud? Your food has arrived. Shall I send up the delivery?"

"Yes. Please direct him to the elevator. Thank you."

The remainder of the evening gave her the rest and relaxation that she needed. The grey sky, the sound of the rain hitting the window and the warm cozy blankets on the couch made it easy to unwind as she enjoyed a good dinner and a movie until her eyes closed without her knowing.

7

Tye went to work refreshed. Ready for business. The meetings that were postponed yesterday took place today in his office. He negotiated a take-over for a business that was once worth 25 million, but they found themselves operating in the black. They were losing money hand over fist and saw no way to stop the bleeding. That's where he came in.

Tye created a win-win situation for the owner and CEO of the failing business. He offered to buy them out but for practically nothing – pennies on the dollar. Nothing close to what they thought the company was worth. Initially they were upset with him and were ready to walk out of the office.

In a calm but firm tone, "Men! You are in a unique situation and I'm here to make sure it works for all of us. Frankly, you have two choices. One choice is to file bankruptcy and lose everything, including personal assets in order to pay out fees to lawyers. In the end, you don't get a penny. In fact, you will still owe salaries to your employees and that will come from your personal savings as well. The second option is to walk away from the business now, not owing anything to a single soul, and you pocket a few bucks."

Tye paused briefly to give them a moment to think about what he said and then went in for the kill as he leaned in closer to them and raised his eyebrows. You could feel the bass in his voice when he said, "I'm the only one willing to give you something for a business that's about to go under." Tye paused and didn't say another word.

This was his way to negotiate, and he did that with everyone. He would paint two bleak pictures, then gave them only one way out where they got money from the deal. Then he wouldn't say a word after painting the picture for them and waited for their reply. He was patient and cool. He wouldn't budge. This made him appear like a wolf waiting for his prey to bleed out so that he didn't have to waste energy attacking.

He once negotiated a business deal where he waited in

silence for almost 15 minutes, looking them in the face until they started to fidget in their chair. He waited for them to speak, despite their seasoned hardnosed approach – they eventually caved in. He took the same approach with these guys now.

They couldn't take the tension anymore. Beads of sweat started to form on their brow and ran down their faces. You could see sweat stains in their armpit starting to form before they couldn't take it anymore and gave in. "Damn it Tye. I guess we don't have a choice, do we? I feel like we're getting shafted for this."

Tye shook his head to give them a sense of relief, "No. You're not. You're walking away from a cancer, scot-free, with more money than you started with 11 years ago and you don't owe anyone a single dime. I'm just helping you to find a way out of a hole that you guys dug yourself. You need to see that." He handed over a pen for them to sign the paperwork.

They instinctively took it, but reluctantly signed the transfer of ownership to Wolf Enterprises.

While they signed the paperwork, he wrote out and handed them a check for 250 thousand dollars and shook their hands, "Gentlemen. Good luck on your future endeavors. May I have the keys?"

They handed Tye the keys and forced themselves to be happy about the decision to sell the business off and left with money in their hand but felt defeated at the same time.

This was a major score for Tye financially. It was a unique restaurant that began as a mom and pop restaurant and they had expanded to several locations, but they moved too quickly and couldn't keep up with the growth. There were seven restaurants in total and they needed help immediately. The main restaurant was located in New York city in upper Manhattan.

Tye had his secretary schedule an important meeting with the staff later in the week to discuss the restructuring of the business. Everyone was to be present where he would announce the exchange of ownership and the restructuring required for its success and he was going to oversee those changes were implemented properly.

Later that evening, as Tye drove the streets of Boston seaport taking in the scenery of the drive, pleased with the way the day went, he stopped at a red light and glanced at his personal phone. He noticed a missed text message from Alexia at 11 am.

"Just landed. On my way to your crib. See you lover."

He took a second to reply to Alexia, "Sorry for the late reply. I was at a meeting. I'm on my way now. Meet me in the arranged place we talked about."

He pulled into the garage at the penthouse where he parked his car reserved for him. As he walked towards the elevator, the echo of his car being armed could be heard several floors up.

He took the elevator to the main floor which was the lobby to the restaurant.

He approached the bartender, "Jose. How are you today?"

Jose turned his attention to Tye, "I'm very well Mr. Wolf. How are you?"

He shook his head, "I'm doing fantastic. Jose, I had a bottle of bourbon set aside. Can you get that for me?"

"Absolutely. It's right here sir." He bent over and placed the bottle on the bar.

Just then, Alexia came behind him and wrapped her arms around his waist and leaned close to his ear whispering with a sexy voice, "Hi, you sexy man. Are you glad to see me? I missed you."

Tye raised his finger and said to Jose while smiling, "Excuse me Jose. You have a good evening."

Jose just nodded and went about his business.

Tye turned around gave her a hug and took her by the hand toward a private elevator at the corner of the lobby. There was a keypad in place of the normal buttons where he punched in a code. It was his own private elevator to his penthouse.

Tye owned the building he lived in. The main lobby area had a number of retail shops and restaurants opened to the public. The entire top floor belonged to him.

The elevator dinged and the doors opened up to reveal luxurious glass elevators lined with gold covered kick plates at the base of elevator where it meets the floor. He motioned her into the elevator. She walked in and turned around and looked at him with hunger in her eyes. There was a look on her face like she couldn't contain herself as the doors slowly closed behind them.

The moment the door shut, Alexia dove down to kneel at his waste and unzip his jeans. Tye reached over to press the button to send the elevator up.

She violently did what she needed to do, to unleash and bare his dick, it was like she was a ravenous animal after raw meat. She licked his cock starting at the head and down his shaft. The sexual tension made him reach for the railing to brace himself.

As they were going up the elevator, he noticed that a few people had a look of shock on their face as they turned to watch him get head from a gorgeous Russian blonde. The higher they went in the elevator, the more aggressive her up and down head movements became until she gagged on his engorged cock. To the people down below, they could clearly see that she was giving him head. They both knew they were being watched and it turned both of them on even more.

He gripped her hair on the back of her head to take charge and move her at the pace he wanted, faster and faster. He shoved his cock inside her mouth until she started to gag and made her saliva drip from her mouth and down his shaft. The breathing in the elevator echoed, it got heavier and faster.

"Mmmm. Oh, that's it baby. That's the way you do it. Swallow the whole cock. Choke it down."

He could feel his rocket ready to explode the faster he moved her head while they were in the open climbing to his penthouse. The elevator bell rang to his penthouse before he lost control.

He lifted her off the floor and led her to the bedroom suite with the bourbon bottle in the other hand. He threw her on the bed, placed the bottle on his nightstand and reached under her skirt and ripped her panties off.

She squealed with delight when he dove in and placed his tongue on her soft delectable pussy. He breathed in her musky aroma, "Oh shit baby. The smell of your pussy is intoxicating."

He placed his hands under her knees and forced her leg up and apart to expose her pussy and ass. She felt vulnerable to him and it turned her on. He took charge of her body and ate her pussy like a desert.

She grabbed a fistful of blanket and threw her had back with her eyes closed to enjoy his tongue. She lifted her hips, "Oh fuck babe. Eat all the pussy you want. Tongue fuck me."

Back-and-forth with his tongue, massaging her clit and in and out of her pussy. It drove her mad and she couldn't help but make sounds like an animal. He ate her out until she begged him to fuck her. She wanted him to fuck her hard, but he wasn't ready.

He reached around to the back of her neck and told her to suck his dick again until he was ready to fuck her hard. She obliged and sucked his cock until he was engorged.

He caressed her smooth sexy body, "Suck my balls too baby" he said as he slipped his fingers in her pussy. It surprised her and she let out a moan of surprise and pleasure.

His hands were strong, and his motion was steady, in and out and hitting her g-spot until she climaxed, not just once, but a wave of them. Her orgasm made her body shiver, wave after wave while he kept fingering her, slipping in two and then three fingers.

She begged him to keep going but he stopped, "Wrap your wet pussy lips around my cock. Straddle me. Lower yourself slowly and ride my cock like a horse." At his command she went ham on his dick.

They were both lost in the moment and the intensity of

his passion drove her nuts. He pushed her off and flipped her over and lifted her by the hips. Her body quivered with every touch. She let out a scream of pleasure when she felt his thick, rock hard cock slip into her ass and fuck her until he couldn't hold it anymore.

"Oh shit. I'm cumming." His body tensed up and his hips thrust forward while his dick pulsed and shot inside her ass and it pushed her over the edge. She thrust her ass back into his pelvic with every squirt he made to intensify her orgasm.

He pulled out and rolled her over and shot the rest of his cum on her pussy. She screamed as waves of pleasure pulsed from head to toe.

They both laid in bed briefly to give themselves a moment to enjoy the feeling and catch their breath. Then Tye rolled out of bed and walked to the bathroom to turn on the shower and get her a towel. He tossed it on the bed to wipe her pussy.

"You can take a shower with me if you want." He gestured toward the bathroom.

"I'm exhausted from the flight and you just wiped me out and drained the last of my energy." She delightfully chuckled.

Tye took his shower and in a flash, the thought of the woman from Morocco came to his mind. Despite having amazing sex with Alexia, he started to fantasize fucking the woman he was looking for and how good it would feel inside. He shook his head quickly to the reality that he was with Alexia and didn't want to live in a fantasy and miss the moment he found himself in.

He got out the shower, dried off and put on his leisure clothes. "Do you wanna go downstairs to grab something to eat?"

"Thanks, but I'm gonna take a nap real quick. Can you bring something back for me?" She said as she stretched out in his bed.

He gave a quick nod, "No problem. I'll take my time. Get some rest."

Tye went to the restaurant and sat in his usual place to eat alone and set aside a meal for Alexia.

After his meal he went back up to find Alexia passed out on his bed. She hadn't moved. He put her meal in the fridge and relaxed for the evening, drinking his bourbon and watching the downtown traffic as night fell.

Early the next morning, Tye woke up and slowly opened his eyes and found himself staring at the ceiling briefly. He took a deep breath and rolled over to glance at Alexia who was starting to stir. He reached over to rub her soft silky skin, caressing her, intentional about touching every part of her. She began to stir as his rough strong hands ran up and down her back. She rolled over to let him rub her thigh and up across her tits. Her breathing got heavier and that's when Tye noticed she was rubbing her pussy.

He struggled to stay in the moment while the woman he has been looking for flooded his mind again. He forgot her name and it bothered him that he forgot. He just remembered that she lived in Boston too and it was that much more bothersome to know they were close but yet so far away.

Just then, the sun shined through the curtains and onto his face. It was refreshing and gave him a boost to get out of bed.

Alexia grunted, "Oh nooo you don't. Where are you going? You can't just touch me and get away with not starting our day off in a good way."

He smirked and gave a quick one breath laugh, "I have a lot of business to take care of today. It's a bit busier than usual today so I gotta get going."

He grabbed his phone and walked into his closet to get dressed as he sent off a quick text to his secretary and asked her to arrange a trip to Dubai for the end of the week next week. Then he asked her to make arrangements to fly to New York to take care of his newly purchased restaurant and arrange a staff meeting for Monday around lunch time. He wanted to hold his meeting during lunch and give them something to eat. It was always good to show your staff how much you appreciate them; in return they would commit themselves to you and your company. He wanted to start things off on the right foot with them.

Tye had a charity auction that he was contributing to a few weeks down the road and he wanted to pick a few things up for them, so he asked Maggie to send his driver over to pick him up. She made the arrangement.

Alexia rolled over to watch him get dressed, "When will I see you again?"

He turned to her as he was putting his tie on, "I'm gonna be busy for the next couple of weeks so maybe at the end of the month."

"Awww." She moaned with disappointment.

"I have something for you." He adjusted his tie and walked over to his nightstand and opened the drawer and reached in.

Alexia smiled, "What is it?"

Tye pulled out a pre-paid master card, "It's just a little gift for you. I wanted to do something special for you."

"That's so sweet Tye." She said with a tone of gratitude. She gasped after she looked down at the card to see the amount was $12,000.

"That should take care of some of your expenses coming all the way from Miami. Plus, there's a little extra for you to getting started to open that designer purse shop you told me about."

Alexia held back a tear, "You have a big heart." She got up to hug him before he left the room.

Tye left the room and went to the kitchen to grab something to eat before he made his way down the elevator to meet his driver at the front of the building, who was waiting to open the car door for him.

"Mike! Good morning, how are you today?" Tye tapped him on the shoulder.

"Very good Mr. Wolf. How are you?" He said in return.

"Fantastic. Let's go for a ride Mike." He said as he got into the car.

Mike shut the door and went to the driver seat. "Where are we off to today sir?"

"The Elite mall. I gotta do some shopping for an upcoming charity." He said with delight.

After shopping at the mall, he told his driver to go to the hardware store.

"Yes sir."

By now, Mike has known Tye long enough to know that this was not unusual for him to go to places that seemed so random. Tye was the kind of guy who like to get his hands dirty.

Tye went into the store and called the manager over to place an order for lumber, tools and paint and have them shipped to his construction company. He made an arrangement with his foreman to donate the supplies to specific shelters around the Boston area.

They drove over to one of the shelters to inform them that a shipment was coming to them to assist with making updates to their facility.

When he arrived at "Humanity House" he noticed a young lady outside working with a volunteer. She looked familiar. He approached her and there was a glimmer of hope that he had found the mystery woman.

He didn't want it to look to obvious that he wanted to see who she was, so he said hello as he walked by her into the building.

She turned to see who was talking to her, "Hello."

It wasn't her. He could sense that she was consuming his mind, and it was a distraction. He nodded but felt disappointment.

He met with the site supervisor and made it known that the supplies to work on the shelter were on its way and asked if they needed anything else before he left.

Tye went to the office to work for the rest of the day. By 4 pm he was feeling a bit stiff around the shoulders. He went to his secretary's desk to have her book an appointment for him.

"Maggie. Can you check to see if there is a massage therapist close to the yacht or penthouse?"

"Yes sir."

A few moments later, she announced to him, "I found one with an opening early this evening near your yacht. I've already made arrangements. Will that be all sir?"

He shook his head, "Yes. That's all. Thanks Maggie. Go home early and have a good evening."

"Thank you, Mr. Wolf. I'll see you later." She gathered her things together quickly and made for the elevator.

Tye went to the penthouse for a change of close before going to get a massage. When he walked into the house, he noticed that Alexia left him a note.

"I had fun babe. I hope to see you again real soon. Thank you for everything."

After Tye read the note he heard his phone buzzing from text alerts. That's when he realized that he had forgotten his phone at home. There were several messages, mostly from women. He silenced the phone and set it aside. Just then, on his business phone, a text came in from Maggie to confirm his travel arrangements to Dubai.

Tye changed his clothe into something more relaxing and got ready for his massage appointment. He went to the garage and got in his Lexus and drove himself to the appointment. He was deliberate about taking his time and slowing down to take in the sunset as he drove over Bunker Hill Memorial bridge as the pink and blue lights turned on at that moment.

He arrived near Marina Bay and found a parking space. He walked slowly toward the office so that he could take in the beauty of the sun setting while he took in deep breathes of the ocean air. There was an air of peace. Tye remembers feeling contentment like this when his parents where alive and they spent time in his father's hometown in Canada.

Memories flooded his mind as he recalled the times when he and his family sat outside his Aunt's home around a campfire overlooking the reservation as the sun set. It was the perfect view of both the reservation, the river and the surrounding mountains. A feeling of tranquility settled over his mind and body.

He announced himself to reception. "I have an 8 pm appointment."

She looked on her computer, "Yes Mr. Tye I see you are booked for 8 pm. Please have a seat and fill out this paperwork." She handed him a clipboard.

He took it from her and expressed gratitude, "Thank you for taking me this late. Not a lot of places stay open this late."

In a pleasant tone, "Your welcome sir. We understand that a lot of people can't come in during normal business hours, so we cater to those people who come in after work."

A few moments went by and she pointed him to walk through the doors down the hall on the right. He opened the door and a beautiful shapely massage therapist had her back to him as he entered the room. She was making preparations for their session. This gave Tye enough time to admire her ass.

She turned around to greet Tye and her eyes got notably wider for a second when she looked at him. She could tell he took care of himself. She was enthralled when Tye walked into the office with an air of confidence, like he was the one in charge.

Her voice was soft and sexy, "Please remove your clothes and lay down on the bench." She exited the room to get his chart.

When he was ready, she came back in with his chart in her hand, "I see that you are tense around the shoulders. I'll focus in that area."

She was very professional about the massage. Her hands were strong and soft. It put Tye to sleep. She told him that his time was up. Tye struggled to open his eyes and wobbled to his feet.

He asked, "Can I make arrangements to see you again? This was probably the best massage I had in a long time."

She said with delight, "Yes. Of course. The secretary can arrange it."

Tye got dressed in front of her while she watched. She grabbed the buttons on her blouse and tugged on them and licked her lips. Just before he walked out the door, she grabbed his hands and prevented him from leaving.

He turned his head to look at her hand and raised his head slowly to look her at her. He could see she was asking a question by the look on her face. With a smile, he gave her permission.

There was no hesitation. She didn't waste a second with him and unbuckled his pants. Her panties were already off the moment he started his session with her.

She decided that sucking his dick wasn't enough, he just needed her pussy. She pushed him down onto the massage table and climbed up on top of him and started riding him hard. The mirror by the window was enough for him to take full advantage of the view as he watched her ass in the reflection bouncing on his lap.

She wrapped her legs around Tye as he stood up and carried her to the balcony to fuck outside. He placed her against the wall and thrust his cock deep inside her and made her scream. To make sure he got deep, he raised her legs up and push himself inside her harder. With every thrust he made she screamed.

"Oh shit, ram that cock inside me. Mad fuck me. Ram my pussy." She screamed louder and louder with every thrust during their rough sex.

It caught the attention of the neighboring office who thought someone was getting beat up next door. They called the cops.

Tye was about to cum, "I see blue lights and my ears are ringing."

The therapist orgasm with his dick still thrusting, "Oh god, I'm cumming."

She heard the sirens and looked at the lights, "That's not ringing. The cops are on their way."

He let her down and shot his cum all over her, spaying everywhere. They quickly went inside to get dressed before the cops arrived and laughed at causing a disturbance in the building.

He watched her scurry to put her panties on and noticed she was rubbing her face, laughing as she reached for a towel.

He couldn't help but laugh too. It made both of them feel like they got caught having sex and they were trying to cover it up. It was naughty, fun and exciting at the same time.

Her laughter grew when she looked in the mirror. "Shiiiit!"

He looked in her direction just as she turned to him. One eye was sealed shut, covered by his sperm.

She frantically tried to get the sperm out of her eye.

Wiping desperately, "Oh fuck, I can't see. Ah ha ha haaaa."

The laughter turned into a deep guttural belly laugh and got louder as she tried to feel her way around the room to the sink to wash his sperm that was dripping from her eye.

The cops were at the parking lot now and were on their way into the office.

Tye did a double take before leaving the room. She had cum shot dripping from her hair and earlobe, and she didn't even notice.

Tye laughed and said to himself, "How the fuck did I shoot her that far up? What a fucking mess. I hope she finds that before they question her or that's going to be one memorable interrogation."

Her laugher got louder when she finally noticed his cum was hanging on her chin like a goatee and jiggled while she tried to talk to Tye.

Tye almost pissed himself laughing when he finally noticed it on her chin too. He scurried from the office laughing his ass off and made his way out of the office and down the hall before the cops entered her office.

One officer stopped him as he was laughing his way out to the parking lot.

He questioned him, "Hey. Are you ok? Did you hear

anyone getting beat up in the building?"

Tye tried to get his composure, and in between laughs said, "No sir. But I heard a couple, fucking each other like jack rabbits and howling like wolves. He must have been pounding that pussy pretty hard."

The police officer tried to keep a straight face and let out a single laugh, struggling to stay poise.

"Ok. Go on. You're free to go."

Tye continued to laugh all the way to his car, but he paused briefly to hear the commotion from the office. He almost pissed himself when the cops asked for the therapist's last name.

She said, "Cumshot...Trixie Cumshot."

Two cops came out of the office laughing their ass off because they couldn't keep it together.

Everyone listened in on the interrogation, they had to hear this one.

A cop's voice asked, "Who did this?"

She said, "Tye..."

The cop asked, "He tied you up and did this to you?"

She replied, "No...his name is Tye...and I would do it all over again. When you find him...give him my number."

Laughter could be heard coming from the office and it spilled into the parking lot.

The chatter from the cops in the parking lot made Tye laugh even more as he got in his car.

"Looks like the 'perp' shot her with his penis. She sustained a non-life-threatening injury to her eye."

The banter continued between the cops.

"Should we call a paramedic to check her eye out?"

"How do we call this in? What is the code for – shot by cum?"

This one made everyone's day, including Tye.

Tye said out loud, "Fuck. That was an awesome fuck...I'm mean...massage session."

Tye drove to the yacht smiling ear to ear. She gave a new

meaning to the phrase - happy ending.

8

Naffilia and her team were sent to Dubai early, to make sure they scouted the area before executing the mission. She has been waiting for this mission and was excited about the adrenaline rush she was going to have. This was a covert operation like she's never experienced before.

Naffilia looked out the window of the plane to admire the City of Dubai from the air just before it landed. It was breathtaking.

In my opinion, Dubai is one of the most beautiful places in the world. What's not to love about the glamorous life of Dubai - with all the skyscrapers and shopping malls, as well as the crazy night life. Wealth could be seen and felt everywhere. Hollywood had nothing on this place. Even the cops drove Lamborghinis. I called it, "The playground for the ultra-wealthy."

I personally loved the people of this area along with the beautiful sandy beaches that are only minutes from the city. There was something refreshing about taking a long walk on the beach admiring the scenery, while taking in the invigorating sea air.

I didn't see anything wrong with taking some personal time to search out the scroll that I knew was somewhere here in Dubai. Besides, I doesn't hurt to enjoy myself as I scope out the area and blend in with the locals one week before our biggest mission yet. One that involved taking out one of the prince's most trusted advisors.

We found out that the prince's second-hand man was Bojangles' arms dealing connection. We didn't know for sure if the prince knew it or not. We suspected that he didn't, but we couldn't take that chance. Iraq has been getting arms from somewhere and we finally narrowed it down to very well-connected people in the underground. This was highly sensitive information, that's why we had to do this mission covertly. We didn't want to create an international incident.

We knew for sure though that at any given moment, this connection to Bojangles and Iraq could incite a biological war with its neighbors and threatened to take war to American soil. This had huge economic implications on a global level. We were here to cut of Iraq's supply chain and the connection was well guarded by the prince and his protection agency. This was our most difficult mission to date and our most important. Time was of the essence.

To keep my head about me, I walked the beaches and embraced that sense of calm from the sound of the incoming waves and took in the cool breeze charged with negative ions. It brought a calm over me every single time.

Besides, I imagined myself walking on the beach with someone special holding hands. Or maybe having sex on the beach, and I don't mean the drink. What can I say? I'm a romantic at heart. I guess I'm a sucker for that kind of thing. Besides, what woman doesn't want to experience romantic things like this every once in a while.

The problem is, for me, life is too busy for that. I've had a fleeting thought that those kinds of things required too much from me – time, commitment and love. Three things that most of the men I've dated wasn't interested in.

My dreams, goals and accomplishments always took precedence in my life. Being creative was part of my nature and I had to explore, and relationships felt like they imposed boundaries. Because of this, I felt like I didn't deserve to be in one or deserved someone special in my life.

I've dated many guys, a few of them wanted commitment and I would run the other way. My job and my life felt like it would have to be put on hold in order to experience that level of relationship. I couldn't live like that. It felt like love put too much demand on me. Maybe it was easier to avoid it.

Several years ago, my father and a few of his best friends who were happily married for years told me that I have the wrong idea of relationships and love. They tried to explain it to me, but I wasn't hearing that. They said something about loving yourself gives you the ability to love others and accept being loved by others. I don't know. Maybe they were right, but I still didn't understand what they meant by that. Love gave me the impression that it made someone out to be weak. I had to take into consideration that I had commitment issues; I just wasn't sure why. Plus, I wanted to find that scroll. I had been looking for it for years and I wasn't going to let anyone, or anything stand in my way. I have to laugh because I admit that I don't have any commitment issues when it comes to pursuing things of this nature. I had no problems committing myself to acquire stuff in my life. Look at where I am in my life. I have everything I've always wanted. Well, almost everything.

Just then a couple holding hands and embracing each other walked by her, and they looked happy and lost in the moment.

Naffilia sighed as she watched them walking with each other seemingly lost in each other's presence, smiling like life was absolutely perfect. She brushed off that feeling of disenchantment and disdain for what they had by turning her attention to the café just ahead as she made her way toward it.

I arranged a meeting with someone who I thought had the best information on the scroll's whereabouts. I heard that he comes from a long line of sage, except he didn't embrace the family business. He took a different route with his calling and career altogether. Nevertheless, I felt he was my best lead yet.

After a long walk I met with my connection at a quant café on a peer overlooking the sea. I only knew him by name and had an older picture of him. I was supposed to meet him around 3pm.

I was a bit early arriving at the café, but that's ok. I could wait patiently, especially with this kind of view. I didn't wait very long. Maybe 5 minutes the most before I thought I recognized the guy. He was asking people's names while he was making his way toward me. They just shook their head.

He stood in front of me. With a curious tone asked, "Naffilia?"

She nodded, "Yes. That's me. Rasheed?"

He lowered his head and put his hand over his heart and spoke with broken English, "Yes. I am Rasheed. I am pleased to meet you."

She gestured for him to take a seat and let him order something off the menu.

Rasheed didn't waste time getting to business, "You are looking for a scroll?"

She nodded.

Rasheed continued in his best English, "My father was a great sage in this area for many years. Being a sage ran in the family for generations. I am told that it goes back to ancient Egypt. They passed down information about a scroll that held the secrets of ecstasy. I heard the story many times. Somewhere in our family history they moved from Egypt to Saudi Arabia, and then here to United Arab Emirates. We have lived here ever since."

He paused as his order was delivered to him, "I have looked for the scroll myself for many years. My family believed it to be here in Dubai. I could not find it, so I gave up. Until one day a light came to my mind."

He leaned in closer to whisper to her. Naffilia leaned in to listen with excitement and anticipation.

Rasheed looked around first then whispered, "It is not here. It is in Egypt."

Naffilia was taken aback, "Egypt?"

Rasheed snorted, "Yah. Egypt. Supposedly the place where the scroll originally came from."

Naffilia leaned back into her chair. Surprised and yet relieved that she was a step closer to finding it.

There was a silence between them, deep in thought as they took a sip of their drink.

"Do you have any idea why Egypt or where in Egypt?" She asked.

He nodded, "It is very likely in lower Egypt. On the outskirts of Cairo. Some say it's north of Cairo in an ancient land called Goshen. Others say it is in the city of Giza."

"That's were some of the pyramids are, is that correct?" She asked.

He nodded and drew a circle on the table with his fingers, "It is around that area and it goes way back to biblical times. There is a mention of some kind of connection between Egypt and Israel. Because of that connection, it is believed that the scroll originated from Goshen around the time the Israelites where salves."

Naffilia was fascinated by the history, "Really?"

Rasheed responded, "Yah. Legends speak of a time when the priests from both cultures collaborated and studied this secret to ecstasy and wrote the scroll together. Their collaboration was thought of as a legend because both cultures weren't supposed to mix. It was forbidden to accept one another's beliefs. A small band of priests from each culture was sworn to secrecy as they met underground to study this myth. It was the combined effort of two separate cultures coming together as one that allowed the secret to be revealed. They each have a perspective of God or the gods and their combined effort led them to discover a portal from heaven to earth through…"

He paused to look around before he continued. She did the same.

"Ah huh?" She said with enthusiasm.

He continued, "…the portal from heaven to earth came through the sexual bond of a man and a woman. But not just any man or woman. It was so sacred and intense that only those pure in heart would survive it and open up that connection to untold ecstasy but also untold truth and blessings. It wasn't just any sexual bond though. There were criteria that had to be met and incantations and prayers that needed to set the stage."

Naffilia was astonished, "Oh my gosh. Are you serious?"

Rasheed shook his head and continued, "Those prayers

and criteria were written on a scroll. The priests believed that it was called - the forbidden fruit. My family heard that the scroll was divided to keep the secret safe."

Naffilia gasped, "This is fascinating. Thank you so much."

She reached into her purse and handed him an envelope.

He opened it up and sifted through the layers of hundred-dollar bills. At a glance, there looked to be fifty bills.

He looked confused, "I was not expecting this much."

"It's ok. I appreciate this greatly. It means a lot to me." She with a tone of gratitude.

Rasheed took his last sip. Placed his hand over his heart and lowered his head, "Many thanks to you. Blessings on your quest."

He left the café.

She watched him leave and noticed while looking in his direction in the distance four Bentley pulling up to a hotel. It was the prince's security. They were escorting the prince and his chief counsel member to the hotel. There were ten bodyguards exiting the car. The agency wasn't anticipating his arrival for another week.

She used her phone to get a closer look at the activity and zoomed in to watch the prince and chief counsel – Jazeer, get out the car. She scoffed and said to herself, "Oh. It's not the prince."

This was a staged practice run before his arrival. Just then she got a text on her work phone. It was from a planted agent inside the hotel.

"Bozo won't arrive till later this week."

She chuckled, and text back. "Thanks. I didn't think the circus was in town yet."

As part of the covert operation they had to send text in code to avoid attention or raise security alerts. She was ready to return to the safe house when she got another text from headquarters back in Boston.

"You need to come back home. It's urgent. We sent you a private plane to get home sooner."

Naffilia put the rest of the plans into the hands of her capable team to stay behind and keep tabs on Chief Counsel - Jazeer. He's been on the agency radar since the Miami mission.

Before taking the flight back to the United States she got a text confirmation from a fellow agent, Danielle, that Jazeer logged onto a Russian sex site to order three beautiful women to join him in Dubai for a party. It was important to remain unidentified, that's why he requested women from Russia. It was an all-expense paid trip. He threw in a bonus of extra money and gifts for making the private party.

Danielle intercepted his Email message that had a private cell phone number and other personal contact information.

The email contained specific dates and times, which included the day of the private party, "Where shall I send my payment and gifts? They'll need to be here on a specific date."

The responding email read, "The girls will be available soon. They have a video shoot to do in Russia first."

His reply to the email read, "To make sure this stays private and to make sure they arrive, I'll send a private plane to pick them up. Where do you want me to send it?"

"You can send the plane to Moscow. There is an airport 48km south of Moscow called Domodedovo international airport. They have private hangers there. You can send the plane there. Once the girls are done with the video shoot, they'll pack their bags and be on their way. Please allow up to 3 hours of delay for their arrival."

Danielle sent the rest of the email correspondence to Naffilia.

Naffilia text her back, "We can use this information to our advantage. We'll have to find a way to get on that plane in Moscow. I'll come up with a plan. In the meantime, I got a text to go back home. You guys stay here and keep tabs. I have to go silent in moment and I'll text you later."

Naffilia packed her bags from the safe house and left to

take the company plane back to the United states.

It was a long fourteen-hour flight back home. Instead of flying her home to Boston, they flew her to New York. The agency filled her in on the reason they were pulling her from the mission to fly her to New York. Her father was in the hospital and the doctors didn't give him much time to live.

The news of her father stunned her, and it drained her quickly. To go from a high-profile mission with adrenaline coursing through her veins, to finding out where the scroll might be, to finding out that her father was on his death bed, was too much for her to bear.

She could feel herself welling up with emotions. She closed her eyes to think about her father but fell asleep from sheer exhaustion. She slept 12 of the 14 hours on the way home.

Naffilia arrived in New York early in the morning. There was a limo waiting to take her to the hospital in upper Manhattan.

She arrived at the hospital and found her father's room. He was still sleeping and didn't want to wake him, so she sat in silence next to him and waited for him to wake up, while she admired her family life, recounting memorable things about her family.

My father is the most amazing man I've ever known. He was always looking out for me. I got my business smarts from him and my risk-taking spirit. He always said that if you want to succeed in life, you have to take chances, that risk was just a thing that needed to be done.

He and my grandfather owned a number of businesses and had big hearts. They always took care of the less fortunate.

I grew up in New York. My grandfather was very influential in his hometown and owned a large tract of land. His contribution to that town earned him his legacy. They named a street after him.

Dad and his brothers had connections to the military as well. I come from a family that believed in serving our country. In fact, my brother was still stationed in Hawaii in the Marines. After the military, my grandfather and father worked for a secret agency and told me some scary shit. He once said to me, "My little betty-boo, promise me you will never take any vaccine shot from any government agency! It's deadly and it's evil. It contains monkey blood."

My father was a part of the division I now work for. He got started after the Vietnam war. Members of his division were recruited to serve the president as well. That's how he got connected with the agent she now works for.

I have such fond memories of my father. I could feel the tears starting to form in my eyes. I couldn't help but reach out to hold my father's hand.

Naffilia held her father's hands and smiled. He felt her hand and it woke him up. He turned his head to get his bearings.

He smiled and struggled to speak, but could only mumble, "Betty-boo."

"Hi dad. I'm here." She could barely speak with the lump in throat. She sniffled.

Naffilia and her father spent the next hour with each other. She did most of the talking because he didn't have the energy to speak. He made an attempt as often as he could.

They talked for about two hours and enjoyed each other's company before a few of his closest friends walked into his room. One of those friends was Naffilia's boss from the agency.

Naffilia stayed a few minutes more to hear about the good old days being shared between her dad and his friends. There was some laughter in the room but also some crying. As the conversation began to subside, she could feel his pain and it was too much to bear. Just then, another round of his friends came in to visit and she took this moment to let him be with his friends and grab something to eat quickly.

She kissed her father, "Dad, I'm just gonna grab something to eat while you visit your friends. I'm gonna be right back ok?"

Her father smiled. He was pleased to see family and friends. "Okay." He said with frailty.

She walked past the nurse's station and a menu on the desk caught her eye. She asked to look at the menu and asked where to get this food. They directed her to a restaurant a block down the road.

When she walked outside, she could see in the distance, a few dark clouds starting to form. It was moving in quickly. She sighed as she turned her GPS on to find the restaurant. She found it quickly and was surprised that it was a nice-looking place. It was eloquent and cozy at the same time. It's something that she would consider patronizing often if they had one back in Boston.

The host greeted her as she entered. "Dine in or take out?"

She needed the break to gather her thoughts, "Dine in please."

"Currently the only open space is on the rooftop because we have an important staff meeting happening right now. I know that it looks like rain is coming in, but if it does, we'll take you inside right away. Is that ok?"

She nodded, "Yes. That's fine."

He led her to the rooftop and seated her. There was a fireplace in the center of the patio that added to the serenity of the place. There was a sigh of relief as she looked over the menu.

The waiter walked over to give her a lemon water and take her order. Just as she handed him the menu, she got a text message.

It's Mya, her agent friend, "Hi girl. How are you feeling? I heard about your dad."

She replied, "I'm good. I spent most of my morning with him and I'm just grabbing something to eat so I won't pass out."

Mya replied, "Ok. I just wanted to check on you to see how things were. Enjoy your meal and I'll get in touch later."

"Thanks Mya." She put the phone aside to sip on her drink and take in the rest of the restaurant and take in the view over the street. She turned and looked inside at the staff meeting. There was a nice-looking man in a business suit at the far end of the restaurant. He looked like a commander at the front. It was unusual to see people eating at the same time while having a staff meeting.

She paused for a moment because the man looked familiar. She squinted her eyes to get her focus. Just then the waiter brought out her plate. "Here you go ma'am."

She didn't take too much time to eat. The more she thought about her father, the harder it was to swallow with a lump in her throat as she held back the tears. Her face became drawn. Naffilia looked as though she was going to cry with every bite and her motion became robotic as it took effort to eat. The clouds began to roll in and cover the sun as the sky became darker. She forced herself to eat a little quicker just in case it started to rain.

Meanwhile, the staff meeting inside was in full swing. The man at the front was obviously the man in charge. He was animated and charismatic. One of the staff members raised his hands to ask a question.

"Mr. Wolf. We just want to know; will this restaurant stay open?"

Tye Wolf said with assurance in his voice, "Absolutely! You have nothing to worry about." Just then, he paused as he noticed a woman on the patio. His heart fluttered for a second because it looked like "Her." The woman he's been looking for. He noticed her downcast expression so he thought that it couldn't be her. She looked a little different.

Tye brushed it off to continue the meeting but kept glancing in her direction.

Naffilia finished her meal and paid her bill. She got up from the chair and turned toward the restaurant to make her way downstairs. She thought she recognized the speaker's voice at the front and took a closer look.

Tye stopped in mid-sentence as Naffilia walked toward the exit and the look on his face said it all, "It was her! Fuck, it was her!"

Naffilia tilted her head and looked Tye in the eyes.

Oh, my fucking gosh! It's him! Of all the places to see him, he's here in New York!

Naffilia stopped in mid-stride and smiled at him.

An employee called out, "Mr. Wolf?"

A couple of people interrupted his gaze and asked, "What were you saying?"

Tye turned his attention back to the meeting.

Naffilia got a 911 text from her boss, "Come back. It's your father."

Naffilia glanced in his direction and then quickly left the restaurant.

Tye looked back in her direction and she was gone. He scanned the room to see where she went. You can tell by the look on his face that he was torn between running after her or keeping his composure to keep the meeting going. He didn't want to discourage his new staff and they had a restaurant to turn around. He looked down at his notes and let out a quick sigh and continued.

Naffilia walked out of the restaurant and to her surprise, the clouds had opened up long enough to walk back to the hospital quickly. She glanced back at the restaurant hoping that he had noticed her and would come out looking for her. But even if he did, she had to get back to be with her father.

She arrived at the hospital and all his friends were standing in the hallway. You can tell by the look on their face that something was wrong. Naffilia could read facial expressions and the long look on her boss's face gave it away. He must have passed.

Shit. No. I shouldn't have left. Damn it. I should've stayed.

Her pace picked up and the look on her face looked worried. She went into his room and there were doctors and nurses scurrying around in his room.

The hospital staff parted and near their father was her brother whom she hadn't seen in two years, holding their father's hand.

"Dad!" She shouted as she entered the room.

Her father reached up with his other hand.

Naffilia ran to hold his hand, "Dad! I'm here."

The tears fell onto his bed as she kissed his hand. "I'm here dad."

Her father gasped for air as he looked at both his kids, "B...B..."

"It's ok dad. We're here. You don't have to say anything. I love you dad."

Her father took a deep breath and spoke his final words, "I...Loooo..." He let out his last breath.

Her world stopped as the sound of the EKG monitor could be heard all the way to hallway where everyone was standing in silence, and it created a ringing in Naffilia's ears. Naffilia and her brother could be heard crying as they held their fathers' limp hands.

9

It was the day after her father's funeral. Naffilia's brother had to go back to Hawaii. They caught up on family matters and consoled each other as best as they could. They agreed that she would take care of his home and clean it up and keep whatever contents were there.

Naffilia stayed in his house since her arrival in New York. Her brother only stayed briefly. They expressed their grief but also shared fond memories of growing up in that house.

After her brother left and she was by herself in the home, memories of her family flooded her mind as she took in every detail of her childhood home. Every object had a memory and a feeling attached to it. The house hadn't changed since she left. The smell. The feel. It brought back years of memories.

Her father and her brother are the last of her immediate family. Her father's passing made her feel alone in the world. Losing a parent creates an empty whole inside, like not having someone watch over you anymore. You feel unprotected. Creating anymore history or memories comes to a screeching halt. It makes your world look empty.

Everything changed. Everything was different now. It hurt when her mother passed away two years ago, and this only intensified the feelings. Everything felt final.

She reluctantly packed her father's personal items because it made it feel like the end of all her good memories. The closure was good, but it made the reality of his passing that much more painful. Any chance to create new memories were now gone. However, it had to be done before the moving company came to pick up all the contents of the house.

She noticed a set of keys on the countertop. With great curiosity she picked them up and looked closely at them. There was one key on the keychain that stood out. She studied the key as if trying to recall a memory, then a smile found its way to her face. She turned slowly to look at the door leading to the garage.

She wondered, "Hmm." The smile remained on her face as she reached for the doorknob and opened the door slowly.

She said out loud, "Oh shit. I almost forgot about this."

She couldn't believe her eyes. It was his 1968 baby blue Camaro with large tires in the back and small tires in the front with custom crown wheels.

"Oh fuck! He's been working on it. The last I remember there was still a lot of work to be done." Her smile got bigger as she approached the car.

"Mmm. Dad had style. How could I have forgotten about this car?"

She reached down to pop the hood, "Oh Shiiiit! Fucking A! He's been working on this car. Look at that chrome Crown engine."

She was overwhelmed by excitement, "Shit there is chrome everywhere under this hood. Way to go dad." A lump formed in her throat. He finally finished the project they started when she was younger.

She opened the garage doors with the buttons. "Ok dad. Let's see what you did." She pressed a button on the keys.

The car started up with a thundering boom. She laughed with excitement. "A remote starter! Fucking ya!"

The roar of the motor sounded like her Ferrari truck. She heard enough and got in to shut the motor off. The smell of the interior brought back memories. She got out of the car and noticed there were pictures on the wall of her and her father working on the car.

There was another picture of her mom and dad standing proudly in front of the car. They looked so young in the picture. I remember him mentioning that it was their first hobby car when they first got married. He kept that picture there for his own memories, especially after mom died.

She laughed at a momentary thought. It wouldn't surprise me one bit if I were conceived in the back seat.

She took a few days to pack everything. Finally, on the last day she made one last walk around the house before the moving company came to put her father's things into storage.

There was nothing left to pack, so she opened up the garage door and started up the car which now belonged to her.

This was the first time she drove the car since she was a teenager. The car had a lot of power and the grip was amazing as it hugged every turn. It felt like she was driving a car that had the power of thunder and lightning. She shouted, "Ha…lightning fast!"

She took her cell phone out and place it on the dash, held in place by a hands-free clip so that she could use the GPS to Boston. "You're coming home with me baby."

It was a 3-hour drive back to Boston, which wasn't too bad. It would give her some time to unwind, recall good memories and regroup.

Before she got onto the highway, she reached down to the CD player, "Let's see what you were listening to dad."

Barry White's, "Love's Theme" blared through the speakers. Naffilia's head bobbed to the beat of the music as tears rolled down her check while happy thoughts flooded her mind.

For the next couple of hours, she played all of his CD's to pass the time and relive much of her childhood memories.

Without realizing it, she was about 30 minutes from Boston.

She said with contentment, "Ok. That's enough. It's time to play some of my stuff."

She played music from her cell phone, pressing random play on the phone.

"Welcome to the Jungle" by Guns N' Roses blasted the car. She belted out a scream of delight and turned up the volume.

Just then, in the rear-view mirror she could see a car roaring up behind her. She moved over one lane to let them pass, as she did, she caught a glimpse of the car as it made its way up next to her.

"Shit. It's him. What an asshole."

They couldn't see each other because of the tinted windows. Whoever it was, paced her for a few seconds, taunting her to race.

"The bad mother fucker wants to race."

She stomped on the gas and took off, letting him know she's not fucking playing today. Of all the days, today is not the day she's in the mood.

"C'mon dude, let's see what the fuck you're in a rush to get to today."

She clearly had the better of him, but she could hear his engine roaring, even with the windows rolled up and the music playing in the background. It turned her on a bit, despite her mood. She rolled the window down a crack to keep her face hidden but enough to hear the sound of his engine as it came roaring up next to her.

Two muscle cars on the highway going toe-to-toe, engines roaring while raw power under the hood could be heard. It started to turn her on. She loved the feel of shifting gears. Whoever this was, they had a knack to make her pussy wet.

She could feel the vibration of the motor through the seat as she pressed her ass into the seat. She wanted her pussy to feel that vibration too, so she pressed into the seat harder, and it made her wet and gushy.

"Mmmm. I can feel my whole body starting to feel the excitement. Shit, I thought is wasn't in the mood for this but whoever that was, they had something special to make me wet like this."

Without warning, a flash of memory came back to her of when her father took her out to race the car.

Then another flash came to mind of her and her father working on the car, when he said to her, "You're gonna love the power of this motor, Betty Boo. There's a lot of muscle under here."

She lost herself in the memory for a second and forgot that she was flying down the highway at 100 mph racing an asshole that turned her on.

When she came to, she didn't notice that the traffic had

slowed down in front of her, so she swerved into the fast lane, out of the way of the car. She slammed on her brakes to get control of the car as she made a quick decision to turn into the breakdown lane if she needed to.

The fast lane was still moving at a fast pace when the car she was racing roared past her, zooming in and out of traffic.

She gathered her wits about her and saw an opening in the slow lane to pass everyone and tried to catch up, but a dumb ass pulled in front of her as he merged onto the highway. She had no choice but to slam on the brakes, almost swiping his bumper.

"You fuckin' prick. Stupid ass mother fucker. Who the hell taught you how to drive? Crusty the clown?"

She shook her head in disbelieve that she almost hit him. If it wasn't for her quick reaction to swerve off the exit near the breakdown lane, she would have hit him for sure. She sat briefly in the breakdown lane at the exit while cars were blowing their horn as they passed by her.

She got off the expressway and took the back-roads home from that point forward. That was an adrenaline rush for sure because her hands had a slightly noticeable shake.

"Wooo. I feel like I just had sex. Thank you, mystery racer! I'll see you in my dreams."

She drove home, pleased that her father's car was still intact. She looked upwards and said, "I hope you turned a blind eye to that one dad." She laughed.

It didn't take long before she got home to relax for the rest of the night.

10

I woke up this morning and it felt like a Mac truck hit me; I had an emotional hangover from everything that's been going on the past few days. It's been a taxing week. One moment I'm in Dubai getting ready for a critical mission and the next thing I know I'm flying home to sit at the hospital with my father one last time and burying him the next day.

The memories of family have flooded my mind daily since then. I feel like I need to run away and escape. I wanna run away from this world and just reset everything. I hate that feeling of waking up thinking it was all a bad dream for a fraction of a second and then snapping back to the reality that it was all true. I gotta blow of some steam somehow.

There's one bright light from all of this. I finally saw "him" after weeks of thinking about him since I last saw him in Morocco, and of all places, New York when I needed a pick me up. What are the odds?

It would have been great to at least talk to him. He looked good from afar. But what the hell was he doing there heading up a staff meeting?

I gotta find a way to shake things up a bit. Maybe I'll fuck with some people just for fun. Let me see what kind of response I got from the dating website I signed up for. Maybe there's someone there that can get me back into my routine or get my mind off of everything that's been going on.

Naffilia logged on to a dating website she signed up for just for shits and giggles before she went to Dubai. There were plenty of options. Lots of men to choose from. She had contacted two potentials and figured it was worth dating a couple of them.

She asked if they were interested in going out tonight. They had no problems being spontaneous and meeting with her later.

Hell yeah, it's on. Let's get ready. Let me set the tone right now with some "Prince."

She cranked up the music on her Bang and Olufsen stereo system to play "International Lover."

Oh yah...uh huh. That's it. I'm feeling it.

She slowly gyrated her hips in a fucking motion, pretending to grind her lover. Losing herself in the music, she did her version of a sexy strip tease as she made her way toward the shower and turned it on. She danced her way to her bed with just her panties on and crawled onto her bed toward the scroll. Lifting herself to her knees and pointing toward the scroll she said, "I'm going to find my lover and make him feel like a man."

She sprawled out on the bed and raised her hips up and down in a snake like motion, like she was fucking the bed. Then she slowly raised her ass in the air, reached her hands down to grip her panties and slide them slowly off her ass making sure her panties tickled her ass as she stripped naked while the music intoxicated her.

She rolled over and sat up in her bed, mimicking the infamous water splash dance scene from "Flash Dance" before getting out of bed to take her shower.

"I'm going to fuck with one of you boys or fuck you. Either way, I win."

After her shower both men replied, and she arranged a movie date with both of them for different times.

What the hell! Dinner and a movie, and maybe some dick.

"Let's meet for a 6 pm show."

The first guy was all for it.

Then she texts the next guy, "Let's meet at 11 pm."

The second guy was all in, almost too zealous. She didn't pay too much attention to it though. They both had potential. On their profile they had their shit together and look like they were fuck worthy.

She put on a sexy dress that hugged her curves and her sexy high heel shoes completed the ensemble. As usually, she accessorized with a watch and earrings. She looked in the mirror and was pleased with what she saw.

"Mirror, mirror, on the wall, what do you think of this sexy doll?" She turned around to look at her ass.

She grabbed her ass and rubbed it, "Oh yeah. That'll get their blood flowing."

She was ready for the evening and went to the elevator. There was another man at the elevator waiting. She could feel him staring at her. She glanced over her should and caught him looking at her ass.

"You takin' a drink with your eyes?" She asked.

He smiled, "You're giving me no choice, aren't you?"

The elevator doors opened. They both got in and he stood behind her as she pushed the button to the garage and he reached around her, invading her personal space to press the lobby button, stealing a sniff of her hair.

As he scanned her from behind, "Girl, you're so fuckin' hot and sexy. I don't think those curves are meant for the average guy. What's your number?"

Naffilia ignored him and acted as though she was nervous. It made him more persistent and aggressive. He thought he had the upper hand.

You could hear him smack his lips, "Mmm. Mmm. I have a package that you're gonna wanna check out baby."

She turned around, looked him in the eyes and reached down toward his crotch and quickly grabbed and crushed his balls. With a sexy voice she said, "Not today Pennywise. I'm not in the mood for a horror story. You fucked with the wrong person today, bitch."

A bead of sweet formed on his forehead as he nervously laughed. The look of fear in his eyes and the nervous expression on his face brought Naffilia satisfaction.

She squeezed harder to make a point, "Don't you ever fuck with me or any woman for that matter ever again or I'll fucking kill you…"

She let go of his balls, "…and I'll get away with it too. You hear me Pennywise?"

He shook his head and scurried out of the elevator as soon as the doors opened to the main lobby. While he wobbled away, he looked over his shoulder like he just got his ass handed to him.

Naffilia smiled and waved goodbye, then flipped him the bird as the door closed to take her to the garage.

Which car am I feeling right now? Dad's muscle car or the Vette?

Mmm hmmmm. The Vette. I'm feeling fast tonight with a touch of class. She got in and turned her GPS on to Gillette stadium movies.

She texts her first date. "I'm on my way now."

On the way over she ran through his dating profile through her head. He's a corporate attorney. Born in Russia. He's tall, dark and handsome. He should be easy to recognize at 6'6". His profile paints a pretty good picture of the kind of guy he his. He's worth a shot.

She pulled up to the VIP section and walked slowly toward the door. He made it early and waited in his car for her. She text him and said she was coming in right now. He looked up and saw her texting.

"Damn she's fine! A quality woman with a smokin' hot body. Shit, I'm in for a treat tonight."

He got out quickly and text her that he was on his way in to. She read the text and turned around to see where he was at. Just then he walked over to her and grabbed her hand.

He remarked, "Wow. You look absolutely beautiful. I'm glad we met in person and that you are everything you made yourself out to be on that website. Most people hide themselves on dating sites like that."

She returned the compliment but was sizing him up. Since Naffilia wanted to burn some stream she contrived a plan that would allow her to fuck him tonight.

They purchased VIP tickets for dinner and for privacy. They ordered their food for the movie and talked in the lounge area for a little while before the movie got started. They had good conversation over a glass of wine and Bourbon.

The movie was getting ready to start so they went into their privacy booth to eat and watch the movie. After their meal and 4 drinks later, she started rubbing his inner thigh and squeezed his dick.

She leaned over to whisper, "Oh wow. Nice hefty meat."

He said with a cockiness, "There plenty of it to please."

She undid his zipper and reached into his pants, "Nice velvety soft sacks."

He said jokingly, "I made sure they smell good too."

She said with a grumble in her voice, "Are you a good boy or bad boy?"

He didn't hesitate with his answer, "I'm both. And it depends on the mood and what you're looking for."

She squeezed his cock, "Good. I'm going in and I'm going rock you."

He was surprised by her comment, "Oh shit! Right now? Right here?"

"Yes. Are you afraid of the dark?"

"No. But there are people not far from us."

She assured him, "Don't worry about that. It's dark enough in our private area and I'm going to sit on your lap nice a slow. We can keep it quiet and not bring attention to our self."

He agreed, "Ok. No problem."

She slipped her panties off and placed it on her finger and twirled it around to show him. Then she climbed on his lap and faced him and slid herself down on top of his stiff dick. She timed it perfectly so that as the loud scenes were playing, she rode his cock hard. The louder the scene, the harder she grinds his cock. Her pussy juice ran down his dick and it made them both lose control as the movie scenes continued to get louder.

The intensity made them forget that there were people close to them and they started to moan. She took her hand

and covered his mouth.

There was a quiver in his voice as he whispered, "Oh shit! I'm coming and I can't stop."

This turned her on and they both cum at the same time. She lifted herself off of him slowly.

"I'm going to the lady's room. I'll be back for you."

He nodded and then went to the bathroom himself to clean up.

When she got back, they both agreed that they were done with the movie and left the theatre.

As they made their way to the car, he asked her, "Will I see you again?"

"Sure. We'll get in touch again." She said it in such a way that left him with some doubt.

Her next date was scheduled for 11 pm and she text him to confirm. He wanted to meet in a theatre in Rhode Island. His profile on the website looked promising as well. He was tall, dark and handsome as well. He had a promising career and was CEO of an up and coming software company. He seemed intelligent and was a health nut. He had potential relationship qualities, but since she needed to blow some steam off, she would settle for another good fuck.

It took her 45 minutes to get there and arrive earlier than him. She texts him, "Where are you? I'm just pulling in. I'll meet you inside hun."

He replied, "I'm inside already. I'm just around the corner."

She asked what he was wearing because she vaguely remembered what he looked like from his profile and wanted to make sure she could spot him.

He replied, "I'm wearing Blue Jeans, a white dress shirt and black sneakers."

There was only one man in the general location wearing what he said he was, and he was nothing like his profile claimed him to be.

She rolled her eyes, "Oh shit. You gotta be kidding me.

I've been catfished."

He was a rollie pollie man who looked like he was a Thor wannabe with long hair and his belly was bigger than his ass.

Her heart sank to her feet and she lost her appetite to eat, never mind watch a movie.

Out of courtesy she approached him and went on the date regardless. After the movie she gave him a hug and a pat on the shoulder.

"Thanks for the movie. I'll text you when I'm home."

He could tell that she wasn't impressed, "Is everything ok?"

She wanted him to be real with himself and others, "That's not your photo on the profile is it?"

He looked embarrassed, "It's my cousin. I didn't think anyone would date me if I put my real photo up."

She touched his heart, "You have to find a way to be comfortable with yourself, and be yourself, and the right woman will be happy to date you."

He appreciated her kind words and watched her walk away.

She made her way to her car. It didn't take long for her to get home. Out of courtesy she text both men to let them know she got home safely and that she had a good time.

For her own sake, she blocked Rollie Pollie but kept Liam the attorney just in case there was something there between them.

She took her shower, turned the lights out and crashed.

In the morning. She did her regular workout and took her shower. She was feeling more herself this morning and cranked the music up before going into the shower. She recalled the fact that she saw Tye at the restaurant in New York and a smile came to her face and started singing in the shower.

When she got out of the shower, she checked her phone, "We changed the meeting. It's an hour earlier."

"Oh shit. I gotta get going." She ate breakfast and left the penthouse quickly. Today felt like the perfect day to drive her father's car.

She turned on some music to put her in good spirits and weaved in and out of the cars on the highway on the way to work. In a playful way, "Where are you today mystery driver?" I'm ready for you. Let's get our race on."

She pulled into the parking lot of her work and revved her engine to admire the sound of the car. She noticed the new recruits were gathered in the parking lot talking. When she got out the car, they turned their attention to her and stopped talking to watch her walking toward the building. Just after she passed by them, they mumbled under their breath, but she didn't acknowledge them as she made her way into the building.

She growled, "I've gotta plan for all you rodeo clowns, and your little clown convention."

She greeted everyone in the office with a smile, "Good morning guys! How are you doing today?"

They all response, "Good morning. We're doing good. How are you doing Naffilia? Are things ok with you?"

They were legitimately interested in her. They knew about her recent loss and wanted to make sure she was doing ok.

With gratitude, "I'm feeling better. Thanks for asking and thank you for the flowers and your condolences."

A few spoke up, "Your dad was an amazing man. I remember when he used to work here. He helped me feel at home when I was a new recruit."

Naffilia smiled, "Yeah. He was a man with a big heart."

Just then, the head of the department walked into the room and pointed everyone into the secured office.

"Ok, let's get down business. Everyone into the office and let's discuss the upcoming mission. There's a lot at stake here."

As Naffilia passed by the chief he inquired, "How are you feeling young lady? Are you up for this mission?"

She nodded, "Yes Sir. I'm good and ready."

Behind secured doors, they mapped out a plan of action to the mission in Dubai. They were given current intel and each person was updated with the plan. The chief gave everyone their assignments.

Naffilia was to go to Russian with two of her friends and collogues, Mya and Chloe, to pose as Russian models. There was a confirmation that the prince's advisor was going to send a plane out to Moscow this week. They needed to pose as the models that he requested and get on that plane.

The briefing lasted 4 hours. At the close of the meeting the chief belted out the order, "Ok. Let's get these girls to Russian and wait for his plane."

On way out of the room Naffilia motioned for Mya and Chloe. "Hey. Can I go fuck with your students real quick? Some of them need an attitude adjustment."

They both agreed, "Sure. Let's go. They're at the gun range this morning."

They got to the range and Chloe watched her students and shook her head, "Tsk. They can't even hit the target. I don't understand how someone could be this shitty at shooting."

The three of them laughed loud enough that the students heard them. When they got done with that round, Chloe yelled out, "You guys need to pay attention to what you're doing. You're making it harder than it really is."

They jeered in her direction and a few scoffed at her. "You act like it comes easy."

Naffilia shook her head and walked over to the student who appeared to be the biggest asshole of the group that was talking in the parking lot. She gestured for him to put his M-16 rifle down and walk away.

Naffilia picked up his rifle changed out his clip and laid down and took aim. She didn't hesitate and took one shot.

Chloe took out her binoculars and shouted, "Bulls eye. Keep going."

Naffilia looked in the asshole's direction, smirked and turned to shoot again. Pow-pow-pow.

After three rapid fires Chloe shouted again, "Bulls eyes again. All three."

Then Naffilia looked at everyone else, nodded her head and shot again. Several rapid fires. It looked like Naffilia was going hog wild on the target. Bang-Bang-Bang-Bang-Bang. Several rapid fires until she was out of bullets.

Naffilia placed her riffle down and went to the next student's lane and changed the clip and started shooting until there was no more bullets. She moved onto the next student.

After Naffilia was done, Chloe looked through her binoculars and laughed, "Clear the line!"

She turned on the red light to signal that it was clear, "Go retrieve your target."

Naffilia retrieved all three targets and handed it to each of the students that chattered in the parking lot. "Here you go Ronald McDonald."

His target had 4 bulls' eye and the words "Ron" spelled out on the paper.

All the students laughed. Then she handed the other targets out to the others – his little groupie. The first student, the leader of his group was stunned to see 'Ron' spelled out and barked to the other two, "Let me see yours."

Their face was in shock because she spelled out, "Goofy and Pluto."

The entire class laughed uncontrollably. Naffilia made her point. After the laughter died down, she had everyone's attention.

She pointed to all of them, "Pay attention to what you're doing right now, not when you get in the field. It will be too late then. Stop acting like dicks and get out of your own mind. Stay focused."

She turned to the others to make an example of them, "Stop being such assholes. At some point you will need to rely on your team members, and you'll need to trust them with your life. Keep up the fucking attitude and disrespect and you will die withing the first year of being in the field.

Show some respect, not just toward others, but what your enemy is capable of doing."

There was a silence in the room and the point was clearly made. It gave all the students something to think about.

Naffilia approached Ronald McDonald and pat him on the shoulder before leaving the room.

Naffilia thanked Chloe and Mya before leaving, "See you in Russia."

11

The private plane was leaving at 5 am. It was going to be a long 15-hour flight from Boston to Moscow. On the way there, there was plenty of time to rest and go over the mission and make arrangements to intercept the plane that the advisor sent to Russia.

Their tech guys had intercepted all the exchanges between the advisor - Bozo and the Russian dating site. The emails and the phone calls had been filtered through their agency so that the girls could intercept the plane. They made arrangements for the agents to take the place of the models who were busy doing the video shoot. Both the Russian dating site nor Bozo suspected that they were making arrangements with the agency to arrange Naffilia, Chloe or Mya as the Russian models to be picked up. The women disguised themselves so as not to arouse suspicions. They made themselves up to look as close to Russian models as possible.

They arrived at the outskirts of Moscow and took a private limo to the other airport for the arranged pickup and waited for the plane to arrive.

The plane arrived as scheduled and they boarded the plane. The flight attendant welcomed them aboard the plane. Naffilia greeted her in Russian. The attendant didn't understand, instead she spoke Arabic. Naffilia acted as though she didn't understand.

She shook her head, "Sorry…I don't understand Arabic."

The attendant spoke broken English to address them.

Once they got seated the flight attendant opened a cabinet and took out a cell phone and held it in front of the women.

She stood in silence briefly and sized up the women and look like she was trying to figure something out, "Who is the one in charge of this arrangement?"

For a moment they thought their cover was blown. Naffilia spoke up, "Pardon me?"

She offered the phone to each girl, "I was told to give this phone to one of you women who was to be a contact point for the client. They wanted me to give you this phone so that he can contact you."

They let out a sign of relief and Naffilia spoke up, "That would be me." She reached out to take the phone.

The phone buzzed and it was a text by the client, "I'm just confirming that the three of you got on board safely and in a timely manner."

She texts back, "We did. Thank you."

The next text came in, "Is there anything that you need or would like upon arrival."

Naffilia text back and gave him their choice of food for their party.

The client text back, "Consider it done. Relax and get some sleep girls, because it's an 8-hour flight to Dubai."

Meanwhile, back at the hotel in Dubai, the other agents who were already there were aware that the mission was a go. They had been monitoring the situation for weeks. They announced to the rest of the team, "It was now, go time."

There were agents outside the hotel monitoring the private security cameras in the rooms and hallway. There were agents posed as security, hosts, cooks and servants. All hands were on deck for this mission and it was in motion weeks ago.

Everyone knew that he had 20 security guards. His security was just as tight as the prince's because he was his most trusted advisor.

The few weeks they were setting up the mission they had gathered more intel on the prince and his advisor. The agency learned that the Chief of Ministry was a traitor and that he had planned to set up the prince, to make him look like he was doing the arms dealing with Iraq and then have him and his family killed. They had enough evidence to take him out and they were going to do without bringing attention to themselves. They were going to put their motto in action.

Back on the plane, the flight attendant offered the girls some Champagne. The girls played the role of partying, acting like they were enjoying themselves, living the high life.

The attendant offered more drink, but they refused in order to keep their head about them, plus they didn't want to wake up with a hangover after their 8-hour flight.

The next day, by noon, the advisor received a message that the girls landed and were being picked up by the limo. The limo driver opened the door for them as they acted like high profile escorts, laughing and having a good time. The girls recognized the limo driver as one of their agents and winked at him.

The driver brought them to the hotel so that they could rest for a little while and get ready for the evening party. As they were on the way, the limo driver rolled down the privacy window to speak to them, "You're all set. The room you're going to isn't monitored. It's been swept of any cameras or bugs."

Chloe leaned into the driver and kissed him on the cheek. "Thanks for taking care of us. We owe you hun."

The driver smiled, "Ok. We're almost there. Good luck girls." He rolled up the privacy glass.

The driver pulled up to the overhang and let the girls out. They were met by a tall thin man holding a clipboard and a burly looking bodyguard.

"Welcome ladies. My name is Saeed. I'll be your host. If you need anything at all, I'll be your contact point. Please follow me and I will take you to your room." He turned and led the girls to the elevator and up to their room.

"Please come down to the lobby at 5 pm and I will escort you to the room. We'll be providing the meal…"

He looked them up and down, "…and you'll be providing desert."

Meanwhile, the agents inside of the hotel and at the safehouse were monitoring their movement. The agents that kept an eye on them to make sure they went to the right room remarked, "The circus is in town. Cue the music for 'Send in the clowns.' They're in the ring getting ready to meet the ring master." The agents monitoring the audios snickered. Another agent remarked, "Better not let 'you know who,' hear that she was referred to as a clown. She'll kick your ass." Light laughter was heard on the headsets.

After they got to their room, they dolled up and put on their sexiest outfit and put on sexy high heels shoes. Naffilia reminded Chloe and Mya, "Girls, security will be checking us for weapons before going into his room. No guns allowed."

Naffilia pulled out the drawer to the nightstand and flipped it over. There were 2 thin needles tapped to the bottom. "We'll be using these. We'll need to inject them into his thigh. The injection point will be too small to catch by quick observation. The chemical will stop his heart within seconds and its untraceable. We also have option B which will paralyze him long enough for us to get the job done. We just gotta time everything perfectly so his guards don't suspect anything."

They went to the lobby at 5 pm. They were dressed provocatively, and they turned heads. Their outfit were see-through and hugged their body. Saeed walked over to the women and tried to keep his composure, "This way ladies." He brought them to a private elevator where two guards stood.

He brought the women to the top floor. When the doors opened there were two guards standing in front of the elevator prominently displaying the guns in their holster by their hip and under their shoulder.

Saeed gestured to the girls, "Please follow me." He walked them toward large double doors guarded by two large men, with a third man off to the side holding a semi-automatic.

Saeed nodded to the guards. One guard nodded back and entered into the room, while the other guard frisked the women. The guard went beyond the call of duty and took the opportunity to feel their tits and grab their ass.

Chloe smiled and turned her head in the girl's direction, "I guess the party started already." The girls giggled.

Mya chimed in, "Are you gonna feel me up too baby? Or

do you wanna just fuck me right here?"

Saeed watched them getting frisked and got a hardon. He found himself distracted by their see-through outfit when he addressed them, "Ok…your nipple…oh, ah, ah…your night with the client is not going to be disturbed. The guards will check on you from time to time. You'll get paid handsomely for your services. Wait here until the guard comes back out. He'll let you in when your client is ready."

He bowed and then walked toward the elevators.

The women giggled and shouted out to him, "Ok Saeed. Thank you for your kindness. Maybe next time YOU can frisk us."

He looked over his shoulders and smirked, "Lucky bastard."

After a moment or two, the guard came out and motioned them inside.

The opulent decor was staggering. The girls acted like they were enthralled by the wealth. "Shit, would you look at this place."

Just then the Chief of Ministry walked in the room with a robe on. "Welcome women. My name is Jazeer. Please make yourself comfortable. I have dinner ready for us."

He was an average looking man. There was no way anyone would have suspected he was an international terrorist. He looked more like a nerd wanna be bad boy. You can tell he wasn't hard core like Bojangles. He seemed to love his life of luxury and without it he would be relegated to be a mere balding single man living in his mother's basement playing video games and going online pretending to be a badass. His wealth propped up his confidence and his cockiness.

He guided them to a dining room where food was laid out in the open like a buffet with all the food they requested. He turned some background music on while they dined.

The girls didn't eat too much but made sure he was full. Afterwards they lounged around the palace and created a party atmosphere.

Naffilia connected the phone that was given to her to the

145

stereo and streamed music that created a sexy atmosphere. All three girls started dancing seductively and making out with each other and grabbing each other's tits.

The advisor was getting turned on when they started to strip their clothes slowly. Mya went back to the table full of food and grabbed a cup of yogurt and stuck her tongue inside the yogurt lapping it in front of the advisor. She then walked over to Chloe and removed her top and smeared yogurt on her nipples, "Come here big boy. Come lick it clean."

The girls stripped down to their panties to dance around the living area. His security guard opened the door to glance in and saw the girls dancing around the advisor. He rolled his eyes and shut the door.

The advisor was already standing at attention, "Girls. Girls. Come here and grab a drink so we can go to my room and fuck, fuck, fuck."

Mya whispered in his ear, "Tell your guard that you are about to get laid and disregard the noise. We are going to make you howl."

The advisor stuck his head out the door, "Give me a moment of privacy. Ok?"

The guard gave a single nod.

Chloe announced, "You are about to get a show that you will never forget."

The girls acted like they were getting drunk and did a strip tease for him. Mya bent over in front of him and pressed her ass into his pelvic, while Chloe danced seductively around him with her hands running across his body. Naffilia came up from behind him and undid his robe so that his dick sprung out. She reached around his waist and shook his cock to spank Mya's ass.

The advisor was overwhelmed by the stimulation and started breathing heavy. He was getting drunk with lust to the point where he didn't notice Naffilia remove the two needles from a lining in her panties.

Chloe and Mya slipped their panties off slowly and danced for him in the living room and put on a show for him while he watched them sucking each other.

They stopped to tell him, "We should go to the bedroom."

He was starting to sway with drunkenness. Naffilia refreshed his drink and slipped him a numbing agent to cause his body to tingle so that he could not tell when they slipped him the needle.

Chloe laid on the couch and spread her legs for him, "Are ready for a new day."

He looked confused, "What do you mean a new day?"

The music was loud, and he wanted them to turn the volume down.

Mya demanded, "Keep the music up, because I'm going to make your night."

He shrugged his shoulders, "Ok."

Naffilia, looked him in the face, "Are you ok?"

"I'm fine." He said as he started to stagger.

Naffilia motioned with her eyes toward the security camera in his living room, "Smile for your camera. Your boys are watching. We are about to give them a show."

He smiled and gave the middle finger toward the camera while "welcome to the jungle" played on the stereo.

The girls insisted, "Let's go to the bedroom."

Naffilia grabbed another cup of yogurt. "Yeah, let's go have desert."

"What the hell. Let's go girls."

He led them to his bedroom where Chloe and Mya laid on his bed as if they were ready to give him 69. Mya hung her head over the edge of his bed and stuck her tongue out like she was ready to suck his cock. Chloe opened Mya legs and laid in between, leaning back on her elbows and spreading her legs for him. She motioned toward Mya's pussy and pointed to hers.

Naffilia guided him to stand over Mya and guided his balls over Mya's face and pushed toward Chloe so that he was leaning in to suck her pussy. The position alone almost made him blow his load before he even got started.

The advisor was lost in the moment and didn't feel Naffilia inject the outside of his thigh with the paralyzing drug. He didn't flinch because of how quickly she did it.

The expression on his face looked like he was about to cum, then he grabbed his heart and fell on top Mya and his face fell into Chloe's pussy. The girls let out a surprised squeal because they didn't expect it to happen that quickly. They also didn't realize how heavy he was.

The guard opened the door came into the palace to check on him. He didn't see the advisor in the living room, so he knocked on his bedroom door and opened it to see his face in Chloe's pussy. The girls were surprised by the guard and Chloe grabbed his hair and rocked his head as though he was eating her out.

Naffilia quickly took a mouthful of yogurt and threw it on the bed for Mya. Naffilia turned toward the guard and acted like she just swallowed the advisors cum. Then Mya stuck her head out from under the advisor with her face covered with yogurt.

Naffilia swallowed then addressed the guard, "Did you come in here to cum on our face too baby?"

Chloe kept moving the advisors head on her pussy and started to squeal, "I'm gonna cum baby, keep going."

The guard was embarrassed as he mumbled with an accent, "'xcuse me." He adjusted his pants to make room for his stiff dick and shut the door quickly.

The girls quickly picked up the advisor before he was rendered completely useless, sat him in a chair and slapped him in the face to wake him up. He opened his eyes momentarily.

Naffilia nodded her head to both girls as they started to clean up and get dressed and then turned to the advisor and said, "Mr. Jazeer – Bozo…I'm gonna recite our motto to you and you have a decision to make. We give all of our victims the option to choose a new path in life…"

Naffilia smiled at both the girls and looked at Bozo, "I love this part of my job…You are either with us or against us.

Do as we demand, believe as we believe, or choose your fate. There is no room in this conversation for free thought. We will do your thinking for you - this is your last chance to choose your fate now…"

He was conscious enough to respond, "What the hell? Who the fuck are you?"

Naffilia shoved a cloth napkin in his mouth, "Shh. Don't interrupt me while I'm working."

She continued, "You have a choice to make right now Mr. Jazeer. You can die by our hands or you can choose to live, but just so that you know, you will lose everything."

She pulled his head closer to her face and made him look at her mouth, "…and I mean everything. Your home, your identity, your way of life and…"

She savored the next statement, "…and the billions of dollars you just made over the years as an arms dealer…"

Naffilia stepped back and gesture like she was handing out something, "…and we will freeze and distribute your assets, your money. Every penny will go to worthy causes as part of your payback to society."

Mya whispered, "Choose life. Choose life. You'll live long enough to watch your money go to help people, instead of kill people. Since you decided to frame the prince and kill his family, we are going to make your life fucking miserable and expose you for the worthless piece of shit that you are."

Chloe added her two sense, "We got some homeless shelters and food banks you can sponsor. Think of all the educational scholarships that you can be a part of."

Naffilia shook him awake, "Make a decision now. Die or live? Or we will choose it for you."

Jazeer started to shake with fear. "Please don't kill me. If the prince finds out what I've been doing or what I planned to do with his family, I'll be beheaded."

Chloe and Mya raised their hands, "He chose plan A. He chose life."

Naffilia nodded to the girls, "Ok. We gave him a chance to change his ways and he took it. Option A it is."

Jazeer was about to say thank you when Naffilia's fist was the last thing he saw before he was knocked unconscious and injected with the rest of the paralyzing drug.

It was going to keep him in a paralyzed state for the next 8 hours. That was long enough to freeze his assets and expose his undercover operation as an arms dealer and notify the prince that he had a traitor in his midst. The agency took his millions of dollars and spread it to all the communities he impacted over the years. They created a buzz in the media to cover up the fact that they were involved in this mission. They made it look like it was an assassination attempt, but it would lead to his demise and expose him.

The girls tried to move his body to the bed, but it fell from the chair and it hit the floor with a loud thud.

Naffilia's eyes widened, "Oh shit."

They acted quickly when the knock at the door happened again. They put themselves in positions on the bed like they were having sex and covered themselves with a blanket and started to moan loudly.

Mya put herself in position under the blanket as though he was getting head, while Chloe was moving Jazeer's head violently. Naffilia held him by the waist to keep his body up while the girls looked like they were getting their fuck on.

Before the guard opened the door, Naffilia rubbed the yogurt on her tits. Just as the door opened, they started moaning and Naffilia was spreading the yogurt around on her tits. The guard saw Naffilia playing with her nipple and turned to the guard and said, "mmm…ya baby…you want to cum on my tits too?"

The guard lowered his head quickly and backed out of the room in a hurry. "No..no…sorry."

The girls got dressed and laid the body in bed and rubbed his body in alcohol and smeared the alcohol around his mouth. They put a few empty shot glasses on his nightstand and positioned him as though he passed out drunk.

The girls got dressed and started to wipe down the house to get rid of any trace of evidence. They were thorough and took their time knowing full well that it was the last time the guard would interrupt them.

The guards on the outside started speaking in their own language, "That's too much woman for him to handle. They'll fuck him to death." Laughter broke out in the hallway.

The guy with the gun chimed in, "I can handle them myself. I could probably fuck them raw."

The guard who kept checking on him said, "The only thing you can handle is your dick. Even then, you probably give yourself 3 strokes on your dick before you're done." Everyone belly laughed at his remark.

The other guard cracked a joke too. "I saw an American TV commercial for Tootsie Roll. A kid wanted to know how many licks to the center of the lollipop to get to the center where the tootsie roll was."

They chuckled, "Yeah I've seen that commercial."

"One. Two. Three. Three licks to the center. That's you…three licks or three strokes and you're done." The laughter grew heavier.

Just then, the loud music stopped abruptly, and it caught the guard's attention. A minute later, the girls pushed the door opened and walked out giggling.

"He couldn't handle the three of us. We exhausted him and he passed out drunk after we fucked him. I don't think he's had Russians girls like us before."

Naffilia turned to the main guard who kept checking on them, "Your little boy is sleeping like a baby. Maybe you boys should have joined us for the fun so that it lasted longer."

Mya added, "He's happy, but we were too much for him. He shouldn't have drunk so much so that he could last longer."

The guards shook their heads and mouthed the words to each other, "I told you."

The girls walked towards the elevator, laughing and shaking their ass, making a ruckus as they went down to the hotel lobby. All the agents were standing by in case the security guards ran out after them. They picked up the pace to walk over to the public elevator and back up to their room to change. They could feel the adrenaline rush and knew that the guards could find the body at any given moment. They took off all their clothes and shoes and anything else that could be used as evidence. They secured the needles and put everything in a bag for the other agents to dispose of.

Quickly, they threw their stuff together, changed and left after a quick sweep of the room and wiped everything down.

Every minute that went by was a minute closer to them being found out. As they walked by the garbage shoot, they threw the bag of evidence down where an agent was ready to retrieve it and burn the evidence. They got down to the lobby and picked up the pace to leave the hotel. Just before they got out the door, they heard someone yell, "Stop!"

They could hear footsteps running toward them.

The girls froze briefly and then turned slowly to see who yelled out.

Saeed had a look on his face like he knew something was wrong, "Wait. I need to have a word with you."

The girls braced themselves while the other agents moved closer to the girls.

He reached into his pocket slowly while the girls kept their eyes on his hands. He pulled out 3 prepaid credit cards. "You can't leave without getting paid."

They let out a sigh of relief, "Of course. Thank you. Saeed, you are very sweet."

He smiled as he handed them the cards, "There's two hundred and twenty-five thousand on each card. This should make your day."

Suddenly he looked confused as he looked at their luggage, "I thought you have more stuff than a single handbag. Where is all your stuff that you packed?"

Naffilia was quick witted and answered, "Honey, with 250K...we'll be buying new stuff. We just tossed those old clothes out to make room for the new."

Saeed was pleased with that answer, "Thank you for your service. I will let the pilot know that you are on your way so he can fly you back to Russia. Have a good flight back home."

They walked out of the hotel and found the limo driver. He drove them to the safehouse to drop them off and picked up three local agents who took their place to fly to Russia.

The limo driver dropped off the stand-in women at the airport and told the pilot to take them back to Moscow and not to ask any questions.

At the safehouse they monitored the guards and kept a close eye on any activity at the hotel, while Jazeer's wealth was distributed in a matter of seconds and they were on standby to handfeed the press whatever information they needed to dismantle his empire.

The guards checked on him and assumed he was drunk, and it didn't dawn on them until several hours later that something was wrong when they noticed a white foam coming from his mouth.

By that time, Naffilia, Chloe and Mya were already halfway home congratulating each other on a successful mission, but clearly wiped.

12

Tye was in his office during his break. He connected with a few of his friends to talk football. They mentioned how much fun it would be to go to a game this year. They agreed that they would make an attempt to make it to at least one game this season.

Just before his break was over his phone buzzed with a text message.

It was Alexia. "Hi sweetheart. I miss you. I wanted to come back to Boston to see you."

He set aside a moment to talk to her, so he replied, "Call me."

His phone rang. Alexia said with excitement, "Hi baby. I miss you so much. I was just thinking about you and how much of a good time I had the last time we saw each other. I can't stop thinking about the elevator ride up to your place."

He disguised his reluctance to show affection, "Hi Alexia. I had a good time too. How've you been?"

She didn't pick up on it, "I'm good. I've been really busy. I've been thinking about you all the time since I last saw you. Do you have any plans anytime soon?"

"Yeah. Actually, the guys and I were thinking about doing a tailgate party for the football game in a week."

He paused for a second then continued, "First, I gotta leave the country to take care of business. But I'll call you when I get back, is that okay?"

With a slight tone of disappointment, "Yeah that's fine."

Tye could feel the disappointment from her response, and he wanted to give this a chance with her and gingerly asked, "Do you...want to come with me and the boys to the tailgate party? Because I think they're going to be bringing their girlfriends and their spouses?"

She said with some hesitation, "Sure. It sounds like it'll be fun."

Tye responded with slight enthusiasm, "Ok. I'll make the arrangements when I get back."

Alexi came back with a comment that made Tye fidgety, "Okay. Then maybe while I'm there we can go shopping and have some bedtime fun."

Tye simply grunted, "Mmm hmm. We'll see."

Alexia seemed cheerful, "Ok. I'll see you later Hon. Have a good trip."

"Ok. Bye."

Tye ended the conversation and took a breath and mumbled to himself, "It may not be too bad."

Tye called his secretary into the office to take some notes for him.

While walking around his office he stopped to look out the window, "Maggie I've got to get out to Dubai this weekend to take care of some business. You arranged the round-trip first-class ticket to Dubai leaving this Friday, right?"

She nodded, "Yes. I booked it last week like you asked. And the hotel."

Then he turned around with a smile on his face, "When I get back, I'm going to have a tailgate party with my buddies."

"That sounds exciting. Let me guess what game you're gonna go to."

She paused and put her finger to her mouth and looked upward, "Hmm…"

Tye grinned and waited in anticipation, "You already know, don't you?"

She jokingly replied, "Of course I do. Everybody knows the game of the season to watch. It's going to be when the Florida Pirates come to town."

Tye put his hand up to give her a high five, "Yeah! You are the best Maggie."

She adjusted her shirt as if tightening a tie, "Yup. I am. Nobody leaves Bean Town and then comes back to challenge us. We'll milk that QB and make some cheese."

They both laughed. Then Tye said with compassion, "Hey…let's not knock him. There's still love there for his time with us."

Tye paused for a second. A serious look came over his face and he looked Maggie in the eyes, "Oh. And Alexia is supposed to come out and meet me so that she can go as well."

Maggie's brow frowned and her head shot back and looked at him as soon as he said, Alexia, "Oh! You're taking Alexia?"

Tye was surprised that she knew her and was inquisitive, "Yeah. Why does that surprise you?"

She cleared her throat, "Well...I've met Alexia. She's come up to your office while you were out. She asked for you."

Tye seemed surprised, "Really? She's from Miami. How many times has she stopped by?"

Maggie replied, "Only once. I had a chat with her and found out you were seeing her. I just didn't think she was your type."

Tye chuckled remembering what they did in the elevator just a few weeks ago. "I'm pretty sure she's my type."

Maggie grinned, "Your type for what reason? Are you just looking for a fun time or are you looking for somebody who has meaning in your relationship?"

Tye snickered, "Okay now Maggie, are you being like my mother looking after me? Or are you just being extra nosy?"

Maggie smiled warmly, "Tye, I've worked with you for a long time and I knew your mom. I'm just doing what she would have done. I'm watching out for you, that's all."

Tye touched her on the shoulder, "Thanks Maggie. I appreciate you. And I'm sure mom would appreciate you looking after me."

Tye changed the subject quickly and motioned like he was throwing a football, "I can't believe that football season is already underway. Before you know it, all the holidays will be upon us. I want to make a few last-minute adjustments on a number of business acquisitions before the holidays are upon us and then I'm going to take a real nice, long deserved break this holiday."

With some excitement in his voice, anticipating the holidays, he nodded in her direction, "Maggie. I appreciate all the work that you've been doing for me. Do you have any plans during the holidays?"

Maggie contemplated, "No not really. I'm just looking forward to the holidays coming up. I'm going to be spending it with family."

Tye reflected, "Family! The good old days. Did I ever tell you how festive it was in our house during the holidays? We had lots of family around to share the holidays. My mother and father would cook up a storm and there'd be food in the centre of the table in the dining room. They really knew how to open up their home and create that family atmosphere."

Maggie reminisced with him, "I remember you telling me those stories years ago. I understand that feeling because my mother and father were like that too, and I've always wanted to create that kind of environment for my kids and their kids as well. It seemed like the older generation really knew how to celebrate the holidays and they were big on family as well."

Tye and Maggie enjoyed that feeling reminiscing family times together, then he looked at his watch, "I'm going to end my day early today. So as soon as you can, send over the information on my flight to Dubai. I'm going to make a phone call to a friend of mine in Silicon Valley. He graduated from MIT and he's been doing pretty good for himself. I was thinking about inviting him to come out for the football game because I haven't talked to him in a while."

Maggie agreed, "That sounds like a good plan. Are you sure this is Alexia's thing, 'cuz she doesn't seem like the type to get into football?"

Tye laughed, "There you go again Maggie, always looking out for me. Do me a favor? Can you call Rich and ask him for 8 tickets in the luxury box for next Sunday's game? Tell him to get us as close to the owner as possible this time."

Maggie replied, "It's nice to have connections in high places huh?"

He nodded, "Yup. I'm really excited about hanging out

with the guys. As soon as I take care of these phone calls, I'm going home."

He pointed to Maggie, "When you take care of all that stuff, go home and be with your family."

Maggie snorted, "There's still 4 hours left in the day Mr. Wolf."

Tye nodded, "Yeah. I appreciate the memories we talked about. We know how to take care of business. As long as it gets done and we work hard, there's no reason to reward ourselves."

With great gratitude, "Thanks Mr. wolf. I'll get that information to you as soon as possible."

Tye called his buddy in California and they had a good half hour conversation. During that time, he arranged for his buddy to come out to Boston a few days before the game.

Tye hung up the phone and took a deep breath and straightened up his area. Just before heading home he waved goodbye to Maggie.

A few minutes later, she text Tye with all of the information that he requested for his flight to Dubai.

Tye's driver picked him up and drove him to his yacht while he called his contact, Rasheed, in Dubai to let him know that he was going to be going out for business and pleasure. They arranged to meet after his business meeting.

He got to his yacht to unwind and made preparations to take his trip, getting ready for business and pleasure. Days later Tye was packed and ready to go to Dubai and made arrangements for the limo to pick him up and take him to the airport.

He made his plane early that morning and nothing was unusual about that day. It felt like business as usual. After 30 minutes into his flight he logged into the Wi-Fi service and connected with his secretary back home to get confirmation on booking 8 seats for the football game. She confirmed his seats and wished him well on his trip out of the country.

Tye landed early in the evening. There was a buzz in the

air. He could tell something was happening. He noticed that the TVs were broadcasting the murder of the Prince's right-hand man, the most important advisor to the Prince. He could hear the chatter of people speculating that the assassination was meant for the prince himself.

Once he got into the limo, he opened up his laptop and saw that the front-page news was all about the assassination attempt on the prince and the murder of the advisor.

The Chief advisor and minister to the prince was staying at the same hotel that he had already pre-booked. Upon arrival of the hotel there was a flurry of people coming and going in and out of the hotel. He pushed his way to the front desk and there were police everywhere, he barely made it inside.

When he got to the front desk the receptionist announced that the advisor was killed just hours before he arrived. He was in shock to hear of the news and immediately got on the phone to text Maggie to find him a flight out of Dubai immediately. Then he turned to the woman at the counter, "I have a reservation for today. I'd like to cancel that."

She emphatically declared, "We're going to have to charge you the full amount and a cancellation because we already booked it off."

Tye awkwardly replied, "That's okay. I don't care. I just need to cancel."

Just then he got a text reply from Maggie, "I'm sorry Mr. wolf but they grounded all aircrafts out of Dubai. Security is tight and they are questioning people leaving the area. Mr. Wolf? Are you ok?"

He replied, "Yes. I'm okay. I just cancelled the hotel reservation. I'm trying to get back as soon as possible. Are there any flights at any airport nearby at all?"

She replied, "There's nothing anywhere. I'm afraid it looks like you're going to be stuck there."

There was a pause between text as Tye rubbed the back of his neck and stared into space trying to gather his thoughts.

Maggie text again, "The guy who was assassinated, wasn't

he your connection? Wasn't he the guy that was supposed to introduce you to the prince?"

Tye text back, "Don't worry about it, Maggie. I'm going to find a way to get back. Okay? I'll text you as soon as I'm on my way."

Tye got in touch with his personal contact, Rasheed, that he was supposed to meet later in the day and told him to meet him right away due to an emergency.

Rasheed arrived at the hotel to pick him up and they left the city to avoid the media and security.

Tye said with some relief, "It's good to see you."

Rasheed greeted him with a heavy accent, "It's good to see you too Mr. Wolf."

They got into the car and drove out of the city. Rasheed said with urgency, "Since we are meeting earlier than you anticipated and you seem anxious, I'll make our meeting really fast."

Tye shook his head, "Don't worry about that, they just shut down all of the airports and it looks like I'm going to be stuck here for a little while."

Rasheed lifted his head and opened his arms, struggling with his English he said, "Ooooh, do not worry about that Mr. Wolf. I have known somebody for a long time who has a private airplane and I'm sure you will have no problems flying home. I think you can afford his rates and have no problem paying for a ride home. In fact, I'll take you to him right now. We'll go, and we can talk along the way. I have some information for you."

Tye said with some relief, "That sounds perfect let's go."

He turned the car around, "Ok. We go. Now...you mentioned to me a while back that you were looking for something. A woman asked me the same question last week."

Tye looked surprised, "You spoke to someone else about this? What did they look like?"

Rasheed raised his eyebrows up and down, "She was very pretty. She was tanned and fit...oooh very fit. I could not stop thinking about her after she left."

Tye was curious, "Really. Do you remember a name?"

He shook his head, "No. I'm sorry I do not. But she was very generous with her gift to me when I gave her some information, but I really couldn't help her. I didn't say much."

Tye was surprised, "So, you really can't help me?"

He replied, "All I can do is connect you to someone in Egypt. You will have better luck there."

Rasheed handed Tye an envelope.

Tye seemed somewhat pleased with the conversation, "I guess this didn't turn out too bad after all. I definitely need to get back because this sudden political upheaval is going to cause a travel nightmare. I'm glad that you're bringing me to your connection for the private plane. Thank you."

They were arriving at their destination, "You're welcome my friend. In fact, we are here now."

He parked the car, "Come. I will introduce you to the pilot."

Rasheed introduced Tye to the pilot and told him that he wants to fly back to the United States. He asked if he could fly him back.

The pilot told him that it was a long flight and that they would have to stop at a couple of time to refuel because their plane wasn't meant for long hauls.

Tye assured him that it was okay, and he was willing to pay, "How much would it cost me?"

The pilot did his calculation, "In order for me to fly you there and then fly back, it's going to cost a total of $110,000."

Tye took a deep breath, looked around him and made a decision. "It's a deal."

He shook the pilot's hand. "Let's get going. I gotta get home. I don't want to be grounded here in Dubai."

The pilot gestured him inside to fill out the contract and to get paid.

Tye shook Rasheed's hand, "Thank you my friend. This wasn't the way I wanted our meeting to go but I do appreciate your information."

"I understand. Your welcome." He said.

Tye took his phone out and texted rapidly, "I just sent you some money. I appreciate your help."

His friend looked down at his bank account, "$5,000? Thank you, my friend. The lady was very grateful as well and gave me $5000 too. You guys must think alike. Blessings to both of you."

Tye seemed relieved and curious, "Do you have any more information on this person? Do you have any idea when she might be going to Egypt or if she's going to Egypt at all?"

He shook his head, "I'm sorry my friend. All I know is she was smoking hot and had the same demeanour as you and carried herself very well. She didn't tell me anything else. Maybe you two should meet someday."

Both of them laughed.

Tye dropped his luggage off in the plane and then went inside to write up the contract. Then they boarded the plane. When he sat down, he let out a sigh of relief.

He texted Maggie, "Maggie, I'm on my way home now. I found a private charter. It cost me $110,000 but I think it's worth it. I don't want to get stuck here in Dubai."

Maggie text back, "Pardon my french, but shiiitt, $110,000? For that price you should buy your own plane!"

The text caught him by surprise, and he responded with enthusiasm, "Maggie!!! That's a brilliant thought. Why didn't I think of that before?"

She replied back, "I was just kidding. I was just stunned by the amount you paid to get back home."

Tye replied, "I understand, but it's still a great idea. I'm getting my pilot's license in a few months. A long-range business class airplane is only 75 million and I could lease it out daily to top executives and it will pay for itself in 3 to 4 years."

Maggie text back, "You're serious, aren't you?"

Tye replied, "I have a friend at Bombardier. Maybe he can get me a deal. I've had my eye on the Global Range 6,000 but the new 8,000 model comes out this year. I'll put that on my list of things to do."

Maggie responded, "Seriously. I was joking. Anyway, I'm glad to hear that you are ok and that you are on your way. I was very concerned because I know that the guy that got killed was your connection in Dubai, and it would have been very suspicious that he was assassinated the day you went to see him. I'm glad you're coming home and that you're safe. I'll see you in a few days."

Tye text back, "Thank you Maggie. I'll see you soon."

He removed his suit coat, undid his tie and asked the flight attendant for a stiff drink. Shortly afterwards, he fell asleep and slept most of the flight. They arrived safely in Boston 10 hours later after stopping to refuel twice.

13

Naffilia went to the office the day after the mission. She and her colleagues were visibly tired from the mission and the long trip home as they sauntered past the chief's office.

The Chief got the girls attention, "Ladies! Can the three of you stop in my office for a moment?"

They looked at each other with curiosity and said, "Sure. What's up boss?"

He gestured for them to sit down, "Ladies. That was a damn good mission all of you pulled off. It got the attention of a lot of higher up. There is a great deal of gratitude expressed by a lot of people."

The girls smiled and appreciated the comment as Naffilia commented, "Just doing our job sir."

He slowly shook his head, "You're modest too. Listen. You girls take three weeks off. There's nothing pressing for a little while. We can cover the classes here and the next mission isn't for several weeks."

The girls nodded their head, Chloe announced, "We could do that."

The boss grinned, "Great."

He paused briefly and the girls knew there was something else he wanted to say, "We pulled some strings for you girls and got you some tickets to the game that's coming up. Everyone under the sun is talking about it. You're on the 50-yard line right behind the bench."

Naffilia, Chloe and Mya gave each other a high five, "Yeah!"

The boss opened his drawer, reached in and pulled out 6 tickets and handed it to them. "Enjoy girls. Take your boyfriend or friends and enjoy the game."

They reached over the desk and snatched the tickets quickly, "Oh yeah baby!"

The room was filled with excitement and relief.

He motioned them out of the office, "Ok. Now go debrief first, and then get the hell out of here and take a vacation.

Have fun. Stay out of trouble."

The girls were giddy, as Naffilia exclaimed, "Alright boss. We'll do our best to stay out of trouble." As laughter broke out in the office.

All three girls were happy to take some much-needed time off after a mission that made international news, and this was a great way to relax and unwind.

After their debriefing the girls made arrangements to meet tomorrow night to have dinner and meet up with a few other friends to relax and kick off their vacation.

Son of bitch, I didn't realize how tired I was until the mission was over. It felt good that I was able to get my mind off of my father's recent passing, but now that the mission is over, the reality of his death is starting to sink in again. I don't like that numbing feeling. This vacation is going to bring that balance back.

She walked out to the parking lot and the sheen of her father's car can been seen from a distance.

Shit, I love my father's car. Dam it brings back good memories. I'm so glad that I took it in to work today.

She took a deep breath of the air, closed her eyes and let the sunshine soak her face.

Yes! I'm on vacation! And the bonus, I'm going to a fucking awesome game next week. Driving dad's car home is going to be liberating today. I feel like screaming at the top of my lungs. What the hell, I might as well.

There was a spring in her step as she made her way to the beautiful 68 Camaro. She got in the car and revved the engine and cranked up the music. She couldn't stop smiling while the bass thumped the interior of the car and smoke bellowed from the wheels as she did a burnout before leaving the parking lot.

Yeah! Fucking A. I love my life!

Naffilia was singing at the top of her lungs driving to the highway when she saw the black Chevelle driving several cars ahead of her.

What the fuck?! Perfect timing! I haven't seen you in a while.

She weaved her way in and out of traffic to try to catch up to the Chevelle. She wanted to see who this person was or maybe get a race on today.

She tailed the car as though doing a stake out. The Chevelle drove to the highway, where she took the opportunity to entice them into a race.

Whoever this person is, in that beautiful muscle, it's the perfect time to race. I get those moments every once in a while, when everything feels complete. Everything feels right in a single moment of time where my mind is at total peace and my body is in complete harmony with the how I feel and what is happening in my life. The world feels free of limitations. Today is that moment. Everything about my life converges into this moment when nothing matters but what's in front of me right now, and that car driving right next to me. I'm fucking ready for that race to get my engine revving.

Whoever this person is, they seem to understand me. They seem to get where I'm coming from and appear to give me just the right amount of excitement to want me to come back again, looking for them over and over again. As strange as it sounds, they feel like a friend. Hell, for all I know, it's probably a man clown. I'm curious and want to know who this is. Maybe we could meet someday at his little circus and get a beer or watch a game.

Even if he's a clown, this person is a friend with no name. And if I had to guess, probably has a lifestyle similar to me. I wish they would roll their damn window down so I could get a look at their face. Fuck! It feels like foreplay, like they're teasing me sexually, slowly bringing me to the edge of climax and then not fulfilling it. Leaving me hungry for more, wondering where this person is.

Naffilia pulled up right next to them and paced them.

Come on mother fucker. Let's take this a few notches up today. The sky is clear and there's nobody on the roads. Let's see what your classic muscle can do against my classic muscle. Head to head. One on one.

Naffilia stepped on the gas to jettison the car forward and then let off the throttle so as to rock back and forth egging the driver on or at least until she got their attention. It worked because they responded the same way by lunging forward then letting off the throttle and getting in line with her.

Then without any signal or warning she stomped on the gas and belted out with delight. The engine roared like a lion displaying power, as the speedometer needle went from 65 to 85 in a matter of seconds. The thunder of his engine could be heard screaming up right next to her. 85 mph was nothing to either one of them.

The Chevelle jettison ahead of her, and it took both of them from 85 to 95 mph and she got turned on the way he handled the car in front of her. It was a thing of beauty.

Just then, "Rollin in the Rear-view" by Headbone played over the radio and started thumping the bass, shaking the windows in the car. The vibration of the motor and the bass from the music could be felt between her legs and her pussy throbbed more than usual.

Naffilia yelled with excitement, "Yeah boy!!! Tease your baby. Wooooo. I like the way you handle that muscle mother fucker!"

Naffilia shouted in ecstasy and lost herself in the moment and throttled the car to 100 mph. She glanced down at the needle and yelled, "Push it baby. You got this. Get your fuck on!"

The needle started to quiver as it approached 110 mph as she caught up and edge ahead of the Chevelle.

Yelling in his direction, "Fuck yeah mister clown boy. You're gonna make me cum. I can handle whatever speed you got. Can you handle mine?"

The Chevelle was not letting up and caught up to her. They paced each other for a few seconds. It was the perfect day to race because there was no traffic anywhere insight, they pushed their engine further as they came screaming down the highway - an easy 120 mph.

Naffilia saw her exit coming up and said, "Fuck it! I'm gonna take this race as far as I can take it."

She remembered that he used to get off one exit before her but this time he stayed on the highway and saw the race all the way through.

Shit ya! He was in the mood to race today! I'm pretty sure he missed his exit as well. Ok muscle guy let's take it to the next exit.

They both instinctively knew the next exit was the last exit to take before they started hitting traffic, so they pushed each other until the next exit. Back and forth, one would take the lead, then the next. It was a match for match race. When one felt like they got the lead the other one would jettison forward.

I'm not sure what was going on in his mind, but for me, I could feel the excitement of this race hit high gear. There was an adrenaline rush, and I didn't think it was in me because of how tired I was just hours ago, yet it didn't seem to stop me from racing today. I don't know. Maybe it was the fact that I was feeling good and I was happy to be on vacation, and that everything felt right at that moment.

One thing for sure, is I don't like to lose and I'm willing to bet he doesn't either, but one of us is going to make it to that exit.

They were both exchanging lanes, from the middle lane to the fast Lane but then when Naffilia saw him pulling over to the far-right lane she knew for sure that was the exit he was getting off at. She didn't want this race end, so she pulled over to the middle Lane and paced him.

It was getting dangerously close to not being able to slow down safely, and she could see that his speed was letting up because he went from 120 down to 85 quickly. Then he went from 85 to 65 as the exit got closer. Despite wanting to win, she remembered how she almost got into an accident the last time they raced. She reluctantly slowed down as well. There was obviously no clear winner on this one and for some reason she was OK with that and thought perhaps they felt the same way as well.

He pulled off the exit before her and she followed. Maybe this is the day that they pull over and actually meet to have a conversation. But where they got off, there was no opportunity to pull over and greet each other. We both missed our exit, so we had to go back in the same direction.

He veered off to the left and down a different road than I did. But he did something different today that he hasn't done in the past. He actually honked his horn and revved his engine before veering off, so I honked back and revved my engine to acknowledge our spontaneous race.

I was pleased that we both took the time to extend this race longer than we ever have and it left me feeling like I had a friend who understood me. I didn't cum, but it left me feeling fulfilled for that day. Like I finally had satisfaction, a climax without having an orgasm. It was fucking weird. Like it was a mental orgasm of some sort because it had been building since meeting this person.

Naffilia noticed that there was a bead of sweat dripping down by her ears. Because she paused briefly to pay attention to her body, she noticed that her pussy was still throbbing. There was a noticeable wet feeling in her panties, and her heart was still racing from the adrenaline rush.

Oh shit, oh shit. I'm about to cum. She tried to maintain control over the car as she went way beyond wet and gushy and cum in her panties.

I definitely have to change my panties when I get home, but it was all worth it.

She took a deep breath and forced an exhale to help her calm down and enjoy the rest of her ride home. She switched the music to something a bit more mellow to help her relax. It was classic music that played, and it made her feel like she was cruising the streets like dad and gramps told her about, how back in the 50's they would go cruising the streets on a Friday night.

She began tapping on the steering wheel in sync with the music she was listening to. A pleasant smile plastered her face and she was humming the song.

This helped her sort through thoughts of what she wanted to do for her vacation for the next couple of weeks.

One of them was to definitely go to the game, but the thought of going to Egypt entered her mind as well. Just then her phone buzzed with a text from one of the men she had gone on a date with weeks ago.

"Hey, just wanted to know what you were up to and checking to see if you wanted to get together again?"

It was the guy who had the best potential, but she couldn't stay focused, the lawyer. She smiled and said out loud, "I wonder if he's into football? Maybe he can come with me to the game. This is my chance to get to know him a little bit better without being distracted."

Naffilia drove by Burger King and it caught her attention and glanced at the sign as she drove by it, "Hmmm. What the hell, I'm on vacation now. I'd might as well grab myself a whopper. I'm taking a break from eating healthy for today. I'll stop at the next drive through before going home and eat a whopper for lunch."

Before getting home, she went through the Burger King drive-thru and placed her order. She set the bag down on the seat next to her so that the smell of French fries and hamburger filled the car. "Mmmm. Yeah. This is what vacation smells like."

She got home and parked her father's car and made her way to the elevator. On her way up to her penthouse the elevator stopped on the main lobby to pick someone up.

It was the creepy guy, Pennywise the clown, who got into the elevator with her.

The look of surprise on his face was priceless but he tried to remain cool and regain his manhood, "Wow! The elevator smells like French fries and hamburger. I didn't think a woman as sexy as you, with that smoking hot body ate that kind of stuff."

She scoffed, "When you work out as hard as I do, you're entitled a splurge every once in a while."

She chuckled while he gave a nervous laugh, but he looked as though he was undressing her with his eyes as he licked his lips.

Pennywise got off the elevator before she did, and he called out to her as he glanced over his shoulder, "Enjoy your BK."

Naffilia remarked, "I will."

Then flipped him the bird as the elevator doors closed, making sure he saw her as she yelled out, "See ya' Pennywise. You fuckin' creepy bastard."

The remainder of the day was all about her and finding a way to chill out for the rest of the day. There was nothing she wanted to do and no place she wanted to be. To unwind she decided to work on her art. No exercising today. Maybe paint something or make a sculpture and listen to some soft music.

She hasn't watched Netflix in a long time. Maybe there was a TV series marathon she could get into that she could consider before retiring for the evening.

The next day, around mid-morning while she was relaxing around the house, a text message buzzed her work phone.

"I know it's not work. It must be one of the girls."

It was from Chloe and Mya from a group chat.

"Hey girl wyd?"

Naffilia replied, "Nothing. Just chilling."

"What's your plans for this evening?"

She responded, "Nothing. What's up with you guys?"

"Let's hang out and grab something to eat at the galleria. 'Bones' is the places to be girl. Me. You. Mya."

Naffilia replied, "Ok. What time are we meeting up at Bones? And does anyone know what the weather is like this evening? I don't want to be melting."

They reply was laughing emoji, "Your makeup won't come crashing down. The weather is cool enough for you girl."

They all responded, "lol"

Chloe text, "Let's meet around 4."

Naffilia, "Why so early?"

"So that we can eat, hang out and maybe see where the rest of the night takes us."

Everyone replied, "Yeah. Ok. That sounds good. See you there."

Naffilia had nothing else on the agenda for the day so she took her time getting ready while listening to some relaxing music. This was girl's night out, so she was going to wear something sexy and nice. She put on sweet perfume, very light. Her makeup and hair were on point. After she pinned up a little hair out on the shoulders, she looked in the mirror, "Ok. Now we're ready for girls' night out."

She walked out of the penthouse with a bounce in her step.

Once she got to the garage, she looked at all her cars, "Hmmm. Which one of you do I take?"

She chuckled because she imaged each car saying, "Pick me! Pick me!"

"The lucky one for tonight is…" She paused, "My father's

Camaro!" She reasoned that the Camaro was very hot and sexy just like her and it matched her outfit and mood for tonight.

She rolled out of the garage and onto the street and revved the engine. "Yeah. Revved up and flexing your muscle. Nice and hard just the way I like my men and my guns."

She drove a few blocks just listening to the sound of the engine.

Yessssss! It feels so good to have the next couple of weeks off. Oh hell ya, I'm going to enjoy myself like never before. I didn't realize how much I needed this vacation.

She connected her Bluetooth and played music to set the tone.

I'm in the mood to listen to the family. Let's listen to 'Little Red Corvette' by Prince, followed by 'The Glamorous Life' by Sheila E..

"Yeah. Now we're feeling it."

She arrived at valet parking and waited for the gentleman to give her a ticket.

When she got out of the car, she did a quick scan of herself, "Yup. Face is good. Hair is good. My shit is tight and I'm ready for tonight."

When she walked into the plaza, she felt sexy and it resonated. People took notice. One older gentleman took a second look at her as he came out of the building and walked right past her. He tripped over the curb and almost fell. Another younger man with his girlfriend almost strained his neck watching her walk by and his girlfriend punched him in the gut.

As she approached the door, a gentleman was leaving and held the door for her. She heard him whisper, "You're so fucking hot."

Naffilia smiled and replied, "Thanks! You have an amazing evening."

For a weekday at four o'clock, the restaurant was surprisingly crowded, and she couldn't find her friends. She text them.

"I'm here. Where you guys at?"

They text from the group chat. "Hey. Come over to the bar."

She looked over and saw them. They waved her over.

She was smiling as she made her way over to her friends and noticed that people were staring at her. She loved the attention and soaked it up.

Chloe remarked, "Girl you love that attention."

They all laughed.

Naffilia chimed in, "I'm not alone. Look at you guys. And I already noticed those guys over there checking you out."

They turned to see who she was talking about and they chuckled.

"Ok. We love the attention too girl."

Laughter broke out between them.

Naffilia made a motion with her head pointing toward the main part of the restaurant, "It's so fucking crowded tonight. What's going on in the city?"

Mya remarked, "I have no idea. Maybe a convention in town showing off the latest gadgets."

Chloe replied, "Probably a concert or a game."

Naffilia agreed, "In this city, probably all three."

They nodded in agreement.

Naffilia pointed toward the tables, "I hope we're sitting inside and not outside."

The girls laughed, "It's natural air conditioning outside Naffilia. You won't melt your makeup off."

She rolled her eyes, "Oh gosh."

They laughed. Just then the reservation buzzer went off and they went to be seated.

The host pointed outside, "Will the patio be ok?"

The girls chuckled as they looked at Naffilia, "It will be just fine, thank you."

All three girls were delighted to be together on a night that wasn't work related and they enjoyed themselves and felt carefree as they walk past a number of people to the patio. They had the attention of the restaurant like a ring master. There were a lot of eyes on them.

Once they were seated the host mentioned that the bartender was bringing a bottle of wine to their table. They sat down and took in the scenery, watching the cars as they drove by and checking out the people as they walked by the patio.

They started chatting about everything under the sun except work. They had an unwritten rule that work, or jobs was not to be discussed on girl's night out. The acceptable topics was makeup, music, family, ambitions and the men in their lives.

Out of respect before going on, they asked Naffilia how she was doing after the passing of her father. She mentioned the various moments of grief, but overall, she was feeling better. They made the conversation light by recalling family memories and the funniest moments in their own life as they were growing up. It was a conversation to get to know each other in a deeper way.

The conversation transitioned to boyfriends and dates. Naffilia chuckled, "So girls. What's the latest on your love life?"

Chloe snickered, "Oh god. Let's not go there."

The girls broke out into laughter.

Mya said, "Yeah girl. Let's go there. What's going on these days?"

Naffilia leaned in toward the center of the table to whisper and drew the other girls in, "I'm horny as fuck lately. I need some dick!"

"Damn!" Chole said as leaned back into her chair.

Mya chimed in, "Me too!"

Naffilia laughed, "Yup it's out there. I haven't fuck since…" she paused to think about it, "Well…damn! It's been about three weeks."

Mya remarked with surprise, "Oh…only 3 weeks? I'm pushing months."

Chloe jokingly said, "I think I'm pushing years."

They laughed their asses off especially when Naffilia said, "Hell girl…don't you have a boyfriend though?"

Chloe remarked, "That's my point. It's like we're a married couple and each of us are too tired or we have a headache half the time."

The girls busted out laughing.

Naffilia said, "Both the guys I had a while back gave me enough to last until a week ago."

"What the fuck?" Said Chloe. "Both?"

Mya said, "Maybe you should have had 3 men so that it lasted 3 weeks."

The laughter was noticeably loud, and they covered their mouth and looked around.

Naffilia chimed in, "Yeah maybe three will satisfied my ass."

They tried to keep the laughter to a dull roar.

Mya made a comment that took Naffilia by surprise, "Or maybe you just need one man who can fill you up, where you don't have to look for two, or three or let me say four guys."

Chloe remarked, "Damn that's a lot of dicks everywhere."

They laughed so hard they all had tears flowing from their eyes.

In between breathes Mya said, "Shit I can imagine that scene. Just thinking about it made me fucking wet."

Naffilia whispered, "Shit. Let's change the subject or else I'm going to pee my pants."

Just then they heard music in the air.

Naffilia announced, "I was just listening to this song on the way over."

The song was, "The Glamorous Life" by Sheila E.

They started singing a snippet of the lyric at the table.

Naffilia paused, "Fuck that! I need a man's touch."

They couldn't stop laughing.

One of the girls said, "Ok. Where is this waiter. We're going to get drunk before our meal comes out. I'm starving now."

The waiter came out and took their order.

Mya continued the conversation about men, as she turned to Naffilia, "What's up with all the clown references that day on the shooting range?"

Chloe giggle, "Yeah! What's up with you and clowns?"

Naffilia responded, "It's my motto for the past year. There are plenty of circus in town, I just need to pick which clown I want to be entertained by."

Mya chuckled, "Yeah. You're right. This isn't the only circus in town."

Naffilia explained, "I'm not interested it meeting a man from Ding Dong Texas, or Booger Hole West Virginia. I Just want to meet a normal guy from a normal place. Not some circus city where he and his guy friends act like clowns. I want someone normal that I can relate to and that can do for me what four men can't."

The girls tilted their head and listened attentively, and Mya said, "I get it girl. But clowns? Come on. There's a story there."

Chloe chimed in, "Yeah. You can't pull that shit with us. What's with the clowns?"

Naffilia laughed, "Ok. I had a bad experience with a clown once when I was younger. I'll tell you some other time."

They started to laugh. "What the hell girl? Did you get raped by a clown or something?"

Everyone laughed at her remark.

Naffilia chuckled, "No! I'll tell you another time. I'm just not fond of clowns and the guys I met lately are like clowns to me."

Naffilia smiled while Mya remarked, "I've dated plenty of clowns too. Most of them were like the Joker to me when I wanted Batman!"

Chloe chimed in, "You think that's bad!? I've been dating

nothing but 'Homey the Clowns' for years until I met my boyfriend."

The laughter got out of control.

The owner of the restaurant noticed the girls were getting a lot of attention, but he also recognized them. He went to the table just as their meal arrived.

The owner greeted them, "Hey girls. I haven't seen you in a while. I'm glad you are having fun tonight. How are you doing these days?"

The girls acknowledge him, "Hey Nelson. It's nice to see you. We've been really busy."

Nelson said, "Well, it's nice to see you back."

The girls nodded.

Nelson offered his sympathies to Naffilia, "I heard about your father Naffilia. My condolences."

"Thank you, Nelson." She smiled.

"Hey girls. Dinner is on me tonight."

Chole, Mya and Naffilia said, "Your too kind Nelson, like always." They thanked him and kissed him on his cheek.

The girls enjoyed their dinner and tipped well. Before they left, Nelson stopped them.

"Ladies, I have some tickets to the ball game for tonight. Would you guys be interesting in going.?"

They were excited, "Hey why not! Let's go."

Mya said with excitement, "Ok. It's on."

Chloe remarked, "They're not bleeder seats, are they?"

Nelson said, "C'mon. C'mon ladies I got you. No bleeder seats for my girls. You're family. You guys take care of me and I got you girls. These for tonight so you better get going."

He handed them box seats next to the lounge. They smiled and gave him a hug, "Thank you Nelson. We appreciate it."

The girls walked toward valet and were excited. They hugged and kissed each other on the cheek. One by one their cars pulled up and the valet driver opened the door for them.

They got in their car and revved their engine before driving off, giving each other the "bar finger." It was their code word for flipping the bird.

Oh my gosh. Shit ya! My day keeps getting better and better. Now I'm off to a baseball game. There's nothing like a great evening ball game in Boston with perfect weather under the lights while they play right into the night with the crowd cheering on your favorite team.

They had the time of their life as they sat in the perfect position to watch the game. They got into the game because of the hype of the crowd. Drinking their beer added to the atmosphere. During the seventh inning stretch Naffilia got a text from Dr. Martin Shraver, one of the professors she met several weeks back at the museum. He told her about an opportunity to sponsor an archaeological dig In Egypt.

She texts him back, "I would love to hear your proposal. How about we meet tomorrow at your office at the campus. I'm at a ball game right now and I have no problems coming in anytime tomorrow. What time do you suggest That we meet?"

He said that he'll be on campus Around 11:00 o'clock so that he can provide more details about what he's doing and how she can contribute.

She agreed to meet tomorrow.

Naffilia relished the remainder of the game with Chloe and Mya. Knowing that she was going to be contributing to an archaeological dig in the area that she knew the scroll was in, added to the excitement of the game and the enjoyment of the evening.

Naffilia took a deep breath and took in the surrounding. She was aware of the cool breeze on her skin on this warm night as park lights came on. Everything but tingled her senses and helped her to live in the moment, made her beer taste better, and made her company that more comforting. It was the perfect way to start a vacation for the three of them. Typically, they would have gone out to the bars or clubbing after a game like this but Naffilia had enough excitement for the day. Besides, she had a meeting to attend in the morning. After the game the girls said their goodbyes to each, giving each other a hug and expressing gratitude for their day. They retired for the evening.

The next morning, after an amazing night out with the girls, Naffilia figured that it wouldn't hurt to get back into her normal routine of working out and then taking a shower to relax a little bit. She had some time on her hands before leaving the penthouse. She was excited about going to see the professor on campus.

She texts him right away to get more information, where to meet him, and he replied back with specific instructions.

She finished her breakfast and decided to take a leisure ride to the campus in her 911 Porsche. The traffic was a bit heavy for this time of year but that didn't bother her because she had nothing else to do. Today is vastly different than what she is used to, and the schedule she usually has.

She arrived on campus relatively early and took a relaxing leisure stroll to his office, admiring the eclectic architecture around the campus along the way and embracing that sense of history that the University resonated. She always loved that history feel. Seeing all of the old buildings gave her a nostalgic feeling, something she has always been fond of.

She found the professor's office and knocked on the door to announce her arrival. She could hear from behind the door, "Come on in. The door is open."

Naffilia entered his office where he was gathering his things together. "Thank you for coming in."

He handed her a pamphlet which contained all of the information required to sponsor an archaeological dig.

Naffilia scanned the walls of his office and noticed his display of his multiple degrees, along with his recent research findings. There was a distinct smell of old books in the office, and it was comforting to her because it made her feel like there was a sense of order, intelligence and genuine character.

He directed her attention to a map on the wall and pointed out Egypt, "This is where we're doing our dig. An associate of ours is in Egypt and they recently found a hidden tomb in the pyramids of Egypt."

Dr. Shraver scoffed at his remark and raised a finger, "You know? After all these years of believing we found everything there is to find in those Pyramids, suddenly one day a small child points out something unusual about a wall in the tourist attraction area of the tombs."

Dr. Shraver continued as he appeared to study the map and shook his head, "Of all people, it was the untrained eye of a child who saw something us professionals didn't."

He turned to Naffilia with his hands extended as if offering something to her, "…just like that, we have a new chamber to explore."

Naffilia was intrigued by the story, "What did they find?"

Dr. Milton shook his head, "Oh nothing yet. We haven't started digging yet due to lack of finances and red tape. We've taken care of the red tape, but now it's financials we need to settle. That's were people such as yourself come into play. We're looking for sponsors to continue the dig, and the University is going to get partial credit for it."

Naffilia inquired, "How can I help?"

Dr. Milton Shraver cleared his throat, "My part is, to approach people of certain financial status, and interest in antiquities, to offer a financial partnership. In exchange, you get a mention as a sponsor. And depending on the level of financial commitment, we can invite you to the opening day for the dig. You came to mind. And here you are!"

Naffilia's eye widened, "Thank you professor."

"You're welcome. I know that you're keen on some of the art in that region of the world, as you expressed several weeks ago."

Dr. Shraver chuckled, "Amazing how the universe lines things up sometimes, huh? It's almost as if we were meant to meet weeks ago."

Naffilia smiled at his obvious attempt at pitching a sale.

She was obviously intrigued by his offer regardless and said, "Please go on. Tell me more."

He motioned out the door, "Let's take a walk. I want to show you something remarkable."

He took her over to the museum that the University built several years ago in one of their new wings.

"This is a new addition to our wing and we're looking to add ancient history from Egypt and Israel. You mentioned something about the art of that time, and you seem to know more than the average person the background information."

He stopped by a few artifacts and gestured to empty places where soon to be art would be placed, "By sponsoring this archaeological dig we would be able to house some of the artifacts here at our museum to attract more students from around the world. Some of the sponsorship will not only go toward the archaeological dig, but most importantly, it will also support the addition here at the University."

Dr. Shraver covered his heart with one hand, "I will see to it personally, that you accompany me on the 1st day of the dig, which is scheduled next week. I can get you specific dates if you are interested."

Naffilia didn't hesitate, "Yes! I can contribute. What is your goal for the contribution?"

Just then they entered into the museum wing where the rest of the art was. They paused briefly in awe of the artwork that surrounded them.

He gave an indiscernible sigh of relief, "Our goal is $2,500,000. This covers all the labour for the dig, plus shipping any artifacts here to the University, and to establish a new wing for the public."

She nodded her head, "How much of a contribution do you need to accompany you on the dig?"

He cleared his throat as he adjusted his tie and hesitated for a second, "The minimum amount to be on the dig is, "$450,000."

There was an awkward silence between them for a second and then he continued, "We will make all the arrangements with a chartered flight to Egypt and take care of hotel reservations. We'll take care of all the food while you are there as well."

Naffilia tried to keep a straight face, "Hmmm. That's a bit out of the range what I can do, but I will still make a contribution."

"That's great! How much are you thinking?" He asked.

She assured him, "I can do $125,000."

He smiled and reached out to shake her hand, "That's wonderful. We greatly appreciate it."

"Would you happen to know the exact day of the dig?" She asked.

"In fact, I do. We are scheduled for next Friday early in the morning." He said without hesitation.

"That's fantastic. Ok. I'm gonna Send $125,000 right now. Via bank transfer." She said as she pulled out her phone.

He pointed at the pamphlet he gave her, "The Bank information for contributions is right there on the pamphlet."

The professor was elated, "Oh my gosh thank you so much. We appreciate your contribution. I'll keep you posted on our progress via the website address that is on the pamphlet as well."

Naffilia nodded with enthusiasm. "OK. That sounds great. You have my information should you need to contact me for any reason."

She shook the professor's hand and bid him farewell.

Naffilia was ecstatic to hear of the archeological dig taking place next week. Although she wasn't invited to the first day of the dig, that wasn't going to stop her from being there. She knew the day of the dig and she had a connection in Egypt, and that's all she needed to be there.

Most importantly, she knew there was a possibility that they were going to be in the area where the scroll might be, and she wasn't going to miss this opportunity.

Things were really looking up for her at this point. Everything was falling into place and all she had to do was make arrangements to go to Egypt.

As Naffilia drove home there was a feeling of glee while she imagined the possibilities of finding that scroll after years of searching for it. She was getting closer than she ever and hadn't felt this way in a long time.

She activated her phone via Bluetooth and made a call to her connection in Egypt and arranged a hotel stay the night before the dig. She was on vacation and made sure that she spared no expense on the hotel and made sure that it was a 5-star hotel.

This has got to be the best vacation I've had in a long time. Not only am I about to go to another country to possibly find the scroll, but I've kicked it off with the time of my life and I still have a football game to go to this weekend. Shit! Life is awesome. All I need is some time at the gun range and that might complete my mental orgasm!

Just then her phone buzzed. It was work.

She said out loud, "Shit. They don't usually contact me unless it's important."

She wasn't going to waste time texting. She called instead.

The secretary answered the phone in a professional but monotone way, "Hello…HQ. How can I direct your call?"

Looked around to make sure nobody was within listening distance, she said, "Agent 254606…Rosebud. Returning a call."

The voice said, "Confirmed. Please hold and I'll direct your call."

A moment later the Chief answered, "Naffilia? It's the Chief."

She held her breath, "I saw that you wanted to get in touch with me."

He said with a jovial tone, "Naffilia. I thought you should know. Your 3 million payment was disbursed this morning for the Miami operation. I figured it would make your vacation complete."

Naffilia said with excitement, "Oh shit…thanks Chief.

That's awesome. That made my vacation for sure. Thank you again."

He spoke affectionately like dad would, "You're welcome dear. You deserve it. You're a good agent and you deserve good things in your life. Enjoy the rest of your vacation."

Naffilia smiled from ear to ear, and fist pumped as she looked up, "Thank you! I guess I'm going on that dig with them after all."

Naffilia returned to the professor and informed him that she was able to contribute the total of $450,000, and that she would like to be included in the dig.

The professor was more than pleased for her donation and her chance to join them on the chartered flight to Egypt. He would keep her informed once the time drew near.

14

Tye was relieved to be back home after nearly being stranded in Dubai. He gave Maggie the details of his adventures. Both of them gave a sigh of relief after he told the story.

Tye remarked, "One thing is for sure Maggie, it's got me thinking about a few other things in my life. I'm just glad to be home."

Maggie was inquisitive, "Did you miss out on a business opportunity?"

He nodded, "Yeah I did, but that's not important right now. I'm just glad to be home. How's things holding up here in the office?"

Maggie replied, "Oh everything is just fine. The restaurant in New York that you recently purchased is doing remarkably well and apparently a lot of the employees are happy with the changes."

Tye looked pleased, "That's good. It's a step in the right direction at least. Maggie please hold all my calls. I'm just gonna make a few phone calls."

Maggie got Tye's attention, "Before you go to your office, I do have to let you know that a professor from Harvard stopped by to get in touch with you. He said he was referred by the curator from the Boston museum. He left this for you."

Maggie handed Tye a pamphlet.

Tye accepted the pamphlet, "Thanks Maggie, I appreciate it. Do me a favor will ya? Can you order lunch for both of us?"

Maggie nodded, "Sure. What are you in the mood for?"

Tye turned away from Maggie as he started to read the pamphlet, "You pick it. I'm not really picky today. I've got a tailgate party that I'm going to this Sunday and I'm gonna be pigging out on steak, maybe chicken or some burgers. So, treat yourself and I'll eat what you eat."

Maggie grinned, "Ok. Hope you like my choice."

Tye raised his voice, "Nothing with artificial crap in it or made of Tofu.”

Maggie remarked about his tailgate party, “It won’t be anything like the food you’re gonna eat this weekend. Sounds like it's gonna be a feast for a king on Sunday.”

Just before he closed the door, “Yep. It's gonna be fun. I'm gonna make arrangements right now.”

Ty retreated to the office to make a few personal phone calls, the first one he made was to his friend in California.

“Hello. Marcus? It's Tye from Boston how's it going?”

On the other side of the phone, “It's going fantastic. How's it going with you?”

Tye said with excitement, “Oh, it's going really well. I'm looking forward to the ball game this weekend. I got some information for you, so let me know when you're ready to write it down?”

Marcus replied, “OK I'm all set.”

Tye continued, “Ok. So, you're flying out the night before the game and what I'm gonna to do is put you up at a hotel near me unless you wanna stay at my place for the night. The choice is yours.”

Marcus said, “If it’s ok with you, I think I'd rather stay at your place. We haven't caught up in years, so I think it would be good just to hang out. We have lots to talk about.”

Tye agreed, “Alright you can stay with me. Then I'll show you around town for a bit.”

Tye continued, “Ok, so you're going to be flying in on Delta flight 117. You'll be coming in Saturday afternoon and then will spend the rest of the day sightseeing for a bit and then will go to my place in the evening and just relax for the day. Then we're going to hook up with a couple more friends of mine and their girlfriend. We'll meet and drive together to the stadium early enough to have a tailgate party.”

Marcus was pleased, “That sounds like a lot of fun Tye. Thank you so much for everything. I'm looking forward to seeing ya.”

Tye inquired, “Did your wife wanna join you for the ball game?”

Marcus said with some disappointment, "She was interested and wanted to go, but she couldn't book the day off for that weekend, so I'll just be coming myself."

Tye was sympathetic, "Oh that's too bad. Ok, no problem we'll still have a good time."

Tye continued, "I'm going to email you this information and the flight confirmation. All you have to do is pick your ticket up at the airport and then I'll pick you up when you arrive."

Marcus injected one last thing before hanging up, "Sounds good. Just so that you know, I've been working on some new software that I plan to launch next year. I can tell you about it if you're interested."

Tye was interested, "Yeah that'll be good. We'll talk when you get here. Alright, I'll see you in a few days."

"Ok. See you too. Bye." Tye hung up.

Tye looked at the pamphlet that his secretary gave him, "Ok. Let's give this guy a call and see what he's up to."

Tye called, "Hello I'm looking for Dr. Shraver. This is Tye from Wolf enterprise."

With professionalism, "Yes. This is Dr. Shraver. The curator from the Boston museum, Mark, connected me to you and thought that you might be interested in a project we are working on in Egypt, and that perhaps you would consider helping us with an archaeological dig and sponsoring a new wing at Harvard."

Tye gave his professional courtesy to present his case, "Ok. So, what did you have in mind?"

Dr. Shraver continued, "We're looking for sponsors to be able to do an archeological dig in Egypt. We recently found a new section of the pyramids that have never been opened. We have a Harvard connection over there and what we'd like to do is dig in that location and bring back any of the artifacts and house them at the Harvard museum."

Tye was inquisitive, "Isn't something like this sponsored by local government and other supporters. Those artifacts belong to Egypt and should remain there. How is Harvard able to bring them back?"

Dr. Shraver was impressed, "Mark mentioned that you were well informed and showed an interest in art of all forms. It's true, that's the normal protocol but we have made important connections to higher ups who are not in a financial position to sponsor this dig, so we took it upon ourselves to raise the funds, in exchange, we get to house the artifacts for 1 year. They also agreed to provide an honorary exchange of art from their country for our new wing for the next few years. Mark was instrumental in making those arrangements."

Tye was surprised, "Was he? Why would he take a vested interest in Harvard acquiring these artifacts?"

Tye could hear Dr. Shraver clear his through, "Mark is an Alumni, plus his Museum gets the benefit of the Egyptian artifacts as well."

Tye was impressed, "He's quite the businessman, isn't he?"

Dr. Shraver agreed, "Yes he is. Anyway Mr. Wolf. Could we count on your support?

Tye responded, "Well, I'm interested in possibly donating. In fact, I've recently become more interested in Egyptian art and artifacts."

Dr. Shraver responded with curiosity, "Really!? What are you interested in?"

Tye generalized, "I'm interested in just about everything."

Dr. Shraver continue, "So, here's how the sponsorship works. Any donations of significant value are allowed to come on the 1st day of the archaeological dig. We will provide all the transportation via private charter and take care of the lodging at a five-star hotel in Egypt and then you'll be able to accompany me and my team on the first day of the archaeological dig. Hopefully we could find something significant on the first day. The money goes toward our goal of 2.5 million for the dig, transporting the artifacts back to the University, and the continued work on the new museum wing. This will attract international attention for the University. Anyone who contributes $450 thousand can accompany us on the first day of the dig."

Tye responded, "$450,000? That's a hefty price tag for one day of digging."

Dr. Shraver defended his position, "We know there are a lot of benefactors out there that can provide that amount. We made it that high to keep the number of people we take to the dig on the low side so that it's not overcrowded. We have a chartered plane that can only hold so many of our team members."

Tye asked out of curiosity, "Who did you hire to charter?"

Dr. Shraver paused briefly to think, "Uhm. It's a new company. They were reasonably priced... 'WE Corporate Charter' I think."

Dr. Shraver paused briefly, "Yeah. Maybe it's, 'WE Charter.'"

Tye smiled and nodded his head, "Good choice. I think I will contribute. Put me down for $450,000 and I'll see you on the dig. Do you have any information and confirmation that you could send me?"

Dr. Shraver was elated, "Yes, I do. Please hold on and I'll text it over to you right now. What's your phone number?"

Ty gave him his work phone number to text over the information and he opened it up and downloaded any PDF information he needed.

The professor added, "You can find any banking information that you need to donate, and I will give you a receipt for tax purposes."

Tye replied, "That sounds good. Ok, so I'm gonna send the donation right now. Please send me a copy of the donation amount plus a tax receipt as soon as possible."

"Absolutely, we can do that for you. Thank you, Mr. Wolf."

"OK. I just sent $450,000 to the account information that you just provided."

On the other end of the phone you can hear the

professor's voice filled with excitement, "Wow that's fantastic Mr. Wolf. We appreciate your contribution. I'll get back to you within the next few days with specific information on flying out and staying at the hotel in Egypt, and we do look forward to having you on the opening day of the dig. Plus, we'll have a sponsor plate that will be engraved and displayed at the Harvard museum for anything that we might find."

"That sounds good I do appreciate it. I'm gonna give you my secretary's number so that you can provide her with any travel information."

The professor was excited, "That sounds good Mr. Wolf. On behalf of the University, thank you, and we'll see you soon."

Tye closed the conversation courteously, "You're welcome. You have a good day."

Tye text Maggie, "I just donated money to Harvard. Keep an eye out for any information from Dr. Shraver. I'll talk to you in a moment."

She replied back, "Yes sir."

Then he called two more of his friends and made arrangements to meet on Sunday morning so that they can drive to the stadium together.

He got in touch with a long-time friend from his hometown, and also got in touch with a business associate that he's done business with over the past several years. They were bringing their girlfriend or wives.

The conversations were brief, just to catch up with each other. He was looking forward to the tailgate party, it was "the game" of the season.

Tye called Maggie into the office.

"Maggie that was professor Shraver from Harvard University that left the message. He was requesting a donation to an archaeological dig. Please make a note that Wolf enterprises donated $450,000 to Harvard University for an archaeological dig and research, and an addition to a new wing at their campus."

"Very good Mr. Wolf. I'll make a note of it and send the information over to your accountant once I get the information."

"Thank you. You can expect some travel arrangements from the professor because he's invited me to Egypt for the opening day for the archaeological dig so please be watching out for that information as well."

"Yes sir, not a problem."

Tye smirked when he said, "They chartered a plane as well."

Maggie smiled and said sarcastically, "Really? I wonder what company they hired?"

They both laughed and went about their business.

He was looking forward to the tailgate party and the trip to Egypt.

A few days passed. He got in touch with his buddy from California and picked him up at the airport that morning and greeted him with a hug.

Tye said, "It's really good to see you."

Marcus replied, "It's good to see you too."

"Let's get your bags Marcus. I'll take you for lunch at my restaurant."

"Wow you got your own restaurant!? That's amazing. What else you got for business?"

They retrieved his bags and walked toward the garage. Tye continued his conversation as they got into the car and drove into the city.

"I got my hands in just about in everything. I've purchased some real estate, I own a few restaurants and hotels, and because I got all these businesses, I started my own law firm, accounting firm and because they all require construction of some sort, I started a construction business as well. They all go hand in hand."

Marcus was blown away, "Shit Tye, you must be

competition for Bruce Wayne or Tony Starks."

They both chuckled, then Tye remarked, "The only difference is…" he paused for dramatic purposes and looked around, "…They're comic book characters…I'm for real!"

Marcus was astonished, "Wow you HAVE been quite busy over the past several years since we last met. Tye, tell me…how's your mom and dad doing?"

Tye paused momentarily, "My mom passed away several years ago. She died from a lung disease and then my dad passed away from a broken heart a few weeks afterwards."

"Oh man…I'm so sorry to hear that Tye. My condolences. I loved your parents. They were good to me."

A noticeable sadness came over his face, "Thank you. I appreciate that. Things haven't been the same since mom and dad passed away. At the time, we didn't have the money to help mom fight the disease. Dad drained his bank account sending her to the best doctors around the world, but nobody could help. It broke our family's heart. Dad lost his purpose after mom died."

Tye reflected on his parents and then forced a smile, "It was because of their encouragement and support, I got this far in my life. They sacrificed a lot for my success. Unfortunately, they didn't live long enough to see it or benefit from it."

Just then, they pulled up to the restaurant and drove slowly past it and into the garage.

Tye said with some relief, "Here we are. This my restaurant."

"Wow this is a really nice restaurant. I like the name too. Very fitting, 'Wolf Appetite.'"

They laughed to relieve the slight tension that built. Tye pulled into the garage and parked at his private parking spot.

"Shit! You even got your own parking spot?"

Tye smirked, "Oh absolutely. Why not? I own the whole building!"

Marcus was astonished, "Fuck, are you serious? That's

crazy."

"Yeah my penthouse is the entire top floor."

Marcus's eyes were wide, "Holy Fuck, you really have made a name for yourself. How the hell did you do it?"

Tye reflected for a second and like a great sage replied, "My father was always a giver. Everything involved opening his hands to anyone in need, whether to help somebody financially, or to pick up a tool and help them. He was always like that and I learned that from him. I put other people first by giving and planned ahead to take care of family. I started giving like my father, and the more I did, the more I was given opportunity to give. He taught me that money was a tool that I used, not to make decision based on money, lack or scarcity. I was not going to be used by money."

"Wow that's incredible. The proof is in the pudding. Your family was truly remarkable."

Marcus expressed his gratitude for his parents too, "Yeah. Dad and Mom supported me while I was in college too. We had amazing parents."

Tye nodded, "That's when you and I met. I took my study seriously especially for business classes. When we met for software development, I thought that's what I wanted to do. I thought I was gonna be a software engineer, but I just got too bored with it, too quickly. I felt like I was doing the same thing over and over again."

Tye parked the car and they both got out and continued their conversation as they walked toward the elevator.

Marcus agreed, "Yeah, I could see how that could be boring for you. Since I've known you, you were always working on something new."

Tye approved the comment, "Yeah I didn't like the monotony. My father always told me to get into business and to work for myself instead of working for other people. That was very good advice on his part."

Marcus said, "Yeah. I could see how that was the perfect advice at that time. It certainly worked out in your favor."

"I whole heartedly agree. I'm the kind of person who likes to start a new project, see it all the way through, get it up and running, and then let somebody else take over and keep it running. Then on to the next."

Marcus chimed in, "It's paid off handsomely and it suits you. I'm impressed Tye. Your Mom and Dad would be proud."

Tye agree, "Plus my other hobby is real estate. My dad got me into that as well."

Tye punched in a code to a specific elevator. When it opened, he gestured Marcus in. "This will take us to my penthouse. We'll drop off your stuff first and then go down to the main lobby to eat."

Marcus was speechless as Tye continued his story, "Dad didn't know anything about real estate, but he was smart enough to purchase the apartment we lived to make sure his kids had a place to stay. He invested in our future."

Marcus recalled, "And your mom always had a big heart. She always took care of me when I needed something. You get that from her. I remember many times when I couldn't get back home, she invited me over for the Holidays. Your family really knew how to celebrate big even though you didn't have much financially."

"Yeah that's true. They really did impact my life significantly. I've done a lot of donations on their behalf. Someone wanted to write an article on me about being a serial entrepreneur, but you know me, I'd rather keep to myself."

"Yeah there's nothing wrong with that. I remember even way back then I always said I wanted to be rich and famous, but you always said - I'd rather be rich, but not famous. I like my privacy. That's when I knew you were going places. I tried to get you out to parties, but you weren't having it, you knew what you wanted and made those sacrifices."

Just then, the elevator door opened to the main foyer and

Tye told him to place his bags outside the door. "It'll be fine right there; nobody can come up this far."

Then they got back on the elevator to go down to the lobby. Tye finished his conversation, "Yeah but we had our share of parties at the right time. We had a good time still."

"Oh, you ain't kiddin' ! Did you ever hook up with that girl from University days? The Italian girl? Florence? I thought for sure you guys were going to get married."

"No, we dated off and on a few months after graduation, but she had plans of her own and I had plans of my own. We just went our separate ways. I guess the problem was, I had issues with commitment. Maybe that's why I'm a serial entrepreneur."

They both laughed and Marcus commented, "Well, you manage to take a commitment issue and make it pay off in your favor, that's for sure!"

The door opened up to the lobby area. Hector the bartender greeted them. "Hello Mr. Wolf. It's nice to see you. It's been a while."

"Hello Hector, how are you?"

"I'm doing good Mr. Wolf."

Tye gestured to Marcus, "Hector this is my friend – Marcus, from California. He's a brilliant software engineer."

Hector shook his hand, "Pleased to meet you."

"Likewise." Said Marcus.

Tye continued, "Hector could you tell the manager that a friend of mine and I will be sitting in my usual spot?"

"Yes, sir right away."

The manager came out to greet both of them, "Hello Mr. Wolf, it's good to see you."

"Thank you, Cliff. How's the wife and kids?"

"They're doing fantastic Sir, thank you for asking," as he gestured them to his favorite area.

"Will you be getting the usual or will you do something different?"

Tye pursed his lips, "I think I might do something

different for a change. Let's take a look at the menu and see what we got here?"

"Very good Sir. I'll be back in a moment. In the meantime, can I get your drinks?"

They ordered their drinks and looked over the menu and did a lot of catching up for the next couple of hours. They discussed some options to acquire a few software companies that were struggling financially. Marcus was surprised that Ty knew a lot about the software companies in his area. Tye assured him that it was his business to know what companies were failing and which ones weren't, that's how he was able to acquire so many businesses.

They discussed the option to partner in developing a new software that worked on cutting edge security.

After they ate, they went to his penthouse.

They went up to the penthouse and grabbed his bags and walked into his suite.

Marcus gasped, "Fuck, you really know how to live life to the fullest. I'm fucking envious of you."

Tye shook his head and remarked, "It's just stuff."

Marcus nodded, "I understand you probably put in a lot of long hours and a lot of long days and sacrificed a lot along the way."

Tye said with relief, "Yeah. It used to be that way years ago, but now things are running pretty smoothly that I have more time on my hands and that allows me to concentrate on charitable work. Back then, I heard a saying - that everyone wants to live like the rich, but nobody wants to make the sacrifices it takes to get that way. Nor are they willing to put in the time to make it happen."

Marcus nodded in agreement as he admired the penthouse and pat Tye on the back.

Ty offered him a drink and he obliged.

Tye filled him on some details of the tailgate party, "So,

we're meeting a couple more friends of mine tomorrow. One is bringing his wife and the other his girlfriend. I'll introduce you to them, plus I have a woman that's coming out to join us as well. Her name is Alexia."

Marcus lifted an eyebrow, "Really? Is this somebody significant?"

"Well I'd like to think so. I'm mean, I'm not opposed to something long-term but as I said, I have commitment issues. She does know how to have fun."

Marcus asked, "Fun? I'm assuming you know how to create your own fun."

Tye said, "Well...I do, but I just wonder if there is anyone out there that fits me to a T without forcing it, if you know what I mean."

Just then, Tye got a text message from Alexia.

"Hi baby. I'm going to be in town in exactly 2 hours. I can't wait to see you."

Tye text back, "Okay. I'll see you in a couple of hours."

He turned to Marcus, "That was Alexia. She's going to be arriving in a couple hours, so I'm going to be heading out to pick her up. Make yourself at home, relax and enjoy yourself. I won't be very long is that okay?"

Marcus nodded his head, "I think I can make myself comfortable here Tye..." he said as he lifted his drink, "...No worries."

Tye pointed down the hallway to one of the spare bedrooms, "You can have this room right here. Alexia will be sleeping with me, if you know what I mean!"

They both started laughing and Marcus said, "It's obvious. I'll be sure to put my earbuds in."

Tye didn't feel like driving so he called for his driver to take them to the airport. He waited at the terminal for the airplane to arrive. Alexia's got off the plane and sped walked over to him and gave him a hug and kissed him on the cheek, "It's so good to see you baby. I'm glad you invited me out. It's been a little while."

They walked over to pick up the luggage.

Tye continued the conversation, "I agree. It's been busy for me recently, but I'm glad you made it. I hope you brought some football gear, otherwise I'm going to have to get you a jersey or something."

Alexia scoffed, "I think I'll be all right."

Tye lifted one eyebrow, "Okay, if you say so."

He walked her out to the limo where his driver was waiting to help with the bags. They drove back to the penthouse, and on the way over she reached over to massage Tye's thigh and gave him a look like she wanted to live on the edge, "We can have some fun tonight if you want to."

Tye reached down to remove her hand from his leg and said, "We're going to have to be a little bit quiet tonight, because I have a friend that's staying with me. He's from California. I haven't seen him in a little while."

She looked confused, "Couldn't he have stayed at a hotel?"

Tye asserted, "I invited him to stay with me so we can catch up. We're gonna be with five other people for the weekend. I didn't have any intention of making this just about us. Maybe we can spend some time alone later."

Alexia said with obvious disappointment, "Okay. We'll have fun this weekend…"

She leaned in to whisper in his ear, "We can still have a good time with somebody in the next room. We'll just have to be very quiet. It's still a turn on."

Tye chuckled, "I think we can manage something like that. As long as you don't scream."

They both laughed.

They arrived at his penthouse and the driver dropped them off in front. Tye gave his driver a tip and expressed his gratitude. Alexia walked into the foyer and her high heels echoed throughout the foyer and the restaurant. The sound caught the attention of few people as they walked by.

Tye smiled as he noticed a few guys gawking. He said to Alexia, "You sure know how to work those shoes and shake that ass."

She was pleased that she got everyone's attention, including his, "Thank you. You know just what to say to get a woman's engine running. We may not be able to get upstairs in that elevator without getting naked."

They both grinned. They made their way over to the elevator and up to his penthouse. When the door opened, Alexia was laughing as though Tye had said something very funny to her, and it caught Marcus's attention. He turned to greet both of them.

"Hello Tye. I take it this is Alexia?" Marcus reached to shake her hand.

Alexia reached her hand out as though he was supposed to kiss the back of her hand. Marcus looked at her hand awkwardly and shook it, "My name is Marcus. It's nice to meet you Alexia."

Alexia smirked and said, "Likewise…"

She turned quickly to Tye so that her hair flicked over her shoulder and said, "Babe, I'm just going to go to your room and change because I am really tired. It was a long day and the flight made me a bit tired. What time are we leaving in the morning?"

Tye said with enthusiasm, "The game doesn't start till 1 but we'll leave around 8 in the morning so that we can meet up with my buddies and get there early enough to setup for the tailgate party. We're meeting with them and their significant other and we'll drive together. That gives us enough time to fire up the grill around 11 and we can party until 12:30."

Alexia said with some enthusiasm, "That sounds like fun. Okay babe, I'm gonna go to your room for a bit so that you and Marcus can catch up on the good old days."

She went to Tye's room to change into something more comfortable.

Marcus watched her walk to the room, and as soon as she shut the door he smiled and said to Tye, "You sly dog…or should I say – sly wolf. Shit! You must be having the time of your life? I'm really happy for you Tye."

Tye smiled back, "I am. I have no complaints. Alexia has her ways and she knows how to have fun."

Tye motioned for them to sit at the other end of the penthouse for privacy and he whispered as they walked over, "…I just haven't found the right person and Alexia seems like the right fit for me. She knows how to get me out of my comfort zone. Every once in a while, I need that. I'm a 'by the books' kind of guy but sometimes I need to live on the edge."

Marcus listened intently.

Tye continued as he handed him a beer and they sat by the fireplace, "Man if I told you the stories of our sexual escapades, you'd wet your pants."

Laughter broke out in the living room.

Marcus stunned Tye with his comment, "Yeah, but…sexual escapades are only one part of a relationship, and the best one's can blind you to the person who is really out there for you."

Tye was taken aback, "I hear you. Perhaps living by my head has blurred my vision to who is really out there."

Marcus nodded, "I made lots of mistakes before I found the perfect fit in Stephanie."

Tye asked, "How did you have your eyes opened up to the one that was really out there?"

Marcus scoffed, "I paid attention to my inner peace, joy and happiness and how far I could go in my life with the women I was with, and that became an indication for me that I was on the right track."

Tye exclaimed, "Holy Fuck Marcus! What are you a relationship therapist on the side? How much do I owe you now?"

Laughter broke out between the both of them as they talked a little later into the night about the past and their future endeavors before Tye yawn and said, "Shit, I'm about to fall out! I gotta get to bed."

Marcus chuckled, "Ah huh. Whatever you say Tye."

They both chuckled.

Marcus said again, "Tye. Thank you for inviting me to the game. I'm really glad you invited me."

They lean in to shake hands and give a bro hug, "No problem Marcus. It was good to catch up. I'll see you in the morning."

Tye walked into his room and Alexia had taken a shower. She shaved her legs and was putting lotion on them while in a see-through red lingerie. She was seated on the pillow top bench massaging her legs as they shined under the light. She looked up at Tye seductively as he watched her rubbing her legs and gave him and inviting smile. She knew exactly what she was doing when she stroked her legs deliberately up and down, and then massaging her inner thighs. She moved her hands slowly as if casting a spell over Tye, seductively inviting him to watch as she moved her hands closer to her panties letting out a moan to tickle his ears.

Tye got that look in his eyes like he was craving that feeling of living on the edge. She stood up slowly to reveal every curve of her body. Her nipples were not hidden, and they were already hard. Alexia felt her body, teasing Tye as she walked slowly and seductively in his direction.

Tye's body gave it away that he was turned on by her body. Alexia looked down at his hardness as it tried to escape his pants, "Baby…go take a shower and then come join me."

Tye licked his lips like an animal ready to eat its prey, "Ok."

She crawled into his bed while he took his clothes off and watched her with intensity while she mimicked a cat crawling, making sure the thong was showcased between her cheeks.

Tye walked into the bathroom and stripped down quickly, covered himself with a towel and turned his shower on. He went back to the door to see what she was doing in his bed. He gasp when he saw her leaning against his pillows with her legs spread open and moved her thong to reveal her pussy. She rubbed her pussy lips slowly and spread them with her fingers and looked at Tye and said, "I can tell you're hungry for a taste of me baby. Take your shower and I'll give you what you want."

Ty grinned ear-to-ear, "I'll be right back."

She played with herself gently, "When you come back, I have something special for you…" then slid her finger inside and moaned, "hurry back."

Tye took his shower and didn't waste time drying off, he let himself drip dry but wrapped his hips with a towel. The droplets were dripping down his rock-hard body when he walked into the room. His muscles glistened under the light and it highlighted his chest and broad shoulders. Alexia gasped at his near perfect beach body and undressed him in her mind, "Oh shit Tye, you've been working out. You look like a fucking Greek god."

Tye grinned slyly, allowing his towel to fall from his hips and letting his shit hang out. Alexia took a breath in. She could smell the testosterone in the air while he let his shit swing back and forth teasing her with every step.

He knew exactly what he was doing, and it drove Alexia wild. She wanted that meat like a wild animal. "Bring that sexy ass over here. I'm gonna get me some dick."

Tye leaned in to untie the lace from her lingerie but Alexia couldn't take it anymore and grabbed his head and pulled him down to eat her out, "Fuck, I don't know how the hell you do it, but you make me crave you like a ravenous animal. I can't drag this foreplay shit out anymore."

She was dripping onto his bed, so he gave her a towel, "Lift your ass and sit on this. You're going to need this."

She quickly positioned herself near the edge of his bed and gave Tye access to her pussy. She wasn't close enough to the edge of the bed for him, so he took charge and pulled her closer, the way he wanted it. The way he took charge of her in bed made her horny. He's a commander in bed and took charge of her pleasure and sucked her clit gently in and out of his mouth in perfect rhythm and made her moan with delight.

She closed her eyes and threw her head back while her body quivered with every suck, "Oh shit Tye...fuck I'm going to cum already."

He manhandled her with his strong hands and turned her body around so that her head hung off the edge of the bed. He lifted her legs close to her ears and he leaned in so that her legs wrapped around his arms. Her pussy was exposed, and he put his entire tongue on her pussy and stoked her with just the right pressure and then surprised her by tongue fucking her until she started to lose control.

She turned her head in delight with her eyes closed to enjoy his tongue. When she opened her eyes, his balls were hanging next to her face. She reached over to cup them and pulled him closer to place his cock into her mouth. The angle of her head as it hung over the edge of the bed allowed him to slide his cock in and out of her mouth deep enough to swallow his whole cock.

He knew exactly how to control her head and give himself pleasure with her mouth. He shoved his cock deep into her throat while he ate her pussy. His moans became louder with every thrust he made.

She stopped and put her pointer finger to her mouth and across her now blood filled sexy full lips, "Shhh. We need to be quiet because your friend is in the next room. It's a turn on knowing that we need to be quiet."

Tye kept the rhythm going until he knew she was close. He turned her quickly so that her legs hung over the edge of the bed. He lifted her legs, leaned in to bite her ass and then placed her legs straight up and against his body and held her in place. He reached under her ass and held her up at an angle to give him deep penetration. He slid his rock-hard cock deep inside her swollen pussy, nice and slow, while she held back her scream. He pulled out and fucked her with the tip of his head - in and out quickly to tease her as she whispered, "Oh fuck baby. It hurts but it feels so good. You are the best fuck I've ever had. I want your cock all the way inside."

Tye, lifted her ass higher and made sure the angle of his penetration hit heaven's arch with every pound. Her body started to quiver while she grabbed a fistful of blanket. Tye took it another level and pounded her pussy until she couldn't take it anymore. It was deep and rough. It brought her to the edge of her mind, and she couldn't take it anymore, so she grabbed his pillow and bit it with her teeth and screamed into it. He pounded her so hard that his bed started to rock. The look on her face turned him on and he whispered, "Oh fuck I'm going to cum."

Meanwhile, in the next room, Marcus frantically rummaged through his bag to find his earbuds, as the sound of the bed thumping and squeaking could be heard through the walls, and it got louder and more intense. He said quietly, "Shit…shit…shit" as he scrambled to put his earbuds in.

The look on Tye's face was intense as he sprayed his cum all over her tits. The heat of his cum turned her on and she squirt all over his chest while she struggled to hold back her scream, she yelled into the pillow, "Oh, my fucking gosh…Tye…"

She sprayed all over his body and made him look like he just came out of the shower again and it turned her on even more seeing a man like that taking charge and making her feel safe, giving her the best fuck of her life and letting her squirt everywhere.

Tye was turned on by her release that he shot his cum all the way to her face. She was turned on even more by how much they let loose on each other. Tye wouldn't stop and shoved his cock inside her again, pounding her pussy again until she orgasm with his engorged cock inside her. "Fill my pussy…fill my pussy. Oh shiiiit!!!"

Tye pumped that pussy until she was full and spilled over onto the towel. Her body quivered and then went limp as he pulled his cock from inside her.

Tye retrieved more towels and gave it to her to wipe herself while he cleaned up and then laid next to her. "It's getting late."

She whispered back as she kissed his shoulders, "Oh shit Tye. If you kept going, I could have had four."

Tye said with a deep sexy voice, "I know. But we gotta get up early tomorrow."

They wound down as he spooned her and rest his dick between her ass cheeks and wrapped his hands around her tits and played with her nipples until they both fell asleep.

It wasn't long before morning came, and they were scurrying around the penthouse to get ready. There was an excitement already in the air as Marcus and Tye high fived each other, excited for the game while Alexia was in the other room getting all dolled up.

Tye and Marcus put on their football jersey and wore blue jeans. Tye put on his favorite ball cap and announced to Marcus as he did, "This cap is a reminder that they are already champions."

They high fived each other again.

Just then, Alexia walked out of the bedroom in a noticeable gingerly fashion. She had a slight bow-legged walk to her. Marcus watched her in silence as she tried to cover up the hobbled walk to the kitchen. He looked away and tried to hold back a chuckle as tears came down his eyes. Then he turned to her and snickered, "You alright?"

Alexia forced a smile, "Uh huh."

Tye covered his mouth to avoid laughing, watching the two of them interact. He took notice of her outfit, and commented on it, "Where's your gear?"

Alexia was wearing a Versace outfit, and couldn't decide if she was going to accessorise with Louis Vuitton or Gucci. She made sure to wear earrings and a necklace that matched her outfit. She was carrying 3 pair of high heels and sat on the couch, trying to decide which ones to wear - Vanessa

Houghton, Gucci or her matching Louis Vuitton high heels. She was dressed up like she was going to a night on the town to a high-profile party.

They both look at her strangely, a bit confused, Tye cocked his head and said, "You know where we're going right?"

Marcus chimed in as he tugged on his jersey to make a point, "We're going to a football game to eat burger and drink beer and cheer at the top of our lungs, maybe swear a few times at some of the missed plays."

Alexia scoffed in his direction, "And?"

Marcus continued, "You're supposed to dress down, not dress up like a princess."

Alexia jeered, "I think I'll be all right, okay?"

Marcus shrugged his shoulders, "Whatever you say."

Tye stepped in to ease the tension, "Alexia? This tailgate party is not the typical party you're used to going to. Do you have something more laid back and relaxing to wear? A sweatshirt or jeans?"

Alexia looked at Tye like she was confused, "Baby! Really? Sweats?"

Tye insisted, "Yeah! Let your hair down and relax."

Alexia stood up and showcased her curves, "I like how this outfit looks on me."

Marcus poured himself an orange juice and then lifted his class as if toasting her, "It does look good on you."

Alexia smiled, "Thank you."

Tye shrugged his shoulders, "Ok…as long as your happy."

They grabbed a quick breakfast and tea before leaving. Tye asked Marcus to help him carry a few things out to the garage. Tye had a cooler filled for the tailgate party. They left to meet the rest of Tye's friends.

There was an obvious excitement between Tye and Marcus. Alexia tried to fit in. There's an unspoken rule among fans on game day, especially if you are going out to party, "No shop-talk. No downer-talk. No work-talk. Just have fun."

Alexia didn't know this rule and couldn't find a way into their conversation as they threw around stats, figures, players and past games. They also talked about everyday life.

When they got to the garage Marcus saw a line of vehicles against the wall that had a sign in front of them reserving that spot with Ty's name on it, "Reserved for Tye Wolf. All other vehicles will be crushed into scrap metal immediately. Don't believe me, test your luck!"

Marcus read the sign and laughed and pointed to all the vehicles, "These are all yours?"

Tye nodded, "Yeah. I like cars, boats and planes. I couldn't park my yacht here though."

Marcus let out a sigh, "A yacht too? Damn Tye. You're my hero. If only every knew where you came from and how you got here, they'd be just as astonished as me."

Alexia took this opportunity to chime in and asked Tye, "Where you came from? What does he mean by that?"

Tye whispered into Marcus' ears without Alexia noticing, "I rocked that yacht a couple weeks ago too. But it is was before Alexia and I decided to see each other again."

They both cheered and fist pump.

Tye paused briefly to scan all the cars and pondered which vehicle to take. He pointed to the recently acquired maroon Mercedes-Maybach GLS 600 SUV, "This is what we're taking today."

He pressed a button and unlocked the doors and popped the trunk. Alexia and Marcus gasped when they looked inside.

Tye looked at Marcus and then pointed to the back seats like he was a host on an infomercial, "These seats recline, and a footrest pops up. Plus, there's a monitor on the seat in front of you to watch tv."

Marcus laughed out of sheer astonishment, "Holy fuuuuck! Are you shitten' me?"

Marcus quickly loaded the trunk and then jumped in the back seat. Alexia took the front seat next to Tye. The look on her face was the same look she had just before she had an orgasm. Tye smiled, started up the car and drove to meet his other buddies.

There was a silence in the vehicle for 20 minutes while Alexia and Marcus touched everything, played with all the buttons and admired the luxury they found themselves in.

Finally, Alexia took a deep breath and asked Tye, "You didn't answer my question. What did Marcus mean by 'where you came from?'"

Tye hesitated briefly and then answered, "Everything you see in my world…everything you experience, that you consider luxury, was non-existent to me and my family. Back then, we just got by. There were times we did without."

Marcus looked genuinely proud of him as Tye made that remark. Alexia seemed shocked, "I can't image going without, or living without these kinds of luxuries."

Tye shook his head, "These things took years of sacrifice and hard work to acquire. They're just stuff that add to the enjoyment of my life. I've lived without it before, and I can live without again if I needed to."

Marcus could be seen in the rear-view mirror nodding in agreement while Alexia shook her head, "Not me."

Tye lifted his eyebrows and said under his breath, "Hmmm."

Marcus changed the subject, "So Tye. The QB is back home. What do you think is going to happen today?"

Tye remarked, "You can't take out a general like him, but you can shake him up a bit. It's going to be a fantastic game."

Tye turned the radio on to play some music for the ride. They pulled into a parking lot where his other friends were standing around a pickup talking.

Tye pulled up and got out of the car to greet all his friends.

"You guys ready? Let's hit the road. Follow me to the highway. I'll show you where to park when we get to the stadium."

They drove to the stadium which took less than an hour to get through with all the traffic. Tye was directed to VIP parking and let security know that there were 2 other vehicles in his party.

They found a good spot. Everyone got out of their vehicles and helped unload everything for the BBQ.

Tye introduce everyone to each other as they set up for the tailgate party. His two friends took the BBQ off the truck and fired up the grill and laid out the cooler for all drinks.

The wife and girlfriend opened up the cooler and shouted, "Let the party begin! Who's ready for beer?"

In unison everyone cheered, hooped and hollered.

The girls were obviously getting into it and noticed Alexia was feeling a bit awkward.

"Hey…what do you wanna drink?"

Alexia looked in the cooler, "Mmmm…I'll take a lite beer."

The girls laughed, "Their aint' no lite beer at this party girl." They pointed to their man, "Do these guys look like they drink lite?"

The guys hooped and hollered again, "Fuck nooo."

Laughter broke out and the music was cranked, and the grill was fired up. One of the girls reached in the cooler and handed Alexi a Bud, "Start off with this and we'll see what we can do for you later."

The women hooped and hollered to the music and random dances broke out here and there.

Alexia became more uncomfortable as the tailgate party got into full swing. All the football talk made her feel more distant and she tried to fit in and asked the girls what they did for work.

One girl leaned in her direction and put one finger up and wagged it back and forth, "Nobody cares about work today sweetheart."

The other girl spoke up and said, "Don't sip your Bud darling, drink it a little faster and move on the next one. That will help you loosen up." She mimicked being drunk and the girls laughed.

Nobody talks work, that's just not the way tailgate parties are. It's about fun and having a good time, but Alexia's thing was shopping and partying in high profile settings. She made a momentary connection when she talked about shopping, but that was it.

Tye noticed that Alexia wasn't have the same kind of fun he was. He tried to help her loosen up and led her by the hand to the BBQ.

"Alexia, we're here to stuff our face with burger, steak or chicken and then watch a game to leave the world behind. You'll be ok to let go just for today." He gestured toward the grill.

Alexia smiled, "Thank you Tye."

She pointed to a burger and Tye gave it to her on a bun.

"If we don't have the drink you want, it will definitely be available inside. Ok?" He pointed toward the stadium with his chin and smiled to help her relax.

Meanwhile Naffilia, Chloe and Mya carpooled to the same game and pulled into the parking lot and waited for the attendant to direct them. They had their music cranked up to add to the excitement of today's game.

Naffilia announced, "My boy is coming back to the hometown, the problem is he's playing for another team."

Chloe chimed in and gave Mya high five and said, "I'll take that boy any day no matter what team he plays for."

All three of them whooped and hollered, "Yeah boy! You got that right."

Laughter broke out in the car, but Naffilia said as she tugged on her Jersey, "I'm still committed to my home team though. I don't want to see his pretty face hurt, but I want him kissing grass all day long!"

The girls chimed in, "I'll drink to that!"

The lot attendant walked over to them, so they turned the music off and rolled their windows down as he directed them to the end of the parking lot. With the music off they deliberately drove slowly to take in the excitement around them, checking out the various tailgate parties that were happening - taking in all the sights and sounds and the smell of all the barbecues everywhere.

There was a general feeling of living in the moment, like nobody gave a shit about anything else but having fun right now. All three girls were living in that moment as you could hear the obvious deep breathes all of them were taking to get a whiff of BBQ.

Chloe belted out, "Fucking 'A' this is life and I'm loving it."

Mya poked fun and laughed as she said, "What are you, a fucking advertisement for McDonalds?"

The girls laughed and Naffilia said, "Now I'm starving for a burger. It worked!"

Chloe laughed and said, "Shit I could feel the energy in the air. It makes me wanna go over there and grab a burger from those guys over there, like they were a part of the family."

Naffilia agreed, "I have no doubt that if we just walked up to somebody, they would treat us like family, and we'd end up partying with them."

Chloe said with excitement, "Shit ya! That's what I love about football games and tailgate parties, because everyone feels like a family."

The girls got out of their car and fit in perfectly with the crowd with their ball caps, jerseys and blue jeans. They gathered themselves together and started walking toward the stadium to get there a little bit early. As they were walking along the way they were chanting, "let's go Boston, let's go."

They incited the crowd and got them into chant as they were working their way toward the stadium. The smell of barbecue was really intense the closer they got to the VIP section of the parking lot and the party atmosphere was thick. Guys and girls, we're acting like it was college days, but the only difference was that some of them had their kids with them participating in the good times.

Naffilia, Chloe and Mya came up to one truck that had a group of three cars parked together and you can tell they were having the time of their life. One guy noticed them walking toward them and called out to them, "Hello ladies! You guys look like you can spice up our party. You wanna join us for a burger or steak and have some beers?"

The girls looked at each other and actually considered it but saw one woman dressed up like she was going to a formal social event with her Gucci bag and high heels. She was hanging all over her man. They couldn't see who she was with, but it was enough for them to pass on the invitation.

Chloe and Naffilia said, "That's Ok. We appreciate it though. Thanks. We don't wanna crash your party."

The man was really nice about it, "No problem girls. You want a beer for the road?"

Naffilia refused, "No that's Ok. They probably won't let us in with the beer anyway."

Chloe started laughing and said, "Naffilia, you know you'll have that beer gone before you get to the gates."

The guys and girls laughed. One guy raised his beer to toast the women, "Cheers. Enjoy the game then."

Naffilia nodded, "Thanks boys. We appreciate it though. Enjoy the game."

As the girls walked past them, Chloe announced, "See, I told you! It's like family here and we could've joined the party."

The girls high fived each other as they agreed they would pig out at the concession as soon as they got inside.

Just then, Tye called out to Marcus and his other friends, "Who you talking to boys? Are you trying to make our party bigger than it already is?"

Marcus called out, "Hell yaaa."

The girls chimed in, "Fuck, the more the merrier."

Tye and his friends lived in the moment and partied, enjoying each other's company and ate plenty of food before packing everything and making their way to the luxury seats.

All of Tye's guest were blown away by the seats they had. Marcus said with excitement, "This is the balls! We're two sections away from the owner. Tye…this is awesome."

One of the guys said with excitement in his voice, "This is a way to see a ballgame. Tye, you outdid yourself. Thank you so much for this."

Everyone gave him a high five while Alexia admired Tye from a distance and appreciated his generous quality. She admired his personal connections that made it possible for everyone to enjoy the game to the fullest.

The luxury seats had premium access to all the food and drink they could want. It came with seating inside or outside right over the 50-year line. They had a TV right behind them so that they had access to the replays as well. Having this kind of luxury provided them their own personal restroom as well.

They were experiencing life as the upper echelon of society would experience it. Through their open door to their luxury seating they watched high profile celebrities walking back and forth, and on occasion they stopped in to introduce themselves. At one point the owner stopped by just to introduce himself. The level of networking was very high and it surprised Tye's friends how my movie stars were fans of the Boston team. Tye's friends were overwhelmingly enamoured by the people that surrounded them, and it almost distracted them from the opening of the game.

A few moments later, music filled the stadium as the opponents ran out to the field and boos could be heard everywhere. After a brief silence a thunderous roar from the crowd could be felt in the chest as a sudden explosion of Ozzy Osborne music blasted the stadium playing "Crazy Train." Everyone got goosebumps the moment the song played and heard the announcer belt out, "Ladies and gentlemen…your world champions - 'Boston Renegades.'"

Then the players came running onto the field lead by the mascot running with a flag to lead the players to center of the football field. The crowd exploded with cheers. Tye and all his friends jumped up and down cheering at the top of their lungs. They all high fived each other.

After the entrance there was a silence as the National Anthem was played and a flyover went right over their heads and the crowd cheered.

The game lived up to the hype of the media as each team went back and forth the entire game. Marcus said in disbelief, "For years I enjoyed having the QB put a spanking to the other teams. I can't believe he's doing that to us now."

Tye agreed, "It sucks to be on the other side at that QB."

The women chimed in, "If I'm gonna get a spanking from anyone, I'd rather it be him than any other QB."

The women started laughing and gave each other high fives as the guys looked at their women wondering where this side of their women come from - they never knew it existed. Maybe it was the beers talking, but who gave a shit?

The husband and boyfriends said to each other, "We're going to get lucky tonight guys...thanks to that guy," they pointed to the field.

One of the guys agreed and said, "...and our women are wanting to get spanked."

The guys and girls laughed.

Just then, the Renegades scored a touchdown and the crowd exploded.

The game was intense, and it stayed close in points. During halftime Tye and his friends mingled together inside their luxury suite drinking from the personal bar.

Tye and Marcus announced, "We're going to take a walk around to check out the scene up here."

Tye walked over to Alexia, "Do you wanna go with us and check everything out?"

Alexia refused, "I'm gonna stay here and refresh myself. My face is probably melting and I'm gonna touch it up."

Tye had a look of confusion when she said that when one of the women nodded in Tye's direction, "She's just making sure her make up isn't running or smutched from sweating."

Tye looked like he got it, "Oh ok."

His friend's wife said to Tye, "That's ok Tye. You go with Marcus. We'll keep her company."

"Thank you," he said with some relief.

The girls did their best to keep Alexia company, but she didn't talk too much, so they took her out to get her the drink that she originally wanted to help her relax.

Everyone came back before the halftime show was done and they got back into the flow of the game. By the end of the third quarter the announcer got the crowd going with chants, the wave went around the stadium a few times and the camera men were scanning the crowd.

Suddenly, on the big screen you could see the crowd cheering. Tye and his friends looked at the screen and then into the crowd to try to figure out the angle of the shot. When the fans saw themselves on the jumbotron they got excited and waved. Everyone's attention was on the big screen while the camera kept panning, until it stopped on three women.

Tye looked stunned for a moment and stared at the screen as the women realized they were on the jumbotron. They got into the moment by waving their hat and jumping up and down so that their tits bounced violently. It was Naffilia, Chloe and Mya. You can tell Mya was getting a bit drunk and she reached down to her jersey crossing both arms and with both hands started to lift her shirt to flash her tits. Naffilia and Chloe's mouth dropped as they laughed and tried to stop Mya from flashing everyone. The crowd went nuts. The cameraman quickly panned away just as Mya got her shirt halfway up, and everyone booed.

On the Tv behind Ty you could hear the announcer say, "Now there's a fan that know how to have some fun. You just can't get naked at a game though."

The other announcer laughed hysterically and threw in his two cents, "It's ok for a painted fat guy to bare his chest, but not an unpainted beautiful woman."

Tye gasped, "Shit! That's her!"

Everyone around Tye turned and looked at him while Alexia asked, "What do you mean that's her?"

One of Tye's friends asked, "Who?"

Alexia chimed in, "Yeah Tye…who?"

Tye could feel his feet get cold when he realized he spoke out loud. It was too late to take it back as he stumbled over his words.

He tried to regain his composure as he said, "I think I know that girl that just popped up on the screen."

The guys started laughing, "Who? The titty flasher?"

Marcus took a jab too, "It wouldn't surprise me if you did."

Tye tried to defend himself, "No the girl next to her with the dark hair."

The women punched their men and gave Marcus a look as they watched Alexia's face become drawn. The men didn't notice the blatant agitation that Alexia was displaying.

Alexia grilled Tye, "How do you know her?"

Tye tried to answer her without any emotion behind it, "I'm pretty sure I met her somewhere in another country. It was a business thing."

"Business?" Alexia pushed.

Tye and his friends tried to pay attention to the remainder of the game as the fourth quarter started and the home team was down by 2 points. It was still anyone's game. Tye was distracted as Alexia got up from her seat a few times to go the bathroom and pace the suite. He looked at her from the corner of his eyes and couldn't take it anymore and asked her to sit down.

She sat down and he asked her, "Is there a problem?"

Alexia scoffed, "Are you fucking serious?"

Everyone around Alexia got a little shifty and Tye held his breath and looked around him in embarrassment.

Alexia stood up, "I wanna go now."

Tye couldn't maintain his composure as the game got tighter, more exciting and Alexia kept insisting to leave. Tye has been in difficult business positions and composed himself like a prey – a king of the jungle, but Alexia found a way to shake him and took advantage of it.

She waved her hand and shook her head side to side and gestured to the door, "I'm leaving. Enjoy your game."

Her high heels had an exaggerated stomping sound to them as she walked toward the door and left the luxury suit.

Tye sighed, "Shit…"

He apologized to everyone. "…I'm sorry guys. I have to go."

There was a brief silence and then his friends said, "We'll take Marcus home after the game. You go do what you have to do. We'll be ok Tye. We appreciate what you've done for us today."

The women chimed in, "Yeah Tye, you go. We're gonna enjoy the rest of the game. None of us wanna miss this chance to enjoy this game. You're a sweetheart Tye. Go!"

"Thanks. Again, I'm sorry."

He nodded to Marcus, "See you later, ok?"

Marcus replied, "See ya. I'll let you know how it ends."

Tye saw the direction in which Alexia walked off and chased after her. He caught up to her going in the wrong direction. "Hey?"

Alexia stopped and looked at him but didn't say anything.

Tye pointed in the opposite direction, "That's the way out. I'll take you home."

Alexia snorted, "Fine."

Tye and Alexia didn't talk as he led her out of the stadium. The crowd was cheering loudly and Tye kept trying to take a glance onto the field or looking at the monitors that were playing around the stadium. Alexia caught him trying to watch the game and shook her head in disgust.

Just then Naffilia paid for her beer at the concession. She turned and took a sip when Tye and Alexia walked by. Naffilia caught a quick glance at the two of them and stopped walking in mid stride.

Naffilia said out loud, "Shit, shit, shit…was that him?"

Watching them walking away, she hoped he would turn around so that she got a better look to confirm it was him.

Neither one of them turned around so Naffilia shrug off the thought that it was him.

Tye and Alexia left the stadium and got into the car. Tye felt the tension grow thicker the further away they got from the stadium. They drove home in silence.

Because Ty is a savvy businessman, he knew the power of silence, so he reached over and turned the radio on to listen to the remainder of the game.

Alexia smacked her lips together and reached over to turn the power off on the radio.

Tye gave her a look and ask her, "Why? Why would you do that?"

Alexia turned her head and looked out of the window at the trees going by in a blur.

Tye then said to her, "You know in my line of work. Lack of communication is bad business and it could lead to a disastrous business relationship."

Alexia turned her head quickly and said, "well this isn't a business relationship now is it?"

Ty said, "Sorry if I caused any embarrassment to you, that was not my intention."

Alexia folded her arms and said, "You didn't embarrass me. I had the impression that we had a thing for each other."

Tye remained silent for the remainder of the drive home when Alexia spoke up and said, "I gave you head a month ago in a glass elevator, and then I let you fuck me like there was no tomorrow last night. Was I wrong to assume that you had a thing for me?"

Ty shook his head and said, "We obviously see life vastly different from each other. I don't think we should be making assumptions about our relationship."

Alexia scoffed and said, "What relationship? Sometimes I feel like I'm your personal prostitute."

Tye remarked, "I thought we were having fun together. More than once."

Alexia scoffed and said, "Oh, so I'm privileged?"

Ty just shook his head - this argument was going nowhere so he remained silent for the remainder of the drive home.

Alexia took a deep breath and sighed as she said, "I want to go home now. I'm just going to pack my bags. I really didn't care about your stupid football game. I just went because you asked me to go. When do we ever do things together?"

Tye remain silent and let her vent.

Alexia continued as she got out of the car and slam the door, "You're obviously a player, and I thought I was okay with that until you made that comment about the girl on the big screen and all of your friends we're rootin' you on."

Tye led her over to the elevator and brought her up to his penthouse and said, "You know? I'll be very happy to take you home. You obviously have other things in mind when it comes to the two of us."

Alexia went to the room and gathered all her things together while he watched her. When she was done, she walked past him with her nose in the air and said, "I'm ready to go. Take me to the airport."

Tye didn't speak another word to her on the way over to the airport and they both endured an awkward silence between the two of them.

He drove her over to the drop-off zone and parked. He popped the trunk and took out her bags and placed them on the ground next to her.

Alexia said, as she uncrossed her arms and put her hand out and said, "Do you have my ticket so I can get home?"

Tye reached into his pocket and pulled out her ticket to go back home.

Alexia looked at the ticket and said, "The return date is for tomorrow! How am I supposed to change a flight, and what if I have to pay for it?"

Tye opened up his wallet and handed her $500 in cash, "If there's any changes or you have to pay for it, this should be more than enough."

Alexia took the money and put it in her purse and reach down to pick up her bags. Tye didn't say a word while Alexia stood before him expecting him to say something.

Tye put his fingers to the ridge of is baseball cap and gave her a salute and walked away.

He got into the car and scrubbed through his contact list, "Let's see... Alexia, Alexia, Alexia. Oh, there you are…"

He pressed the ignore button, "...You've just been ghosted."

As Tye drove off in his car he turned the radio on hoping to catch the end of the game when the announcer said with over exaggerated excitement, "Folks! That was an incredible game. If you're just tuning in now you missed the game of the century."

Ty was pissed off, "Shit! Of all the games to miss why did it have to be that one? What the hell was I thinking inviting her to that game?"

Tye turn the radio off and drove home in silence reflecting on the day and what just happened.

Just as he arrived, home Marcus called him to let him know they were on the way home to drop him off at his place. Tye let him know that he'll meet him outside. He waited at the bar in the lobby and watched the highlights and the other games that were playing.

Shortly afterwards, Marcus text him to let him know that he's a few minutes from his place. He went outside to greet him at the door.

Marcus got out of the car and so did his other friends.

They approached Tye and asked, "Is everything okay Tye?"

He remarked, "Yeah everything's alright. I dropped Alexia off at the airport so she can fly home. I just wish it didn't happen like this, especially at a game like this."

His friends were sympathetic and said, "Yeah. Sorry it went down like that. Bad timing. Are you and Alexia going to be okay or is there something you want to talk about?"

Tye shook his head, "I'm ok guys. I don't think I'm going to be contacting Alexia anymore. I haven't been with her long and I thought she would have been okay going to a game. I obviously had to learn the hard way it wasn't meant to be."

The girls gave Tye a hug and said, "Tye when a girl dresses up like she's going out to a high-profile party, she obviously doesn't get where you're coming from and doesn't understand your culture. That's not a good way to start a relationship. You're such a sweetheart and you'll find someone special."

Ty's friends affirmed what their women were saying, "We agree with them Tye. You'll find that one. It's just a matter of keeping an eye out. Which brings me to the next question. Who the hell was that girl on the jumbotron you commented on?"

The group responded, "Yeah. Who was that girl on the big screen? She's obviously something worth getting a fight over!"

Tye smiled, "Honestly, I don't remember her name, but I met her several months ago in Morocco and had an interesting conversation. There was something about her that just enamoured me, and I've seen her a few times after that but never got a chance to talk to her."

Ty's friend said, "She obviously likes football and was dressed for it, that's a start. She's right up your alley. Use all the resources you can to find her. Who knows? That might be the one you've been looking for."

They all agreed, "Yeah. She obviously would understand your culture if she was at the same game as you - flashing her tits to the world."

Tye snickered, "She isn't the one who flashed her tits."

Laughter broke out among and then Marcus chimed in, "Yeah and you missed one hell of a game."

He turned to Marcus and said, "Oh man, don't remind me about the game. Let's go upstairs and watch the highlights and then we can watch the remainder of the games playing today."

Tye shook the hands of his friends and gave them a hug goodbye and thanked them for bringing Marcus to his penthouse. They expressed their gratitude to Tye for treating all of them to the game and giving them an amazing experience. After exchanging pleasantries, they got into their pickup and car and honked their horns and drove off cheering, carrying on that air of celebration.

Tye gestured for Marcus to go inside. On the way to the elevator Marcus said, "So you brought her to the airport, huh? She's gone?"

Tye gave a quick remark, "Yep she's gone."

After they got to the penthouse, Ty turned on his big screen TV and grabbed a beer for him and Marcus and watched the highlights of the game and the remainder of the games for that day.

Marcus filled Tye in on the portion of the game that he missed as they watched highlights on TV.

After a brief silence between the two of them Tye turned in Marcus's direction and asked earnestly, "How did you know that your wife was the one?"

A grand smile came across Marcus's face as he said, "Trial and error."

They both laughed.

Tye shook his head, "Well if that's the case then I'm in for a long haul looking for that one who fits me perfectly." He said with a tone of futility.

Marcos quickly cracked a joke, "Yeah but at least you can have a shit load of fun looking for the right one. You don't seem to have any problems connecting with women. And by the sound of it last night, you have no problems making sure they're happy while you're looking for the right one."

They laughed heartily.

Tye said apologetically and with surprise, "Wow! I'm sorry about that. Sometimes I forget how noisy it can be for both of us."

Marcus quickly replied, "Don't worry about it Tye. The only thing I regret is not putting my earbuds in fast enough and not having noise cancelling technology."

Tye laughed and took a jab at him, "Of all the techies I know - you're the techiest and you don't have noise cancelling earbuds? What the fuck, buddy! Get with it."

Marcus changed the subject, "Seriously Tye, what was it about that woman on the jumbotron that made you remember her from one meeting months ago?"

Ty cleared his throat and leaned back on the couch to reminisce, "As I said, we met in Morocco at a restaurant while I was on a business trip several months earlier and she came across as being very intelligent. She had a very sexy, soft spoken voice…"

Tye raised one eyebrow, smirked and motioned like he was talking on a phone with his thumb and pinky, "…like the voice of a phone sex woman."

They both laughed.

Tye continued, "…yeah it was soothing, and her voice tickled my ears and made my dick hard in an instant. Fuck that's a rare thing for me."

Marcus laughed, "Shit! If she had that impact on you, she must have been sexy."

Tye nodded, "…and she seemed like she was a low-key kind of person, the kind of person who could handle her business but knew how to let her hair down. She had a subtle way to show her sexy side through her intelligence and life experience, but at the same time knew how to draw out of me the sexual side without even trying. She just gave off that air of having her shit together. That alone was a turn on."

Marcus asked, "Was she an entrepreneur like you?"

"I have no idea. We didn't talk long enough to find out." He said with regret.

Tye continued, "She knew how to tease me. It was like she was reading me the whole time. It felt like we were having sex just by the way we talked to each other. I gave her my number, but I don't know if she lost it or not. Since then, I've seen her a couple of times, and to be honest with you, she is so fuckin' smoking hot that I find myself dreaming of having crazy sex-capades with her. I nearly wet my underwear just thinking about her."

Marcos nodded his head, "Wow! She sounds really sexy. A woman like that is right up your alley and that's pretty observant of you to make those kinds of assessment on somebody who's a total stranger."

Tye nodded his head in an exaggerated way, "Do you see why I reacted that way now?"

Marcus' eyes were as wide as saucers, "I do!"

Tye sighed and looked at Marcus, "So what's your story? Tell me about you and your wife."

Marcus cleared his throat, "My story, how my wife and I hooked up is quite an adventure."

Tye leaned in his direction, "I'm all ears. Maybe I can get some pointers from you."

Marcus' head jolted back, "Pointers from me? Fuck, I should be getting pointers from you on how to make a woman cum several times in less than 15 minutes. You should be a sex therapist."

Ty laughed, "As a matter fact, I saw a therapist just a few weeks ago."

Marcus looked confused, "You saw a sex therapist a few weeks ago? What the fuck for?"

Ty teased him, "It saw a massage therapist…"

"Oh." said Marcus, then took a sip of his beer.

Then Tye smirked, "…but we ended up having crazy sex and I shot my cum in her eye. So, I guess you can call her my sex therapist."

That caught Marcus off guard and made him laugh. It made him shoot beer through his nose.

They both laughed hysterically.

Marcus tried to get his composure as he wiped his face, "What the hell? You shot your massage therapist in the eye with your cum? Damn Tye, you're my fucking hero."

After the laughter died down Tye encouraged Marcus to continue.

Marcus continued to talk about the ups and down of his relationships. He went through a time of depression because of the multitude of relationships. He emphasized that none of them worked for him for years.

Tye felt bad for him and said, "I'm sorry I wasn't around for you at the time."

Marcus nodded, "It's okay. I've learned a lot since then. I've learned a few things along the way."

Marcus sat up straight on the couch and began to talk about his relationships, "Many of these relationships lasted either 2 weeks or 16 months. It was the ones that lasted longer that hurt the most and it felt like I got my heart ripped right out of me. I thought they were the one, by virtue of how long they lasted. I found out that the common problem was a lack of communication between both of us. That's where the problem came in. To make matters worse, I lost myself in the relationship. We both did. That's when we started drifting apart."

Tye said with surprise, "Wow! 16 months! That's a long time to be with somebody and then start drifting apart."

Marcus agreed, "It is, but I learned some things. After that length of being with someone and calling it quits - it rendered my heart. I had to rethink things in my life. I paid attention to my mistakes and applied it to my life. That's when I met my wife."

Tye gave Marcus his full attention, "Our connection was immediate. We spent time getting to know each other for a period of time. The similarities were refreshing, but the differences were too. We maintained our individuality. We didn't have sex until we were comfortable, but when we did…"

Marcus took a deep breath and shook his hands like they were on fire, "…oh shit…she is a wild one in bed. We explored our sexuality and we were comfortable with each other, enough to communicate what we wanted."

Marcus lifted his finger to emphasis a point, "Communication."

Tye shook his head in agreement.

Marcus continued, "We've been together for 4 years. We got married on the third year. We've learned a lot being together. We went through personal relationship stages before learning that we had our own love language."

Tye looked confused, "What do you mean?"

Marcus continued, "We were drawn to each other and initially spent all of our waking hours together. We immersed ourselves in each other's lives and loved learning about each other. After a while, we got used to each other. The familiarity ushered in monotony and we stopped paying attention to each other. It felt stale and the threat of distance between us was real - until we learned that each of us had our own love language. That's when I discovered that every person expresses love differently. Then the sex was out of this world because we connected on a multitude of levels."

Tye struggle to understand, "Can you explain what you mean by that?"

Marcus explained, "When it comes to expressing oneself to or for another, each person says things or does things to express that love. There is a give and a take in this relationship when it comes to verbal and nonverbal cues. Because of that, there's room for interpretation. Let's use your parents as an example." Marcus paused briefly and went deep into thought and then continued.

"For the limited time that I knew your mother and father I don't recall them telling you verbally that they love you or giving you physical expressions of love, like a hug or a kiss, like my parents used to do. How many times when you came over to my place my mom would give you a hug and a kiss and even my father would kiss you on the cheeks?"

Tye nodded emphatically.

"Each person expressed their love differently as the giver, and we as the receiver interpreted that love differently. How did your mom and dad express love to you? What were the telltale signs?"

Tye didn't hesitate to recall those moments, "For my father he would do things with his family and do things for me. He got me started in martial arts and we did martial arts together. He paid for all my lessons until I got my black belt. For my father it was clear that it was doing things with his kids. I don't know how many times we went canoeing and fishing."

Tye smiled as he reflected on his relationship with his father. Then continued, "For my mother it was taking care of our physical needs. There was always a meal on the table. Also, because my mom was more of an academic, there were many times she stayed up late with me helping me with homework. For both of them there was the occasional telling me that they're proud of me."

Marcus agreed, "Exactly. That was your parents love language to you and you understood how to interpret it properly. People outside looking in wouldn't have figured that out because they experience it differently, like myself who got hugs and kisses. When it comes to a relationship, each person expresses their love or affection differently. Some people buy gifts, some people like to receive gifts, some show it by constant physical contact, others show it by sacrificing their time, and others show it by paying attention to the details of your life. The problem is, as human beings, we're not versed in interpreting that love language. That's where the problem comes in. That's where communication fills that gap. Sexual expression is just one part of it, and unfortunately a lot of people put a lot of weight on that part and don't consider the other things."

Tye was engrossed while Marcus stood up and started mimicking like he was a motivational speaker at a convention, "When a couple stops engaging each other and challenging each other or supporting each other's individual goals, or when each individual is lost in the relationship and lose their own individuality, or when they get used to each other and stop telling each other what they want for excitement in their life - that's when distance between a couple starts to happen and they take the easy road and look elsewhere outside of their relationship. That's when broken hearts become inevitable. But if you take time the time to understand each other's love language and have an open line of communication to spice things up or connect on a deeper level – that's when things really take off. To make my point, I'm willing to bet you figured out how a woman speaks to you nonverbally in bed."

Tye smirked, "Yeah I pay attention to all of her nonverbal cues - how I touch her to get a reaction, where I touch her and how she responds. If I see that I've touched her a certain way or said something a certain way that drives her crazy, then I continue doing that because it tells me that she likes it. I also take charge of the bedroom and do things the way I want it done. That has worked out in my favor about 90% of the time. But the most important thing is - I give them what they want and that's a big turn on for me. I try to engage all of the senses, hers and mine, when it comes to having sex with a woman, and because I don't like doing the same thing twice, it's always different and new for them."

Marcus' eyes widened, "It seems you figured out how to understand the nonverbal cues when it comes to sex. The same principle applies when it comes to mental, emotional and spiritual connection as well. That's what I mean by interpreting their love language."

Tye looked as though he got it, "Ok! I see what you're

saying. So, in Alexia's case I could have picked it up from the beginning that because she wanted to go shopping instead of going to a ball game - that was her way of connecting with me. Gifts and shopping are her avenues of affection. Where with me, it's experiences and doing thing together, and having an incredible sexual encounter. Because of that, we're not reading each other properly."

Marcus lifted his finger straight up and then lowered it down to point at Tye and said, "Yep that's it! And a lot of times…and I'll speak from a man's perspective…men or couples miss that simple point."

Tye chimed in, "Obviously there's more to it than that, and it can't just boil down to one or two things. It's more comprehensive than that, and more fluid and engaging. People who are looking to fulfill a fantasy can sometimes miss that simple point. A fulfilling relationship can't be just about fulfilling a fantasy alone - it simply isn't enough. Look at me! I feel like I live a fantasy life with crazy sex, but I'm still missing the deeper connection and I'm still looking."

Marcus nodded, "You understand…" then he sat down and let out a breath like he was relieved.

He continued, "That took me a multitude of relationships and many years to figure that out. Since then I have paid attention to the finest details of my wife, and it made a huge difference at every level of our relationship - including in the bedroom. We're not afraid to push each other sexually and we communicate that all the time. She has learned to tell me what she wants when I simply don't get it. I'm not perceptive like you – that's for sure."

They both chuckled and nodded in agreement, then Marcus jokingly said, "I don't know how many times it would have saved my ass if most of the women I dated just told me outright what was wrong or what I did wrong, because honestly, there were many times I was oblivious. Not because I didn't care - but because I didn't know how to pay attention. Most of the time I was too focused on one thing - how quickly could we get our fuck on. I missed the process of getting there and connecting along the way. My dick said, 'fuck the foreplay'. I didn't take the time to start the process of her orgasm in her mind and imagination first. That's where I missed out connecting with all those women before my wife came along."

They both laughed at his remark as if trying to cover up something embarrassing.

Tye turned up the volume on the TV, "You should consider writing a book or taking on a second career in relationship development."

Marcus smiled, "Thanks I appreciate that. The funny thing is, this is what my parents have been trying to tell me all along, but I wasn't paying attention to what they were saying - and they were married for over 50 years."

Tye agreed, "Now that I think of it, my parents tried to tell me the same thing."

Marcus threw in one more remark that got both of them thinking for the rest of the night, "What throws a wrench in everything we talked about, is, if someone experienced a tragic event at any point in their life, it can negatively influence this whole process and it wouldn't be obvious to either party and they would misinterpret what was happening between each other. I've seen that kill a relationship after years of being together. It's sad."

They both agree. Tye took everything he said to heart. After a brief silence, Tye lifted his beer and offered a toast, "To us. To the women we have in our life. To success in our life. And to another Superbowl run this year."

They tapped their beer cans together, took a drink and watched the remainder of the games until evening came and they retired for the evening.

15

After the game, the girls hung around the stadium pub to watch the other games that were playing across the league. They talked about what they planned to do for the remainder of their vacation.

Naffilia mentioned how she was going to Egypt for a business and personal trip. The girls were excited for her.

After most of the games were played, they stopped at the plaza to do a little bit of shopping until early evening.

On their drive home, Naffilia, Chloe and Mya chatted about how good the game was. There was a moment when Naffilia was lost in thought reminiscing the game and the thought of having possibly seen him. The thought of seeing him with another woman made her pause briefly and give life a second thought and what she wanted for her future.

Just as they pulled up to Naffilia's penthouse Chloe said, "Ok girl, here's your spot."

Mya asked, "When are you coming back from Egypt?"

"I'll be back within a week."

"Ok girl, have fun and be safe." Said Chloe.

"Love you girl's" Naffilia said as she opened the car door to get out.

"We love you too." Chloe and Mya said in unison.

Naffilia walked into her penthouse, stripped naked and threw her clothe in the washer. She ran the hot water in the shower for a minute before jumping in.

Wow! What a day to remember? It was such a blast with those girls. What an awesome way to start a vacation. And to top it off, I'm pretty sure I saw him. I can't remember what the hell his name is. Fuck, I can't believe I misplaced his contact information. Shit! Shit!

Naffilia's mind began thinking about him and just as she was washing her thighs, she brushed up again her pussy and it excited her briefly.

What the fuck is it about this guy? Shit, I gotta stop. I have to wake up early tomorrow and meet the professor and catch my flight to Egypt. That scroll has to be in that area and it's been over a year since I've had a good lead.

She finished her shower and put on a t-shirt and panties. Before jumping into bed, she set her alarm clock for 5:00 AM. Exhausted by the eventful day, Naffilia passed out in minutes.

She woke up the following morning and laid out her clothes to pack quickly. After refreshing her face with a little makeup, she got dressed in her pants, suit and jacket. The quick and easy thing to do was pull her hair in a baseball cap to manage it. Before leaving she grabbed her sunglasses and a nice bag.

As usual, Uber was taking her to the airport. Five minutes before they arrived, she locked the doors and went outside to meet them. Just as she walked out of the building, they were just pulling up.

She waved him closer and jumped into the car. On her way over to the airport she text all of her contacts in Egypt to inform them that she will be arriving later in the evening. Then she text the professor and any relevant contacts in the local area to let them know she was on her way to the airport.

She made arrangements with Will, a local auto detailer that she knew personally, and wanted him to stop by this week while she was away to wash and detail all of her cars. She wanted to come home to a nice clean drive.

Will replied, "Will do. Be safe and have fun."

She replied, "Bet. Thanks."

She arrived at the airport and asked to be drop off in the VIP section of the airport. She hasn't been to this part of the airport and they drove in slowly before coming to a security checkpoint. They confirmed her arrival and the driver dropped her off at VIP drop off. Her headspace was a big foggy from the night before and took a moment to get her bearings before tipping the driver.

"Here ya go" handing him a $50 bill.

The driver was shocked, "Thanks you so much. Have a good flight."

She nodded and walked towards the VIP drop off area and check in her bags where they were already waiting for her. She walked in the tunnel area that connected passengers for a chartered private plane.

This is the area where I've seen all those businesspeople coming from. How many VIPs, CEOs, company executives and high-profile people have walked this tunnel? Shit, this is nice.

As she got to the end of the tunnel, she saw the professor and a number of people she didn't recognize at the gate. He greeted her.

She greeted the professor and mentioned she's a little bit tired because she went to a game and stayed up late last night and that she may fall asleep on the plane.

The professor replied, "It's Ok. It's going to be a long flight anyway. There's plenty of time to rest." He patted her on the shoulder.

He gestured her toward the plane, "Go aboard and find yourself a comfortable seat. There's no seat assignment."

She climbed aboard and was enthralled by the luxury throughout the plane and admired how beautiful everything was. She took a seat by the window near the back. The stewardess gave her a blanket and a pillow and said, "Is there anything else that you need? A drink or something to eat?"

She nodded, "Can I just get a bottled water?"

Naffilia got her bottled water and took a sip. She pulled her ballcap down over her eyes and leaned her chair back. She could hear the professor talking to other passengers on the plane.

"There's one more person on the way who will be joining us for the dig. We're just waiting for him."

After waiting a few more minutes, the professor let the stewardess know that it was ok to leave, and they couldn't wait any longer for him. Then the pilot announced that they were preparing for take-off.

Everyone took their seats before the plane taxied to the runway. The sound of the air blowing overhead and the chatter among the passengers made Naffilia fall asleep.

The plane took off at high speed. They were on the way to Egypt and the excitement on the plane could be felt. Naffilia woke up just in time to look out the window and watch the take off. Once they got over the clouds, she put her Air Pods in her ears to listen to soft music over the muffled sound of the chatter taking place on the plane. It put her into a deep sleep for most of the 17-hour flight, only waking occasionally to use the rest room and snack.

They finally arrived in Egypt and the professor leaned in to Naffilia to wake her up. "We just landed in Egypt."

She smiled, "I hope I didn't bother anybody with all my snoring."

The professor laughed, "No. You were sound asleep like a baby. You didn't snore one bit."

She was relieved, "That's great. I can't wait to check into my room now."

The professor informed her that the dig is going to be early in the morning. 9 am to be exact. "It's 12 miles from Cairo to the pyramids. So, it would be wise to get a good night's rest. Eat well and be ready for the day. Be sure to dress appropriately for this weather. We have you at a Four Seasons Hotel. Our driver will take you and everyone else to the hotel."

She knew she wanted to wear very light clothes, nothing dark, and nothing heavy but also go prepared. You never know what's out there. She would think of it no differently as if she were at work. She got her bags together and got into the limo with a few other people to go to the hotel. On the way there, as she took in the scenery she was lost in thought.

This time, this moment, is finally my mission. I'm gonna treat this like my personal mission to find that scroll. After years of searching I'm that much closer to finding a myth.

She found herself in a place of peace as she took in the area and they pulled up to the hotel. Her smile hadn't left her face since getting off the plane.

After checking into her room, she opened the doors to the balcony. The view took her breath away because she could see the pyramids in the distance against a beautiful sunset sky.

Watching in awe as the sun set behind the pyramids and fell below the horizon, she said with a tone of admiration as though she was praying out loud, "Dear god, this is an incredible work of beauty."

The menu and a mint were prominently placed on her pillow, so she took the initiative to lay on the bed and order room service for some light eats.

After ordering, she scanned her surroundings and looked out the balcony and said out loud with joy, "This is the life. How can this possibly get any better?"

While eating, Naffilia opened her curtains and shut off her lights to get a good look at the lights coming from the city and take her time eating.

After eating she remarked, "Ah…time to take a shower."

After a nice hot shower, it felt liberating to lay across the bed, butt naked, and roll back and forth in the cool sheets, embracing that feeling of not having a care in the world. She felt like she was exploring the world without any limitations. Every concern in her life melted away.

"Shit, shit, shit, I feel so free. I'm sleeping naked tonight on these nice soft cold sheets."

It was getting late, so she made a point to go to bed early and get rest for the big day.

Morning came quickly. The phone rang at 7 am.
She answered, "Hello?"
"Good morning. This is your wake-up call."
"Oh. Ok. Thank you."
Naffilia got ready quickly to go downstairs and grab a continental breakfast and enjoy doing some people watching while she waited for the ride to arrive.

When she was finished with her breakfast she went outside to talk with the other members of the dig and got a chance to know everyone. The van arrived and Dr. Shraver got out of the van to greet everyone.

"One again, I'd like to welcome everyone to Egypt. I hope you had a good night's rest. We're in for a real treat today. Today is a very special day, as it is our first day of the archeological dig that each of you had a part in sponsoring. Please load yourself into the van and they will take you out to the pyramids. It's going to be a short 12-mile ride so sit back and relax and enjoy the scenery. There's a second van coming out to meet us, but we can get out there first and get set up. Everyone, enjoy your trip and let's take in the sights."

It was a leisure van ride as the professor acted like a tour guide, giving us details of how they found the new tomb, along with providing a history of the area and what to expect for the dig. Naffilia and the others arrived and waited by the pyramids for the professor to get his things together. The group chatted with each other as mild sandstorm swept in.

Admiring her surroundings, she took a mental picture of the sand swirling around the pyramids, in awe of how beautiful they looked. It was picturesque. To her, there was nothing that could add to the amazing moment.

Just then out of the sandstorm a large Jeep broke through the cloud of sand swirling around and it looked like it appeared out of nowhere. Naffilia, the professor and the group watched as the Jeep stirred up a trail of dust, adding to the already brewing sandstorm. The jeep pulled up to them kicking up a heavy blinding dust as the wind whirled around the site. All you could see were the silhouette of several people getting out of the Jeep. You could barely make out the people through the dust, but as it settled you could begin to make out the people walking toward them.

The last person to get out of the Jeep placed his Timberline boots into the sand and braced himself as he stepped out. Naffilia could sense that the man had a presence about him as a few people huddled around him. She couldn't make out who it was until his silhouette began to fade as he walked out of the settling sand toward them. She could tell he was a nice-looking man from a distance, that knew how to carry himself and wore the shit out of those sexy shades and rugged clothes.

The dust whirled around him and made him look like Jesus walking out of a glory cloud straight toward Naffilia. She could swear she heard a choir of angels singing as the sunrise shined brightly from behind him through the dust cloud as if he stepped out of heaven onto the earth. Maybe it was Moses coming back to Egypt in full glory. "Oh Lord! Is that him? Did I just die and go to heaven?"

The professor squinted his eyes to get a good look and said with surprised, "Oh there you are Mr. Wolf. We thought we left you back home. We waited as long as we could for you."

Naffilia looked hard at who he was talking to. Her knees got weak momentarily and was stunned to see that it was him.

"What the fuck?! It's him. His name is Wolf?" she said under her breath.

The professor eagerly jogged over to greet Tye and said, "Mr. Wolf. We're so glad you made it. When did you get in?"

Ty chuckled and said, "I got in at the same time as you. I'm the one that flew the plane."

The professor was astonished, "Oh my gosh. Are you serious?"

"Yes, I'm serious. You chartered the plane from my company, and I was one of the crew members."

The professor was stunned, "Well don't that beat all. You're full of surprises Mr. Wolf."

Naffilia heard the conversation and remarked to herself, "Son of a bitch! He's a pilot and owns the company. I was in the plane with him the whole time. Shit! I'm glad I brought plenty of panties with me."

The professor turned to the group and introduced everyone, "Ladies and gentlemen, I'd like to introduce you to Mr. Tye Wolf of Wolf enterprises, who graciously gave us a discount to fly on his chartered plane to Egypt."

The group applauded and Naffilia had a smile on her face that she couldn't hide. This surprise was the icing on the cake, and it couldn't make her day any better.

Tye scanned the crowd of people that stood before him and noticed Naffilia. He lowered his sunglasses to take a look at her with his own eyes and muttered under his breath, "You gotta be shittin' me?"

Tye and Naffilia's eyes locked on each other as Tye slowly walked over to her. There was no hiding it between them that they were excited to see each other. All of the chatter that happened around them seemed muffled to both of them and paused as they pushed everyone aside to make their way toward each other.

Ty reached out with a smile to shake Naffilia's hand and said to her, "Pardon me. But it seems to me we've met somewhere before."

Naffilia smiled back at him and said, "I believe we did meet. It was in Morocco."

Then Tye said without hesitation, "You're the one that I met. I've actually thought about you since then, and I thought I saw you a few times as well."

Those words made Naffilia melt on the inside, that someone like him has thought about her since then and she couldn't help but giggle.

Oh shit! Did I just giggle? What the fuck?! I feel like a schoolgirl having a crush moment. I gotta get hold of myself.

She kept the conversation going, "I thought I saw you in New York."

Tye said, "Did you stop at a restaurant in New York to have lunch?"

"Yes, I did. That was me." She said delightfully.

Tye said out of curiosity, "Did you happen to go to the game yesterday?"

Naffilia was surprised by the question, "As a matter of fact I did."

"Seriously? That was that you on the screen?" He said with surprise.

She laughed, "That WAS me."

Both of them laughed with delight. Naffilia felt like a kid in a candy store talking to Tye while he himself could feel his knees slightly knocking. Naffilia asked him his name again.

"My name is Tye Wolf. Please, tell me, I have to know your name."

"Naffilia Rosebud."

Naffilia asked with delight and curiosity "You thought of me since we first met?"

"Yes, I have. I gave you my personal contact information and I thought you ghosted me." He said with curiosity in his voice.

She quickly defended herself to ease his mind, "No. I actually misplaced it. I must have forgotten it at the hotel in Morocco."

Giddily she repeated herself, "Yup, I noticed you a few times afterwards as well..."

Naffilia paused briefly and she started to blush, "I actually thought about you as well."

In an instant each of them could feel their bodies tingle the moment they admitted to each other what they were thinking. Naffilia was speechless for a moment, lost in thought, lost in the moment.

I was speechless and at a loss for words. I had thought about this moment for several months. I daydreamed about the conversation we would have. I thought about the impact that this total stranger had in my life and how many times I fantasized about him, just then, at that moment, one of those fantasies awakened my pussy and it sent a tingle up and down my spine. I tried not to shiver as I thought about Tye doing things to me that I've only fantasized about.

This was my chance to get to know him and find out the

kind of man he is. I don't wanna make any assumptions and I didn't take for granted that we both met again halfway around the world, exactly where I believe the forbidden scroll of sexual secrets can be found, and here was this fucking hot guy looking me right in the eyes telling me he thought of me since our last meeting.

It's taking a lot of self-control on my part not to fuck him right now. But I'm not going to miss this opportunity to ask questions and get to know him. His good looks and strong athletic body were a distraction, but I wanted to know who he was. Why was I drawn to him like a predatorial animal in the wild hunting for food? Shit, even his name turns me on. With a name like his, it stirred my primal nature. Fuck! If he could hear my thoughts. I wanna fuck you, right here, right now baby!

Tye gestured to the entryway of the tomb as they both walked in together and continued their conversation. They followed the lead archeologist and the rest of the team into the new area of the pyramid.

Tye asked her, "So. What are you doing here?"

She replied, "I'm here probably for the same reasons you are."

Tye pointed in the team's direction, "I'm here because I sponsored this archaeological dig."

Naffilia chimed in, "I sponsored the dig too. I love being a part of something special like this. Especially when they are about to discover something brand-new. This is very exciting."

Dr. Shraver announced that some of the sponsors can participate in the dig and ask them to take things slowly. He handed the sponsors a small shovel and brush and a flashlight and allowed them to participate. He declared the standard protocol for digging and made it clear how things were to be handled, outlining procedures for an archeological dig. Then he sent us in pairs.

After an hour of Naffilia and Tye working together they came across an earthen clay jar. They were both excited about the find and savoured this moment as they uncovered history for the first time in centuries. Tye took a deep breath and said, "look at this a jar."

Standard protocol for an archeological dig is that you are supposed to notify the archeologist and leave everything in its place for documentation purposes. Unearthing artifacts was a slow and meticulous job to preserve the find.

They were both excited about the find and their curiosity got the best of them that Naffilia reached out to grab the jar. Tye looked around to see if anyone was looking and cleared his throat.

She held the jar for him to explore. He pulled the top off and reached inside. Naffilia and Tye held their breath to see if there was something inside.

He looked puzzled, "I don't feel anything."

He took his flashlight and shined it in the jar. "Oh…there's something inside."

Her hands were smaller, so she volunteered to reach in. If a scroll was going to be in there, she wanted her hands on it. She put her hands in slowly and carefully and moved her hand around until she felt something.

She pulled out a scroll. They gasped simultaneous at the find. She cautiously opened it up as both of them held their breath.

It was clearly an important artifact with Sanskrit text. Naffilia's hand was holding the scroll open when Tye reached over and unintentionally touched her hand while he took his turn looking at the scroll.

Naffilia scanned the scroll quickly and sighed without Tye noticing. She knew that this was not what she was looking for.

Tye said in a matter of fact way, "This is exciting. I'm sure this is an important historical find. We should probably put everything back in its place and tell Dr. Shraver."

Naffilia said with a hint of disappointment knowing full

well that this wasn't what she was looking for, "Absolutely. This was an exciting find."

She rolled up the scroll and handed it to Tye. He reached out and accidentally touched her fingers to receive the scroll. Naffilia looked down at his hands. Tye wouldn't remove his hands as he looked her in the eyes. There was a moment of silence between them as they were both at a loss for words and held that moment between each other as long as they could.

Tye broke the silence, "Let's get this in the jar and put it back the way we found it."

They both approached Dr. Shraver and told him about the clay jar they found.

Naffilia guided the professor to the spot, "Right here."

The professor gasped and quickly rummaged through his backpack and took out a small camera and notebook. He took pictures and documented the location of the jar.

He was giddy. Like a kid in a candy store and said with a smile on his face, "Thank you very much."

Dr. Shraver took over and removed the artifact to catalogue it while they stood by to watch.

Ty and Naffilia continued to participate in the dig the remainder of the day with no significant finds. By noontime the remainder of the team gathered together to eat lunch and talk about what was found for the day.

The professor mentioned to everyone that they were going to be digging in that location for three to six weeks or until there was nothing left to be discovered, and he would keep all of the sponsors informed of any archaeological finds.

After their lunch, before going back to the pyramids for the remainder of their dig Tye pulled the professor aside to have a private word with him.

Naffilia was just out of range to hear the conversation between them distinctly, it was a bit muffled. There was an exchange of cards between both of them. Tye's gestures didn't give Naffilia any indication of the conversation. He was a smooth communicator and it looked like he was in charge of the conversation. Dr. Shraver kept nodding his head.

Tye reached out and shook his hand and returned to where Naffilia was standing.

She spoke up out of curiosity, "It looks like you and Dr. Shraver are friends."

Tye nodded, "I have a curator friend back in Boston who is interested in some of the things we find here at this dig. I sponsored this dig as a gift for the Boston Museum who is opening a wind in honor of my parents. I asked to stay informed."

Naffilia was intrigued and wanted to keep talking to Tye when each of them was interrupted by a few people. Tye got pulled into a conversation with another team member while Naffilia was distracted by another person from the team.

Each time they tried to end the conversation and turn toward each other to talk, someone would ask them a question or someone else interrupted. They looked at each other from a distance in their own group, smiled and shrugged their shoulders.

They could feel a growing agitation by the petty exchanges each time they were interrupted. Eventually they were distracted by the glances they gave each other as they stood a few feet apart from each other, divided by people who wanted their attention.

Tye couldn't take it anymore and interrupted his conversation to approach Naffilia, "Pardon me. Sorry for the interruption. Would you like to leave dig and take in the sights of the city with me for the rest of the day?"

Naffilia's pulse started racing and she disregarded her conversation and said, "Absolutely."

Tye smiled, "Great. Let's let Dr. Shraver know that we are leaving."

Tye smiled at the people around them and lowered his head, "Pardon me. Will you excuse us?"

They both walked over to the professor and announced that they were going to be leaving the dig for the remainder of the day and spend the rest of the time back at the city.

Dr. Shraver nodded his head and told them, "I'm glad you spent most of the day with us. Enjoy the rest of the day and I'll see you tonight at the hotel."

Tye approached the driver of the Jeep and asked him to bring him and Naffilia back to the hotel.

Naffilia said, "You're staying at the same place?"

Tye nodded, "Yah. I'm surprised I didn't see you earlier."

"Me too." Naffilia said with curiosity in her voice.

On the drive back they agreed to meet each other in the lobby after they showered and changed into something more comfortable so that they can take in the sights of the city.

They got back to the hotel. Ty stepped out of the Jeep first and then quickly turned around and reached for her hand to assist her from the Jeep.

Oh my gosh, he's a gentleman. He's nothing like the clowns I've dated for the past year. He's already rounded second base in my book, and he doesn't even know it yet.

Tye escorted her to the lobby and then said, "Meet you back here in an hour?"

Naffilia tried to cover her enthusiasm, "Yes, that works out perfectly. See you in an hour."

There was a bounce in her step as she walked through the lobby to the elevators and went to her room. Once she got to her room, she let out a pent-up response to her day, "Shit, shit, shit! Of all the places to see him - it's here…"

She walked over to her balcony and look out, "…On the other side of the world in this beautiful country, and now we're about to spend the rest of the day taking in the sights. This is fucking unbelievable!"

I'm gonna wear something sexy and make sure I smell nice. I'm gonna enjoy every moment of this day and make sure every one of my senses are stimulated so that this time is etched in my mind forever. Shit! I have fucking butterflies. What the hell?! I feel like a schoolgirl dating a jock waiting to spend the day with Tye. I haven't felt like this since...well, ever.

Naffilia took her time taking a shower and getting dressed, making sure her legs were nice and smooth, giving them a little shine by putting some oil on her skin. She wanted to be extra soft tonight. She put on a sexy red dress, nothing too formal so that she was comfortable, and she put on her favorite perfume. To top all of this off, she made sure to accessorise properly. The butterflies intensified while she was getting ready and she giggled to shake them off.

Wow! Fucking unbelievable! I feel like I'm in a romance novel meeting someone who seems like the perfect guy even though he's a stranger to me and I flew halfway across the world to meet him. Not only that, he's a pilot and owns the airplane that we chartered to get here. Shit, he owns the private airline company! I wonder what else this guy does besides own a privately held airline. I guess I'm gonna have the time of my life finding out tonight. I should write a book about my life. I'm living in my own unbelievable fantasy world.

Naffilia laughed out loud over her thoughts, and then went down to the lobby where Ty was already standing there wearing blue jeans with a dress shirt and nice casual suede shoes. He accessorized very well. I noticed the watch he was wearing. It was an A. Lange Sohne watch with white gold and it had a blue genuine leather strap. It stood out to me like a peacock spreading his feathers.

I know my accessories, and this one was noticeable. He wore it well. His accessories told me that he liked nice things. This one is at least $75,000 nice. It told me something about his style and his financial status. Someone with this status probably has everything he needs or can get anything he wants. Now I know for certain that he's a far cry from the clowns I've been with for years, especially talking with him for most of the day.

There was something that caught my eye and I probably wouldn't have noticed it if I didn't gaze at his handsome smile. It was his neck wear. It was something I haven't seen on very many people. It was rather rare to see it on a man today. Instead of a tie, it was what looked like a Native American choker. The way it was crafted, it was inconspicuous, not ostentatious the way most men wear their accessories.

I was very curious as to his choice of neck ware, because that too spoke volumes about his personal choice of style. Maybe there was something there that I could learn about him.

The way he looked standing there waiting for me, I could have had an orgasm just looking at him. His lightly bronze color skin and athletic stature and how he carried himself made me throb as I approached this good-looking man waiting for me.

I couldn't smell cologne until I was in his personal space. I took a deep breath. It was probably noticeable to him, but I didn't care. I wanted him to know that I liked the way he smelled. I just didn't want him to know I was going to have a fucking orgasm in the lobby in front of him. He already captivated all my senses except one – taste. Up to this point, I had only imagined what he tasted like.

Tye walked me past the lobby doors where his Maserati was waiting and opened the door for me and let me in. He got on the driver side after tipping the lot attendant.

He drove us around the various sites of Cairo. We stopped at points of interest that both of us appreciated about the culture, and saw - Tutankhamun's mask, the grave mask of King Amenemope, Pyramids of Giza, Valley of the Kings, King Tut Exhibit Egyptian Museum.

Along the way we stopped at a coffee shop to sit and talk and experience the local foods. We explored what the local artisans had to offer. To my surprise, we even took a classic camel ride through the dessert.

The conversation was engaging as we talked about what we liked about the area, mixed with talking about more personal things. I rarely told anyone about my personal life but Tye made it very easy to open up and share with him. My comfort level with him made it easy for me to be myself.

I learned that his last name – Wolf, is not just his legal name but was his clan name from his Native American heritage. I was intrigued not only by his history but enamored by the intelligent conversation I could hold with him. We got wrapped up in the moment that we didn't notice that time had passed, and we were getting hungry. He suggested that we eat at a local restaurant. He seemed fond of local establishments, Tye was like me in that way. Franchises don't serve, nor have the authentic local flare that a local restaurant does. Ty asked me what kind of food I like, and I mentioned to him that I was very much into seafood and the occasional barbecue.

We found a few options that served some of the best seafood in the area overlooking the Nile River to enjoy the scenery of the boats going up and down the Nile.

The evening felt like a dream. I could hardly believe my day. Here I was less than a few days earlier, hoping that by flying halfway across the world I would find a scroll that had the answers to fulfillment. Yet, here I am with a man who embodies many of the great characteristics of all the other men I've ever dated, and I continue to live in the moment, satisfied and feeling fulfilled, despite not having a scroll in my hand.

He has a sexy bass voice and it was soothing to my ears, especially as we sat in a private area with very little noise to disturb us. As odd as it sounds, his voice and presence made me feel safe. He seemed to have command over his life and knew where he wanted to go. Tye achieved many of the things he put his mind to and that turned me on.

We started talking about our personal lives but what I gathered, he didn't have someone special in his life. It didn't seem like he was in a relationship.

I don't know what happed to me and where my mind was, but what I blurted out next stunned me. I was in shock as it crossed my lips, as if I were in a trance and I couldn't help myself, "Are you seeing anyone?"

Oh my fucking shit! What the fuck did I just say? What the hell did I just ask him? Are you fucking crazy Naffilia? You just had a fuckfest a few weeks ago with two strangers and you are asking if he is seeing anyone?

To my relief, I noticed a smile on his face. I can tell by the question I asked, he was happy I did. There was a sense that he wanted to ask me the same question but some for reason he held back.

Tye shook his head, "I don't have a girlfriend, if that's what you mean. But I've seen a few women in my past. There was one woman who I dated twice."

I broke the ice, "Wow. You went on two whole dates?"

We both laughed nervously.

Tye paused briefly. By the look in his eyes he made it clear that he was interested in me. With most other guys, you can see it on the face, that they only wanted sex. Tye's look was different.

Tye added, "Two dates was enough for me. I'm keeping my eye out for someone special. She'll show up."

We were both at a loss for words briefly.

Tye asked, "What about you? Are you seeing someone?"

Sheepishly I replied while my voice squeaked slightly, "Me? No. No one at the moment. He'll come along."

My response put a larger grin on his face, while he looked down at his food as if lost in thought. He seemed pleased with my response and I heard a sigh of relief.

The look on his face changed and I saw that look in his eyes that guys get when they know we are about to have sex. I know that look of hunger. The pupils dilate and there is a sheen in the eyes. He had that look but you can tell he held back, he reigned it in. If he had let loose, I would have fucked him right on that table right now.

As odd as it sounded, I could feel a sexual inferno coming from him. He was throwing off some heat by the way he looked at me once he found out I was single. Yet he remained a perfect gentleman in my presence.

Tye reined it in with his sense of humour, "You made that camel happy today. He seemed happy that the two of you went for a walk. My camel tried to spit in my eye because I wasn't a beautiful woman like you."

We both laughed.

Tye and I had an amazing dinner. During our dinner conversation he found out that I liked walking along a pier. Afterward, we drove to a spot on the Nile River that had a small pier and beach that we could walk. Tye touched every mental and emotional button of mine and he seemed to do it naturally, as if he knew what I wanted.

For the first time in a long time, I lost myself in the moment with his company and felt myself losing track of time. I didn't care what time it was.

Evening came quickly and he drove us to a spot where we could watch the sunset over the pyramids. It was breathtaking. Here I was with a man who knew how to read me like a book. There was something about watching a sunset like this that made me want to reach out and hold his hand. I anticipated and hoped that he would reach for mine. I must have said it with my eyes because when I smiled at him, he looked down at my hand and did exactly that.

I could feel the electricity between us. I knew that he wanted me. I'm sure he knew I wanted him, but I didn't want this to be a one-night thing. I wanted this moment to linger in my memory and I wanted it to make a difference in my life.

As the sun dipped below the horizon, it cooled very quickly. We got back into the Maserati and headed back to the hotel. We admired the beautiful lights along the way. There was a cozy, comfortable feeling in the air as we drove past the various coffee shops along the way. Our conversation went to things about our life that made us feel cozy. This was not a conversation that I'm used to having with anyone, but Tye pulled it out of me. It made me recall my youth.

When we got back to the hotel the lot attendant opened the door for us to let us out and parked the car for us. Tye gave him a tip and turned toward me to reach for my hand.

Ty led me into the hotel and walked me to my room. I wanted him to come into my room. Oh, Fuck ya, I wanted him to come to my room. My pussy was primed the moment I saw him and to spend the whole day with him…Hell, I was ready hours ago.

Both of us knew we wanted the same thing. I could tell that he wanted to cross the threshold of that door as well but something inside both of us wanted this to be special. Both of us wanted this new and unexpected feeling inside to last and sear our memory of the day we had together.

Tye reached for my hand and I gave it to him. He leaned in to kiss my cheek and with bass in his voice he said, "I had an amazing day today. Thank you for making it special for me."

I fuckin' melted inside. My legs were like jelly and I could barely stand. I blushed and could barely get my words out, "Thank you. I had an amazing day too. You made it special for me."

I kissed his cheek and noticed that it was soft and warm. I put my cheek against his and paused momentarily and was tempted to kiss his lips.

We pulled back simultaneous and Tye said, "I'm going back to Boston tomorrow. When are you supposed to go back?"

"We were supposed to be flying back two days from now on the charted jet that we came in on. That you flew!"

"I wasn't planning on staying long. I have other pilots who were supposed to take over. They are flying me back tomorrow. Since I'm flying back tomorrow would you like to fly back with me?"

SEXUAL SECRETS AND THE FORBIDDEN SCROLL

In my mind I screamed, "Fuck...Hell yeah."

But I was cordial and said, "Yes. Absolutely. I'll go back with you. What time shall we meet?"

He said he wanted to meet at 8:00 AM and that he already arranged a ride over to the airport. I agreed fervently.

Tye said goodnight to me, and he retreated to his room.

Once I closed the door I ran over to the bed and dove in the air and landed on my belly to bounce on the bed. I rolled over and kicked my feet in the air as though I was doing a bicycle ride and let out a squeal of joy, "My life is amazing!"

Naffilia took a shower and laid on the bed butt naked. She was astonished and pleasantly surprised at feeling fulfilled for the first time in a very long time. And she didn't even have sex.

It was an unusual feeling but my craving for sex was somewhat subdued. I wanted to fuck Tye. Oh, shit did I want to fuck him! But somehow that inner urge seemed satisfied even when we didn't. It was as though I had an orgasm already, except it was a mental and emotional orgasm.

It sounds strange to think of it that way but that was the best way to describe it. Tye managed to settle that inner tension that grew over the years.

I wasn't going to overthink it, however. I'm going to enjoy this feeling of being settled and content.

Naffilia settled in to enjoy a good night's rest on the cozy cold sheets, thinking about the day she had with Ty. She struggled slightly to prevent her mind from going down the road of sexual fantasy, at least for the moment, because she wanted to enjoy that romantic feeling that engulfed her and settle the storm inside. She got her deepest sleep in months.

16

The next morning was a glorious morning in both of their eyes. The sky was bluer, the air smelled fresher and the peace in their mind and heart was deeper. Naffilia snapped awake and danced her way to the shower. Tye is a morning person and had already gone down to the lobby for breakfast before the sun come up and admired the tranquility of his world.

Tye had pre-arranged a limo ride to the airport, it was due to arrive by 8:30, so he took his time eating and checking out. He brought his things to the lobby and sat to have a coffee.

Naffilia took her shower, gathered her things together and took them to the lobby. She saw Tye already downstairs drinking coffee. He looked at peace. His aura intrigued her.

Naffilia checked out and greeted Tye, "Good morning."

Tye nodded his head, "Good morning."

He gestured to the chair across from him, "I ate already. We have about 30 minutes before the limo arrives. Have something to eat."

Naffilia sat down and ordered a light breakfast.

Waiting for the limo, Tye and Naffilia had idle chit chat while she ate a light breakfast.

The limo arrived on time. They gathered their bags to load them in the truck. Both admired the scenic drive until they arrived at the airport where the jet was ready for them to board.

As they boarded the stewardess greeted them, "Welcome aboard Mr. Wolf."

She turned to Naffilia and acknowledge her as well, "Welcome aboard."

The captain announced the flight according to protocol, "Welcome to 'WE Charter Airlines' and we are happy you chose us for your flight…"

There was a brief pause and then the pilot continued, "…Actually we're glad you own this company Mr. Wolf and have chosen us to work for you…" Laughter could be heard at the front of the cockpit.

This set the tone for the entire flight home. It was laid back, happy and enjoyable.

The pilot announced, "Prepare for take-off."

Naffilia turned and asked Tye inquisitively, "'WE Charter?' Who came up with that name?"

Tye smiled, "Wolf Enterprises!"

Naffilia understood, "Oh…Wolf Enterprise. You own more than this airline?"

Tye nodded, "There's more. We have plenty of time to talk about that later."

Just then the plane took off. Once they reached cruising altitude the flight attendant served them drinks and snacks.

They had a long 12-hour flight ahead of them which gave them plenty of time to get to know each other even more. They were both engaged in deep conversation asking personal questions about each other. The conversation wasn't forced. It flowed from one topic to the next.

Tye leaned in toward her, "I want to know about you. Who are you?"

Naffilia was tickled that someone was interested in her, interested in what makes her tick.

Shit! Is this really happening? I feel like I'm dreaming. Here I am again, sitting across a fucking smoking hot guy with a tight ass and a good head on his shoulders and he is waiting for me to respond because he is actually interested in me - my past and what I want in my future. This isn't just about wanted to fuck me for shits and giggles. Shit, shit, shit – I can feel my face blushing.

Naffilia took a slow, deep breath, "I'm not going to give you a list and I don't want us to share a list. The reason why is because a list of attributes seems way too confining to me. I'll say that I'm attracted to a real person whose aura and character so resonates with me. What matters most is how we make each other feel, the passion, excitement, energy, tension, and simply enjoying each other's company."

Naffilia paused to emphasize the next point, "Rare, I know, but for my array of shortcomings, I'm what some would call 'overly optimistic.' I choose to maintain my individuality while exploring my world and enjoying life, taking everything in stride and living in the moment. The other person, whom I consider my match, will come along and we'll fit like a puzzle."

Tye's gaze was locked on my eyes and mouth and his attention was on every word I spoke, "I'm a super active, youthful looking and thinking woman who has both sides of the brain constantly abuzz. I am interested in virtually everything…the indoor and outdoor, travel, music, food, sports, and a whole lot more that I want to explore."

Naffilia paused and shrugged her shoulders, "But hey, if it's not fun, I'm not going to do it. Fortunately, I am pretty easily entertained so there are a lot of things that qualify and meet my standard."

Naffilia paused and gestured as if offering something, "We've already done a few of them in the past 24 hours and I am so blown away by it. Thank you for that Tye."

Tye nodded, "Your welcome. Tell me more."

Naffilia smiled, "Laughter is for the mind, body and soul. A sense of humor is refreshing and has healing effects. I like to take a 'relaxed' approach to life and find laughter daily."

Naffilia continued, "As for work…" There was a long pause as she contemplated giving him anymore information.

Tye looked confused, "Work? Is there something you don't want to tell me?"

I was lost in my thoughts momentarily about work. My identity needs to be protected at all times. I work for an agency called - Global Assassination Sector. G.A.S. for short. G.A.S. protocol was to never reveal who you work for and to keep your identity hidden. This was a top-secret organization that was considered a fabricated division. That's what they wanted. It helps keep them unknown.

The name itself was to invoke doubt. For fuck's sake, who names an agency "GA.S.?" We've had fun with this name for years. We been cracking jokes at each other and our agency name since its inception. In fact, my grandfather was one of the original agents who participated in naming it. Dad was part of the organization too. Hell, "G.A.S" runs in my family! All of us at HQ got gas!

I chuckled at my own thoughts while Tye tried to decipher my facial expression and thoughts. I wanted to tell him about what I do. I even wanted to tell him my real name. Everyone that knows me, calls me Naffilia Rosebud. Gramps, Dad and family know my real name. I wanted Tye to know about my world, but I just couldn't go there. He would be the first person outside of the agency who would appreciate what I do. It would feel so good to let out this monumental secret with someone I could trust. Still, I don't know much about Tye. I'll keep this part of my life secret and tell him later if we continue to meet.

I wanted to tell him, but I found a way out, "…Well, it's just that my work is kind of in the realm of government and I can't talk about it much. Let's just say that I work for a gas company and I take care of the leaks before things blow up."

Tye gave me a surprised look, "Oh. Ok. No problem. Don't worry about it. I understand."

Naffilia continued, "I enjoy the challenges that come with a fast-paced work environment. I pride myself in my work, accomplishments, and continue to be success driven. However, I always allow free time to pursue other passions in my life. I enjoy art and music or getting out on the beach to clear the mind, and the tranquility of losing myself just kicking back and playing my violin. I have great friends and am very happy with my life but am not a woman to brag. People see me as a variety of things - bold, self-confident, laid back, non-judgmental, honest, physically fit, and humorous."

She paused briefly and then said, "...But I've always considered the whole 'Who am I' thing to be kind of limiting. I'm more than a list of things I like and want."

Tye was impressed with her response, "Wow. I like that approach. There's no pre-defined way to express who you are. You don't feel boxed in that way. That's an amazing way to look at yourself. I like that."

Naffilia continued, "The word, and the concept of family and true friends have a special meaning. It's a philosophy I learned from my father and grandfather. I don't take it lightly because they add to the beauty and appreciation of your life. When I think of family or friends, I extrapolate good memories and moments that add to who I am as a person. Family is the framework in which to grow from. I came from a good family and we shared our life with each other, our love and our sorrows as well. Family were always there for you, at least...most family."

Tye nodded his head, "Exactly. I was close to my family to. But unfortunately, there are people who don't come from that vantage point. Sometimes they miss out on the benefits of family and it leaves a gaping hole that feels like it needs to be filled. I've known people like that, and my heart goes out to them."

You could see the compassion on his face as he said it.

His face became light and contemplative, "What you see around you...,"

He motioned to the plane and all its contents, "...came from the love and support of my family, and I don't mean they drained their bank account from me. They had very little, but their love and support and their concept of family was very rich. It allowed me to keep my focus and work hard to achieve the things I did."

My heart melted when I saw and felt his compassion. He seemed genuine and very appreciative of family. I knew, that somehow, I tapped into something deeper with Tye. I gave him room to speak from the heart, but he was a perfect gentleman and allowed me to finish my thought. I could tell he connected with what I was saying and simply wanted to affirm my thoughts and feelings. He knew – he fucking knew what I was saying and feeling! He lived it. He comes from the very same family philosophy that I did. This was fucking unbelievable that a man lived a similar life.

By the pause he gave, I took it he wanted me to continue but I waited.

Tye smiled and said, "Thank you. Tell me more Naffilia."

A warm smile came to Naffilia's face as she thought about what she wanted to say next, "I'll be honest with you. I've been looking for someone who is ready to open his heart and let me in. Someone with a positive attitude and good heart. Passionate and very affectionate. Good communicator and open minded. Someone who believes in love and is trustworthy. Someone I can count on for everything. Spontaneous and adventurous."

Naffilia paused and thought twice about what she was going to say next, "…sexual attraction…"

Tye's eyes got wide and he leaned in toward Naffilia, waiting anxiously. The look on his face was as if he was waiting to get a surprise gift.

Naffilia brushed her hair back and started to stroke her legs slowly, seductively. The look on her face and the glean in her eyes transitioned to a look of hunger – it was sensual, "…Sexual attraction and physical attraction are very important to me - emotionally and psychologically. I like a sensual man. I like a great kisser."

Naffilia's sexual gestures and soft-spoken voice put Tye in a trance. His imagination took him to another place as he struggled to pay attention to her words as his eyes fed on her sexy legs. In his mind he could see her reaching over to touch his thighs. She placed her hands on his thighs and slowly ran them up to his crotch.

His dick grew the closer she got to his zipper. She gave him a sensual smile and unzipped his pants and reached in to pull his dick out. This was their first time to have a mile-high experience.

The stewardess walked in on them, "Oh…I'm sorry." Her face turned red and she turned around immediately and went to the back of the plane.

Tye pulled Naffilia closer and she undid his pants. Tye stood up so that she could pull his pants off and let his shit hang out for her. She licked her sexy full lips and tried to contain her craving for him. Naffilia wrapped her hands around his hard cock and swallowed it slowly, sucking and kissing his cock until he couldn't keep his moaning at bay.

Naffilia got off her knees and stood up in front of Tye and slowly slipped out of her dress. Tye's eyes filled with drunken lust as she stood before him in her lacy panties and bra. He caressed every curve of her body as she undid her bra and let it drop to the floor.

Tye held her hips as she turned around and bent over in front of him as she slipped her panties off slowly to tease him. He leaned in to kiss her ass and caress her legs. She stayed bent over so that he could press his face into her ass and stick his tongue out to taste her already wet lips. He inhaled slow and moaned with pleasure. It was just a sample of more to come.

Naffilia turned around and placed her hands on his shoulders to brace herself as she straddled his lap. She leaned in closer so that her tits hung in front of his face, "I'm gonna ride you until we create our own turbulence in this plane."

Tye reached up to grab her tits and leaned in to suck her soft nipples. His soft tongue massaged her nipples as he ran his tongue in a circle around her nipples and sucked them gently. She took a deep breath and moaned as he gently squeezed them between his teeth.

He ran his fingers up and down her body. Her breathing got heavier. Her pussy was throbbing and her craving for Tye became too much for her to control. She reached down to grip his dick to help guide herself as she slowly lowered herself down until her dripping lips wrapped tightly around his head of his cock. She raised herself and lowered herself, controlling the depth of his penetration so that it was deep enough for the head of his dick to give her pleasure.

Just then, the plane hit an air pocket and she slammed down on his cock and took it deep. They moaned with pleasure at the surprise. They looked into each other's eyes and saw pleasure as her warm wet pussy squeezed his cock. Naffilia rode him hard while he sucked her tits. Suddenly the turbulence kicked in again at the perfect time and assisted with her bounce. He took advantage of it as she bounced her graving pussy on his rock-hard cock. Their moaning got louder until they came to the edge of orgasm.

For the first time, Tye and Naffilia weren't just fucking, they were making love. They gave themselves to each other with sheer pleasure. She grinds the fuck out of his cock, and he took it stride for stride with her. Naffilia swayed her hips back a fourth while her grabbed her plump, round ass to help her grind him. He pushed her harder than any man she's been with and it made her uncontrollably horny until she let out a squeal that turned him on.

He was about to blow his load inside her, and she knew it. She leaned back to thrust her pussy into his pelvic. The moment her squeezed her ass to pull her closer she felt him pulsing inside. He was filling her tank and it made her cum on his dick.

She scream his name, "Tye!...Oh shit, Tye! Ah ah ahhhh. Oh shiiiit!"

They cum simultaneously with great pleasure and it send a shock wave up through their body. She stood up quickly and he was still spraying, and it turned her on so much that she squirt all over his lap, screaming in ecstasy.

Naffilia's orgasm kept going as she called out his name, "Tye...Tye."

Tye came back to his senses and snapped out of his imagination when Naffilia called his name again, "Tye? Are you with me?"

Tye was slightly embarrassed, "Oh ya...sorry. I was just thinking of something."

Naffilia knew that look and suspected that he was making love to her in his mind. It turned her on.

Tye cleared his throat and shifted his body. He was trying to give himself some room in his crotch without bringing attention that he was getting hard.

Naffilia recognized that move that men do, and it confirmed that Tye's mind was fucking her. She noticed his dick filled his pants and it turned her on. She wanted to continue with the sexual talk but didn't want to make him uncomfortable. Tye refrained from displaying or making any sexual innuendos because he wanted to show his respect for her. She loved it and it turned her on even more.

Naffilia eased the sexual tension, "Political stuff...I absolutely believe everyone has a right to their own opinion. What I don't understand is why people can't express their opinions in a respectful, intelligent manner. I can hold a conversation about politics but it's not my go to subject. I don't gauge a person by their political persuasion."

Naffilia nodded her head, "How's that for a summary?"

Tye smiled warmly, "You seem to know exactly who you are and what makes you tick. Being self-aware is a characteristic that takes people years to develop. You're interesting and intriguing."

Naffilia blushed, "Thank you."

Tye took a breath before asking her the next question. It was almost as if he knew that it was going to be too deep, "Naffilia? How did you get to where you are in your life? What's your history? As you pointed out, family is the foundation of who a person is."

I had to admit that Tye knew how to ask the right questions. He could probe better than some of the agents back home. It's almost like he was an agent himself. He was asking something that required more thought and it was going to go deep into my life. I wondered if I was ready to give him that personal information yet. I'm certain I he could sense my hesitancy. I wanted both of us to take all the time in the world to get to know each other.

There was a silence between them as they scanned each other up and down, obviously checking each other out.

The flight attendant came just before the silence got awkward and asked them if they were interested in having lunch yet.

Over lunch, they had idle chit chat about various things in their life and current events. The conversation didn't go much deeper than that because that's as deep as she wanted to take it. He was less revealing of his past. Without realizing it, Tye dominated the flow of the conversation – it was his way of directing the flow of conversion away from him. Both of them lost track of time and eight hours had flown by quickly.

This time, Tye and Naffilia weren't going to lose touch with each other. They agreed to exchange cell phone numbers and get in touch more often.

The moment they flew into United states, each of them were getting text messages from various people. They tried to stay focused on each other, but the text interruptions were frequent and annoying for both of them.

They laughed it off each time their phone buzzed. Tye shrugged his shoulders, "I'm just going to put my phone on silent for a bit."

Naffilia chimed in, "Yeah, me too."

As they flew over Boston, Tye said suddenly remembered to ask her a question, "Hey...I have to ask you. Did you enjoy the game last weekend? I was surprised to see you there."

Naffilia answered, "Yes. Best game in years. Me and my girlfriends had a blast."

Tye said with excited, "I was blown away when I saw you on the jumbotron. You and your friends. I got myself into trouble when I made a remark."

Naffilia chuckled, "Really?"

She leaned in as if telling a secret, "I think I saw you with a woman there. She was dress up to go to a party. Bougie. She didn't seem happy."

Tye snickered, "Yeah. That was our second date, but she wasn't into it. Then, I made a remark when I saw you, and hell broke loose."

"I take it a third date didn't come out of it?" Naffilia joked.

Tye chuckled, "No. That's ok though. I guess I was trying too hard to make the date work when she wasn't into football."

Naffilia was surprised, "Not into football?! How can you not be into football?"

Tye's eyes widened, "Yaa…I guess I took the wrong girl."

Naffilia moved her hair out of her face and smile, "I guess you did."

They both laughed.

The plane landed and taxied to the private charter end of the airport. It was a fresh experience for Naffilia to land and taxi to that area of the airport. She contemplated how a few months ago she wondered about this part of the airport and what people did for a living to allow them to be privileged to use this area, and now she was one of those people using this area.

When they arrive in Boston a limo was ready for them. Mike greeted Tye, "Welcome home sir."

Tye was cordial, "Thank you Mike. This is Naffilia. We'll be taking her home."

Mike tipped his hat, "Pleased to meet you Naffilia. I trust your flight was pleasant?"

"It was. Thank you." She said.

Mike helped each of them put the luggage in the trunk.

Tye got her address and instructed the driver to take her home.

They arrived at her address and both Mike and Tye got out of the car to assist her with the luggage.

Tye reached out for her hand and she gave it to him. He pulled her close and kissed her on the cheek.

"We have each other's number. I would like to have dinner with you this week if you don't mind." He said inquisitively.

She blushed, "I would like that."

He was excited, "That's great! I'll text you tomorrow and we'll make arrangements."

Just before Naffilia took her bags Tye stepped forward and announced, "I'm glad I met you Naffilia. I'm blown away that we met halfway around the world twice! And all along you live right around the corner from me. Well, at least within driving distance."

Naffilia agreed and chimed in, "That's incredible that we had to travel around the world in order to meet each other." She hugged Tye and kissed his cheek.

Tye and Naffilia parted ways but double checked that they had each other's contact information.

17

Naffilia and Tye kept in contact, regularly texting each other and talking to each, often times until 3:00 o'clock in the morning.

Tye and Naffilia found themselves lost each other's conversations, oftentimes their phone would buzz from previous dates wanting to hook up, only to be nothing but annoying.

It got to the point where Naffilia started ghosting the men because her phone buzzed constantly. The same thing was happening to Tye.

Tye paid attention to every detail of Naffilia's life and admired her passion for art, culture and history. They revealed to each other the things that matter to them most.

Fall was almost over as the leaves had reached their peak. New England in the fall time offered not only cooler days and even colder nights, but it was surrounded by the beautiful color of the leaves as festivals could be found anywhere across several states. It added to the ambience of their exciting life and the time they spend together.

Naffilia and Kyle explored the beauty of New England and not once during their time together had sex. Instead, they teased each other verbally with sexual innuendoes. They respected that about each other, and it was rare for both of them to go that long without fucking someone. They were too distracted by how they enamored each other.

One cool day, over a lunch date at Naffilia's favorite restaurant at the pier, the one that Bucky the clown ruined, Tye made up for it.

He reached over to her and touched her hand, "Will you take a weekend trip with me?"

"To where?" She asked with delight.

"To my cabin retreat in New Hampshire. This time of year, it is absolutely beautiful. The perfect place to lose yourself."

Naffilia didn't hesitate, "Sure. Let's go. When?"

Tye said delightfully, "That's great. We'll leave this Friday."

Naffilia and Tye enjoyed their dinner and got lost in conversation.

Neither one could wait until Friday.

Thursday seemed to drag out. Finally evening came and Naffilia packed her bags and couldn't wait until morning. Friday seemed to drag itself in. Finally, in the morning, Tye called her early, "Good morning, are you ready?"

"Absolutely" She said delightfully.

"I'll be by in 45 minutes to pick you up. I'll text you as soon as I'm right around the corner from you."

Naffilia double checked her bags and made sure she had everything she needed for the weekend. Her phone buzzed and Tye let her know he would be arriving within 10 minutes, so she went downstairs to meet him as he pulled up outside. He pulled up in his SUV and got out of his car to open the door for her. Tye has been a gentleman since they first met, and he never stopped being a gentleman and took her by the hand to assist her in the car and close the door behind.

Naffilia was turned on and impressed that he continued to be that way even weeks after knowing each. Most of the guys she had known would stop being that knight in shining armor after getting comfortable with each other, but not Tye, it was a part of him.

I was excited, and despite my recent crazy high adrenaline missions, I still felt a flutter of nervousness about going to his cabin retreat. You'd think with all the missions that I've been on I would be able to stay calm and relaxed simply going to a cabin of a man who's fucking hot. Hell, I haven't even had sex with him...at least not yet. Maybe that's why I was nervous.

I guess the problem is - we both know we want it, that's what makes me so nervous. It's going to happen this weekend and I'm overthinking it.

Sex with Tye was always on my mind but for some reason, we didn't cross that line. We only talked about it and we banter back and forth a lot. We sexually tease each other all the time and that's been a turn on. This was foreplay for sure.

Tye's SUV was powerful and smooth and made me forget we were driving. The ride to New Hampshire was relaxing and he made me feel comfortable. We got to New Hampshire quickly and the scenery beautiful. He was spontaneous and drove by beaches. We stopped to take in the scenery along the way and have a meal on the pier.

We enjoyed the journey to get to his place, stopping at cozy places of interests to explore so that I could take pictures for my own personal collection of art. As the day got closer to dusk, we drove deeper into New Hampshire. We drove through the back roads of the forest, driving through small quant towns. I could see the mountains from a distance getting closer.

Ty's cabin retreat was secluded, out of the way - far from the city and it felt far from civilization. We were headed toward the base of a mountain when Tye took a quick right turn down an unfinished road.

I was a little bit nervous as to where Ty was taking me, even though I had been in tight places before, and tough situations, and I can handle myself pretty good. But I still felt nervous. I reasoned that being with a man that I trusted made me feel vulnerable and made me feel a bit nervous down in the pit of my gut. I guess it's safe to assume that I'm nervous because I was going to willingly give myself to him for the first time since meeting him.

The further we drove down this unfinished road, the darker it became. The road was surrounded by thick tall trees. We were literally headed into a forest which lead to absolutely nowhere. However, I noticed an occasional red beam across the road, and I knew for sure it was some form of security. Tye obviously took security seriously. It wasn't a joke to him, but I don't understand why.

The further down the road we got, the darker it became,

and suddenly out of nowhere he took a left turn and the road was paved and we came upon a gated compound. I was surprised that the gate did not appear luxurious and lined with gold. It was opposite of what I was used to seeing since I met him. The gate looked like something from a horror movie. It was huge, dark, cold and very intimidating. It made me feel like we were entering into a graveyard. I guess that's what he was going for, something uninviting and it worked.

Tye pulled up to the gate and pressed on the center of a stone. It moved slowly – sliding downward like some kind of Indiana Jones secret passage. It looked like something that would have been designed for our division. A screen appeared and he put his thumb on a pad. The gates creaked slowly open – exactly like a horror movie so that we could drive in. What the fuck was happening here?

Naffilia was impressed with his sense of security, utilizing theatrics to beef up the security, but she wondered why this compound had that level of security and it made her suspicious.

Now her heart was racing out of nervousness for who this man really is and what he's capable of, which is vastly different from other men she's been with. He managed to remain a mystery.

Within minutes they pulled into a broad driveway and what appeared before them was a large log cabin compound.

The logs were oversized and gave an air of security. It didn't look like anyone lived there but his lawn was perfectly manicured with gardens that abound. To the far right was an impressive seven car garage doors.

Shit, shit, shit, a 7-car garage. His cars had their own private home. Something I haven't seen before, even with the amount of wealth I've seen around the world. I thought the guys in Dubai flaunted their wealth, but this was the epitome of what I knew of Tye.

Tye pushed a button on his SUV and one of the doors

opened up slowly and he drove the SUV into his temperature-controlled garage.

Unlike most garages, this one had plenty of room to walk around. He walked around to the other side of the SUV and opened my door and took my hand and assisted me as I stepped out of the vehicle. When I stepped out, I glanced down the row of cars. I looked at the last car at the end of the row and my pussy instantly throbbed. My panties started to get wet. What got me, was that I almost ship my pants the moment my eyes focus on the car at the end of the row.

At the end of all those luxury cars was a black 69 Chevy Chevelle. I gasped for air when I took a closer look. In my head I screamed out, "Are you fucking kidding me?"

But what came across my lips was, "Oh my gosh!"

Ty looked at her a bit confused, "What's the problem? Too many cars?"

"No. It's the one on the end, the 69 Chevy Chevelle. How often do you take that into the city?"

"I take it every so often."

She walked over to the car to admire the muscle and it brought back a flood of sexy memories of their last few races. She felt her panties getting wet and her heart started to pound, "Ty? You're the guy I've been racing on the highway for the past few months."

Tye looked stunned by her comment as he looked her up and down and asked, "You're the 68 Camaro?"

"Yeah, I'm the 68 Camaro. You made my day every time we saw each other." She said it with a look in her eyes like she wanted to fuck him on the hood right there.

In her mind she was screaming, "You made my pussy throb every time we met on the highway."

Ty smiled and licked his lips like he was ready to eat a meal, "I've enjoyed our races on the highway. You don't know how much I've enjoyed the adrenaline rush of our races."

Naffilia smiled and undid the top button of her blouse to let out some of the heat her body started to throw off.

Again, in her mind said, "You've practically given me an orgasm every time we've gotten on the highway."

Instead she said, "I've enjoyed our races too."

Tye ran his hand over the hood of the car and hovered it inches above the car as if teasing with his touch and said, "Naffilia, there's power under this hood that I like using."

Naffilia nodded her head and smiled as she remarked, "If you have the power, you might as well use it for the right reasons, Right?"

Her panties were wet, and she could feel herself blushing. She turned to walk away but accidently brushed his crotch with her hand and felt his dick – hard as a rock.

"Oh my gosh. I'm sorry. I gotta use your restroom."

Tye tried not to make much of it but he wanted to shift himself. The erection was obvious, and he didn't want to adjust himself, but it needed more him in his pants.

"Oh…yeah. Right over here."

He pointed to the bathroom in the garage. He has a heated bathroom in the garage!

Naffilia kept her composure as she retrieved her overnight bag and went to the bathroom.

Shit, shit, shit. Oh, my motherfucking gosh. I gotta change my panties. It's the good thing I brought 7 pair for the weekend. She scurried to change her panties and rolled them up nice and small and put them in a plastic bag and placed them in her bag.

Damn girl. Get a hold of yourself.

She splashed her face because sweat started to form on her nose. Looking in the mirror she said, "Ok…cool off. You got this girl. Your good."

SEXUAL SECRETS AND THE FORBIDDEN SCROLL

She was ready to go back out to Tye.

Meanwhile, Tye scramble to adjust himself and whispered to himself, "Oh shit. Easy boy!"

He struggled to find a comfortable spot. Too late. Naffilia walked out of the bathroom and he quickly took his hands off his dick.

I couldn't believe the reaction of my body when I saw the car, knowing that Tye was the one that drove it that whole time. I was so turned on because now I knew that Tye could handle anything with power, which means he can handle me more than the average man. It showed in the way he led me into his house and the way he treated me and paid attention to every detail of my life - of who I am.

Tye asked, "All set?"

My reply was short and sweet, "Yup."

We walked into his house and immediately it opened up to a large living room with an open concept kitchen. Luxury abounds in this house. Every detail that Tye put into his house was meticulous and it added to the opulence of his home. The way the windows were framed, the way the furniture was arranged, how the fireplace was the focal point of the room and the stones that were used for the fireplace screamed out romantic and sexy winter fun. The giant windows were custom made so that a lot of light came in and you can see the mountains in the background.

I walked over to the window and gasp when I saw the vastness of his property with a brook running through it and wildlife running free in the back with a view of a mountain. Ty had a secluded compound like nothing I've seen before. I imagined myself running naked on his land, feeling free and not a soul was around for miles.

I was enamored by the natural beauty that surrounded us and told Tye how much I admired it. It was an absolute dream.

Tye spread his arms out and invited her to walk around the house and take a look. He gestured to the paintings on the wall and invited her to take a look.

I couldn't believe my eyes, to see that he had authentic and original paintings from various artists around the world. He had replica paintings of Rembrandt, Dante, Picasso and modern-day artist all throughout his house. Each of them was framed by a professional and had its own lighting. I felt like I was in my own personal museum and I was stunned by his appreciation for art. It wasn't just paintings throughout his house, there were sculptures and statues all handcrafted by some of the best artists around the world.

I was drawn to his erotic art as well and it turned me on. I got lost in one painting of a man and woman intertwined. Somehow, the woman looked eerily like me and Tye.

Based on my quick assessment of what I saw with the home and all of its contents, my calculation was he was worth more than 500 million dollars, given the level of wealth I've seen so far. If I had to guess, I'm willing to bet I was standing in the presence of the first unrecognized and unmentioned billionaire - dare I say he approached the trillionaire status?

The way he held himself in public, and what I knew of him, material wealth did not have a hold of him, and he didn't appear starstruck by high profile people but had pictures of him and a countless number of high profile people all over the house in various places. After getting to know him, he was clearly not a materialistic man, but he knew how to acquire wealth and how to use it.

In the middle of my speculation as I stared at the erotic art, he went to the kitchen and opened up a bottle of Don Perion, "Care for a glass?"

"Yes. Thank you." She said with her sexy voice with a hint of enthusiasm and delight.

He handed her a glass and motioned with his head toward the refrigerator, "I have some strawberries too. Would you like some strawberry?"

"Absolutely."

He took the strawberry out, washed it, and immediately

took charge of my thoughts and emotions and took control of my body as he took the strawberry and slowly touched the tip of the strawberry to my lips. With a deep bass voice said to me, "The strawberry is sweet. Take a bite."

I opened my mouth very slowly and watched his facial expression. He was pleased with my response to his demand. I could see that he looked like he was lusting after my lips, so I stuck my tongue out very slowly and touched the tip of the strawberry and then open my mouth very slowly and wrapped my full luscious lips around the strawberry, very slowly, as if stroking the strawberry with my lips until I got to the end and took a bite.

Tye licked his lips and smiled because she knew how to turn him on and Tye naturally brought it out of her.

She chewed on the strawberry slowly and as she did he took a sip of his Don Perion and then put it on the counter leaned in toward her, put both his hands up behind her neck, ran his finger up behind her neck and behind her ears and ran his fingers in her hair and held her head in his hand as he leaned in to kiss her lips.

His strong hands grab my neck and pulled me into him, and I lost feeling in my body. It was like my ears were ringing and I could see stars as he pulled me into his mouth and kissed my lips in a very sensual way. His lips were so soft and supple. He probed my mouth with his tongue with the flavor of the Dom Perion on his tongue and it tingled my mouth.

This is a man who knew exactly how to get my body to react. I closed my eyes to enjoy the passion behind his kiss with a subtle hint of lust and electricity - that I knew both of us felt. That was my first real kiss that I've given a man and I was willing to let it go for him. I could feel my body go limp as he continued to kiss me with my head in his hand and he reached down and put his hand around my waist and pulled me into his tight body.

There was no coming back from this and I pressed myself up against him making sure he felt how big and firm my tits were, and then he reach down behind the small of my back, rubbed it until he went down to the crack on my ass, and pulled me into his pelvic so I can feel how stiff he was.

I could have fucked him right there and not had to wait for any kind of foreplay from him. I had waited for far too long for this moment, weeks even, but I didn't want to lose this feeling and I wanted to enjoy it for as long as it took.

I felt his hand reach around my waist and slide up to my blouse to undo the buttons and exposed my bra. He stood back to take a look at my body, to drink my body with his eyes while I reached over and undid his belt buckle and pulled his belt off.

I wanted to assure him that I wanted him, so I reached down and massage his bulging cock until I heard him starting to breathe heavier. He rubbed the flesh of my waist, all the way to the small of my back and ran his hand and fingers up my spine until he got to the hook of my bra and unsnapped it in an instant, like he had been doing this for years. He knew exactly what he was doing.

Tye reached around, placed his finger above my navel and ran his hand up my belly and up to my tits and reached under my bra to massage my nipples that were already hard, and I couldn't help but moan with pleasure from his rough and strong hands.

He paused and gave me my Don Perion while he finished off his. I didn't want him to stop doing what he was doing. I needed him to finish what he started but he knew how to tease me, he knew how to take me to the edge. This was something that I've been longing to experience with a man.

He gave me a moment to compose myself as he dimmed the lights in the house so that we could watch the sunset through the big custom windows, and he turned the fireplace on. I took my bra off and left my blouse open covering my nipples to tease him so that he could see my tits bouncing as I walked closer to him. I wanted him to enjoy the show I could give him. I wanted to please him the way he pleased me.

He never spoke a word, but he said a million things with his eyes and the way he touched me, I knew that he cared, and I knew that he wanted me, and he knew exactly how to express it.

Tye led me to his room and that's when I began to shiver because I knew something was about to happen when I walked into his room. I gasped again at the enormous size of his bedroom and the bed that faced the balcony with a view from heaven.

I thought he was guiding me to the bed but to my surprise, and to my delight he led me to his balcony and slide the door open. To our left before walking out to the balcony was a door to what looked like his closet. He opened the door next to the balcony.

I knew that Tye was gonna be able to handle me and that I was going to be the woman he needed to take his sexual experience to new heights. I was prepared for anything that he was going to do to me.

As the door opened all the way, it revealed a large dark room that he used as his personal secret getaway, keeping theme with his hidden retreat cabin.

I felt my body get a chill of excitement and nervousness when I thought I was looking at his lounging area, but as my eyes adjusted to the darkness, in the middle of the room facing the balcony was a tantric chair, similar to the furniture found at club Orgy. Along the walls was erotic art, accentuated by professionally crafted and decorated ropes, chain and leather used in conjunction with low lights to highlight the art, but it was also functional.

This was a man who hid his sexual passion very well from the world, and somehow, he knew I could handle whatever he wanted to do and invited me into the room – the room looked unused, waiting for someone special in his life.

He affirmed my suspicions and said this room is reserved for someone that he wanted to expose his heart too. He led me to the balcony and open up the doors, and along the balcony as the sun was setting there was a fireplace that he ignited. The air was cool, and I could feel it on my bare skin as he placed his fingers in between my tits and ran them up and down.

Tye could see that I had goosebumps. He had a smile on his face and leaned in to kiss my breastbone and reached up with both hands and grabbed my neck and ran his hands down my collarbone as he opened up my shirt and exposed my large round tits to the cold air and pinched my nipples.

Tye licked his lips before he kissed mine, then suck on them and preceded to kiss my neck, my shoulder, my collarbone and worked his way down to my nipple. He focused on my nipples and sucked them, teasing them by twirling his tongue around my nipping. I moaned involuntarily.

Tye placed his hand on my navel and walked behind me, and as he did, he slid his hand around my waist and came up from behind me and grab my chin, lifted it up so that my neck was exposed and he put his tongue on the side of my neck and then sucked it.

Then he kissed my back starting at the base of my neck and worked his way down my spine as he lowered my blouse. He kissed every inch of my back down to the base of my back just above the crack of my ass until my blouse fell to the floor. He paused briefly to look at my lower back.

I leaned back with delight onto his shoulders as he reached around with both hands and ran them down my navel and undid my skirt and slowly slid them down as he rubbed his hands along my hips and down my thigh until my skirt fell to the floor.

The cold air now touched every part of my body and I stood near the balcony in my panties, barely able to feel the heat from the fireplace.

I got lost in the erotic moment in my mind and I was ushered into a new world as I let Ty have his way with me. He continued to touch every part of my body as though examining every square inch like he was admiring a rare sculpture.

I got lost in the moment and felt like I was his own personal artwork - a living artwork that responded to every stroke of the master painter - and he stroked every part of my body perfectly.

I wanted the same pleasure, so I turned around and kissed him passionately while I undid his pants and undid his shirt.

I exposed his strong muscular chest and rubbed it lightly, the way I handled my artwork, as though I was molding a new sculpture.

I undid his pants and lowered them along with his underwear while I lowered myself down until I was even with his cock and balls. He stepped forward out of his pants and underwear while his shit swung freely in front of my lips. I reached up around his waist and pulled him close to me. I wanted to tease him the way he teased me and placed the head of dick on my lips the way he placed the strawberry on my lips, and I can tell that he enjoyed it. I tasted his now swelling head.

He pulled me up from the kneeling position and carried me into the room and pushed me up against the wall next to his erotic art on the wall next to ropes. He pinned me and I couldn't move. Our breathing got heavy. The look in his eye told me he wanted to fuck me hard. He came in close to my lips and then looked down at my panties.

He took me by the hand and guide me over to the tantric chair, placed me down on the chair facing him. He lifted my legs in the air and placed them on his shoulders and reached down to pull my panties off and expose myself to him. He slipped my panties off me like a pro and removed my legs off his shoulders but spread my legs open. The position I was in made me feel vulnerable and he was obviously turned on by the fact that I was already dripping.

I was expecting him to finally fuck me. But he picked me up, carried me to the wall again and pinned me against it and lifted me off the floor like I was weightless and kissed me passionately. I was surprised, stunned that he didn't fuck me on that chair.

My instinctual sexual reaction was to wrap my legs around his waist, and I made sure my pussy pressed up against his erect cock. My pussy finally felt his dick and the sound of my wetness as my lips opened up for him to slip inside turned us both on. We got lost in the passionate kissing and it shocked both of us when he lost control and shoved his cock inside me, using the wall to brace us.

"Oh, fuck." We both yelled out together.

He pumped me hard. I felt my body lift several inches as he fucked me like we were having mad sex and it fucking turned me on so much that I stuck my tongue in his mouth. The moaning and wet passionate kissing made both of us horny as hell. I could feel my eyes roll to the back of my head the harder he fucked me against that wall. He mad-fucked me with perfect rhythm and my body melted every time he lifted my body in the air while my thighs squeezed his hips. I was lost in the moment. I've never had my pussy pound that hard, yet that passionately. Like he actually cared about me and it came through with every thrust.

He gave me a sexy smile and reached past my head for something on the wall. I turned and saw him grab a rope next to me. He put me down and lead me to the tantric chair and laid me down on my back.

Tye stood over me like a conqueror and it made me melt into submission. He grabbed my wrist and pulled my hands behind the tantric chair and tied them together. I haven't felt this vulnerable with a man, nor have I given a man this much control - and he had all the control right now.

I can tell by his body language that he wanted to talk dirty to me, but he wanted me to feel like a woman too and it made me feel appreciated, desired and fulfilled for the first time getting my fuck on.

I wanted him to let loose, so I guided his words, "You wanna spank this bad girl. Don't you?"

Tye felt what I was doing for him, "Yeah…I wanna spank this bad girl and pound your luscious pussy all night long."

This was too much foreplay for both of us, so he lifted my legs in the air, bit my ass, slapped it and then straddled the tantric chair.

He spread my legs wide open until you could hear my pussy lips making a lip-smacking sound, "mmm. Talk to me baby. Your beautiful pussy is inviting me in."

Without warning me, slid his rock-hard cock inside of my primed pussy. Both of us simultaneously filled the room with howls like wolves, and I screamed with pleasure as he shoved his cock deep inside and slap my ass with his ball.

I let him know how I felt, "Oh fuck! Tye! Your cock feels so good. Slap me with your balls."

We howled until we could hear the echo outside.

With his deep sexy voice, he said to me, "Oh shit, you are so hot and wet. I am so fucking turned on…" as he pushed himself deep inside of me, giving me just enough pain for my pleasure.

Then he changed his angle and every thrust he made hit heavens arch with erotic perfection and sent a wave of electricity across my whole body, satisfying my pussy for the first time as my tits bounced rhythmically for his viewing pleasure.

The angle he positioned me in and the control he had over me was something few men have done for me before, especially because he paid attention to detail. This was new. This was different, and this was what real power felt like between my legs and it made me want to let go completely and let him do whatever he wanted to me for his pleasure and mine.

I couldn't hold it anymore. Every thrust he made with his thick hard cock sent me over the edge and in a matter of minutes I couldn't contain the ecstasy I felt and belted out a scream of pleasure.

Instinctively I screamed out, "Oh fuck…my pussy is craving you. Drive that cock inside me. Ahhhhhh ah ah ah yaaaaa."

Wave after wave I cum on his cock. It sent shockwaves through my whole body. It was unbearably intense, and I wanted him to stop so that I could catch my breath, but he was ravenous and kept going.

He stopped briefly to untied me and rolled me over the edge of the chair into a new position to arch my back and raise my ass in the air. He gave himself access from the back, gripped a handful of my hair and slapped my ass before he shoved himself inside me again.

My skin became sensitive and I could feel his rough hands massage the small of my back. He seemed pleased at what he saw.

"Your tattoo...," He said as he fingered it and didn't lose his pace thrusting himself inside me, "...is a fucking turn on for me."

He was losing control as all of his senses were on overdrive. Knowing that he was losing control because of me...over me...fucking turned me on even more and he brought me to the edge again. I never craved a cock so much. It was him I graved, because of everything he made me feel in that moment. I could feel my pussy dripping out of control onto the chair as I let myself go and howled again and screamed with delight.

He wasn't done. He kept going and turned me over to lick the milk that flowed from my pussy down my thighs. I could feel the passion as he sucked and licked my inner thigh until the tip of his nose pressed my clit.

He stopped to inhale deeply the aroma of my pussy and turned me on with his words, "Mmm, your perfume is intoxicating baby." He closed his eyes and inhaled deeply my fragrance and tasted me with pleasure. His lips glistened with my juice and I watched him licked them slowly.

"Oh shit...Tye..." is all I could say.

His eyes were filled with lust and it ignited his imagination and mine. I felt his desire for me, not just for my body, but for who I was deep inside and he wanted to please me. He untied my hand so that I can participate now.

He pulled my body down low so that he could delight me with his cock and shoved it deep down my throat. I reached around his waist and squeezed his ass. I had a hand full of that tight ass and a mouth of his shit and pulled his ass toward me until he fucked the back of my throat. He moaned with pleasure as I deep throat him, and it turned me on.

Tye paused to look at my lips, "Your lips are swollen. Oh, shit you are so sexy." He ran his fingers along my checks and up to my earlobe and then grabbed the back of my head and shoved his still swollen cock into my mouth and controlled the motion of my head for his pleasure until he moaned with ecstasy. I can tell he wanted to fill my mouth with his cum so that I could swallow it. Instead, He pulled out to unleash his cream across my face. He kept going and let it go on my tits. I was swimming in his cum. He gently wiped my face with his hands.

He could feel himself losing control over his body with the pleasure I gave him, and quickly ran his strong callused hands up my legs to grab me by the waist and flip me over to fuck my plump round ass.

He gazed lustfully at the tattoo on my back covered by goose bumps from his touch.

She returned the favor to please him. Her luscious full sexy lips lightly touched and kissed his body, exploring every part watching his response to her lips to find what pleases him. When she found it, she took the tip of her tongue and touched him gently on that spot, kissing and sucking, conveying her passion for him through her lips and tongue. Tye was pleased and she could see in his eyes how pleased he was that she took her time to know his body. She took her time to please him and it moved him.

She kissed, licked and sucked his inner thigh until the head of his cock was swollen with excitement. Naffilia placed her lips on his head then wrapped her lips around it and lowered her head until she had his whole cock in her mouth.

He could feel her passion for him, and then shift to please him and herself. She went ham on his dick. He's both pleased and surprise how hard cord she went down on him. She was like a tiger attacking a wolf. It turned him on that this woman tiger was eating Mr. Wolf. She was everything he imagine she would be for him.

She was pleased that he was pleased and moaned on his dick, taking it in like a professional slut. What turned him on was that she was doing everything right and doing everything naturally to please him. She was genuinely enjoying herself.

Tye was beside himself and couldn't believe that this was happening to him. He thought, "how can a woman know me this well and do everything the way I wanted it without telling her how to make it happen?"

She was turned on because of the reaction of his body and knew she was blowing his mind by blowing his cock, stroking his cock and sucking it until she drooled down his shaft.

He lost himself because she made him feel wanted and moaned out his thoughts to her, "Damn! Baby this shit feels so fucking good."

It turned her on and it made her go faster and faster.

The breathing was loud between both of them. He closed his eyes to focus on the feeling of this sexy woman going down on him like no other woman. It was what she was doing, it was how she did it and how she cared how it made him feel. With his eyes closed a flash of a thought entered his mind that he could see himself wake up next to year every day.

He had to tell himself to come back to the moment and thought to himself, "Open! Open your eyes and watch her suck this master dick."

He looked down at her and said, "Ooooo baby please don't stop."

He played with her silky black hair and massaged her head. He took the bobby pins out of her hair and threw them to the side. Her long black hair fell down the backside of her body and he grabbed a handful of hair on the back of her head to feel and enjoy the movement of her head. The feel of her hair against his skin was erotic and it stirred him.

He got lost in his thoughts, "Fuck! Her hair is so silky and smells beautiful." It turned him on so much that he lost control and he grab a handful of her hair and pulled her face into in dick, making her go ham on his cock. Faster and faster. Everything about her was a turn on for him. At one point he wasn't sure if he was dreaming or if this was really happening.

They both knew they could have anyone they wanted but it felt good and right that they craved each other. They knew what each other wanted. They knew when to dominant and when to be submissive. They took turns in perfect harmony going from dominant to submissive, and it was a turn for each of them to be vulnerable to each other.

Tye got caught up in the moment and said, "Oooo baby. Darling the way you make sweet love to me, makes me feel so good."

In that moment it brought a tear to his eye and it fell to her body. She felt it, but thought it was sweat.

Both of them could feel they weren't' holding back from each other. They were letting their feelings spill over in their love making and their words.

Tye wanted to bust a nut in her month but held back to show his respect for her. The way she fucked him made his thoughts go wild.

He thought to himself, "Shit! This is the most intense feeling I've ever had. What the fuck is going on here? She's a fucking freak!"

His thoughts were confirmed the moment she said, "Oh baby. Fuck. Fuck. Fuck my fucking head until you are all the way down my throat."

It turned Tye on so much, he was like a ravenous wild wolf. In that moment, he was strong enough to scoop her up and made her wrap her legs around his head and hung her upside down, laid back on the chair down and supported her shoulder and ass in a 69 position. He invited her to swallow his cock while he enjoyed the smell and the view of her pussy in his face, sucking her lips.

Naffilia thought to herself, "Oh my fucking gosh. He's more of a freak in bed than I thought." It turned her on more

283

and added to her pleasure of sucking his balls and swallowing his cock.

Tye said out loud, "Ooooo shit. Shit. Baby you are making my legs shake." His breath got heavier as his dick touched her tonsil.

He let her down and she looked at him with curious eyes and said, "Hey. You ok? You good?"

Between breaths he said, "Yes. Yes, I'm good."

She took her freak another level on him, "Good. Now turn around," she said.

Tye didn't know to expect. That was the exciting part about fucking Naffilia. She flipped him over to lay on his stomach. She gave him a new experience as she slapped his ass and started to talk dirty to him.

Tye was curious as to where she was going with this. On the one hand, he was nervous, on the other, he was grateful for answered payers.

Naffilia used her agent skills to entice him as she said, "Do you trust me?"

Tye sheepishly replied, "It depends on what you're going to do to me."

She didn't want that answer and said again, "Tye! Do you trust me? I'm not going to stop what I'm about to do to you."

Tye thought to himself, "Oh dear lord. What the hell is she going to do to me? Did I update my life insurance? I maxed out my policy and updated my next of kin."

Naffilia slapped his ass again then Tye answered quickly but his dick got hard from the excitement, "No!"

Naffilia laughed playfully, slapped his ass and bit it, "Baby! Do you trust me? Do you need a minute to think about it?"

Tye answered with excitement, "I don't need a minute to think about it. Yes. I trust you. Whatever it is, I hope you're gentle."

To build his excitement and expectation she paused and didn't say a word. Then leaned in and stuck her face into his ass and put her tongue in his ass. His ass cheek squeezed from surprise as he took a breath.

Tye caught his breath, "My ass is a virgin. I need a second to relax."

Naffilia caressed his ass and legs to help him relax, until he felt comfortable. She went in with her tongue, back and forth as he caught his breath and let out moan. She massaged and suck his ass until the intensity built and precum dripped from his cock. He couldn't take the intensity anymore and stopped her.

He manhandled her and flipped her over to fuck her throbbing pussy from behind while she stuck her round ass in the air for his pleasure. The ecstasy they felt was overwhelming. The smell of sweat and sex filled the air and it made both of them that much hornier.

They sounded like a pack of wolf crying for one another. Tye couldn't hold it anymore, "Yeah. Yeah, I'm cumin baby. I'm cumin. Yaaaaaaaaah."

Naffilia couldn't hold it either as she screamed, "I'm cumming. Keep going. Pound my pussy. Yaaaaaah."

Tye filled her pussy with his cream and pulled out to cover cum cover her tattoo. Tye paused long enough to rest.

Tye reached around to my tits and took his own cum to lube my ass. Then he took the cum on my tattoos spread my ass cheeks to lube my asshole and slip his cock inside. I took a deep breath as he slid in, "Oh, shit Tye. Fuck my ass as hard as you want."

I couldn't help but think, "Oh yeah. Tye is definitely a freak in bed. I finally found a real man who can handle and please this pussy."

Tye watched her tattoo violently shaking as he pounds her ass with his rock-hard cock. All of his senses were engaged, and he was turned on by her scream with every rhythmic thrust.

He was on the edge again, until she said, "Fuck! Tye! Tye! Your cock feels so good. Fuck me harder. Pound that ass."

Tye said, "Oh shit! Your pussy is so wet and gushy. I'm

about to cum."

Naffilia could barely speak, "Oh shit, I'm gonna cum. Stay inside. Fill me with your cream. Give me what I want."

He was turned on by the electricity generated touching her tattooed silky skin and slapping her heart shaped ass and then wrapping his hands around her waist to pull her forcefully into his pelvic.

He banged her ass and made her tits swing violently. She screamed with pleasure and squirt all over the chair. He laid her in her fluid and positioned her to pound her pussy. He was a machine and it turned her on. He shoved himself inside and it made her scream with painful pleasure when he went deep. She kept squirting until she begged him to stop. The moment she begged, he unleashed his load again inside of her and pulled out to mingle his cum with her juice.

They felt a deep unbreakable connection between them, like paradise was within reach. They were drained from the ecstasy they hadn't experienced before. Tye let himself down to the floor and she rolled over and collapsed onto his hard body and into his arms. Their naked sweaty bodies covered by cum and pussy juice somehow continued to generate electricity between them.

This was just the beginning of their sexual hunger for each other. Their insatiable craving for each other and their satisfaction filled them up more than ever. They were like wolves who ate a satisfying meal of raw meat.

Just then, Tye's voice could be heard as if coming from a distance, "Naffilia? Naffilia, are you OK?"

I came to my senses realizing that I had been staring at an erotic painting on the wall in his living room the whole time. I lost myself in my imagination - fucking Tye.

Ty brought over the Don Perion and gave it to me, "You sort of zoned out for a second there, are you tired?"

Naffilia shook her head to come back to the moment, "No. I was just admiring your erotic art on the wall and I kind of got lost in it."

Just then, out of the corner of her eyes, Naffilia saw a very special framed piece of art on the wall and it drew her attention. She walked over to it very slowly and her eyes widened the closer she got.

Her jaw began to drop the closer she got to it. It was professionally framed, and it was lit up so that it became his centerpiece for the entire house.

Tye noticed that she was drawn to it, and the closer she got, the more surprise she became. She examined it very closely and gasped, dropping the glass of wine to cover her mouth with her hands - to prevent her from gasping too loudly.

Tye approached her quickly with a look of concern and was shocked at her response, "Naffilia are you ok? What's the matter? You look like you saw a ghost."

Naffilia turned to Tye with overwhelming surprise and said, "Tye? What is this? You've got a scroll that confirms the ancient legend of sexual ecstasy. What the hell are you doing with this scroll?"

The End

ABOUT THE AUTHOR

N.R.R.P is a seasoned writer, entrepreneur and advocate for non-profit organizations and gives to family non-profits close to heart.

www.ingramcontent.com/pod-product-compliance
Lightning Source LLC
Chambersburg PA
CBHW070656180626
46817CB00006B/2397